"Melanie Rae Thon give[...]ho long to love while they w[...] [...]ibune

"Thon weaves a Faulknerian tale. . . . It is her considerable achievement that she is able to lay bare the scarred psyches of both men and women."   —*Boston Review*

"Vivid, passionate and intense . . . a fast, gutsy, windows-open ride down a western highway—and it's a literary adventure to be savored."   —Michael Dorris

"Combines a view of heartland America reminiscent of 'The Last Picture Show' with a look at brutal family and sexual relations akin to Dorothy Allison's *Bastard Out of Carolina*—but strikes a tone that is singularly Thon's. . . . expert and beautiful."
—*Publishers Weekly*

"In prose of passionate intensity, Melanie Rae Thon takes us on a journey into the peopled and animaled heart of White Falls, Idaho. She quarries her way toward the very soul of her heroine, exploring the strangely erotic, and vibrantly lyrical, world she inhabits. Thon has a distinctive and dazzling voice."
—Caryl Phillips

MELANIE RAE THON is the author of *Meteors in August* and *Girls in the Grass*, a collection of short stories. She has received grants from the Massachusetts Artists Foundation, the St. Botolph Club Foundation, and the National Endowment for the Arts. She lives in Syracuse, New York, and teaches in the Graduate Creative Writing Program at Syracuse University.

IONA MOON

Melanie Rae Thon

A PLUME BOOK

PLUME
Published by the Penguin Group
Penguin Books USA Inc., 375 Hudson Street, New York, New York 10014, U.S.A.
Penguin Books Ltd, 27 Wrights Lane, London W8 5TZ, England
Penguin Books Australia Ltd, Ringwood, Victoria, Australia
Penguin Books Canada Ltd, 10 Alcorn Avenue, Toronto, Ontario, Canada M4V 3B2
Penguin Books (N.Z.) Ltd, 182–190 Wairau Road, Auckland 10, New Zealand

Penguin Books Ltd, Registered Offices: Harmondsworth, Middlesex, England

Published by Plume, an imprint of Dutton Signet, a division of
Penguin Books USA Inc. This is an authorized reprint of a hardcover edition
published by Poseidon Press, a division of Simon & Schuster. For information
address Simon & Schuster, 1230 Avenue of the Americas, New York, NY 10020.

First Plume Printing, October, 1994
10 9 8 7 6 5 4 3 2 1

Excerpts from this novel originally appeared in *Threepenny Review*, *Ontario Review*,
Hudson Review, and *Antaeus*.

 REGISTERED TRADEMARK—MARCA REGISTRADA

LIBRARY OF CONGRESS CATALOGING-IN-PUBLICATION DATA
Thon, Melanie Rae.
    Iona moon / Melanie Rae Thon.
        p.   cm.
    ISBN 0-452-27280-7
    1. Idaho—Fiction.   I. Title.
PS3570.H6474I58   1994
813'.54—dc20   94–17418
                                                   CIP

Printed in the United States of America

PUBLISHER'S NOTE
This is a work of fiction. Names, characters, places, and incidents either are the
product of the author's imagination or are used fictitiously, and any resemblance
to actual persons, living or dead, events, or locales is entirely coincidental.

ACKNOWLEDGMENTS

Alice Lichtenstein and Mark Robbins read an early draft of this story with extraordinary care and insight; I am thankful to them for all they saw. I also thank Antje Lühl, Ann Patty, Elizabeth Searle, Clare Alexander, Miles Coiner, Caryl Phillips, Fanny Blake, Matthew Archibald, David Gewanter, Irene Skolnick, Fiona McCrae, Andre Dubus, Wendy Thon, and Mary Pinard for their faith and wisdom. I am indebted to Elizabeth Domholdt Shoemaker for her expert opinion on medical questions.

Several sections of this novel first appeared in literary journals; I thank Wendy Lesser, Raymond J. Smith, Joyce Carol Oates, Dan Halpern, and Paula Deitz for their support.

The words of Walt Whitman are from the poem "To a Stranger," included in *Walt Whitman: The Complete Poems*, edited by Francis Murphy and published by Penguin Books.

I am grateful to the National Endowment for the Arts and the St. Botolph Club Foundation for their generous support of this project.

For Mary and Miles and Matthew

I am not to speak to you, I am to think of you when I sit alone
  or wake at night alone,
I am to wait, I do not doubt I am to meet you again,
I am to see to it that I do not lose you.

—WALT WHITMAN

IONA MOON

1

꧁ *Matt Fry couldn't go home,* so he lived in the abandoned shed down by the railroad tracks. Willy Hamilton
and Iona Moon each knew part of Matt's story, how his troubles
began the day his brother died. But Willy and Iona didn't talk
to each other, and Matt Fry wasn't talking to anyone, so there
were pieces no one knew, secrets locked in the boy's body.

At Everett's funeral, Iona watched Matt squirm, scratch his
crotch then sit on his hands. He kept glancing over his shoulder
as if he expected to see his brother come strutting down the
aisle, head held high, medals gleaming. *Just a flesh wound. Ugly
scar, but girls like a man with something to show.*

Hearse to grave, six men carried Everett up the hill. Matt
shuffled and smirked, pinched himself but couldn't stop smiling.
The sun was white. Dry leaves skidded across the yellow grass.

Sharla Wilder sobbed like a widow, softly and to herself.
Other girls cried too, clinging to one another—to keep from
falling, Iona thought. Matt thrust his hands in his pockets and
kicked stones toward the hole. All those words. *Beloved son, war
hero.*

Everett Fry had gotten out of Vietnam alive in '66, nothing
worse than that scar on his shoulder where shrapnel tore skin
and muscle but left bones unbroken. He'd had a hero's welcome
in White Falls, Idaho, where people believed any man in uniform

was doing a good thing for the country. But a month after he came home, Everett still hadn't looked for work. In his parents' house on the Kila Flats, he paced the attic room, wore nothing but his underwear, kept the blinds shut tight. Sometimes he got dressed and drove to town, parked on Main and stared at women who passed his truck. He made them nervous. With his hat pulled down over his brow, he looked like a man who meant to go hunting.

More than one young lady said she had dreams about Everett, dreams that made a girl giggle and hide her mouth, dreams that made her cry out in her sleep till she woke with her damp nightgown twisted up around her waist.

Iona knew that Sharla Wilder was one of the girls Everett had watched, one of the girls who'd had those dreams. Last summer, when Everett was still alive, Jeweldeen Wilder bolted the cellar door to tell Iona. They squatted in the dark, puffing cigarettes that Jeweldeen had stolen from her sister's purse. "Sharla says that when Everett stares at her, she feels like her whole body's about to catch fire, like she's been doused with gasoline and he's got a match. In this dream, she's naked and he just stands there looking 'cause a woman's body doesn't do a thing for him. Finally he touches her, just one finger on her belly or maybe her forehead. His hand is cold, the way metal gets so cold it sticks to your skin. She shatters like hot glass, like a bomb goes off inside her. The pieces fly in Everett's face. His eyes are bleeding. Then my sister has to lead him around by the hand. She's alive, you see, and not exploded, 'cause it turns out the whole thing is Everett's dream, not hers."

Jeweldeen and Iona sucked on their cigarettes. "I think my sister's crazy, having dreams like that. One night she went sleep-walking. Came down here in the cellar where you can't see your own nose if you look cross-eyed. She woke up and started hollering. Daddy and I ran around the house looking for her. She's standing here wearing nothing but her own goose flesh, yelling her fool head off, saying, 'Don't bury me. I'm still alive.' She keeps rubbing her eyes because she thinks they're full of dirt and that's why she can't see. Daddy says he's gonna put her in a special school if she doesn't straighten up. He says he can smell the sickness in her. He says girls go crazy just like animals—something like rabies but it only happens to females."

Iona thought of Sharla's dream, the way Everett shattered her. She imagined Everett staring at them all now, getting ready to toss a grenade into the crowd. They'd wake up dead. Sharla would think she was sleepwalking again. She'd scream and scream, but this time her father wouldn't run down the stairs, wouldn't say: *Cover yourself.* But Everett Fry didn't throw the grenade. He held it instead. Stuck it in his mouth and pulled the pin.

Iona never told Jeweldeen how Everett gave her a dollar one day to run across the street and buy him a pack of cigarettes. He didn't stare at her, because she was just a scrawny kid with no butt. Sharla Wilder had too much ass but nice tits, that's what Iona's brother Leon said. Even Jeweldeen had breasts big enough for a bra, but Iona's ribs still stuck up higher than her chest when she lay on her back. Maybe that's why she wasn't scared of Everett Fry and didn't have any crazy dreams either.

"Don't get any smart ideas about running off with my money, you little shit," he yelled.

She whirled in the middle of the street and stuck out her tongue. *Well how'd I know what he'd do?* She brought him the cigarettes and change. He started to roll up his window but she stood there waiting.

"What you gawking at?"

"Thank you," Iona said. "You're supposed to say thank you."

He handed her a quarter. "Now get lost," he said.

Willy's father was the first one to see Everett Fry, and his mother was the last.

"You never saw such a mess," Horton Hamilton told his wife. He was on duty that Saturday morning and took the call alone. "Blood spattered all the way to the ceiling."

"Careful," Flo said. "The children."

But Willy already knew. The wailing siren hours before had sent Willy and Jay Tyler flying on their bikes, pumping and panting to catch Horton as he sped out east of town. Rumors whipped across the Flats. Now neighbors stood silent in the Frys' front yard; like stumps, Willy thought. No one moved. That morning, Everett Fry had locked the bathroom door, put on his uniform, double-knotted his shoelaces, sat down on the toilet, and shot himself in the mouth.

Jay stood on Willy's shoulders to see inside the bathroom. Horton Hamilton spotted the tuft of blond hair, the fingertips clutching the sill. He snapped down the blind. "Damn kids," he said later. "That's all this town needs—boys bragging that they saw Everett."

Jay didn't tell anyone but Willy. They pedaled all the way back to town as if racing a flood, as if the gorged river swelled behind them and any moment they might be swept away, no more than sticks in the roiling water.

When they were lying in the damp grass in front of Jay's house, staring at the blank sky, Jay wished a dog would bark. He hoped his mother would yell at him to come inside, but there was nothing except the quiver of bare branches and the sound of Willy's breath. "I didn't think it was gonna look like that," Jay whispered.

"My mom says everybody has his own way of dying. Some folks smile like they just told a good joke. And some folks grit their teeth like they got a hot poker up their behind."

"Everett looked like he couldn't believe it," Jay said. "But he did it. Why should he be surprised?"

"Maybe he didn't know how it was gonna feel."

"Shit. You can jump off the bridge, you can take a handful of your mother's pills. You don't have to make such a goddamned mess. Somebody has to clean that wall. I wonder if he thought about that, his own mother on her knees, wiping the tiles."

Willy said, "Maybe he wanted her to see how much it hurt."

"Your mom gonna fix him up?"

"I s'pose."

Jay whistled through his teeth. "Jesus," he said, "sweet Jesus."

Sooner or later Flo Hamilton saw most everyone in town. She scraped under their fingernails and sponged their feet, swabbed inside their nostrils and wiped the sleep out of their eyes. Ladies got lipstick and rouge. Baldwin's Funeral Home had pink and red, one shade of each. She couldn't do anything fancy. She had to shave the men because their beards grew for a day after they died. Everett Fry had such tender skin she lathered him up twice. Mr. Baldwin said, "No need to go to all that trouble, Flo. Nobody but the good Lord himself is going to see that face."

But she shaved him anyway. "Just like a boy," she told her husband, "just like Willy."

Willy thought of the pig, how they'd poured scalding water over its back and shaved it with the edges of spoons, shaved it until its skin was pink and smooth and softer than his mother's own cheek when she kissed him goodnight.

"I never knew there was so much blood in a man," Horton said. "All my years, I never saw anyone do it that way."

Flo said, "They'll have to have a closed casket. It's a shame, such beautiful skin."

Willy remembered watching his father cut the pig's neck. Horton Hamilton was a big man. He wore size twelve shoes, extra wide; he could pin you to the wall with one hand. He had hair up his nose and hair in his ears. But he was no match for a three-hundred-pound pig that knew it was going to die. That animal kicked and squealed, rolled on its side and flailed at the air with its stubby legs. Finally Willy and his sisters and his mother got on top of the pig and Horton jabbed the knife into its throat. Such a small cut, but the blood flowed into the basin, so much blood, and the basin was emptied and filled again; still it came, thick and dark, and the pig lived but no longer struggled—no, made a suckling noise and seemed to slip into some sweet dream of his mother's teats, eyes half closed, tongue lapping. Willy's father worked the foreleg to keep the blood pumping through the heart, and Willy's mother said, "I never knew there was so much blood in a pig."

The minister said: *Suicide is sin, but God forgives, as we must forgive.* Matt Fry kicked another stone. It hit the lip of the grave and tumbled, banged against the coffin lid, left a small dent in the perfect, polished pine. *Judge not lest ye be judged.*

Mrs. Fry smacked Matthew as they climbed into the long black limousine. Men pound you with their fists, Willy thought, blacken your eye or break your nose. Women slap you with an open palm and leave the red marks of their fingers on your face.

Two weeks later Matt drove his mother's Buick into the Snake River and let it sink. He set fire to her drapes three days after that, but his father got the hose in time. In early December, when the ground was hard but no snow had fallen, he stole the lights from the lawn of the funeral home.

Willy was cruising with his father that night, pretending they might get lucky and find some trouble. They caught up with the boy down by the Miller Creek bridge. His white face rose, a moon above his dark coat.

Horton Hamilton climbed out of the patrol car, one hand on his hip. Thick fingers unsnapped the leather band that held the pistol safe in its holster. Matt's eyes glazed, blind as stones in the twin beams of the headlights. "Don't you be gettin' any ideas of makin' like a jackrabbit, boy—I got a gun." Willy knew his father had never shot a human being. A man doesn't shoot peeping Toms out of trees or pull his gun on drunken girls reeling through the woods. Once he'd fired off a round to scare a badger off poor Mrs. Griswold's porch, and Willy thought he

might do that now, might blast the ground just to show the boy
he took what business he had seriously.

Horton Hamilton was the one to drive Matt up to the state
school for delinquents in Cross City. The Frys told the judge
they'd lost control of their child. *Wits' end,* they said. *No sense
sending him home.* So Willy learned that if you did a bad enough
thing your parents could decide they didn't want you. Horton
told Matthew: "You're getting a second chance, son. Next time
they'll judge you as a man and it won't go so easy. Take my
advice—learn something useful. You end up in prison, all they
teach you to do is stamp license plates."

But the boy didn't take to his education. Willy heard whispers
at home, stories at school. Matt Fry always was the kind who'd
throw a kid to the ground for looking at him too hard. He had
a reputation and finally lived up to it by biting off a piece of
another boy's ear. He got solitary for that. "Lucky for him it
was only the hole," Horton said. "They shoot dogs for less."

Eighteen days later, when they dragged Matt Fry into the
light, he was like this: lame in one foot, skinny as a coyote at
the end of winter. He'd forgotten how to talk, forgotten he was
supposed to unzip his pants before he took a piss. Willy wondered: *What did the guards do to him when they pulled him off
the boy with half an ear? How hard did his head hit the gravel,
and how many times?*

Matthew returned to White Falls that spring to find the
basement windows of his parents' house boarded shut and their
doors locked.

Now he lived in the shed by the tracks. The shack was big
enough for one man, two sheep and some chickens—if a person
could stand the smell. Old man Hardy had lived that way for
40 years. He died in '63, and in the end, it was his smell that
drove the animals out.

Willy followed Iona Moon and caught her doing things with
Matt Fry. He watched through the window of the shed while

they ate cold soup from a can and smoked cigarettes. Matt's head bobbed up and down; spit dribbled from his slack lip. He was more of an idiot than Roy Wilkerson, who was born with those slanty eyes. When Matt tried to eat a cigarette, Iona had to pull it from his mouth.

Another time, Willy saw Iona cover him with a tattered blanket and curl up behind him, belly to butt. She held that filthy boy in her arms and kissed his dirty hair. She pressed herself against his torn jeans, damp with piss and smelling like a body died in them.

Iona didn't mind the smell. Her brothers were always making her pick up dead things. Once she carried a pack rat home by its hairless tail. Mama yelled and Iona cried. Her brothers vanished and she took the licking alone, stood naked in the cold bath water while her mama scrubbed her hands with a brush, soaped her face and wasn't careful of her eyes. But Iona didn't fuss. She was done crying. And she didn't wail when Daddy came home and took his belt to her bare behind. Her brothers watched and she never told on them. She was eight when it happened, and now she was eleven. She still didn't mind the smell of dead things—but she'd learned not to bring them home.

She didn't try to bring Matt Fry home either. She knew what Mama would say if she saw him. *Always was a bad influence, teaching my sons things they didn't need to know.*

But Iona remembered Matthew a different way. He and her three brothers said they had a surprise for her in the gully. They blindfolded her and led her into the trees. *Count to fifty, Iona.* And she did. When she pulled the bandanna down around her neck, they were gone. She sat on a rock, counted to fifty again, but there was no surprise. She sat still as she could, waiting for something to happen.

When Matt circled back, he found her curled on the ground,

holding her knees to her chest, her face blotched and salty. "Come on, Iona," he said, "I'll take you home."

She said, "I'm not lost."

"Then why you been cryin'?"

"I wanted—" She choked on her words. "You said you had a surprise." Matt didn't laugh at her. "I just wanted to *see* something."

He knelt beside her. She'd been sucking on her hair and he pulled the wet strand from her mouth. "I'll show you something," he said.

He knew a secret place, a cave he'd dug in the earth at the edge of the woods. He took her there and no one found them. They barely fit down the narrow mouth and had to lie chest to chest, not moving, faces close, legs entwined. The hole was damp with decaying roots and leaves; it smelled like the inside of an animal, her father's bloody hands, a calf just born. She liked being swallowed. She liked this boy with sour breath and skinny arms. He held her tight but didn't rub against her, didn't make her jeans chafe her thighs, didn't bruise her ribs the way her brother Leon did when he paid her a dime to lie down with him.

Days later, she tried to find the cave alone, but a hard rain had made the roof collapse and filled the opening with silt. They could have been buried alive. She thought about that a lot. When Mama swore or Daddy pulled his belt from the loops, she said to herself: *I could have died.*

Willy knew his mother blamed Horton for the whole thing. "You never should have cuffed him," she said.

"I wanted him to understand."

"What if it had been your boy?"

"I would've whupped his ass."

"You should have taken him home instead of locking him up."

"How was I supposed to know his folks would leave him there all night?"

"You shouldn't have told them the lights cost so damn much. The boy was just pulling a prank."

"I don't make the laws, Flo. I just follow them."

"Why not chop off his hand?"

"Huh?"

"Eye for an eye, Mr. High and Mighty."

"I wasn't the judge. I didn't send him to that school."

"You cuffed him like a man. Took him to jail. You called it a felony."

"I do my job. I do what I think is right."

"And if some boy loses his head because you're doing what you think is right, well that's just the price of justice."

"I can't see the future, Flo."

"You can't see your own hand in the dark."

"What's that supposed to mean?"

But there was no explanation. Willy's mother put on her coat and said she was going for a drive. Horton sat down at the kitchen table, his head in his hands. Willy wanted to go to him, wanted to sit beside him in the dark and say: *Let the thief no longer steal, but rather let him labor, doing honest work with his hands.* He knew the words from Sunday school, knew that all men were sinners, all were dirty. Only by God's grace would the chosen few be spared. He wished he could tell his father what he'd seen Iona Moon do with Matt Fry. *If anyone touches an unclean thing, he shall be guilty.* Why should decent folks feel any pity for people like that?

Willy's sisters sneaked up behind him while he stood watching his father. Lorena grabbed his legs and Mariette knocked him over. They pinned him to the floor and started tickling. They weren't strong, but they were both fat. Once they were on top of him, he couldn't move. Willy heard the back door snap. Horton wasn't going to have any of their nonsense tonight. But his father's presence was still in the house. *Don't hurt your sisters,*

Willy. Lorena was crushing his bladder. *Never hit a lady.* Mariette
shoved her fingers into his ribs, not tickling but jabbing, making
him writhe. *A man is stronger than any woman. Stronger in his
body, stronger in his mind.* He had to pee. Lorena had her big
butt right on his pelvis. His arm was twisted behind his back.
He felt tears sting his eyes, the hot shame, his bed wet again.
Jesus, Willy. His mother so tired, stripping the bed, stripping
him, buying the rubber sheets that squeaked when he turned
in bed, that made him sweat even though the cotton sheets
covered them. How old was he then? *Too old to wet the bed.*
And now Lorena was bouncing and laughing, loose flesh of her
legs jiggling, pink dimpled skin, small eyes squinting shut in
delight, and Willy's tears were rolling into his ears and the wet
spot was spreading on his jeans and Mariette was squealing,
"Willy peed his pants," and his sisters were both standing, covering their mouths, shaking with laughter, and Willy was on
the floor, burning, seeing Iona Moon pressed up tight to Matt
Fry, knowing exactly how he smelled. Exactly.

Around midnight, Willy heard two shots and hung his head
out the window. Flo's car still wasn't in the drive. The moon
was low and almost full, flattened on top like a smashed pumpkin. His father stood in the yard with his pistol drawn. He
seemed to waver in the yellow light, and at first Willy thought
he'd shot himself in the foot.

By the time Willy got downstairs, his father was underneath
an elm at the edge of the lawn, staring at the raccoon he'd shot
out of the tree.

"Damn vermin," he said without looking at the boy. "That
coon made a mess of our garage last winter. Stole half a bushel
of apples before I got wise to him."

"How do you know this is the one?" Willy said.

Horton whirled to face Willy. "How do I know?" He cleared
his throat and spit on the ground. "What the hell else could it
have been?"

Willy backed away from his father. He saw the big man's legs tremble, saw the glint of the gun against his hard thigh. The boy looked at the limp body of the animal, the masked bandit eyes, the pointed nose, the clean paws, delicate as the hands of a tiny woman. He turned and sprinted toward the house, the crushed head of the moon so bright he had to close his eyes.

2

Jeweldeen Wilder pedaled her bike two miles across the Kila Flats to tell Iona what her daddy had done.

"Locked Sharla in the cellar. Says she's not coming out till she tells him who got her in this mess. And she keeps saying the same thing: Everett Fry."

"Everett's been dead a year and a half."

"Every time she says it, Daddy just gets madder."

Jack Wilder was a fat man with no hair who sweated when he thought too hard. Even his fingers were fat. Iona imagined his red face and damp shirt as he stood nose to nose with Sharla, making her say the name one more time.

"Come on," Jeweldeen said, "we can look at her."

They raced their bikes down the rutted road, even though Sharla wasn't going anywhere in a hurry.

"Where's your daddy?" Iona said when they got to the Wilder place.

"Spreading manure."

"Hot day for that."

"He don't mind the smell."

"Isn't he afraid you'll let Sharla out?"

"Said he'd break my arm if I did."

"So you won't?"

"She never did much for me."

They crept around the back of the house to peer down into the cellar. Iona remembered hearing about a man overcome by gas while shoveling fertilizer on a warm day. He fell face down in the stuff and smothered in two inches of shit. She thought this might be a fitting end for a father who locked his own daughter in a hole.

"There she is," Jeweldeen said.

The tiny window was speckled with dirt. "I don't see her."

"On that sack of potatoes in the corner."

Iona could barely make out the lumpy shape of the girl in the shadows.

"She's a mess," said Jeweldeen. "Thank God my mama isn't here to see this. Daddy says Sharla would put her in her grave for sure if she weren't already there."

Maywood Wilder had died of pneumonia before Jeweldeen could walk. Now her picture hung on the wall above the television. Jack Wilder liked to remind his daughters that their mother was watching over them, just like God. Such talk could bring Sharla to tears but had no effect on Jeweldeen.

"Mama would have died at least a hundred times if we put her in her grave every time Daddy says." Jeweldeen puffed out her cheeks and lowered her voice to mimic her father. "Your mama would fall down and die if she saw how filthy you are, Jeweldeen. It'd burst your mama's heart to hear you take the Lord's name in vain, Miss Sharla." Jeweldeen crossed her arms over her chest and became herself again. "*Geezus,*" she hissed, "my mother has turned over in her grave so many times she's halfway down the hill by now."

Iona smashed her nose against the mud-spattered glass. Maybe Sharla was fatter, but she always looked soft because she was so fair, skin pale as uncooked dough, hair wispy, almost white. When Sharla was hot, she blotched from her neck to her forehead. Nothing so fine or flattering as a blush ever rose on her cheeks. Jeweldeen was much prettier and knew it. Her hair was thick and wavy, gold as hay. *For my blue-eyed sweetheart,* the man at the candy store always said, touching Jeweldeen's shoulder as he gave her a free bag of sour balls or a long rope of licorice. Even Leon liked Jeweldeen, said she was *dangerous,* and Iona wondered how a thirteen-year-old girl could be a threat to a grown man.

Sharla clutched her knees to her chest and rocked. "She could go crazy down there all by herself," Iona said.

Jeweldeen clicked her tongue against the roof of her mouth. "Go crazy? She *is* crazy. Says she got knocked up by a guy who's been dead since November before last."

"You think she believes it?"

"Came to her in a dream. Everett weighed nothing at all, but she felt him all the same, like the air just got thicker in that one place."

Iona tried to imagine this. When Leon climbed on top of her, he'd felt heavy as a cow.

"She says he didn't talk but she heard his voice in her own skull. He told her he was tired of being dead and he was sorry he shot himself."

Leon didn't talk much either, as Iona recalled, but she'd never known her brother to be sorry about anything.

"That's why he wants Sharla to have his baby. He means to be reborn."

Leon unzipped his pants but kept them on. Having babies wasn't the point of the whole thing.

"No wonder Daddy locked her in the cellar. Imagine Sharla telling people Everett bumped her."

Iona remembered Sharla's other dream, the way Everett touched her, the way she exploded. Jack Wilder thought she was cracked long before she expected a dead man's baby. *Like a sick animal,* he said, *but it only happens to females.*

Iona wondered if female animals went crazy from having kids or not having them. After the five-legged calf died, Angel rolled on her back, rubbed the hair off her hide till she bled. Later, she charged the fence, and Iona's father had to hold her while Leon pulled the barbs out of her flesh. Free at last, she tried to jump Leon, the unexpected object of her strange desires.

Iona's father said a cow had a big head, but no brains, nothing but tongue filling up all that space.

Iona peeled potatoes while her mother fried hamburger for a shepherd's pie. They were last year's potatoes, the skins wrinkled and dusty, the flesh a bit too soft, already sprouting tough violet shoots. She meant to tell Hannah now, while they were alone, but something stopped her: the line of her mother's mouth, or the way she held her hands under the warm water long after they were clean.

At dinner, Iona told the story. She knew what her brothers would think.

"Could be anyone's," Leon said. He was nineteen but looked thirty. The skin under his eyes was pouched; he'd already lost a patch of hair over both temples.

"She's done half the senior class," said Rafe.

"You hush," Hannah said.

"It's no secret." Dale's mouth was full of pie.

"She's blaming it on a dead man 'cause she forgot to keep a list of the possibilities," Leon said. "Poor Everett can't even deny it, and he's probably one of the few guys in town who didn't pop Sharla."

Iona stared at Leon, trying to decide if his nastiness came from being one of the few or one of many.

"You hear me?" said Hannah. "I won't have you talking that way."

"I heard you, Mama. I just don't see the point."

Iona's father said, "You sit at this table, you mind your mother. That's the point."

Leon stood, let his napkin fall. "I'm done anyway," he said.

Iona lay in bed wondering how Everett looked when he came to Sharla in her dream. His picture in the paper after he died showed a proud young man in uniform. The flag waved behind him, out of focus. Everett's mouth was firm. *I do what I'm told to do.*

The picture didn't look a bit like the Everett Fry Iona knew. That Everett Fry parked on Main for half a day at a time, staring at women, making them jittery for weeks afterward. That Everett Fry wore a red and black plaid hunting cap with the ear flaps pulled down and the visor shading his eyes. His hunter's vest bulged; he had something hidden in every pocket: knives and grenades, leather straps and dried beans, a half-dozen boxes of shells. He smoked filterless cigarettes down to a nub so small he could barely pinch the hot butt between his yellow fingers.

Then there was the third Everett Fry, the clean-shaven one wearing his uniform again. His eyes were startled, opened wide. His mouth was open too, revealing jagged chips of bone: his teeth shattered by the blast. If Sharla put her hands on his head she'd discover the back of his skull was gone. Iona wondered if men bled in dreams or if the wound would be nothing worse than a hole, surprising and strange but not too terrible to touch.

Iona rode her bike along the dirt road to Jeweldeen's. She stopped pedaling near the Zimmerman place, coasting to look at Al's bulls. Muscles rippled over their buttocks. They had thick necks, twitching tails. She knew the scent of a cow wafting across the field could turn them mean. Sometimes even her smell made them paw the ground under the fence. But this day was still, and the bulls chewed their cud, gazes blank as her father's when he looked at her without seeing. He had more important things on his mind: potatoes and corn, beets and beans. He worried: *Too much rain or too little?* Even in June he had to figure what he'd do if they got frost in September.

Iona wondered if Sharla had given up and told her daddy the truth, or at least something halfway believable. The afternoon was hot; dust flumed under her tires. Iona's father would fret about the heat, remembering the year the topsoil dried up and blew away. He was sixteen years old. The potatoes shriveled in the sun. *Like horrible little heads,* he said.

Like her own head when she got lice last fall and Mama had to shave off all her hair. Hannah grabbed soap and scissors and hauled Iona out to the back steps. She yanked a clump and cut, then another and another, wasting no time on tenderness. Soon Iona's long hair lay around her in limp, dark swirls. Her head felt light and sore. Hannah rubbed Iona's scalp with kerosene. The oil burned, and the pain spread to her neck, a fire radiating through her shoulders to her arms to the tingling tips of her fingers. The heat shot down her spine and her legs prickled— just as they had when she fell in the briars and her daddy had to twist the spiky thorns out one by one with his pointed pliers.

But her parents hadn't done these things to hurt her, so she was lucky in a way, not like Sharla Wilder, who'd been locked in the cellar for a solid week.

"No end in sight," Jeweldeen said when Iona got off her bike. "Every morning he goes down there and asks her who done it, and every morning she gives him the same answer. Yesterday he took a stick to her legs, said he'd beat the truth out of her. She said 'Everett Fry' about a hundred times before he stopped."

Hearing Everett's name out loud made Iona touch the back of her own head.

"I broke the cellar window with a rock," said Jeweldeen. "You can look at her if you want."

Sharla sat crushed in the corner, exactly where she'd been the last time Iona had looked. "Does she ever move?"

"You should see her jump when she hears Daddy on the stairs. And she was sure dancing yesterday when he whacked her with the stick. You never saw a fat girl move so fast."

"Why doesn't she bolt the lock from her side?"

"He'd bust down the door and whup her good if she tried that." Jeweldeen peered through the jagged hole in the glass. "Hey, Sharla," she said, "somebody's here to see you."

Sharla shuffled over to the window, old already, dress torn at the shoulder, legs blue with bruises.

She climbed on an empty crate. "More cake," she said.

"It's all she'll eat," said Jeweldeen. "I made her one yesterday and one the day before, and they're both gone. Daddy would thump me if he knew. He means to starve the truth out of her."

"I'm hungry," Sharla said, raising her hands toward the window.

"Honestly," said Jeweldeen, "you're gonna drive me straight up this wall with your begging." She banged her fist on the side of the house. "I already told you, cake's gone. You ate it, Sharla, the whole damn thing."

Sharla stared at her sister. "You talk to her," Jeweldeen told Iona. "I'll go see if I can find her something sweet." She wagged her finger at Sharla. "But I am not making you another cake. You're too fat anyway."

Jeweldeen was right about Sharla being too fat. Her breasts and belly were already bloated, twice their usual size. "You can tell me," Iona said. "I won't breathe a word to your daddy; I won't even tell Jeweldeen."

Sharla cocked her head and her brow wrinkled. She put her hand over her mouth and Iona saw the chipped red polish on her nails. Living in the dark, eating nothing but cake, waiting for her father to come down the stairs—no wonder Sharla was starting to go off. "I know why you're acting this way," Iona whispered. She remembered the day her father put Angel down. Hannah wanted him to wait. *Dry a year,* he said, *and now she's worrying the others.* But he was sorry to do it, and Iona saw him in the field, stroking Angel's head.

Jeweldeen returned, carrying two slabs of bread with butter and sugar. Sharla snatched them from her sister, stuffed a whole piece in her mouth and scuttled to the corner. No amount of coaxing could lure her back to the window.

"I'll bring you another slice," Jeweldeen said. "With honey this time. Or strawberry jam. You'd like that, wouldn't you?"

Sharla squatted and chewed. "Forget it, then," said Jeweldeen. She grabbed Iona's arm. "Honestly," she said, "I don't know what you find so interesting."

Iona found everything about Sharla Wilder interesting. Maybe she did make love to Everett Fry before he shot himself. Maybe it felt like being with the ghost of a man and now she couldn't get it out of her head. No matter how many times her daddy smacked her legs she was going to keep on telling him the same name. Everett Fry. What good was the truth? No one in his right mind was going to marry Sharla in her condition—even if Jack Wilder did hold a shotgun to his head. Maybe that was the real reason Sharla lay the blame on Everett. He'd turned the gun on himself and was safe from her daddy.

Iona stayed clear of the Wilder place for the rest of the week. She wanted to see Sharla alone and planned to sneak over there some night. She'd ask Sharla what it was like to make love with Everett Fry, to feel the scar on his shoulder with her fingers, the place where the flesh was puckered and hard.

Did a dead lover whisper your name, or was silence the most important thing? Did you hear the wind in the grass? Did the branches beat against your window? Did he smell like a man, like your own father, or was his breath sweet as cinnamon and almonds?

Iona never got the chance to ask these questions. On Sunday, Jeweldeen appeared. She still wore her church clothes, though it was late afternoon. Her little white anklets and patent leather shoes were speckled with mud. It had rained during the night, and Jeweldeen had ridden straight through the puddles.

"Sharla's not pregnant anymore," Jeweldeen said, puffing as she tried to catch her breath. "She's sick though. Too hot to touch. Daddy found her on the floor of the cellar when we got home from church, bleeding like a stuck pig. 'Well that's that,' he says, and we carried her upstairs. My hands were burning. Fever a hundred and four, I'd say, but he won't call the doctor.

'Leave well enough alone,' he told me. We put her in a tub of cold water. The bleeding slowed down but she's still hot." Jeweldeen climbed on her bike. "I better get back there before Daddy sees I'm gone."

"I'm coming with you."

"He won't like it."

"Since when do you care?"

Jeweldeen shrugged and Iona ran to get her bike.

They rode fast without talking. The day was already dark, the air heavy with low clouds. Al Zimmerman's bulls rammed their heads into the electric fence as the girls passed. The shock made them rear back but didn't stop them from charging again, digging at the dirt with their sharp hooves.

Jeweldeen peeked down the cellar window as they propped their bikes against the side of the house. "Look at this," she said. Iona was afraid Sharla's father had already forced her back down the stairs. But it was nothing like that. It was Jack Wilder himself, on his hands and knees, scouring the place where Sharla had curled into herself hours earlier.

They found Sharla in the living room. All the shades had been pulled down, and the place smelled musty. She lay on the couch, wrapped in a white sheet, wide awake. The cold bath had brought her temperature down. Her face was bloodless, pale as always. In fact, she seemed a lot more like herself than the last time Iona had seen her.

Sharla's eyes looked red and sore, but she didn't blink. "Don't you stare at me," Jeweldeen said. "I didn't do nothing."

Sharla breathed hard. Iona thought she had something to say, but all of a sudden she was wailing instead, punching and kicking at the sheet from inside till she'd beaten it away from her. She clawed at her white breasts and her white belly as if she wanted to tear off her skin too. Iona tried to grab her wrists, but Sharla was quick. She slapped at the air and kicked Iona in the stomach. The sheet was stained underneath Sharla's rump, and her thighs were streaked with dried blood. "You better get some towels," Iona said to Jeweldeen. The sight of her naked sister startled Jeweldeen enough to do what Iona asked.

"Look at her," Sharla said. She pointed to the picture of Maywood Wilder above the television. Iona did look. The head floated, bigger than life, cut off at the shoulders. She wore glasses that magnified her eyes but left them out of focus. Someone had erased all the wrinkles, leaving her face unnaturally smooth, unmotherly in a way Iona couldn't define. The picture had no color, and the woman's lips looked almost black; Maywood Wilder smiled without enjoying herself.

"She's watching me," Sharla said. "Daddy told me—just like God." She laughed. Her cheeks didn't seem swollen anymore; she was shrinking back to her normal size, and her voice was tight and clear. "He's glad I took care of it." She swallowed hard. "He was afraid it might look too much like him." Her throat was dry but she didn't whisper. "He kept tryin' to make me say somebody else did it. Ain't nobody gonna know now. 'Cept my mama. She knows what he did. I told him so too. She knows."

Jeweldeen had come back in the room in time to hear the last three sentences. "Get out o' here," she said to Iona. She dropped the pile of towels on the floor. Iona wanted to push Sharla's damp hair off her face. She wanted to promise that everything would be all right. She wanted to hold Sharla's hand or at least help Jeweldeen get those towels underneath her. But there wasn't time for any of that, before Jeweldeen said, "I mean it, Iona—now."

Sharla's eyes opened wide, but she didn't move, didn't make a sound. Iona walked out into the yard and Jeweldeen followed. It was drizzling again. Rust-colored rivulets cut the muddy drive. Jack Wilder knelt by the cellar window, nailing a board over the broken glass. He glanced at Iona and Jeweldeen but didn't stop pounding. Iona thought of his short, fat fingers.

"My sister's crazy," Jeweldeen said. "She's just trying to get back at Daddy, telling you those lies."

Iona nodded.

"You don't believe her, do you?"

Iona shook her head.

"My daddy's not like that."

Jack Wilder stood and wiped his bald head with a handkerchief. He was too far away to hear them. He dumped the bucket
of water he'd used to wash the cellar floor. It trickled down the
drive, the same color as the red brown mud.

"Don't you dare tell anybody what she said or I'll swear you
got lice again. Nobody'll touch you. Nobody'll even talk to you."
Jeweldeen took a deep breath and waited. "Well?"

"Well what?"

"What Sharla said—are you gonna tell?"

"No."

"Cross your heart?"

Iona drew an *X* over her heart with her finger.

"And hope to die?"

"Yes," Iona said, "I hope to die."

She didn't tell, not that summer and not that fall when Sharla
disappeared. Who would she tell? Jeweldeen Wilder was her
only friend. She wanted to tell her mother, but she remembered
overhearing Hannah's words on the phone one night: *I can't
stand one more thing.* Iona considered her mother's afflictions—
surely there would always be one more thing: a hard rain in
August to destroy the corn; a blight to pock every potato in the
field; a husband sitting in the dark drinking whiskey, breaking
glasses in the middle of the night; a calf with five legs and a
brooding cow tangled in barbed wire; three sons who guzzled
beer and drove to the dump at dusk to plug rats, who seemed
bound to shoot off their own toes—sooner or later; the shame
of a daughter sent home from school with a head full of lice.
One more thing, and one more. Iona was afraid and always
wondered: *What will be the last thing, and will I be to blame?*

3

Willy Hamilton never did like Iona Moon, not when they were kids and not now that they were sophomores in high school. He said country girls always had shit on their shoes and he could smell her after she'd been in his car.

Jay Tyler said his choice of women was nobody's business, and if Willy didn't like it, he should keep his back doors locked. Choice of women, Jay said that so nice. He thought Iona was a woman because the first night they were together he put his hand under her shirt and she didn't stop kissing him. He inched his fingers under her brassiere, like some five-legged animal, until his wrist was caught by the elastic and his hand was squished against her breast. She said, "Here, baby, let me help you," then reached around behind her back to release the hooks. One hand on each breast, Jay whistled through his teeth. "Sweet Jesus," he said. He'd had plenty of girls in the backseat of Willy's Chevy, girls who let him do whatever he wanted as long as he could take what he was after without any assistance on their part, without ever saying, "Yes, Jay," the way Iona did, just a murmur, "yes," soft as snow on water.

In the moonlight, her skin was gold, her breasts small but warm. Jay cupped them in his palms, touching the nipples with the very tips of his fingers, as if they were precious and alive, something separate from the girl, something that could be frightened and disappear. He pressed his lips to the hard bones of Iona's chest, rested his head in the hollow between her breasts and whispered words no boy had ever spoken to her.

"Thank you," he said. "Oh God, thank you." His voice was hushed and amazed, the voice of a drowning man just pulled from the river. As his mouth found her nipple, he closed his eyes so tight she thought he wanted to be blind.

Iona believed that the distance from the Kila Flats to White Falls depended on age more than miles. For a kid on a bike it took an hour of hard pedaling, but a teenager in a pickup could make the trip in twenty minutes. You were in town before the muck on your shoes dried. If you rolled all the windows down, you got there with grit in your teeth and dust in your hair, but the warm smell of the pregnant sow who brushed up against your leg in the yard never blew away. You saw her in your mind as she tottered on her short, ridiculous legs, her wavering bulk too much for her small feet. You could stay in town all night, but the Kila Flats were close as your own breath.

She knew Willy was right about her shoes. No way to avoid it—in the field, in the barn, before school every day. She couldn't recall exactly when her mother had stopped milking the cows and the duty had become her own. One morning after a storm, Iona had to shovel her way to the barn. Waves of blue snow fluttered across the yard. A drift blocked the door, and she bent over, dug like a dog. The first stall was empty. She ran to the next, shining her flashlight in every corner, trying to imagine a cow could hide in a shadow, small as a cat, but she knew, even as she ran in circles, she knew they were in the fields, that her brothers had just assumed an animal would head for shelter on its own. They didn't understand cows the way she and Hannah did. A cow's hardly any smarter than a chicken; a cow's like an overgrown child, like the Wilkerson boy who grew tall and fat but never got smart.

She heard them. As she ran across the fields, stumbling in

the snow, falling on her face more than once and snorting ice through her nose, she heard them crying like old women. The four cows huddled together, standing up past their knees in the drifts. Snow had piled in ridges down their backs; they hadn't moved all night. They let out that sound, that awful wail, as if their souls were being torn out of them. Iona had to whip them with her belt to get them going. That's how cows were: they'd drop to their knees and freeze to death with their eyes wide open and the barn door barely a hundred feet in front of them.

Later, Iona took Hannah her aspirin and hot milk, sat on the edge of her bed, and moaned like the cows, closing her eyes and stretching her mouth wide as it would go. Hannah laughed, breathless, holding her stomach; the milk sloshed in the cup and Iona had to take it. Hannah had a bad time hanging on to things. Her fingers were stiff and twisted, and that winter her knees swelled up so big she couldn't walk.

Iona told Jay how it was in winter on the Kila Flats, how the wind had nothing to stand in its way, how the water froze in the pipes and you had to use the outhouse, how you held it just as long as you could because the snow didn't fall, it blew straight in your face; splinters of ice pierced your skin and you could go blind or get lost just walking to that little hut twenty-five yards behind the house. Her brothers tied ropes from the back door to the outhouse and the barn so they could feel their way. She told Jay she kept a thunder mug under her bed in case she had to pee in the night. But she didn't tell him Hannah's arthritis was so bad she couldn't get to the end of the hall, didn't say her mother had to use a bedpan all the time now, and Iona was the one who slid it under her bony butt because Mama thought it wasn't right for a husband to see you that way.

Jay and Iona parked down by the river with Willy and Belinda. Willy Hamilton liked girls who accidentally brushed their hands against a guy's crotch, girls who flipped their hair and almost closed their eyes when they said hello, girls who could pull you right up to the edge and still always, always say *no*.

That's why he liked Belinda Beller, a good girl who wore braces and stuffed her bra with toilet paper. She was in the front seat saying, "No, honey, please—I don't want to." Jay slid his knee between Iona's legs and kissed her hard to keep her quiet. Willy said, "I'm sorry." He stopped pawing at Belinda and sat with his hands in his lap, pretending they were tied, remembering how his father cuffed Matt Fry, talking all the time, his hand on the gun, using the low rumble of his voice to hold the skittery boy in one place, like a farmer trying to mesmerize a dog that's gone mad so he can put a bullet through its head. Then the snap of metal, cold on the wrist.

Belinda leaned over to peck Willy's cheek and whisper, "It's all right now, honey."

But it wasn't.

Matt Fry had been home four years and still slept in the shed by the tracks. If you saw him by the river and said, "Hey," he didn't look at you.

Belinda started sweet-talking, stroking Willy's neck, messing his hair, calling him *baby;* but when he kissed her again, his lips were dry and his heart chaste.

Iona had no sympathy for Belinda Beller's point of view. What sense was there in saving everything up for some special occasion that might not ever come? How do you hold a boy off if his tongue in your ear makes you arch your back and grab his hair?

Iona thought, *You hang on to something too long, you start to think it's worth more than it is.* She knew enough to be careful; you could end up like Sharla Wilder. But she was never tight with the boys, on account of having three brothers and being the youngest. When she was nine, they took her to the barn and gave her pennies to dance for them. Later they gave her nickels to lift her shirt and let them touch the buds that weren't breasts yet. And that one time, when she and Leon were alone in the loft, he paid her a dime for lying down and letting him rub against her. She was scared, all that grunting and groaning, and when she looked down she saw that his little prick wasn't little anymore: it was swollen and dark and she said, "You're hurting yourself." He clamped his dirty hand over her mouth. Finally he made a terrible sound, like the sound a cow makes when her calf is halfway out of her. His eyes bulged and his face turned red, as if Iona had choked him. He collapsed, a dead man, and she lay there, pinned, clutching fistfuls of straw, wondering how she was going to explain to Mama and Daddy that she'd killed her brother.

Hannah Moon knew Iona had a guy. She made Iona tell her that Jay Tyler was on the diving team. He could fly off the high board backward, do two somersaults and half a twist; he seemed to open the water with his hands, and his body made a sound like a flat stone you spin sideways so it cuts without a splash. Mama worked the rest of it out of Iona too. Jay's father was a dentist with a pointed gray beard and no hair. Jay was going to college so he could come back to White Falls and go into practice with his dad. Iona said it like she was proud, but Mama shook her head and blinked hard at her gnarled hands, trying to make something go away. She said, "If I was a strong woman, Iona, I'd lock you in this house till you got over Jay Tyler. I'd rather have you hate me than see some boy from town break your heart."

"Jay's not like that," Iona said.

"Every boy's like that in the end. Dentists don't marry the daughters of potato farmers. He'll be lookin' for a girl with an education—even if all he wants her to do is serve afternoon tea."

• • •

Willy thought that just listening to Jay Tyler and his father might be dangerous, a bad thing that took him too far from home and made his stomach thump like a second heart.

White Falls stretched down the north side of the river for two miles but was only twelve blocks wide. Some people—like Willy Hamilton—lived on numbered streets, and others—like Jay Tyler—lived on roads named after trees: Elm and Spruce and Willow Glen. If you crossed the bridge to the south side of the river, the street was Route 2 and led to a trailer park, an eyesore, Horton Hamilton said, and Willy agreed: the lime green and brilliant silver of the little box houses could make your eyes smart on a sunny day. Route 3 was a dirt road to the Flats. There was no Route 1.

Everything was close, but on nights like this one, Willy believed that the distance between his own table and the Tylers' front porch was unfathomable. Willy's father had been late for dinner—which was why the peas were mushy and the roast overdone, which was why Flo stood at the stove and muttered, "Everything's ruined," softly, so only Willy heard.

"Got a call at the last minute," Horton said. "Woman and her son strollin' out of Pick-n-Pay with their groceries stuffed under their shirts." He smiled. It was the worst crime of the week. "Said they were hungry—that was their excuse: they were hungry."

"Maybe they were," Flo said.

"Woman had two cartons of cigarettes and six batteries."

"What about the boy?"

"Bag of Fig Newtons and a box of pretzels."

"So *he* was hungry." Flo looked at Willy as if to ask: *Would you steal for me?*

Now, sitting on the Tylers' porch, Willy was having the same conversation with Jay and his father. When he told them there was one right and one wrong and all you had to do was look in the Bible to see which was which, Andrew Johnson Tyler stroked his beard and said, "Well, Willy, I tell you, it's hard for a *medical man* to believe in God." Jay nodded, understanding what Willy did not, the secret reverence of the words *medical man.*

Jay's mother floated across the veranda, her footsteps so soft that Willy had to glance at her feet to be sure they touched wood. The folds of her speckled dress fell forward and back, and he saw the outline of her thighs before he looked away. "All this talk," she said. "How about some lemonade? I swear I don't remember another May as warm as this one." Everything about her was pale: her cheeks, flushed from the heat; the sweep of yellow hair, wound in a bun but not too tight; a few blond tendrils swirling at the nape of her neck, damp with sweat; the white dress with tiny pink roses, cut low in front so that when she leaned forward and said, "Why don't you help me, Willy," he saw the curve of her breasts.

In the kitchen, she brushed his hair from his eyes, touched his hand, almost as if she didn't mean to do it, but he knew. He scurried out to the porch with the lemonade on a tray, ice rattling against glass, a woman's laughter rippling from the cool shadows of the house.

Willy lost his way on the Kila Flats. All those dirt roads looked the same. Jay told him: turn left, turn right, take another right at the fork; he sent Willy halfway around the county so he'd have time in the back seat with Iona Moon, time to unhook her bra, time to unzip his pants. Willy kept looking in his rearview mirror; he'd dropped Belinda Beller off hours ago. He imagined his father cruising Main and Woodvale Park, looking for him. He thought of his mother at the window, parting the drapes with one hand, pressing her nose to the glass. She worried. He knew she saw a metal bumper twisted around a tree, a wheel spinning a foot above the ground, headlights blasting into the dark woods. She washed the blood off the faces of the four teenagers, combed their hair, dabbed their bruises with flesh-colored powder, painted their blue lips a bright pink. That was back in '57, but she saw their open eyes and surprised mouths every time Willy was late. "Forgive me, Lord, for not trusting you. I know my thoughts are a curse. I know he's safe with you, and he's a good boy, a careful boy, but I can't help my worrying: he's my only son." She unlaced her fingers and hissed, "I'll thrash his hide when he walks in that door." She said it out loud, because God only listened to prayers and silence.

Jay said, "Shit, Willy, you took the wrong turn back there. I told you *right* at the fork." And Willy said he did go right, and Jay answered, "We'd be in front of Iona's house if you went right." There was something in Jay's voice—a crack, one high word that gave him away. Willy slammed the brakes and sent the Chevy into a quarter spin. "What the hell?" said Jay.

"Get out," Willy said.

"What?"

"You heard me."

Jay zipped his pants and opened the door; Iona started to climb out after him. "Just Jay," Willy said, and he got out too. The front window was open far enough for Iona to hear Willy say, "You're gonna get me grounded because you wanna fool around with that little slut." Jay shoved Willy over the hood of the car, and Iona watched the dust curl in the streams of yellow light, waiting for the blow. But Jay didn't hit him; he held him there, leaning on top of him, ten seconds, twenty; and when he let Willy up, Jay clapped him on the shoulder, said, "Sorry, buddy, I'll make it up to you."

Jay stood on the diving board, lean and tan, unbeatable. Willy was almost as good, some days better; but next to Jay he looked undefined, too thin and too white. Jay rolled off the balls of his feet, muscles flexing from his calves to his thighs. He threw an easy one first, a single somersault in lay-out position. As he opened up above the water, Iona gasped, expecting him to swoop back into the air.

Willy did the same dive, nearly as well. All day they went on this way, first one, then the other; Jay led Willy by a point and a half; the rest of the field dropped by ten.

Jay saved the backward double somersault with a twist for last. He climbed the ladder slowly, as if he had to think about the dive rung by rung. His buttocks clenched like fists. On the board, he rolled his shoulders, shook his hands, his feet. He strutted to the end, raised his arms, and spun on his toes. Every muscle frozen, he gritted his teeth and leaped, clamped his knees to his chest, and heaved head over heel, once, twice, opened up and twisted, limbs straight as a drill.

But in that last moment, Jay Tyler's concentration snapped. By some fluke, some sudden weakness, his knees bent and his feet slapped the water.

Iona thought she'd see Jay spit as he gripped the gutter of the pool, but he came up grinning, flashing his straight white teeth, his father's best work. Willy offered his hand. "I threw it too hard, buddy," Jay said. *Buddy.* Iona stood outside the chain-link fence; she barely heard it, but it made her think of that dusty road, stars flung in the cool black sky, Willy pinned to the hood of the car, and Jay saying: *Sorry, buddy, I'll make it up to you.* Only this way, Willy would never know. It was just like Jay not to give a damn about blame or forgiveness.

Willy's dive was easier, two somersaults without a twist, but flawless. He crept ahead of Jay, and no one else touched their scores. They sauntered to the bathhouse with their arms around each other's shoulders, knowing they'd won the day.

Standing in the dappled light beneath an oak, Jay Tyler's mother hugged Willy and Jay, and his father pumped their hands. Willy wished his parents could have seen him, this day above all others, but his father was on duty; and old lady Griswold had died, so his mother was busy making her look prettier than she'd ever been.

Iona Moon edged toward them, head down, eyes on the ground. Willy nudged Jay. In a single motion, graceful as the dive he'd almost hit, Jay turned, smiled, winked; he flicked his wrist near his thigh, a wave that said everything: *Go away, Iona. Can't you see I'm with my parents?* Willy felt the empty pit of his stomach, a throb of blood in his temples that made him dizzy, as if he were the one shooed away, as if he slunk in the shadows and disappeared behind the thick trunk of the tree, its limbs drooping with their own weight.

He was ashamed, like the small boy squinting under the fluorescent lights of the bathroom while his mother stripped his flannel pajamas off him with quick, hard strokes and said, "You're *soaked,* Willy; you're absolutely *drowned.*"

Upstairs the air was still and hot. Hannah couldn't stand the noise of the fan and told Iona, "No, please, don't turn it on."

Iona said, "I'm going to town. You want anything?"

"What's in town?"

"Nothing. It's just too dark out here—black fields, black hills. I get this desire, you know, to see a blaze, all the streetlamps going on at once—like something's about to happen."

"Don't go looking for him," Hannah said. "Bad enough he doesn't call—don't make it worse by being a fool."

"I'm just goin' to town, Mama. You want a treat or something, maybe a magazine?"

"Take a dollar from my jewelry box and get me as much chocolate as that'll buy. And don't tell your daddy, promise?"

"Promise."

"He thinks it's not good for me."

"I know."

"I think I've got to have some pleasure."

Iona's father sat on the porch with Leon and Rafe and Dale. They rocked, each with his pipe, each with the same tilt of the head as if a single thought wove through their minds. A breeze high in the pines made the tops sway so the limbs rubbed against one another. The sound they made was less than a breath, a whisper in a dream or the last thing your mother said before she kissed you goodnight; the kiss on your forehead was a whisper too, a promise no one could keep.

Iona buzzed up and down Main, feeling strong riding up high in the cab of the red truck, looking down on cars and rumbling over potholes too fast. Her father kept a coil of rope, a hacksaw, and a rifle in the back behind the seat. She had no intention, no intention at all, but she swung down Willow Glen Road, past Jay Tyler's house. She honked her horn at imaginary children in the street, stomped on her brakes and laid rubber to avoid a cat that wasn't there; but all that noise didn't lure anyone out of the Tyler house, and no lights popped on upstairs or down. In the green light of dusk, the house looked cool and gray, a huge, lifeless thing waiting to crumble.

She sped toward Seventh, Willy Hamilton's street. She might just happen to roll by, and maybe in the course of conversation she'd say, "Are the Tylers out of town?"

Sure enough, Willy stood in the driveway, hosing down his sky blue Chevrolet. Iona leaned out the window. "Hey, Willy," she said. He wrinkled up his forehead but didn't answer. She was undaunted. "You wanna go get an ice cream with me?" The spray from the hose made a clear arc before it splattered on the cement and trickled toward the gutter in muddy rills.

He still didn't like her, and he didn't think he could stand the smell of her truck; but he told himself to be brave—it wouldn't last that long, and it was the right thing to do, a small, kind gesture.

When they'd finished their cones, Iona headed out the river road. Willy said, "Where are you going?" And she whispered, "The river." He told her he needed to get home; it was almost dark. She said, "I know." He told her he meant it, but his voice was feeble, and she kept plowing through the haze of dusk, faster and faster, till the whole seat was shaking.

She swerved down to the bank of the river where all the kids came to park; but it was too early for that, so they were alone. Willy stared at the water, at the beer bottles bobbing near the shore and the torn-off limb of a tree being dragged downstream. "I'm sorry about Jay," he said.

"Why're you sorry? He's not dead."

"He didn't treat you right."

Iona slid across the seat so her thigh pressed against Willy's thigh. "Would you treat me right?" He tried to inch away, but there was nowhere to go. Iona's hand rested on his knee then started moving up his leg. Willy batted it away. "You still think I'm a slut?" She touched his thigh again, lightly, higher than before. "I'm not a slut, Willy; I'm just more *generous* than most girls you know." She clutched his wrist and tried to pull his closed hand to her breast. "Don't worry," she said. "You won't be fingering Kleenex when you get a grip on me."

Willy felt the pressure in his crotch, his penis rising against his will. He thought of his mother putting lipstick and rouge on old Mrs. Griswold after she died, but even that didn't help this time.

Iona pounced, kissing his mouth and locking the door at the same time. She fumbled with his belt, clawed at his zipper. He mumbled *no*, but she smothered the word, swallowed it up in her own mouth.

Willy thought of his sisters, Horton saying: *Careful, son.* Even if they both jumped him, Willy was the one who was supposed to go easy.

He clamped Iona's arms, but she broke his hold. "You know you want it, Willy," she said. "Everybody wants it." But he didn't, not like this, not with Iona Moon. She bit at his lips and his ears, sharp little nips; her fingers between his legs cupped his balls dangerously tight.

He shoved her back and wasn't careful, flung her hard against the dashboard—stunned her. He had time to unlock the door, leap from the truck, and flee. But he didn't get far before he heard the unmistakable sputter of tires in mud, an engine revving, going nowhere. Slowing to a trot, he listened: *Rock it,* he thought, *first to reverse, first to reverse.*

He heard her grinding through the gears, imagined her slamming the stick, stamping the clutch, thought that by now tears streamed down her hot cheeks. Finally he heard the engine idle down, a pitiful, defeated sound in the near darkness.

Slowly he turned, knowing what he had to do, hearing his father's voice: *A gentleman always helps a lady in distress.* She's no lady. *Who are you to judge?*

He found small dry branches and laid them under the tires in two foot rows. One steady push, his feet braced against a tree, one more, almost, third time's charm; the front tires caught the sticks, spun, spit up mud all the way to his mouth, and heaved the truck backward onto solid ground. He wiped his hands on his jeans and clumped toward the road.

"Hey," Iona said, "don't you want a ride?" He kept marching. "Hey, Willy, get in. I won't bite." She pulled up right beside him. "It'll take you more than an hour to get home. Your mama'll skin you. Now get in. I won't lay a hand on you." He didn't dare look at her. His face felt swollen, about to explode. "What I did before, I didn't mean anything by it. I never would have tried if I thought you wouldn't like it. Willy?" He glanced up at her; she seemed no bigger than a child hanging on to that huge steering wheel. "Willy, I got a gun. Right here behind the seat, I got my daddy's gun." *Don't you be gettin' any ideas of makin' like a jackrabbit, boy.* He knew there was no real threat, no reason not to get in the truck—except his pride, and that seemed like a small thing when he weighed it against the five-mile trek along the winding road, his mother's pinched face, the spot of grease from her nose on the windowpane.

White Falls lay strung along the river, a fearful band of lights drawn taut for the night, a town closed in on itself. Iona said,

"I almost died once. My brother Leon and I started back from town in a storm that turned to a blizzard. Everything was white, like there was nothing in the world besides us and the inside of this truck. Leon drove straight into a six-foot drift; it looked just the same as the sky and the road. We had to get out and walk, or sit there and freeze like the damn cows. We stumbled, breaking the wind with our hands; then we crawled because the gusts were less wild near the ground. I saw the shadows of houses waffling in the snow, right in front of us, but they were never there. A sheet of ice built up around my cheek and chin, and I kept stopping to shatter it with my fist, but it took too long; Leon said: *'Leave it, it will stop the wind.'* I thought they'd find me that way, the girl in glass, and they'd keep me frozen in a special truck, take me from town to town along with the nineteen-inch man and the two-headed calf. But Leon, Leon never thought for a minute we were going to die on that road. When I dropped to my belly and said I was warm now, he swatted my butt. 'Not this way,' he said, 'not this way, God.' And then I wondered if he'd whispered it or if I heard what he was thinking. Leon talking to God, I thought; that was more of a miracle than surviving, and I scrambled back to my knees and lunged forward.

"Just like a dog, Leon knew his way. I forgave him for everything. I swore in my heart I'd never hold a harsh thought against him, not for anything in the past or anything he might do later on, because right there in that moment, he was saving our lives.

"When Mama wrapped my hands in warm rags and Daddy pulled off my boots to rub my toes as hard as he could, I knew that nothing, nothing in this world was ever going to matter so much again." She punched the clutch and shifted into fourth. "Do you know why I'm telling you this?" Willy nodded, but he didn't know; he didn't know at all.

It wasn't until Iona Moon eased into her driveway and shut

off the engine that she remembered the chocolate, Hannah's last words, the ragged dollar bill still crumpled in her pocket. She thought of her mother awake in the dark, waiting for her. *I think I've got to have some pleasure.* A single sob erupted, burst from between her ribs as if someone had pounded his fist against her chest. She fought her own cry, choked it dry, and was silent.

4

Muriel Arnoux didn't even like it, that was the shame of this whole mess. Not that she'd put up any fight. All summer long she'd watched Jay Tyler throw perfect somersaults off the high dive, leaps that made girls gasp. When the water closed around him, tears welled in Muriel's eyes, as if she'd seen him jump from the bridge over the Snake River. He surfaced, hair plastered flat, the laughing boy, and Muriel clapped, brought to ecstasy by this small miracle, a man spared by the grace of God, his body not broken on the rocks or dragged to the reservoir.

In August, a girl might cry when she imagines you've risked your life for her delight, but she won't like you half as much when you're parked down by the river, shivering in November. No, in the back seat of the Chrysler, there was no clapping and no ecstasy, no double twists in layout position, no graceful entries. There were only rough hands and stubborn zippers, grunts in the dark and the terrible silence when he was done.

Plenty of girls had hopped in the car with Jay Tyler. They wanted to be seen dragging Main, but only one ever liked Snake River, only one ever unhooked her own bra. *Here, baby, let me help you.* Iona Moon wanted it. Too bad they never got the chance. Jay didn't have his license back then, so Willy was at the wheel, with Belinda Beller in the front seat saying *no.* Belinda's mother was one of those women who thought boys only married virgins. *A virgin takes what you give her and doesn't complain.* Guys said it all the time. They didn't like the idea that a girl might have some basis of comparison. But when you thought about it logically, the best you could hope for was a girl who had the good sense to lie. Most guys said they'd done it and most girls said they hadn't. That meant a couple of girls were getting an awful lot of action. It was possible but not likely.

Iona Moon was all elbow and knee, bony ribs and hardly any breasts at all. Her dark hair held the odors of the barn: sweet, grassy scent of cud and sting of cow piss. Willy was right about one thing: country girls had a dangerous grip, the strength to break a chicken's neck and no qualms. Iona's skin was yellowish, the color of a sick baby. She was nothing to look at, but she knew what to do in the dark, and her nipples felt hard as stones in your mouth.

Muriel Arnoux had a soft belly and clean fingernails. Her hair caught the light; her skin smelled of soap. You could take a girl like Muriel home to meet your parents even though she was only fourteen. Willy would cuss over that. *Shit, Jay, you can go to jail for foolin' with a girl that age.* Sanctimonious bastard. *My father said he'd string me up by my balls if he ever heard I was baby-snatchin'.* Horton Hamilton was a man of his word. Now Willy was talking about following in his father's footsteps, being a policeman, but he was never going to fill his daddy's size twelves. Jay got a kick out of that. Good joke, but Willy didn't laugh when he heard it. Pain in the ass. Jay was glad he didn't have to depend on Willy anymore. He had his own license and his mother's car.

Jay regretted the missed chance with Iona Moon. Her fingernails had left red marks on his back. She sucked up little pieces of flesh on his neck and he had to wear his shirts buttoned to the top for days. But she wasn't the kind of girl you wanted to eat lunch with in the cafeteria; kids still remembered her shaved head in sixth grade, how three boys pushed her down in the street and stole her scarf. Girls shrieked and ran away. All day the boys chased them, saying: *I touched her, now I'm gonna touch you.* And you couldn't take her home to meet your folks. She had bad teeth for one thing. *Show me a mouth like that and I'll show you a farmer's daughter.* That's what Jay's father would say, and he should know. He'd seen the insides of enough mouths. Jay knew what Andrew Johnson Tyler would say about an abortion too. He was a medical man. After all. *Nothing but a cluster of cells at this stage.* He'd pull on his pointed beard and think so hard that his hairless scalp would wrinkle halfway back his skull. *I know a doctor in Boise. Owes me a favor too.*

But it was no use thinking about what his father would say, because Muriel Arnoux wasn't going to have any abortion. Jay had waited for her outside the church. She never did get up the nerve to talk to the priest. She said, "I confessed to God and he gave me his answer." Jay looked at her white ankle socks, her thin, pale calves. "I was praying, Jay; when I opened my eyes, I saw Jesus hanging on the cross behind the altar and he couldn't see me because his eyes were carved. Jesus has wooden eyes and won't ever look at me again if I do this."

Jesus. Jay heard his father's words on that topic. *The Catholics drive their girls crazy, all that muttering and confession, fondling beads and crawling into a little black booth with a priest, being forgiven so they can go out and sin again. I never knew a Catholic girl who wasn't touched, half in love with her priest or ready to die at the feet of Jesus.*

Muriel called and told him to come by at eight. "And bring the money." Her parents had found a place for her to stay till the baby was born. She wouldn't tell him where it was. "Out of state," she said, "no one will know me." He had two thousand from his grandfather in Arizona, but he told her he only had five hundred. "Bring it all."

• • •

"You're getting off cheap," Muriel's father said. "I'd take it out of your hide if I had my way." He had a potbelly and pug nose, burly arms from loading freight for thirty years. Muriel's mother sat in a blue armchair, blowing her nose. The chair was covered with plastic that made farting noises when she moved. She looked like Muriel: all the curves turned to rolls of fat, milky skin gone pasty, ankles swollen, but the same clean, small hands. The girl was locked in her room, forbidden to come downstairs while *he* was in the house. Jay imagined her, kneeling, fingering beads, naming the sorrowful mysteries, seeing her Jesus nailed to the cross. *For me, Jay, he died for me, for my sins. And look what I've done.*

"You're never going to see my daughter again. You understand that?"

"Yes, sir."

"Well?"

"Sir?"

"The money, Mr. Tyler."

Jay pulled the crumpled envelope from his pocket.

"You know how old my daughter is?"

"Yes, sir, I do."

"And she's gonna have her first child. She's gonna let that baby go, and she's never gonna be the same again. Five hundred dollars just bought you your freedom, but I'll kill you and go to hell without regret if you ever come near my family again." Above the mantel hung a painting of Jesus, not yet crucified but already heavy with knowledge, his white robe parted to expose a brilliant heart. This Jesus had beautiful hands, delicate and pale, but the heart was ridiculous, the shape a child would draw and much too large.

Muriel's mother blew her nose so hard she really did fart. Jay held out his hand to Mr. Arnoux. It was a stupid gesture, something his father would do, his way of saying he understood how troublesome women could be. Muriel's father showed him the door.

Jay knew that if he turned and looked up, he would see Muriel at the window, her palms flat on the pane, waiting to mouth the words: *I'm sorry, Jay.* She was sorry about everything. Sorry about being born and sorry about being female. Sorry she let him do it and sorry she didn't like it. Jay thought his father was right about Catholic girls. He didn't bother to turn around.

In the car, Jay stared at the hand Muriel's father wouldn't touch. He thought about swinging by Willy's, saying, "You wanna go for a ride?" They'd park on the bridge and drop rocks in the river, wait for the sound, count the seconds a stone takes to fall. They hadn't talked for months. Willy would know something was up and Jay would spill it. Then he'd have to listen to all that crap about giving a blind man a dollar in change when you owed him five, knocking over gravestones, and tipping cows when they were asleep. *I told you this would happen.* Willy Hamilton knew Jay's crimes like the fingers of his own hand: crouching in a tree to watch Sharla Wilder take off her bra, telling the Wilkerson boy he could improve his thinking by drinking a cup of his own piss every day for a month, watching him down the first warm gulp, laughing so hard the tears rolled down Jay's cheeks and Roy Wilkerson knew he'd been duped. *See, you're getting smarter already.*

That was the subject of his last conversation with Willy Hamilton, back in December. *Somebody's gonna pin you to the ground someday and piss on your head. Let you know how it feels.* The lights were on in Willy's room. Horton's cruiser was in the drive. Jay slowed down but didn't stop. *You just bought your freedom with five hundred dollars.*

Jay's father sat in the living room, smoking his pipe in the dark, watching television with no sound. Jay knew what that meant, knew his mother had locked herself in the bathroom upstairs.

He stayed with his father, but he turned on the lights because he couldn't bear that deep, disembodied voice. No, better to see the mouth move, lips and teeth, tongue and spit, just a man after all, smoke curling above his head.

"Man is ruled by impulse," Andrew Johnson Tyler said. "Underneath it all, we're just animals that decided to stand up."

How did he know?

"An animal is ruled by smell, really—the smell of food or fear, the smell of a female."

Maybe they told him at the bank: *Your son withdrew five hundred dollars.*

"Instinct is stronger than reason. That's why we have laws. Men understand punishment, or the threat of it."

Now his mother was at the top of the stairs, wearing her pearls and black stockings.

"I hope your mother's life is a lesson to you, son."

He didn't know about Muriel. He didn't know anything.

Delores Tyler clutched her beaded purse and fur stole. Jay breathed hard. He already caught a whiff of her perfume, Southern Rose spilled between her breasts, dabbed behind her ears and knees. His father packed his pipe with fresh tobacco, gave the match and those first sweet puffs his full attention. Only five more steps. She wobbled on her spike heels. Her smell filled the room.

"I'm going into town," she announced as she stood at the door. The seams of her stockings made crooked lines up the back of her legs.

"They've done experiments with rats," Jay's father said to him. "A rat will take certain drugs until it kills itself. It will starve by choice. A male and female in the same cage will fight instead of fornicate."

"Don't expect me home tonight." His mother's voice was husky from cigarettes.

Jay and his father knew there was nowhere for her to go in

White Falls, no place to dance till dawn, no place to hold your shoes in one hand while you shuffled in your stocking feet, too tired to stop. There was no place with piped-in piano music where a woman could meet a stranger, a man who whispered tender obscenities. No, there was only the Roadstop Bar with the jukebox blaring, all the familiar faces, wolf whistles, and propositions shouted above the din.

In an hour, Jay saw himself walking half a mile down the road, finding his mother slumped at the wheel. He'd bring her home and help her climb the stairs, tuck the dancing shoes under her bed. An hour after that, he'd cruise down the River Road, hands tight on the wheel.

"I think I'll retire," Jay's father said, knocking the ashes out of his pipe. "You should get some rest too, son." Jay nodded but didn't follow.

He waited until he heard the toilet flush to crack the door and slip outside. The night was cold, moonless; he needed his jacket but didn't dare go back. He found his mother just where he thought she'd be.

"I lost the keys, baby."

"I'll look for them later, Mom."

She draped her arm over his shoulders. Her body was soft, her skin warm. His father said she was fat, but she felt nice, a good flesh hold, hot breath on his neck, and the sweet burp of brandy. The cold had weakened her perfume, and she smelled as she used to smell years before. Late at night, after parties or bridge, she'd come to Jay's room, lift him to the dizzy height of a dream with the scent of bruised flowers, wake him with her cool kiss and say: *Don't worry, baby, I'm home.*

They stumbled together. Black trees lined the drive, trunks long and straight, leaves numb as praying hands. The Milky Way swirled, a storm of stars, but the earth was unbearably still, strange and soundless, without wind or the rush of water, without the comfort of a car passing, that temporary light throwing elongated shadows, willowly human shapes. "I should've put the porch light on," Jay said. His mother clung to his arm. "I like the dark," she murmured.

She giggled at the bottom of the stairs and took off her shoes. "Don't want to wake your father."

Jay put his arm around her, his hand just below her breast.

At her door he said, "Three more steps." She fell onto the bed, her body limp and heavy.

"Do you think I'm pretty, Jay?"

Your mother dresses like a whore.

"You look nice, Mom."

"Not too fat?"

Puffed up like Marilyn Monroe.

"No, Mom, you look fine."

She was an alcoholic too, you know.

She patted the soft bulge of her belly. "I used to have a flat stomach, but having you took care of that. That doctor your father knows in Boise wrecked my muscles cutting you out. Stitched me up like the Bride of Frankenstein too. I should have sued, but your father said he couldn't do that to a friend, another *man of medicine.*"

"I know, Mom, you told me."

"He was a butcher."

"Yes, you should have sued."

"My father said I was the prettiest girl in White Falls." She lay very still, eyes closed. "Any boy I wanted and I end up with a man who hates me."

"He doesn't hate you, Mom."

"Lie down next to me, Jay. I caught a chill out there in the car." He stretched out beside her on the bed. She wasn't cold at all, but he stayed. "You know what they did to me when your father sent me to that clinic in Wharton, that *spa* for worrisome wives?"

"You told me, Mom."

"Did I tell you I thought I was blind?"

"Yes."

" 'Just a little jolt, Mrs. Tyler. This won't hurt at all.' But they put a piece of rubber in your mouth so you won't break your own teeth."

"Sssh, Mom, don't think about it. Just go to sleep."

"I heard my spine crack."

Jay put his arms around her. "You're safe now."

"I could feel my blood burning my brain. The doctor said, 'One more time.' That's when I died, Jay. I swear to you I died. When I woke up, I kept thinking about your father and his father, walking me up the steps, one on each side, the last day of my life. I looked at your grandfather. His face was tan and wrinkled, his teeth too white when he grinned. I said, 'Please don't leave me here,' and he said, 'There now, be a good girl, Delores, and don't put up a fuss.' "

Jay found the keys down the crack of the seat. He could have taken the car home, parked it in the drive, awakened in his own bed, but instead he drove toward the Snake, all the windows down, March wind blowing through his hair, the radio blasting: a pair of dueling banjos that made Jay pound the wheel. He longed to fill the night with noise, but beyond this car the only sound was the slow water of late winter.

He knew every curve of the road, every bend of the river. His life eddied at the banks with the beer cans and the drowned cat. He pressed himself to the hard chest of Iona Moon; her fingers moved to his crotch. He hit sixty and felt good. He had steady hands. *I can control myself.* It didn't even last that long, didn't feel that much better than what he did alone in the bathroom—no, it was worse because Muriel lay there so still, and he had to ask, "Are you okay?" Then she looked at him as if nothing was ever going to be okay again. *Don't worry. I pulled out in time.* Iona Moon pulled the cat out of the river and tossed it up on the bank. *I've touched plenty of things that were dead longer than that.* The Chrysler could still do eighty on the highway. He pushed it to sixty-five. Muriel said, "I'm pregnant, Jay."

He raised his arms to save his eyes. She came out of nowhere, leaped onto the road as he barreled around the curve. He couldn't stop or swerve in time. The high beams of his headlights cut the night and struck her eyes, paralyzing her thin legs. Her body flopped on the hood, the most terrible sound he'd ever heard. Her small feet shattered the windshield. The car spun and the doe hit the pavement. He tried to get out but couldn't move his legs, couldn't even curl his toes without the pain shooting all the way to his skull. He didn't know if the blare in his brain was his stuck horn or his own screaming.

Jay's right leg was fractured in three places, his left in one. Shards of the windshield had cut his arms and hands, left slivers embedded in his cheeks. His eyes were spared.

"You broke your own legs," the doctor said, trying to offer some comfort or lay the proper blame. "You would've been all right if you'd just relaxed. People punch the brakes and go rigid. Just your luck to have such strong thighs."

"Yeah," Jay said, "I'm a lucky guy."

All that spring Jay waited for a disaster, an avalanche or a flood, a search for survivors that would make his father turn up the sound on the television. He wished his mother would get off her bed and knock on his door, so he could hear himself say: *Leave me alone*. Any day, he thought, a car will turn in the drive, just by mistake.

The grass grew greener. Leaves unfurled. The air grew hot and his skin itched under the casts.

Muriel came in August. "My father would whip me if he knew I was here," she said.

"You shouldn't have come."

"I had to see you, Jay."

He stared at the wall. He wanted her to go.

"I feel like I lost a part of myself," she said, "like my arm's been cut off, but the missing thing is inside."

"Yeah, well, you're lucky," Jay said.

She looked at his legs, the right one still huge and heavy in the dirty cast, the left one withered and white. "I'm sorry," she said. "Sometimes I'm so stupid."

"I hate it when you say that."

"When I say what?"

"Sorry. Why the fuck are you so sorry?"

"I didn't mean—"

"Forget it."

At his bedroom door, she turned. "It was a boy," she said, "if you want to know."

Days shortened. Crickets sang. One night he broke his dinner plate, flung it across the room, saw it splinter against the wall. The sound split the air, but no one ran to his room and nothing changed. His father and his grandfather still walked his mother up the steps; he still had Muriel Arnoux pinned to the backseat of the Chrysler. When he closed his eyes, the doe leaped out of the woods. He saw her dark, startled gaze, her thin legs. *Why didn't she run?* He slammed the brakes, but there was no way to stop.

5

Iona Moon wasn't exactly happy when she heard what had happened to Jay Tyler, but she wasn't sorry either. He never came back to school that spring, and he still hadn't returned by fall. So he wasn't going to college like Mama had said. No educated girl with light hair and straight teeth was going to follow him to White Falls.

Iona had imagined Jay Tyler's life with one of those pink-skinned women who played afternoon bridge with the ladies. She'd cut the crust off the tiny sandwiches and serve cookies no bigger than Iona's little finger. All the women would kiss her soft cheek when they said goodbye. But at night this same pretty woman, loved by the ladies, would lie beneath her husband like driftwood, her limbs smooth, her body cool and hard.

Later, there would be blond children, and everyone would say Jay Tyler was a lucky man to have a beautiful wife and beautiful babies. Certainly an educated woman would be clever enough to have one boy and one girl. She'd grow waterlogged and heavy with love for them, devoting her days to matching their socks and wiping their runny noses, combing the tangles from their silky curls and sewing fur collars on their little wool coats. Every night, exhausted by the endless needs of her children, she'd sink into sleep as wood sinks to the bottom of a lake.

Some evening Jay Tyler might find himself dragging Main, looking for a girl like Iona Moon, the kind who didn't mind the cold vinyl of the backseat, a resourceful girl who knew how to find her own way home.

But none of this was going to happen, because Jay had locked himself in his room. He wasn't going to be a dentist like his father or marry a woman who looked like his mother. Only a rich boy could afford the luxury of staying sick on purpose, that's what Hannah said. He drank his tea from a porcelain cup; he ate baby peas with a silver fork. But he might as well have bars on his window because he was just as much a prisoner as Iona's mother was. Only Jay was worse: he chose. So he was a damn idiot besides.

Iona started to think that no one she knew ever escaped White Falls. Everett Fry was the last one who'd left for good, and he had to kill himself to do it. Sharla Wilder nearly killed herself too. She bled on her daddy's couch for two days before he gave in and took her to the doctor. When she recovered, she packed one bag and headed to Seattle, but she was back home in six months. Now she had an apartment in town and worked grave-yard shift for the phone company. At least she'd gotten off the Kila Flats and out of her father's house.

Hannah said there were three ways out: the river, the tracks, the long, winding road. Iona remembered the summer Leon jumped a train. Bruised and broke, he called three days later. Frank said, "You got your ass to Portland, you can get your ass home." And it was true. Getting back was easy if you didn't mind the hunger, the cold night wind blowing through the slats, the steady clatter of the boxcar.

One March, when the river was fast, a woman leaped from the bridge to the water. She twisted like a cat in midair. When she hit, her body lost all grace, crumpled on the hard surface. The kids in the bus watched her red coat swept downriver and thought she'd disappear. But even she was saved, brought back, raised up, revived against her will.

In the winter, Iona's brothers moved to Missoula to work at the pulp mill. Every year they said they might stay on, but every spring they sat on the porch again, waiting for the ground to thaw. They reminded Iona of the three mongrels Daddy kept on tethers in the yard. The dogs had big heads and long tails, hair the color of mud. Yipping and dancing in the cold morning light, they bounded after one another. But the ropes were always shorter than they remembered, and the spikes that held them were planted deep. Chains tightened around the dogs' necks, and the animals fell back, squealing and betrayed. They butted their knobby heads together and nipped at their own legs, lashed their tails and hopped on one another's haunches.

A fine layer of snow blew across the fields, exposing patches of bald earth. Iona wore the coat Hannah had always worn for milking, Frank's fur-lined jacket. The zipper had broken last year or the year before; now Iona hugged herself as she ran to the barn.

She whispered to her cows, scratched their heads, murmured in their ears. *Don't ever sit down at an animal's rear end without letting her see who you are,* Hannah had said the morning she taught Iona to milk Ruby. But the cows knew her footsteps, recognized her breath. *A cow knows everything she needs to know. When her udder's full, she's glad you've come to milk her. When you're old, she'll feel your cheek against her flank, soft, unchanged. When she's old, your touch will bring her more comfort than the grace of God.*

Iona gripped Ruby's warm teat, remembering her own small hands moving beneath her mother's hands. *Breathe when she does,* Hannah said. The dense smell of cow shit made her light in the head. It was almost sweet if you liked it, and she did.

Cows have no God, so they don't fear the future. Ruby's milk rang against the metal pail. She groaned, an almost human sound, soft and satisfied, from somewhere low in the belly. *A cow has no wish to be anything other than herself.* Except for Angel after the five-legged calf died.

Iona remembered that February morning, the hay in Angel's stall damp with her water. Frank put his whole arm inside the cow. "She's not ready," he said, pulling himself free. He turned to piss in the gutter. Hannah whispered to Angel and held the cow's head in her hands.

The barn was cold. Wind cut through the cracks; the other cows moaned, but Angel only breathed, her whole body heaving.

Iona's father tried again. "I have it," he said. He gripped the calf's legs, tugged two hooves to the gaping mouth of the cow's vagina. He slipped ropes around the legs and used his full weight. The hair of his arms was matted, dark with blood and mucus, like the hair of the calf's legs. At last the head emerged, eyes already fluttering beneath the lids. Angel turned, anxious to use her great tongue, to lick the eyes open, to lick the calf's genitals and know for herself.

Only then did they see the flaw, the short fifth leg protruding from the calf's belly, as if there had been twins and one calf had swallowed the other in their mother's womb. "We'll have to kill it," Hannah Moon said. "Five-legged animal's a curse."

"Waste not, want not," Frank answered.

By dawn, the calf had four legs and a bandage on its belly, but he was spindly and weak from the start. Two of his mother's teats went rotten. The calf died and Angel's milk was thin for months, not worth the milking.

Cows have no God. Iona kept hearing the words. Angel rubbed herself raw, snared herself in barbed wire. Frank said he had no choice: he had to put her down. *Cows don't fear death. They're terrified by fire, but not the idea of fire.* Hannah said it was a blessing to live this way, to be able to look a man in the eye even as he raised the gun.

But now Iona wondered.

• • •

She took her time with the cows and still had fifteen minutes to sit alone in the kitchen, drinking her coffee with cream skimmed from the milk. She knew the exact moment she would hear her brothers on the stairs, so she was already on her feet, sliding biscuits in the oven, dropping sausages in the pan.

Soon they sat at the table. Dale looked sleepy and dim. His hair was thick, but his eyebrows were wisps, so he always seemed surprised. Sometimes Iona wanted to put her arm around him, and sometimes she wanted to hit him. Rafe smiled to himself, remembering a dream or thinking up ways to steal Dale's sausage. He was hard. A little tree, Iona thought, muscles tight as burls. Leon's brow furrowed into three deep creases. He worried about the day ahead of him, and the one after that. He couldn't sit still waiting for biscuits to bake, so he rolled a cigarette and took his coffee to the back steps. Iona watched him. He was built just like their father, thick through the chest and not too tall; his arms bulged, but his legs were skinny and his butt flat.

Frank was the last to sit at the table. He wore a flannel shirt and blue jeans, just like Iona's brothers. *A matched set,* Hannah called the four men, and for some reason this never failed to amuse her. Frank Moon had one wild eyebrow. A tuft of hair whipped up in rebellious glee over his right eye, silent mockery of a serious man. He slicked his dark hair straight back, exposing his high forehead and the blue vein that throbbed in his temple.

Leon came inside, and Iona filled his plate. He grunted. She closed her eyes and turned back to the stove. *What made Leon so afraid?* She knew the answer: the rest of his life, all the mornings just like this one. He couldn't imagine a wife or a child, a life that was his own. One day soon he would sit in his father's chair, thinking his father's thoughts. He saw himself old and he saw himself dead.

When Iona turned around again, all the chairs were empty, as if the men had simply vanished. They'd left dirty plates and half-filled mugs, pans to scrub and food to put away. And it was late. Mama was awake by now, ready for her white coffee:

one quarter coffee, three quarters milk. If Iona wasn't standing on the road in half an hour, she'd miss the bus to school, and Mr. Fetterhoff would call again to remind her she had eight absences. *The year's hardly begun, Miss Moon, and already I wonder if you'll graduate.*

"I'm glad they're gone," Hannah said to Iona. Frank had driven the boys to town and put them on the bus for Missoula. "Rafe will push his brother too far someday. The crazy thing is, Dale loves Rafe. Like part of himself. Like you love your own arm."

Iona sat on the edge of Hannah's bed. She wouldn't say she loved her own arm, but she thought she knew what Hannah meant about another person being part of herself. Sometimes when she slipped the bedpan under her mother, she felt the sting of the sores as if they were on her own rump.

"Are you warm enough, Mama?"

"Yes."

"You want another cup of milk?"

"I'll float away."

"Anything?"

"Just keep talking." Iona reached under the covers to hold her mother's hand. "It's quieter with them out of the house," Hannah said.

"Yes."

"But I worry about your father."

"Leon chopped enough wood to get us through two winters."

"That's not what I'm talking about," Hannah said. "I saw your daddy chase a bear one night. He ran out of the house wearing nothing but his nightshirt and his boots. The bear was having a time for himself. He'd knocked over the garbage and was batting tin cans across the lawn. He was twice the size of your father, but he took one look at that crazy little man waving the flashlight and headed for the hills. Literally. I remember thinking, Frank Moon has the skinniest legs I ever saw, but he is brave."

Iona glanced at the wooden figures on the dresser, the ones Leon had carved for Hannah before Iona threw his knife in the river. There was a miniature farmer wearing a wide-brimmed hat, a farmer's wife with a long braid, a stooped bear no bigger than the man, a rooster half the size of the woman.

"Later people told me he'd done a stupid thing. You shoot a bear dead or stay in the house. I was sixteen, just married, and I already knew my husband was a fool in a nightshirt, a man with the legs of a chicken and the brains of a loon."

"He's not a fool, Mama."

"No," Hannah said, "he's just a man who used to be lucky."

Pancreas. Hannah Moon mouthed the three soft syllables. *Whoever thought of you?* "It started in the pancreas," the doctor said, "but it's spread."

"I thought I had rheumatism."

"You do." The whites of the doctor's eyes were yellow. *He doesn't look so well himself.* "And this too," he said.

"So take it out," said Hannah.

"That's what I'm trying to explain to you, Mrs. Moon." The doctor fingered his stethoscope. His hands were large and pale, freckled with deep brown spots. "It's spread," the doctor said again. "Metastasized, we say." *We say? Did you create it? Did you give it a name and call it into being?* He wasn't looking at her. *What did he see across the room?* Hannah turned her head. *The bare wall.* "I can't take it out."

There were kidney stones and gallstones. Heartache, heart-break, heart attack. It all came to the same thing. Blood clotted in the brain, appendixes burst, lungs collapsed, spleens ruptured.

"You could see a specialist in Spokane."

"A specialist? And who would pay for that?"

The doctor stuffed his stethoscope in his bag. Hannah could see he was anxious to leave. "I just want to go home," she said.

The young man pursed his lips and nodded. He thought it was a bad decision. "As you wish, Mrs. Moon."

. . .

Iona stood on the road, looking for the school bus. The wind whipped her hair across her face. Her brothers had been gone eight days, and Hannah was right: everything was quieter. It was seven-thirty, more dark than light; she wore her jeans under her skirt and a denim jacket with flannel lining, the collar turned up. She'd forgotten her gloves, so she blew on her hands then thrust them in her pockets.

The bus was warm with bodies. Jeweldeen had saved a place on the inside, and Iona climbed over her legs. "You look like shit," Jeweldeen said. "Your father make you sleep with the cows last night?" Jeweldeen herself wore dark lipstick, ruby red, painted beyond the lines of her lips so her mouth looked full from a distance and smeared if you sat beside her.

The bus was slow, behind schedule because of the icy roads, but Iona and Jeweldeen still had time to duck into the girls' room for a smoke.

Iona peered in the mirror as they passed the cigarette between them, wondering if she did look as if she'd slept in the barn. She saw her hair first, dark and wild, long but not thick, moss hanging from a tree, hair that brushes against your face and scares you when you walk through the woods at night.

She hiked up her plaid skirt and pulled down her jeans. She was a tough girl in a denim jacket. Jeweldeen handed her the cigarette again, and Iona took a deep hit. They kept the ash on the butt as long as they could, hot-boxing the cigarette so the rush of nicotine was a good high that made Iona flushed and dizzy, a little sick to her stomach. She was skinny and yellow; her knees looked dirty, though she'd bathed last night. Yellow-skinned. A kinder person might have said golden. But she wasn't kind and neither was Jeweldeen. Blond Jeweldeen. Plump, pretty darling of old men in candy stores and boys in Mustangs. *You've been wearing that skirt since eighth grade, Iona. Nobody, I mean nobody, wears pleats anymore.* Iona saw her mother bent over the sewing machine, measuring and tacking each pleat, basting the waistband. *No one will ever know it didn't come from the Mercantile.* Except it was more beautiful than anything from the store downtown. Iona twirled through the living room, the skirt spinning around her legs, floating, the pleats opening and closing like an accordion. Yes, she heard the rustle of the cloth against her skin, and it was a kind of music, the sweet sound of fine wool, light and warm, the best skirt she'd ever owned.

One glance at the face, Iona could bear that. But she looked at herself as a scolded dog looks at its mistress, quickly, afraid of the hand that might slap its head. Two eyes, one nose, not a freak. Crowded teeth but no overbite or underbite, thank God for small mercies.

The long ash of the cigarette collapsed. "Light another one," Iona said, though her throat burned. She moved toward the mirror.

"What the hell are you doing?" said Jeweldeen.

"Seeing if I look like shit."

"Jesus, Iona, it's just an expression."

Iona leaned over the sink. "I have my father's nose," she said. She turned and reached for the cigarette. "Watch this." She took a long drag. Smoke curled from her parted lips, and she breathed, slowly, evenly: it was easy if you had the patience. Now her nostrils flared and the smoke whirled up her nose.

"You don't look so bad," Jeweldeen said.

"Thank you. I really appreciate you saying that." But sarcasm was wasted on Jeweldeen. Iona flicked the butt in the sink and was lighting another when Belinda Beller sashayed into the bathroom, arm in arm with Susie Endicott. They bounced as they walked, springing off their toes. Their breasts moved, but in a way that was oddly independent of their bodies. Iona thought they must stuff their bras with something heavier than Kleenex these days, packets of some dense, gelatinous fluid that could burst at any moment, leaving those perfect white blouses stained and damp, stuck flat to their chests.

Belinda pinched her nose when she saw Iona and Jeweldeen.

Iona wasn't sure if she was trying to make a point about the smoke or something less specific. "Come on, Susie," she said, "I can hold it."

"I can hold it," Jeweldeen sang after them. They were such clean girls. In those seconds, Jeweldeen had realized that her own skirt was too tight, her stockings too dark. The makeup was wrong too, but it was too late to start again. "I hope she pees her pants in homeroom."

"No," Iona said, "she most definitely can hold it." She thought of that night down by the river, Belinda playing hunt and peck with poor Willy a week before she dumped him.

The bell was ringing. "I'm going to Sharla's after school," Jeweldeen said. "She's off tonight, so she can drive us home."

"I can't."

"Shit, you've been running straight home every day since school started. You hiding a boyfriend in the barn?"

"I just can't," Iona said.

"Fine," said Jeweldeen, "but I'm not asking again."

Iona stepped into a stall and flushed her cigarette. Jeweldeen waited by the door, but Iona stayed at the toilet, watching the butt swirl. She didn't tell Jeweldeen that her mother's hair came out by the fistful, that she had to hide the brush so Hannah wouldn't see her yellow strands in the bristles. She didn't say how Hannah hated the bedpan because her own urine burned her skin. Iona powdered her butt like a baby's and tried to keep her clean. She could have told Jeweldeen's sister. She could have said her mama didn't even brush her teeth anymore because her gums bled. Sharla would understand. She wouldn't be disgusted, wouldn't say: *How do you stand it?* In her kitchen on Rosewood Drive, Sharla Wilder would pour two rum and Cokes; she and Iona would sit at the table till dusk filled the room; they'd listen to the refrigerator hum and watch the lights pop on in houses across the street. But this never happened, so no one knew.

"We'll be late," Jeweldeen said.

"Go ahead."

"You are a piece of work, Iona Moon. I'm not lying for you this morning in homeroom."

"I'm not asking."

"Fine."

Jeweldeen kicked the door open so it swung wide, flooding the bathroom with the jabbering and shuffling of the hallway. Iona closed the door of the stall and sat down on the toilet. Voices dimmed. One by one, doors shut, echoing down the empty corridors.

Iona pulled off her skirt, stuffed it down her book bag, put on the jeans again. She glanced over her shoulder as she passed the mirror. The dark-eyed girl looked mean, a cornered dog about to bite. The face was small, sharp at the chin. The mouth drew into a clean line of resolution. Someone had asked a question and she had answered. Everything was decided.

Iona Moon climbed out the window and sprinted across the frozen schoolyard.

Iona lay in her bed, too weak to talk. Her mother sat in the chair, sewing by the dim light. The cloth was blue. Her hands white. Someone was playing the same note on a piano again and again. Iona closed her eyes and sank into a fever dream.

She woke ten years later. She'd been dozing in the chair beside her mother's bed. Hannah slept. The sun was almost white. All the blue had bled from the sky, leaving it white too. The last gray leaves flickered in the wind.

Her mother's hands clutched at the blankets like claws, the joints stiff, swollen into knots of bone.

Her forehead was high and white, and her skin seemed translucent, blue-lighted, fragile as the wing of a moth.

Her eyelids wrinkled, soft as crepe. Every day her eyes sank deeper in their sockets, her gaze turning slowly inward.

Only her ears were unchanged, joyful and pink.

Iona went to the window. *This is my life,* she thought, *the foothills, the fields, the blank sky; a fence, a dirt road; the specks of distant animals, the smoke of distant chimneys.* All day her father had been repairing fences. Dead cornstalks lay on the ground around him, a collapsed forest, pocked and rotting, gold gone to brown and gray. He gathered up his ax and hammer, a roll of wire. He didn't know Iona watched him. If he had, he would have walked faster, carried his load with ease. But she saw how heavy it was, how it dragged him down. He favored his left leg. His spine curved under the weight.

Now, in the fuzzy stillness of dusk, father and sky and ground blurred at their edges, each a part of the other. But soon the night air would turn hard as black glass. In the yard, the naked maple would stand sharp and solitary against the sky, a duller black. Iona's father, sitting in his chair under the lamp, would be collected and solid, no bigger than himself.

The morning began like any other. Iona milked the cows and drank coffee alone in the kitchen. She heard her father on the stairs and cracked two eggs on the side of the pan. The whites bubbled in the hot grease. The bacon stayed warm in the oven; the biscuits were in a basket on the table, covered by a white cloth.

"Raspberry or huckleberry?" Iona said as her father sat down.

"Huckleberry."

She put the jam on the table. The smell of grease and bacon made her queasy. She ate a biscuit, thinking of her mother. Hannah ate only white food: warm milk and macaroni, biscuits and saltines, four bites of oatmeal if Iona held the spoon for her. She couldn't weigh more than ninety pounds. *Never lose more weight than you can carry.* This was Hannah's idea of a joke.

"It's late, Iona," her father said.

"Yes."

"You'll miss the bus."

"Yes."

He nodded. "Just as well."

• • •

The phone rang three times the first week. The truant officer had a thin voice. She tried to threaten, but Iona knew a woman like that wore high heels and would never drive out to the Kila Flats in winter. Leon called to leave a phone number and address. He asked how much snow they had and if the wood was covered. Jeweldeen called. "I got three days' detention for trying to cover your ass," she said. Iona didn't answer. "You sick or something?" said Jeweldeen.

"No," Iona said, "my mother."

After that the house was quiet. There were no visitors and no calls. Iona was not unhappy. Her days had order and sense, a clear purpose. Milking at five, her father's breakfast at six-thirty. By seven, Hannah was awake, and Iona fed her too, or tried to make her eat. Hannah grew weary toward the middle of the morning, so Iona had time to wash the breakfast dishes before she started lunch. At noon she made a sandwich for her father, or heated leftovers. With some coaxing, Hannah might drink a bit of broth, but more often she said she was still full from breakfast.

Every third day, Iona gave her mother a spit bath, wiping her frail arms and sore bottom, sponging her knobby back and sharp shoulders. Once a week, she changed the sheets, rolling Hannah from one side to the other so she never had to leave the bed.

At first Iona tried to keep the house clean, but soon she gave up and let the spiders weave their sticky webs. Her father tracked mud and snow through the kitchen. For days Iona could see each footstep, her father's small journeys, but soon he had crossed his own path so many times the entire floor was marked. A blue ring appeared in the tub, a yellow one in the toilet. Dust settled on the shelves and under beds, across windowsills and along the iron frame of Hannah's bed.

By the third week, Iona had stopped cooking dinner. Mostly she and her father just opened cans and ate quickly, trying not

to look at each other. One night it was pork and beans, heated
so fast they'd burned on the bottom but were still cold on top.

"Should I call your brothers?" Frank said.

"She won't like it."

"They should be here."

"There's time," said Iona.

"I dreamed your brothers came home," Hannah said when Iona
took her a cup of hot milk. She'd taken two painkillers at noon
and had slept the rest of the day. "They floated above my head
like balloons; they stuck to the ceiling and couldn't get down.
Their bodies were fat and round, like babies' bodies; they flapped
their stubby little arms, but it didn't do any good. They wore
their white baby dresses, as if they'd just been baptized. I saw
their bare behinds and tiny genitals. But they had the heads of
grown men, too heavy for their puny necks. They hated me.
They squinted their eyes and said, *Who's that old woman in our
mother's bed?* Their bodies smelled sweet, but their breath was
smoky and stale. They hadn't shaved for days."

Frank Moon shuffled down the hall. He paused at Hannah's
door.

"What is it, old man?" Hannah said. "Are you afraid to look
at me tonight? Your mama was right after all. Skinny girl like
me—I wasn't worth the spit it took God to put my bones
together."

Iona's father came into the room, but he kept his distance
from Hannah's bed. "She never said that."

"Not to you."

They fought often, about things his mother had said and
things she hadn't. "She told me I didn't have the hips to carry
a child," Hannah said. "She wasn't surprised the baby died."

"Hannah."

"You know it's true. 'Two months early, poor little thing
never had a chance,' she said."

"She didn't mean to be cruel."

"No, she just was."

Hannah knew it was wrong to be uncharitable to the dead, because you can't ask for forgiveness. Usually she'd hold her tongue, but for Frank's mother she made exceptions.

Later, after another painkiller, Hannah let Frank sit beside her. "Remember," she said, "I had to teach you."

"I'd had women."

"You'd *paid* for women."

"I knew what to do."

"It's not the same."

Hannah turned to Iona. "He was scared because I was so young. I had to take his hand and put it on my belly. *See,* I said, *see how warm it is.*"

By morning Hannah was herself again, saying that Frank's damn dogs had kept her awake half the night. "Just like that winter you went to Seattle," Hannah said.

"We only had one dog then."

"He barked enough for three. I didn't get a whole night's sleep for four months."

"I had to go."

"Yes, I know."

They'd had a bad year in '57: the potatoes were small from a dry stretch in July; night winds kept the corn from ripening. Frank went to Seattle to work on the docks. He left Hannah alone with the three boys and two-year-old Iona. The pipes froze and they had to use the outhouse for three weeks straight. Hannah melted snow for water, and Iona got a fiery rash on her bottom and thighs from too few proper baths. Then he blamed her: "I told you to keep the water running at night. How many years have you lived on the Flats?"

"A hundred," Hannah said.

Those were the last words of the day, but the fight lasted years. In 1962 it rained before they got all the hay to the barn. Frank had gone to town, *Fool's errand,* Hannah said. A thunderstorm caught them by surprise. This was just one more example of Frank Moon not being there when they needed him. In 1965, the potatoes sprouted in the cellar and were rotten by March. Frank claimed Hannah was always leaving the door open, letting in too much light. And of course he couldn't stop himself from saying that she'd lived on the Flats long enough to know better.

They argued even now—as if the potatoes had sprouted this very morning and the clouds had burst this afternoon. Tonight the pipes would freeze. They both knew it, but neither one could keep it from happening again and again.

"Talk to her," Iona said, though she knew there was no end to the argument. Memories were a web in her mother's body, catching her father every time he moved. He'd avoided her for two days.

"All she wants to do is fight."

"She wants you to stop being afraid of her."

That evening he climbed the stairs to Hannah's room and stood at the foot of her bed. "Angel would have recovered if you hadn't been in such a hurry to put her down," Hannah said.

"You can't know that."

"I had a dream."

"And what else happened in this dream?"

"She had a calf that grew to have eight teats."

"Instead of five legs."

"And she gave forty quarts of milk a day."

"That *was* a dream."

"It could have happened if you hadn't killed her."

"Go back to sleep and have another dream. Maybe your cows will grow wings. Maybe they'll jump over the moon."

She closed her eyes. "Turn out the light, old man. I do want to have another dream."

• • •

Hannah woke thrashing, kicking the covers off herself. Iona was afraid to try to hold her down. She kept muttering at someone to wash his hands. "Just a bad dream," Iona said when her father came to the door.

Hannah grew calmer as she woke, and Iona leaned over her mother, whispering nonsense as she washed Hannah's head with a cool rag.

"Don't you come in here," Hannah said to the shadow in the doorway. "I saw you digging."

"You had a dream, Mama."

"And I kept saying: *It's deep enough, she's so little, it's deep enough.*"

Frank took one step into the room to tell her again: "Not last night, Hannah, twenty-five years ago."

She'd dreamt of the child, not the cow.

"Why did you dig so long?"

"I had to bury her."

Frank came to the bed and Hannah turned her face to the wall. "I wanted you to stop digging," she said.

"You stood at the window."

"Yes, I wanted you to put her in the ground and be done with it."

"I thought you wanted me to go deeper. I thought you were watching me so I wouldn't stop."

"No." Hannah looked at him now. "No," she said again. She lay limp and exhausted, one arm and one bony leg exposed.

Frank touched the blankets. "You'll get a chill," he said, and she let him cover her.

"She was too small for a grave," Hannah said. "She should have stayed in my body and disappeared."

"Everything has to be buried."

"I felt the dirt hit her chest."

"So did I."

"Every time you lifted the shovel."

"What could I do, Hannah?"

"I heard you come inside."

"Yes."

"But you didn't come to my room."

"I couldn't."

"It was still so light outside."

"I remember. "

"How could it still be so light?"

Frank Moon sat down on the bed, and Hannah didn't tell him to go away.

Chickens squawked and dogs yipped. Frank had fallen asleep on Hannah's bed, and the noise confused him as he struggled to remember how it happened that she'd let him stay. He heard the snap of the dogs' tethers. They ran against the ropes so hard he thought they'd break their necks.

As soon as he was outside, he heard the hens flapping against the walls of the coop. He grabbed the shovel by the back door and nearly fell down the steps.

The weasel had a chicken by the neck and was trying to drag it out a tiny hole at the back of the shed. The first blow of the shovel stunned the thief; the second crushed its skull. But the man didn't stop. He gouged its stomach and hammered at the splintered head; he battered the creature as if it were ten times its size and still half alive. Hens fluttered around his head in silly despair, and he swatted at them with one hand while he swung the shovel in the other.

The dogs howled in the yard, and the man stopped long enough to see that the weasel was nothing more than fur and blood. Only the legs and tail still resembled the animal it had been.

He tried to scoop the creature onto the shovel, but it stuck to the floor. He had to scrape it up in pieces and carry them outside. The dogs bounded toward him, flying to the end of their ropes until the chains tightened around their necks. They whined and snarled, frenzied by the smell of blood. He saw he was ridiculous. The thing he'd killed was smaller than a rat.

In the henhouse, Frank Moon kicked straw over the bloody patch on the floor. The chickens clucked at him and puffed their feathers. Four were dead. The weasel had slipped through a knothole and had tried to pull its fat prey through the same opening. It killed another and another, and would have pierced the neck of every hen in the shed without ever understanding its mistake.

Iona found her father washing his hands at the kitchen sink.

"You cut yourself," she said.

"No, a weasel," he said, "in the henhouse."

She didn't understand.

"I killed it with the shovel."

She stared stupidly at his hands as he scrubbed, at the pink lather of the soap, the murky water swirling down the drain.

"Did it get anything?" she said.

"Four."

"The little bastard."

"Will you do it?" he said. The soap slipped from his hands.

She didn't know what he meant. His wild eyebrow curled upward, gleeful traitor, laughing at his misery. Specks of blood dotted his forehead, and she knew exactly how he must have pounded at the weasel, how he'd beaten it long after it was dead, how he hated the little murderer. She wanted to wipe his face.

"Will you call your brothers," he said.

She nodded and they stood at the sink watching the water stream over his hands, waiting for it to run clear.

"What was all the ruckus this morning?" Hannah said. Frank had changed his clothes and shaved. Even his fingernails were clean, and his wet hair was combed straight back. Now he sat beside his wife's bed, holding her warm milk.

He told her about the weasel.

"So, it's come to that," she said. "The bear chaser has become a weasel killer."

She licked her chapped lips. Her mouth was dry, so sticky she could barely make the words. He offered her the milk, but she waved her hand.

"It could have been a coyote," she said.

Yes, he thought, *and that would have been worth killing.*

"I've heard howling in the foothills all week."

"I haven't," Frank said.

"They're coming down from the mountains."

"No," Frank said, "it's just the dogs you hear."

"They're hungry," said Hannah.

"It's too early."

"When you hear them this soon, you know the winter will be hard."

"No," he said.

"I saw a pack of coyotes bring down a cow. I was just a girl. An hour later it was nothing but bones. Picked it cleaner than buzzards. Even took its eyes. I don't know how."

"Please," he said.

"What is it, old man?"

"It's only the dogs you hear," he said.

The thought of the coyotes excited Hannah all day. She was hungry herself. She ate two biscuits with huckleberry jam. She rolled the berries in her mouth, sucked the flavor from them, and spit the skins in a napkin. She asked Iona to comb her hair. "Harder," she said, "it feels so good." Later she made Frank carry her to the window. She put her nose to the glass. "It's cold," she said. He stepped back. "No—I like it."

She's better, Iona thought. *What do doctors know?* She'll gain weight. By spring she'll walk to the bathroom alone. By summer she'll sit on the porch.

Iona woke in the middle of the night and heard her mother coughing. She ran down the hall. Frank was already there, making Hannah sit so he could pat her back. At last she gagged, spitting up the mashed potatoes and chicken broth and applesauce she'd had for dinner, the most she'd eaten in a month. The coughing stopped. Hannah said, "You'll have to change the bed, Iona."

The white hills blazed with fresh snow. Nothing moved. Even the cows were silent, and the dogs cowered in their house. Hannah didn't want the boys to come home. "Why?" she said to Iona. "So they can hover at the door and watch me puke? So they can feel sorry for themselves, like your father? I suppose this was his idea. Does he want the doctor to come too? Maybe he'd send me to the hospital. Your father would like that, wouldn't he? Does he want my smell out of the house?" She imagined she heard him, scuffing down the hall. "Hey, old man," Hannah said, "you can throw me out the window when I'm dead. You can burn the sheets. You can burn the whole damn bed. But until then you'll have to live with me."

"Shush, Mama, he's not there."

"No," she said, "of course not."

Frank Moon sat with Hannah in the dark. She was asleep at last and couldn't fight him.

He remembered a girl he saw on the road one summer. Her legs were dirty, her feet bare. He asked her name, and she glanced over her shoulder as if she hoped a brother might appear suddenly to swoop her up in his arms and carry her away from the stranger.

He counted the years between them. He was twenty-four; she was ten. The days he'd have to wait for the child seemed impossible, but the decades of his future collapsed and his whole life seemed terrible and quick.

No brother came. She told him her name. The wheat moved in waves across the field behind her; her hair waved too, the

same color as the grain, and he felt the wind on his face for the
first time, though it must have been blowing all day.

He knew her people. They lived in a trailer near the woods,
six of them in a tin shack at the northern edge of the Flats. Her
father hauled junk from the dump, cleaned it up, and made it
work long enough to sell it in town on Saturdays. Frank had
seen Clayton Cislo parked in the lot at Pick-n-Pay, his truck
bed crammed with toasters and bicycles, rewired lamps, a chair
with one new leg, a pot with a makeshift handle, knives freshly
polished and oiled, so the blades eased from their sheaths, gleaming in the sun. *Riffraff,* Frank's mother said.

He must have seen the girl many times, sitting in the cab of
the truck with her older sister, but the glass blurred her features
and kept him from seeing what he saw now. She was too skinny
to be pretty. It was nothing as simple as that. The bones of her
face were sharp, without disguise of baby fat, so she looked at
him as a woman, her mouth closed, lips tight, as if to tell him
she'd answered enough questions for one day.

The boys arrived on the bus the next day, and Frank drove to
town to pick them up.

Rafe and Dale crowded each other in Hannah's doorway,
each one shoving for his share of space, a better view, but neither
one bold enough to come near his mother's bed.

Leon leaned against the windowsill, his thumbs hooked in
his pockets, staring at the old woman, his mother, forty-one and
wrinkled, skin gray and dry as paper.

Hannah's eyelids fluttered. Iona thought she only pretended
to sleep. She remembered the dream, how the boys floated above
the bed with their fat baby bodies and their grim adult heads.
She felt sorry for them now as she watched their useless childish
gestures and pathetic faces. She saw that each of her brothers
was ludicrous in his own way. Rafe wore a pair of loafers, silly
city shoes that would do him no good now that he was home.
Dale's down vest made him look even fatter than he was, and

Iona wanted to tell him to take it off. Leon had grown a scrubby beard and was chewing tobacco. Every few minutes, he had to leave the room to spit. She wished they would all go downstairs so that Hannah could open her eyes.

They left soon enough, and Iona saw that Hannah wasn't pretending. She counted the painkillers in the bottle and realized that her mother must have taken five or six before the boys got home.

Frank stayed with Hannah all day, hoping she might wake for a moment. Even if she told him to go away, that would be something. Once he thought he heard her mumble a word or two, and he leaned close but couldn't make her repeat it. "I'm afraid," he whispered. Her gnarled hand batted the covers and she clutched his fingers in her sleep.

Iona tried to give her water, but it dribbled out her mouth.

The brothers sat in the living room, smoking their pipes, waiting for Iona to come downstairs and cook their dinner.

That night, Hannah Moon curled into herself and began to dream of cows with wings. When Frank tried to take her hand, she pulled it away and hid it beneath the blankets, tucked it against her own chest. Even Iona's touch startled her, made her jerk in fear. "Don't," Frank said, "please don't." And Iona didn't know if he was talking to her or to Hannah.

He went to the window and pressed his fingertips to the cold glass. He saw a barefoot girl with yellow hair. She ran down the road. He ran after her. And he was ashamed of himself: he wanted her to fall so that he could pick her up.

Iona touched his back. "What is it, Daddy?" she said. "What do you see?"

At the bottom of the hill there was a creek covered by thin ice, at the edge of the woods a grave where Iona's sister was buried. Shadows in the trees moved like women.

Just before dawn, Hannah Moon gasped and opened her eyes wide, remembering the most important words. Iona and her father leaned close. She breathed hard but did not speak. She died instead, as if she had seen the day ahead of her and could not face the struggle.

Frank and Iona were surprised when the light did come: it was neither terrible nor loud. Clouds lay low and thick on the horizon, so the passage from the night was merciful and slow, and they felt it had been this day forever.

They washed the body of Hannah Moon. Her bloated feet were milky and blue as fish underwater. Frank sponged them, tenderly, though they seemed strange to him, not at all like the long knobby feet he thought he remembered. He washed her swollen knees and fleshless thighs; he washed between her legs. The pubic hair was gone, and he saw that the distance between girlhood and old age was painful and brief.

Iona couldn't look at her mother's body, though she had seen the shriveled breasts and sharp hipbones every day for months, though she knew each sore on her mother's buttocks. Now she washed Hannah's face and imagined her as only her father knew her: as a child on the road, as the girl in his bed, as the woman who reached for his hand and pulled it toward her belly, as the wife who said: *See how warm it is.*

Iona's brothers slept in ignorance while Iona chose stockings and shoes, a pale green dress, a pair of gloves, a ribbon to tie in her mother's dry hair.

Later, after an uneaten meal, the boys all sat around the table and watched a plate slip from Iona's hands and shatter on the floor forever and ever.

Alone, she stood in the kitchen as a drip from the faucet filled a cup in the sink. Each drop made the surface tremble, and she felt the water move in her own body. The thin golden light of winter streamed through the window, so beautiful she wanted to lie down and die in it.

Visitors came and went. Hannah's sister Margaret arrived from Boise. She wheeled their senile mother through the house. "At least Hannah got to live her own life," Margaret said. "Look at me, tied to this old woman." Iona thought she saw her grand-mother's face twist with understanding. Margaret stooped in front of the wheelchair and wiped drool from her mother's mouth with her own sleeve. "But you're a sweetheart, aren't you, baby? You don't give me any trouble." The old woman grinned, a great toothless smile that made her whole body strain and quiver. She didn't know why she was here; *Hannah* was just a name like any other.

Hannah's two brothers paid their respects, then sneaked out back to drink whiskey from the silver flasks they kept in their pockets. Quinte and Ray Cislo had fifteen fingers between them—a man and a half, they liked to say. Their wives stayed in the kitchen, chopping vegetables and making pies no one wanted to eat. Iona heard their chattering complaints, their endless gossip and weightless threats: *I told him my bag was packed.* But when Iona opened the door, they hushed and looked at her in a pitiful way that made her ashamed.

Her father's sisters called from Wolf Point and Sheridan. The roads were bad; they weren't coming. They sent their love. Everyone said that. *I send my love.* What did it mean?

Frank's parents were dead, but that didn't stop them from visiting the house. Iona hated them for her mother's sake. *Marry a young one,* Delbert Moon said. His wife sat beside him on the sofa, her arms folded over her big chest. *I told you she was too frail to outlive Frank,* Eva said. *I'm surprised she lasted as long as she did.*

Clayton Cislo came too, drunk as he was the night he died. He winked at Iona. *She thought she was too good for us,* he said. *Couldn't wait to get away from her ma and me. Well you can see where it got her.*

The unnamed child found her mother, brought her tiny bag of bones and laid them in the hollow of the woman's pelvis. Iona was jealous of the baby and longed to be cradled, body within a body, just that way.

• • •

Iona's brothers didn't go back to Missoula that winter. No one asked why. Every night they sat at the table, each one in his place: the father at one end, Leon at the other. This never changed.

No one but Iona noticed how the mother's absence filled her chair, how her hand fumbled with the fork. No one else saw her rise from the table to close the faded curtains and block the glare of the setting sun.

Iona sat beside the empty chair. The sun made her blink and squint. She stood and moved toward the window. Her limbs floated, her bones were water. Slowly she drew the curtains and said, "Sun's in my eyes." Her own voice made her dizzy. One of her brothers burped. None of them stopped eating. She had to lean against the sink. *Whatever happens, happens again and again.* The sun flared as it set, and the trees at the crest of the hills seemed to catch fire. Her father's spoon scraped across the bottom of his bowl, and Iona Moon sat down to keep from falling.

6

Jay Tyler knew the woman was dead. His mother had clipped Hannah Moon's obituary from the paper and left it on the kitchen table. He wondered if she knew about him and Iona, or if she was just trying to make a point about what could happen to mothers, even young ones. He felt sorry for himself and then angry, as if Delores wanted to blame him somehow.

Willy Hamilton talked about it too. He sat by Jay's window and Jay lay on the bed. Willy hadn't been to see Jay since the second cast came off, since the day Jay had said: *I don't need your fuckin' pity.*

Willy said, "I just keep thinking of Iona pulling that cat out of the river, saying she'd touched plenty of things that had been dead longer than that."

Jay remembered Iona Moon touching him, the part that was dead now. He wanted Willy to leave. "I'm tired," he said.

Willy stared out the window, at the bare black trees and the icy street. "She touched her too, after she was dead, I mean."

Jay felt Iona's long hair brush his cheek, the warm rag on his chest, imagined her washing his body as she had washed her mother's body. "It's late," he whispered.

Willy stood up. "I should go," he said. The room was dim, full of shadows, and Jay was glad for that. Objects lost their outlines, furred, and grew indistinct, as if they were crumbling slowly in the night air. He'd wake to find himself outside, lying on the frozen ground, the house and everything they owned fallen down around him. "I saw Muriel Arnoux at school this week," Willy said. "She looks all right—if you want to know."

It was a boy—if you want to know.

He didn't want to know anything.

He drank himself to sleep and saw a dirty girl in overalls grab a chicken by the neck. She swung it over her head in great windmill loops. Bones snapped. The chicken fell to the ground and ran twenty feet, its head dangling, before it collapsed in the yard.

He woke cursing Willy Hamilton. What did he care how Hannah Moon died, or what Iona touched. What did it matter if Muriel Arnoux looked all right when she'd already made it clear she was never going to be all right again.

He had taken his mother's car twice since the accident. Every time he hit the brakes he felt the stab in his shin and knee. Once he drove to South Bend and paid a woman twenty dollars for a blow job. He didn't want to take his clothes off, didn't want to see her face or feel her breath at his ear; he just wanted to unzip his pants, close his eyes and leave his body. But he couldn't come. She gave him half an hour and finally said, "Look, baby, I don't have all night." Weeks later he headed north to the gorge where the cliffs plunged sixty feet and the squeezed river grew fast and wild. He thought of the woman who'd jumped from the bridge and was saved—bad luck or bad planning; people miscalculated all the time.

Now he took the car again. He parked by the high school three days in a row before he spotted Muriel. He didn't know what he wanted. Slouched in his seat, he hoped she wouldn't notice the Chrysler.

She walked with her head down. She looked more like her mother already, puffed up in a down parka so she seemed thick through the middle and slow, taking tiny steps, afraid of falling on the ice. *She looks all right.* It was a lie. *If you want to know.*

He parked in the same place on Thursday and again on Friday. Both days she passed him quickly, without seeing. She was still a clean girl, Jay thought, but if he held her in his arms and pressed his nose into her hair, he thought she'd smell of wet leaves and damp earth.

He couldn't find her on Monday and wondered if she'd seen him after all. He worried that she might be sick and envisioned a long illness that would leave her body wasted and her mind fogged. It was very important to see her before this happened.

The next day a letter came for him at noon—a small, square note with no return address. His name and street were printed in careful, tiny script. Though he couldn't remember seeing Muriel's handwriting, he was sure the letter was from her.

He took it upstairs to his room, locked the door, sat down on the bed. He wanted to tear it open but restrained himself, easing one finger under the flap gently, the way he knew Muriel would.

He hoped the letter contained some secret message, some words he could not imagine until she spoke them, a line of forgiveness to heal him, a burst of longing to make him whole.

The note wasn't signed and didn't begin, *Dear.* There was only one sentence: *Stop it, Jay.*

He wished he could have been kinder to her that day last August when she'd come to the house to tell him that their child was a boy. If he had, she might speak to him now, might sit beside him in the car and feel some tenderness or regret. For two days he stayed home, but on Friday he waited again. At three-thirty he glimpsed her in the rearview mirror and knew she saw him too. She looked startled, about to run. He thought he'd have to chase her, but she walked toward his side of the car, her stride swift and deliberate. He rolled down his window, and she said, "Leave me alone."

He stared at her quilted blue coat, trying to remember his hands on her belly. "I just want to talk."

"My father'd beat me if he caught me with you."

"Then get in and put your head down." Jay was surprised to hear himself say it, and even more surprised when Muriel walked around the back of the car and did what he asked.

He hadn't worked it out this far, had no plan of where he'd take her, but he drove toward the river, as if by going back to the place it all started, he could begin again and change the past.

Already the white winter sun sank through thin clouds near the horizon, leaving sky and river the same metallic gray streaked with gold. The far shore was black, and the line of trees appeared in the perfect mirror of water. Jay thought everything could be turned upside down and still look exactly the same. The river could open above them, and the sky could flow toward the dam at South Bend. Whether trees grew upward or hung from their roots made no difference. He wanted to explain this to Muriel so that she would understand how solid things could be made insubstantial and the past could be washed away.

"What do you want?" she said. She leaned into her door and rolled down the window even though the air was frigid. He rolled his down too, to show her that anything she did was okay. Anything. And he would do the same. Whatever she wanted.

"What?" she said. He was staring. He saw now that she was scared. Her voice quavered. Her nose was red as if she held back tears. He was sorry. He didn't want her to be afraid of him. He reached for her hand, but she jerked away and held her own hands in her lap, fingers tightly laced.

Jay thought about the slivers of glass in his cheek, how they worked their way to the surface for months after the accident, how they made hard knots before bursting through the skin and dotting his face with blood. "I don't want anything," he said.

"Then take me home," said Muriel, "and stop waiting for me. You don't know. You don't know what my father will do." Tears welled and her eyes glistened. *I'll kill you and go to hell without regret if you ever come near my family again.* Jay knew what Francis Arnoux would do to him. He moved toward her. He wanted to kiss the tears from her cheeks and say, *I hurt too.* He wanted to touch the back of her neck, under her hair.

But when he put his fingers on Muriel's face, she pulled away, as if his hand burned. She looked at him, eyes wide, mouth tight. He forgot how sorry he was. His touch was vile to her, he saw that now. *Look, baby, I don't have all night.* And to her too, Jay thought, to all of them. *Mommy has a headache.* He wanted to slap her. He wanted to kiss her hard, force her lips apart. He thought of the river at the end of winter, ice heaved up on the shore, great broken chunks, the relentless river, green and black and slow. He'd brought her here to make everything all right, and now she had ruined it again. He had thought of her so tenderly, like a child. Now he wanted to grab her legs and pull her toward him. If he repulsed her, all the better. She was cruel to make him behave so badly, to make him see himself this way.

But his hands were shaking. He was afraid too, and the tears streamed down his face though he didn't know why he was crying. Once his mother had shown him a tree in the woods that had been cleaved and burned by lightning. There was a wound in the trunk, and the tree had two trunks after that, growing out of the scar, forever joined and forever separate. He didn't understand then, but he did now.

He thought there were two kinds of people. The distance between who he was before the accident and who he was after was insurmountable. He had crossed a boundary. He wanted to tell Muriel that she was here, on the other side, with him, that they couldn't go back and be what they were in the past, that the people who loved them then couldn't love them now, could barely see them, in fact; so they should try to love each other because they were twin trunks of the same tree, their lives scarred by the same wound.

What do you want? She despised him. *Nothing.* She wasn't even pretty anymore, and never would be again. *Nothing.* He headed back to town. It was just past five but already dark.

"Christ was whipped thirty-nine times for a question he couldn't answer," Muriel said.

He laughed, a loud bark from the chest. "I'm no Jesus," he said.

"I was thinking about myself," she whispered.

It was only after he'd dropped her three blocks from her house that he realized what she meant. He imagined her father waiting behind the closed door. He heard the insistent, unanswerable question: *Where the hell have you been?*

Jay knew that Muriel thought he'd ruined her life. *No one will marry me now.* That's what she said. She was planning her spinsterhood at fifteen. She was going to live at home, take care of her parents, nurse them in their old age. *I can't ever make up for the pain I've caused.* He thought they should be grateful to him for what he'd done; now she'd stay, humbled and ashamed, forever their servant—no, slave.

He drove back to the place where they'd parked. A light snow was falling. Jay Tyler reviewed his crimes. He thought of the frog he'd caught when he was seven. He whacked it on the head to stun it, torched a wad of papers and threw the frog on top to see it explode.

He remembered things he'd seen that he had no right to see: Everett Fry's hat blown off his head; Sharla Wilder sitting half naked on her bed; Roy Wilkerson curled into a ball on the sidewalk.

Once, when no one was home, Muriel had led him through her house. In every room there was a different image of Christ: a blue Jesus hanging in the bathroom, hands nailed to the cross— even his blood was tinted blue; Jesus opening his own chest in the living room to reveal his throbbing sacred heart; scattered crayons and the Jesus coloring book spread on the kitchen table: Jesus rolling a stone from a tomb, calling to a man four days dead; Jesus multiplying loaves and fishes; Jesus talking to his disciples at the last supper—*one of you will deny me, one of you will betray me.*

Jay had laughed about the coloring book, but now he thought how good it would be to sit with Muriel's little brother and sister, trying to stay within the lines, how peaceful to come to some understanding as the pictures emerged, as color gave them shape and sense.

There was so much he didn't understand. Why didn't the frog explode—why did it only hiss and shrivel and turn black? Why did his mother touch him so tenderly, then go away? What good did it do to lock herself in the bathroom and let the water run and run? What had Iona Moon told him about winter on the Kila Flats—*Absolute zero, no degrees.* Frozen pipes. Her mother's frozen legs, no, only swollen: she couldn't walk. Same thing. The outhouse. Don't sit down all the way—your ass might freeze to the seat. Don't stand up. You know what will happen.

There was a place in the center of his body that was this cold. Absolute zero. He wanted to lie down with Iona now, to drift without moving, rest without sleeping, to feel the hard bones of her chest against his chest, skin against skin. He didn't understand this either, didn't know how she would heal him, or why, except that she was the only one who wasn't afraid. If he'd had any courage at all, he would have gone to her and tried to explain.

Iona saw the boy as he ducked out the henhouse door. Even in the half light of the January morning she knew the skittish shadow was Matt Fry. He sprinted across the white field, hugging a small bundle to his chest.

A thief has to steal, she thought. A hungry boy doesn't give a damn about what other people say they own. Better to come here. Al Zimmerman or Jack Wilder might shoot first and ask questions later. Matt Fry's own father would shoot for sure.

She heard Hannah say: *All your kindness is never going to change him.* Now she saw that this was true. If her brothers found out about the eggs, they'd go up to the shed and slap Matthew around—*Teach the little shit a lesson*—as if they'd forgotten he was once their friend. But their meanness wasn't going to change him, either. One more blow to the head wouldn't knock any sense into him.

Iona thought it was unfair that her brothers sat around all day waiting for the ground to thaw, while she had to go back to school. They weren't up early enough to expect her to make their breakfast, but they still counted on dinner—even if all they'd managed to do during the day was drive to the dump.

The worst of it was the fact that she'd flunked every class in the fall. That meant summer school with dummies or an extra semester next year. Thinking about it as she stood on the road waiting for the bus made Iona want to forget the whole thing. What good was a high school degree to a girl like her? She wasn't going to college and she could already read.

The bus rolled up before she had a chance to decide to go home, and as she climbed the steps she figured going to school was better than staying in the house with her brothers. Sometimes she was afraid to be alone with them, afraid of what she'd do. She might stick the knife in Leon's belly this time instead of throwing it in the river.

Jeweldeen hadn't saved her a place. Why should she? School had started three weeks ago. She didn't know Iona was coming back. Jeweldeen had been at the funeral, but they didn't talk. Iona couldn't remember if she'd spoken to anyone that day. All she could recollect was being kissed by ladies she knew and ladies she didn't. They smelled of face powder and waxy lipstick. They said she was a good girl to take care of her mama the way she did. She nodded and they squeezed her arm, dabbing at their noses with white handkerchiefs.

Sharla Wilder sobbed as hard as she had the day they'd buried

Everett Fry, and Jeweldeen dragged her weepy sister out to the car.

Iona didn't care. She was sick of being kissed, sick of being told she was a good girl. What was so good about sliding a bedpan under your own mother's bottom while she yelled that she couldn't stand it, that the metal felt like a razor, that she'd piss in her bed before she sat on that damn thing again. What did the powdered ladies know. What right did Sharla have to carry on that way while Iona stood outside her own body, dry and thin as air, feeling nothing.

Maybe Sharla thought they had something in common: she'd watched her own mother die. But Maywood Wilder had had the good sense to go fast from pneumonia. She still had all her hair when they buried her. Sick as she was, Maywood Wilder stayed plump.

Mrs. Wilder's casket would have been left open. People must have passed and whispered about how lovely she looked, how serene, dear Maywood gone to her Maker with the smile of an angel on her face.

Hannah Moon's face could offer no peace of mind to the living, so the pine box stayed closed. Her wrinkled mouth would have said that no one leaves without screaming. Her twisted hands would have made the rosy ladies rub their own joints; her withered breasts and swollen feet would have made the men look at their wives too hard.

Iona wanted to push the women away when they bussed the air near her cheek. *You haven't seen her.* But her father stood beside her, holding her hand so tightly that the tips of her fingers went numb. She thanked the ladies for their kindness. Did she really say that? Liar. Only one person knew enough to say something true. Flo Hamilton had stripped Hannah Moon at the funeral home, had sponged the skin with alcohol and dressed her again. "You took good care of your mother," she whispered. Flo Hamilton said the same words as a dozen others, but she'd seen the sores and knew Iona had tried to keep them clean. She saw the ribbon Iona had tied in her mother's brittle hair; she saw that each toe had been washed.

Jeweldeen sat with Bonnie Zimmerman on the bus. Bonnie was the only other high school girl who came from the Flats. They waved to Iona, but Iona pretended not to see. Kids quieted down when she passed, as if they were afraid of her. She found an empty seat near the back, hunched down and stared out the window at the ripples of snow that had blown across the fields and frozen in hard waves.

Iona was the last one off the bus. She figured she'd go straight to homeroom and wouldn't have to talk to anybody all day. But Jeweldeen was waiting.

"Fetterhoff's gonna be glad to see you," Jeweldeen said.

"I can hardly wait."

"I can hear him already: 'Miss Moon, how good of you to honor us with your presence.'"

"Sonuvabitch."

"Fetterhoff never had a mother—he's just a worm that crawled out of a hole."

"We could cut," Iona said, "go hang out at Sharla's."

"You wanna be in high school till you're twenty?"

Iona shook her head. It was bad enough to be in school at seventeen.

In February the cold broke for three days in a row. Iona and Jeweldeen and Bonnie Zimmerman sat on the concrete wall at the edge of the parking lot trying to smoke as many cigarettes as they could before lunch break was over.

"Chicken?" Iona said.

"No way," said Jeweldeen.

"Then roll up your sleeves."

"I said, *no way*."

"I thought you meant you weren't a chicken."

"I meant no way I'd play chicken with someone as crazy as you."

"What's with you two?" Bonnie said. She was short and pudgy, cute in a little-girl way.

"Iona plays this stupid game," Jeweldeen said.

"*We* play this game," said Iona. "We play lots of games." She nudged Jeweldeen, thinking of the summer they were ten years old, the summer they locked themselves in the cellar and took off all their clothes every day for a week. They rubbed against each other and rolled on the dirty floor. They kissed and pinched each other's nipples. Sometimes it felt good and sometimes it didn't. The last day Jeweldeen said, *You have to touch me—here.* But when Iona did what she asked, Jeweldeen didn't want to play anymore.

"What kind of games?" Bonnie whined.

Iona wanted to tell her about the cellar so that Bonnie would run off and not bother them again. Jeweldeen saw it coming. "Don't you dare," she said.

"Chicken," said Iona.

"Shit," Jeweldeen said, pushing up the sleeves of her sweater to expose her forearms.

Iona rolled the sleeves of her denim jacket past her elbows, took one last hit off her cigarette, then laid the burning butt on the wall.

"One inch," Jeweldeen said.

"Anybody can do an inch," Iona said. "I bet Bonnie can do an inch."

Jeweldeen and Iona jumped off the wall. The idea was to see which one of them could bring her forearms closer to the smoldering cigarette. Jeweldeen put one arm on each side of the butt and brought them closer and closer, until her arms were an inch apart, just like she'd said.

"I wanna play," said Bonnie.

"This is no game for pussies," Jeweldeen said.

"I'm not a pussy." Bonnie's voice was even higher than usual.

"I'm not a pussy," Jeweldeen squealed.

"Let her do what she wants," said Iona.

Jeweldeen backed off and Bonnie stepped up to the wall. She moved fast, thinking it would be easy to get closer than Jeweldeen, easy to hold her arms there longer. But the heat scared her and she leaped back, inspecting her arms for singed hairs.

"Told you," said Jeweldeen.

Iona squinted at the glowing butt. "Half an inch," she said, "half an inch between my arms."

"You'll never do it," said Jeweldeen.

"I could touch it," Iona said. "I could pick it up."

"You're crazier than I thought."

"She's not gonna do it," Bonnie said.

"Dollar says I will."

"I got a dollar says you're full of it," said Bonnie.

"How about you?" Iona said to Jeweldeen.

"I'm not paying you to burn yourself."

Iona took it slow, focusing on that cigarette as if it were the only thing in the world, its fiery ash the only light, its sharp smoke the only smell. She watched her arms move closer and closer. They belonged to someone else. They were part of Sharla Wilder's dream, the one where Everett Fry doused her with gasoline and lit a match, the one that became Everett's dream in the end: so he was the one to burn and Sharla's skin remained untouched.

A bell rang. A boy yelled. Bonnie squeaked like a pet rabbit being squeezed by a child. Jeweldeen cussed. Iona Moon didn't feel a thing, but she couldn't see the cigarette, couldn't watch the red hot end because the butt was between her arms and her arms were pressed tight together.

The bell was still ringing somewhere far beyond them, in Everett's dream.

Jeweldeen tried to pull Iona's arms apart, but Iona had locked her hands together and wouldn't let go. The bell stopped. Iona relaxed her grip. The cigarette was out.

"Jesus," Jeweldeen said.

"I'm not paying," said Bonnie. "We never shook and I'm not paying you a friggin' dime, Iona."

Iona turned her arms to look at the burns. She still didn't feel them, though she knew they should hurt, because the sores were already blistered and dark and the smell reminded her of a pig on a spit.

"You owe me a dollar, Bonnie," Iona said.

Bonnie's eyes were watery and red. She pulled a ragged dollar out of her purse and threw it at Iona's feet.

"I hope you're happy," Jeweldeen said as Bonnie ran toward the school.

Iona rolled down her sleeves. "I am," she said, "I'm fuckin' ecstatic." She plucked the money off the pavement and stuffed it in the pocket of her jacket, patting it smooth, as if that dollar were something precious, close to her heart.

In early March, the ground began to thaw. Mud oozed up through the melting snow until the Kila Flats became a bog. The smell of it made the cows impatient. They butted against their stalls in the morning. Ruby stamped on Iona's foot when she came to milk her, and Iona had to slap the cow's flank to make her move.

Frank Moon grew impatient too. It was too soon to plant; they were sure to have another freeze—might last two nights or two weeks. He remembered the year the thaw came in February. It got so warm the sap started to run in the apple trees. When they froze again, they froze dead. By spring their limbs were dry and black. He and his father chopped them down, sawed them to pieces. His mother wept for the trees, though she'd seen many things die.

Iona's brothers were anxious in their own way. They wanted

to enjoy the last of their idleness. Night after night they loaded their .22s, piled into the truck, and drove to the dump. The shadows writhed with rats. The boys kept score by the squeals they counted, and Rafe always won.

Iona didn't like being in the house alone with her father. They couldn't look at each other without thinking about all those nights they'd stood over Hannah's bed or at her window. After supper, Iona went to her room, and Frank sat on the porch, smoking his pipe until the boys came home.

Frank Moon and his sons planted the potatoes the second Saturday in April. Iona scrubbed the kitchen floor. Even after the mud was gone, the tiles still looked gray. She scraped at the splatters on the stove and scoured the sink. One room every Saturday; she'd be done in June and could start over.

She thought about the soil, loose and grainy from ancient volcanoes, how potatoes grew to huge perfection in the dark earth. Not like those puny lumps from Maine, her father always said, crushed by clay and pocked by stones. When the men came back from the field, she caught them at the door and made them leave their boots outside. The brothers laughed at her, but Frank told the boys to do what she said.

Later, she looked at the four pairs of boots, soles crusted with dirt, old leather cracked, laces knotted where they'd frayed and broken. Each pair was unmistakable, leather worn to the shape of one man's feet, rubber heels rubbed down from his weight and stride. They were part of the men, her brothers, her father. They seemed almost conscious, and Iona had to close the door.

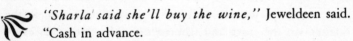

7

"*Sharla said she'll buy the wine,*" Jeweldeen said. "Cash in advance.

She and Iona were planning a little party for themselves before graduation. Iona still hadn't told Jeweldeen that she had nothing to celebrate. She couldn't decide whether to go to school this summer or next fall—or whether to forget the whole thing and try to get a job at Woolworth's.

"How many bottles?" said Iona.

"She won't buy us more than two."

"We'll barely get a buzz."

"Don't worry," Jeweldeen said, "we won't go thirsty."

Iona convinced Sharla to buy three bottles of wine. *In case we make some friends.* Jeweldeen stole a pint of her sister's rum and five packs of cigarettes from a carton in the refrigerator.

Sharla insisted on taking them to the river. "I don't want to hear the sirens," she said. "Bad enough I know what you're doing without worrying about you sailing off the bridge." She looked like the photograph of her mother: hair curled tight to her head, lipstick much too dark. Maywood hung in Sharla's kitchen now, and Iona wondered if Sharla had swiped the picture from her father's house or if he'd given it up gladly. Maybe he got tired of his wife watching over him every time he plunked down to have a look at the news. If he thought the woman knew what he'd done to his daughter, he was probably relieved to get them both out of the house. Remembering what Maywood knew made Iona ashamed: she should have gone back that day, despite Jeweldeen's threats.

"You meet me right here at midnight," Sharla said when she dropped Jeweldeen and Iona. "And don't keep me waiting."

"Yes'm, Miss Sharla."

"Don't be a smartass, Jeweldeen. I'm doing you a favor."

"If she only knew," Jeweldeen whispered, cradling the stolen rum under her jacket. *Yes,* thought Iona, and she wanted to tell Sharla but wanted to get drunk more. She started down to the water. Sharla rolled up her window, and Jeweldeen waved.

They weren't alone. Lots of kids had the same idea. Today was Friday; they'd survived the last day of school. Monday was graduation. Iona didn't give a damn. None of them had anything to celebrate. Who was leaving town to start a new life? Half the girls would be married by September. *The first child can come anytime; after that it takes nine months.* Jeweldeen had had a few boyfriends but no real prospects. She could stay on at the farm and cook for her father the rest of her life, or she could try to get a job at the phone company and live in town.

Catholic girls were lucky: they had other choices. They could always go to some convent and spend their lives doing kind deeds for sick old women and neglected children. If they were smart enough they could teach school, floating between the rows of chairs in their black habits, knowing exactly who they were. But most of them weren't smart. They got married like everyone else, had six kids by the time they were twenty-five, then bought a single bed.

"Wait up!" yelled Jeweldeen, trotting to catch Iona. "You trying to ditch me?"

"Just trying to get away from the crowd."

Jeweldeen stumbled in a rut and swore.

"Better let me carry the rum," Iona said.

"Not a chance."

Iona recognized most of the cars. Twyla Catts had brought the drill team. She was Catholic but didn't have a hope of being a teacher or a nun. She thought she was lucky: she could take her pick. Half a dozen guys had already lined up for the captain of the drill team. But Iona knew that no matter who Twyla Catts married, her life was going to end up just the same.

Twyla's friends sat on the hood of her Pinto, guzzling beer. How all eight of them had ever crammed in the car, Iona couldn't guess. But they wouldn't have to worry about stuffing themselves back in to get home. Already the boys were circling.

Iona spotted Willy Hamilton's Chevy near the end of the road. She knew for sure that Willy wasn't drinking. But he still took his pals wherever they wanted to go. Except Jay. Nobody drove Jay Tyler anywhere now. Iona was glad she knew one other person who wasn't going to graduate. She wished Jay were here. She remembered his hands on her ribs and thought they'd feel good even now—whether or not he liked her at all. Darryl McQueen leaned against the trunk of Willy's car. He was too lanky to be a strong diver, too tall to lock his limbs and go down straight the way Jay did. But that turned out to be Jay's whole problem—being able to lock his legs.

Luke Sweeney and Kevin Burch sat in the backseat of the Chevy with their doors open. Willy was in front with his door shut and his hands on the wheel.

In his boots and black jeans, Darryl McQueen didn't look half bad. Maybe his knees bent when he tried to do somersaults in layout position, maybe his narrow white feet slapped the water like fins, but he looked just fine tonight, much better than anyone else Iona had seen. At least he wasn't making a fool of himself, skulking around Twyla's car, drooling like a dog.

"Hey, Darryl," Iona said as she passed.

"Hey," he said, "what've you got?"

Jeweldeen jabbed Iona. "Don't you go making any trades," she hissed.

"Not enough to share," Iona said.

"That's not what I heard." Darryl grinned. He had a big mouth—and big hands. The bottle of beer he held looked small. "I hear you're a generous girl." He was still smiling.

"You've been misinformed." Iona stopped ten feet in front of him.

"I don't think so," said Darryl. "I have a very reliable source." He looked serious now. "At least you could spare a cigarette, couldn't you?"

Iona pulled a pack from her jacket pocket and tossed it to him. He caught it with his left hand. "Got a light?" he said. She threw a plastic lighter and he caught that too.

Iona and Jeweldeen started down the path to the water.

"Hey," Darryl said, "don't you want the cigarettes?"

Iona waved. "Keep them."

"How about the lighter?"

"It's your graduation present."

"I owe you," Darryl said.

"Yeah," Iona said to Jeweldeen, "he owes me."

"You started it," said Jeweldeen.

"I always do."

At the bank of the Snake River, Jeweldeen and Iona crouched under a weeping willow. Its thin branches trailed in the water, rippling the surface. Iona knew she could have Darryl McQueen if she wanted him, exactly the same way she'd had Jay Tyler: in the backseat of a car or the back row of a movie—as long as she bought her own ticket and met him after the lights went down, as long as she could find her own way home and keep her mouth shut, as long as she didn't have some stupid romantic notion that they'd walk out of the movie together holding hands. If she remembered all that, she could meet him five Saturdays in a row and then forget the whole thing. She thought of Darryl standing there on the high dive in his scarlet swim trunks. He wasn't so hot then. He was as scared as anybody and might as well have been naked for all his suit could hide.

Girls' cries carried across the water. Headlights blazed on the road as more seniors came to celebrate. Glass shattered on metal and a boy with a high voice said, "You fucker." Iona hoped Darryl had smashed his beer bottle on Willy's hood. She hoped he'd scraped the perfect blue paint and that Willy had laid him out flat. Another bottle cracked and then another. The boys were laughing now, nothing but a game, one more thing she'd never understand.

Iona and Jeweldeen took turns with the rum and chased it with wine. They smoked cigarettes to stay thirsty. Iona lay down in the grass. If she concentrated, she could hear the water splashing against the riverbank, louder and louder, lapping over bottles and stones, twisting in the dark as it dragged tires and the bloated bodies of dead dogs toward the dam at South Bend. Everything stopped at the concrete wall. Sometimes Iona wished she lived in South Bend so that she could go down to the dam and see what the river gave up. Missing children and careless fishermen surfaced at the wall. Drowning wouldn't be so bad, she thought. When you went under for the last time, the water would close above your head. You'd realize that the place you'd found was dark and safe, that the water flowing between your legs and over your breasts felt cool and good, and there was no sense in struggling because you were already moving too fast.

"You're hogging the rum," Jeweldeen said.

Iona farted. "You said it."

"You're disgusting."

"Comes naturally."

"No one will ever marry you."

"Thank God."

"Yeah? And what are you gonna do with your life, Miss Independence?"

"Join the circus."

"As what?"

"The girl who gets sawed in half."

"I'd rather get married."

"I suppose you think you're gonna meet some prince—live happily ever after."

"It's possible."

"And where are you going to find this man?"

"My own back door," Jeweldeen said. "Or maybe yours."

"You want one of my brothers?"

"I might."

"Which one?"

"I haven't decided."

"I'll give you all three." Iona remembered what Leon had said years ago—that Jeweldeen was dangerous.

"Sssh," said Jeweldeen, "there's someone on the path."

"Iona?" It was Darryl McQueen. "Iona Moon?" He sang her name. "Are you out there?"

"Goddamn it," said Jeweldeen. "Thanks to you, we'll be stuck with that mooch all night."

"He can have half my share."

"You already drank your share."

"Iona Moon, I'm looking for you." Boys sounded so sweet in the beginning.

"Over here," said Iona.

Darryl fell to his knees beside her. "I've been looking for you for half an hour," he said. "Got another cigarette?"

"I gave you a whole pack."

"Yeah, with six left. Luke took two and Kevin had one. I'm out, babe. What d'you say?"

She gave Darryl an unopened pack. "You owe me for that one," Jeweldeen said to Iona.

"Yeah? How much do you charge for cigarettes you rip off from your sister?"

"I'll just take a couple," said Darryl.

"Forget it," Iona said. "I gave you the pack. Jeweldeen doesn't mind, do you, Jewels?"

"Screw you."

"See? She doesn't care."

"Wanna go for a ride?" Darryl said. "Sort of a trade for the smokes?"

"Some trade," said Jeweldeen.

"I'll go," Iona said.

"We have to wait for Sharla, remember?"

"We'll bring you back," said Darryl.

"Come on, Jewels."

"Don't call me that."

"Well, I'm going."

"I'm not."

"Fine," Iona said.

"Yeah, fine."

"You can sit here all by yourself, jump half out of your skin every time a twig snaps."

"I will. Thanks."

"I'll be back by midnight."

"Don't bother."

"Have it your way." Iona took another pack of cigarettes and what was left of the rum. "You can keep the wine," she said to Jeweldeen.

"Don't come knockin' on Sharla's door in the middle of the night," Jeweldeen said. "I'm gonna tell her not to let you in."

Willy wasn't happy to see who Darryl had dragged out of the woods. He didn't want to take them for a ride, but they were going. Luke and Kevin argued about who had to ride up front with Willy and who got to hop in back with Darryl and Iona. Both those idiots would have wedged into the back if Darryl had let them, like Iona Moon was some kind of prize and Willy was nothing but the guy who drove the car. He knew damn well they didn't like her any more than he did. Darryl already had his mouth all over her face and his hands under her jacket; he was making awful sucking noises as Willy backed over the ruts. But Willy knew for a fact that the same Darryl McQueen had never even said hello to Iona Moon at school.

Willy believed you shouldn't talk to a girl you didn't like, even in the dark, even if she did decide to put out for you. He felt very pure and certain of himself on this point because he could have had Iona, right here, summer before last, and no one would have known.

In the rearview mirror, Willy could see that Kevin had one hand on Iona's leg and one on his own crotch just like some old geezer at the movies who gets off on the couple beside him instead of watching the show. Luke leaned over the seat to watch.

Eighteen years old and those guys were already nasty as goats. Kevin was tall and blond, a bit too fair but handsome enough. He could have had a real date. He could have made a run on Twyla Catts and her friends. Not like Willy—or Darryl, for that matter. Maybe Luke Sweeney had a tougher time because he was so short. Girls ran their fingers through his hair but didn't want to dance with him. Still, being five-foot-three was no excuse for turning into a pervert before you were out of high school.

Iona laughed, pushing Darryl away. "Slow down," she said, "you're gonna wear yourself out."

"This guy never wears out," Darryl said.

But Iona held him off and lit a cigarette. Willy didn't know what was worse: listening to those sucking noises or breathing in their smoke. She and Darryl passed the cigarette back and forth. Kevin asked for a hit, and then Luke wanted one too. Pretty soon Iona had lit a cigarette for each of them and Willy was practically choking.

Darryl said he wanted to go somewhere quiet, somewhere they could relax with the rest of the beers and Iona's rum; he didn't want to meet up with half the senior class again. "Morons," he said, "I bet you five bucks Willy's father will bust them before midnight. Ol' Horton'll haul them all down to the jail and call their parents. What a scene."

The thought of it made Willy sick to his stomach; for a few

seconds the road blurred. He felt as if it were slick with rain
and he was skidding toward the ditch. He imagined his father
yanking him out of his own car, counting beer bottles and
cigarette butts, saying: *I'm disappointed in you, son.* Willy could
swear he hadn't had a drop. *So you know it's wrong.* Yes, he
knew. *But you drove your friends around all night.*

If Willy cut out now, Darryl would figure the crack about
Horton had gotten to him. They'd all have a good laugh. *Coward.*
It was true. He'd just drop them somewhere private like Darryl
said, then he'd get his butt home. By midnight he'd be asleep
in his own bed with the covers pulled over his ears.

"How about that shed up by the tracks?" Luke said. "The
one where old man Hardy used to live."

"That place stinks," said Iona.

And your boyfriend lives there, Willy thought. She could fool
everyone else in this car, but not him.

"No one will come up there," Darryl said.

"Except Matt Fry," said Kevin.

Luke leaned over the seat. "I thought he died," he said.

This made Darryl and Kevin hoot. Iona lit another cigarette.
"I'm telling you," she said, "Hardy kept his goats and chickens
right in the shed. There's three inches of dried shit on the floor."

"Maybe we should just burn it down," Darryl said, "do the
county a favor."

"And have Willy's dad screaming up here for sure."

"She's right," Willy said. He hated siding with Iona Moon.
He wanted to tell Darryl what Matt Fry and Iona used to do
together, what they probably still did.

Willy did head up toward the tracks, but he stayed a good
mile from the shed. As soon as he stopped, the boys opened the
doors and leaped out, howling like wild dogs. Willy saw no
sense in pressing their luck even though they were miles from
town. If he left now, he could be home by ten-thirty. But he'd
never live it down. This was his last summer on the diving
team, and he couldn't stand the thought of being razzed for

three months, called little-miss-goodie-two-shoes: *only girls are prudes*. Wait till they heard Horton was putting him on part-time in September. Wait till they figured out that next June he might be rounding up drunken seniors with his father. In two years he'd have enough experience to go to the academy in Pocatello. That was one more reason not to get caught tonight.

Kevin wanted to build a fire, and Darryl said, "You're stupider than you look, Burch. You should have gone out for football."

"The thicker the neck, the smaller the brain," Luke said.

"Yeah," said Kevin, "and the smaller the foot, the shorter the dick."

Everyone stared at Luke's tiny feet. "Score," Darryl said. Iona sat down in the high grass and opened the rum. It was still half full, and the boys had eleven beers between them. Willy stood by the car with his door open.

"You're making me nervous," Kevin said. The dome light glowed yellow, the only bright spot for miles.

"Yeah, shut the door," said Luke.

"Let him be," Darryl said. "Chauffeurs are supposed to stay by the car."

Willy slammed the door, thinking of the day he'd have a blue light and a siren.

Darryl rubbed his hand up and down Iona's thigh and kissed her neck. "I used to charge my brothers a nickel for that," she said.

"For what?"

"For touching me. A penny to watch me dance, a nickel to touch my tits."

"I've got a quarter," Luke said.

"What'll you do for a dollar?" said Kevin, digging in his pocket.

Willy knew the answer to that. He'd heard what she'd done to get a dollar from Bonnie Zimmerman.

Darryl put his hand under her shirt and cupped her breast. "I'm not paying for something I can get for free."

Iona knocked his hand away, but Willy remembered how she tried to make him touch her, just that way. She'd probably do it with all of them before the night was out. What did Darryl call it? *Pulling a train.* Willy wasn't going to stick around to see. And he wasn't going to try to stop it either. *You make your bed, you lie in it,* his mother always told him. He knew his father's words too: *A man who watches a crime has helped commit it.* Willy thought of Mrs. Stiles at Sunday school, a passage she wrote on the board and made them copy: *I hate the company of evildoers, and I will not sit with the wicked.* It was that simple.

But he stayed a moment longer because he'd heard what his mother had said after Hannah Moon died. Flo whispered to Horton in the kitchen, not knowing Willy stood at the door. "She couldn't have weighed more than seventy-five pounds. I don't know how she lived as long as she did. And she was clean. I washed her, but she was already clean. The girl's been taking care of her all this time."

It was hard to believe that the same Iona Moon who bathed her sick mother and dressed her bedsores was selling kisses to Luke Sweeney and Kevin Burch, letting Darryl McQueen collect the nickels.

She was a dirty girl who just happened to be kind to her mother. So what? Even a murderer might be nice to his parents. Willy got in the car and started the engine. If anyone wanted to come with him, this was his chance. Iona pecked Luke and Kevin before she fell in Darryl's lap and took another pull of rum. Willy hit the lights. Last chance. He'd even take Iona if she made a run for the car. That's how open-minded he was. Didn't Jesus shelter Mary Magdalene? Iona was standing, swaying as if tossed by wind. Maybe she was going to come with him; maybe she had the sense to save herself. No. Iona Moon twirled in the beams of light, dancing in front of the boys for free. She waved to Willy, blowing him kisses, saying, "Bye-bye, Willy—bye-bye."

* * *

He was too mad to go straight home. If his mother was awake, she'd see that something was wrong. She'd say, "Willy, baby, what is it?" He'd feel his heart tearing deep in his chest because she'd look at him so sweetly, as if he were still a child and she could still make everything all right with a kiss. He dragged Main for an hour. He wanted to buzz out the River Road again, just to see who was still there and if anything had happened. But the guys were probably right. Any minute now he might hear the cry of his father's siren and know that half those kids would get away and half wouldn't. The unlucky ones would have to wait down at the jail for their humiliated parents to come and drive them home. For weeks afterward those kids would do Saturday chores for the city: picking up litter and clearing out rain gutters, mowing the grass in Woodvale Park.

He thought of paying a visit to Jay too, just dropping in on his old buddy. He'd tell Jay all about Iona Moon. Jay would say she'd wanted it since she was thirteen, and Willy could stop feeling like he'd done something wrong, leaving her up there by the railroad tracks with his three pals.

But he knew it was wrong. He knew Iona didn't have a chance, and even if she did want it, that didn't make it right. So he was driving back to the tracks because he had to be sure. Even if they laughed at him, even if by some fluke his father came up there instead of down to the river, Willy Hamilton had no choice.

He didn't find anything except empty bottles and a pile of cigarette butts. He pointed his headlights right at the place where he'd left Iona and the boys, but there wasn't a clue: no signs of a struggle, just the flattened grass where they'd sat and a hole someone had dug in the dirt for the cigarettes. He was a jerk to worry about Iona, a girl like that could take care of herself, a girl like that got just what she deserved. He could go home now and sleep in peace. In a week he'd start diving practice and the guys would tell him what he'd missed.

He had the key in the ignition when he heard something move in the grass. *Just my imagination,* he told himself, and he knew that all he had to do was start the engine to keep from hearing the sound again. But it was already too late. He got out of the car and called her name. He heard it again, a hissing noise. "Iona," he said, "is that you?" And he prayed no one would answer.

He walked toward the sound and nearly tripped over her. She scooted away like a spooked dog. He knelt, just as he would to show an animal that he was no threat, and held out his hand even though he had nothing to offer. "Did they hurt you?" he said. Stupid. He wished he could swallow his question. Her shirt was torn and her jacket was gone, but her pants were still on, her belt still buckled.

"My shoes," she said, "they took my fucking shoes."

Willy inched closer and Iona jerked back. "I'm not gonna do anything," he said. He sat down cross-legged to show her he was telling the truth.

She touched her right eye carefully. "I think Darryl gave me a black eye."

Even in the dark, Willy could see that her face looked bruised. He hoped it was just dirt. Darryl McQueen wouldn't slug a girl. "Tell me what happened," he said.

"They got carried away."

"*They* got carried away? I didn't see you objecting."

"You're an asshole."

"Yeah, right, and I'm sitting here talking to you because I'm an asshole. I drove all the way back up here because I'm an asshole."

"Spare me."

"Gladly," Willy said. He stood up and brushed himself off. His headlights still blasted the place where it had all started. *She wants to be left alone so I'll leave her,* he told himself, but he couldn't keep from turning and calling out, "Come on, Iona. Let me give you a ride."

"Fuck you," she said.

Sometimes it wasn't easy to do the right thing. "I mean it," he said. "I'll take you home."

"I don't need any favors from assholes."

Fine. It was fine by him if she didn't sit in his car. He didn't want to look at her. He didn't want to get lost on the Kila Flats. And he never did like the way she smelled.

Willy started to town but didn't get far before he spotted his friends on the tracks, at the bend where the road ran beside the railroad for half a mile. They'd gone to the shed and found Matt Fry after all. Willy slowed down and turned off his lights. They must have made Matt drink the rest of the rum because now his legs were limp. Darryl and Kevin each had one of his arms draped over their shoulders so they could run with Matt between them, dragging him back and forth, letting his feet thump against the ties. Luke Sweeney ran behind, too short to take a turn.

Willy pulled over on the shoulder and ran up the embankment to the tracks. Kevin and Darryl dropped their load, and the boy crumpled.

"What the hell are you doing?" Willy said.

"That bitch was holding out on us," said Darryl, "and she got her claws in me besides." He turned to show Willy a long scratch down his left cheek.

"This is why she didn't want us to come up to the shed." Kevin kicked the lump, but it didn't move.

"Must be her sweetheart," Luke said.

Willy crouched to feel Matt's neck. There was still a pulse. "Let's get him off the tracks," he said.

"Why bother?" said Darryl. "Nobody gives a damn."

Willy wrapped his arms around Matt's chest from behind and pulled him off the ties. The skinny boy was heavier than Willy expected. "Help me get him back to the shed," he said. He looked at Luke, figuring he was the best bet. Luke shook his head.

"Leave him," said Kevin. "He'll crawl back in the morning."

Darryl slapped Willy on the back. "Glad to see you, buddy. We could use a ride back to town."

All three of them piled in the backseat, and Willy drove slowly, trying not to call attention to his car, just in case his father was still patrolling the back roads. He hated the girl hissing in the grass and the boy passed out by the tracks. He hated the three guys crammed in the back of the Chevy. He hated Jay Tyler for not being there, and he hated himself for driving down to the river tonight where all of this began.

Iona knew she could walk home in a quarter of the time it would take to get to Sharla's. But the dogs in the yard would bark, and Frank would meet her at the door. She was afraid he wouldn't yell, afraid he wouldn't notice that her shirt was ripped and her feet bare. He'd say, "Where's the truck?" And that would be the end of it.

But it was the dogs she kept seeing in her mind, straining at their leashes; they were the ones she cursed, those whining, foolish mutts. Sometimes she wondered how they found the wits to chase a rabbit or flush a pheasant. They were bred for one use, indifferent to love. If her brothers slaughtered a pig, the dogs grew wild with the smell of blood; they'd rip one another's throats fighting over warm entrails and pig's balls. At night they piled in a heap, nuzzled together only for warmth, just as her brothers had once huddled together on a hillside, caught by a snow squall in early November. They survived that night of wind and snow, cradling their useless guns in their laps; they kept one another warm and alive, but no more tenderness grew between them for all of that.

She did find her jacket and one of her shoes. The boys had tossed them down in the ditch by the road. The jacket was dirty but not destroyed. She could mend the sleeve where Darryl had torn it away from the shoulder. Her shirt was another matter. Definitely ruined. Just as well, Iona thought. She didn't want too many things around to remind her of the celebration for the girl who wasn't going to graduate. It made sense that the night had turned out the way it did. She carried the shoe for half a mile before she gave up hope of finding the other and heaved it toward the woods.

It all happened so fast after Willy left. Darryl grabbed her breast, and she twisted away, still laughing. He got hold of her jacket. She heard the low rip of denim as he pulled it off her. Luke snagged an ankle and Kevin gave her a shove. Then Darryl jumped her, pinned her to the ground. Kevin held her feet while Luke untied her shoes and took her socks. She was more afraid of him than she was of the others, afraid of the cigarette in his mouth, what he meant to do to her naked feet. She writhed, got one arm free and clawed Darryl. *Fucking bitch.* He popped her eye so hard her head banged against the ground. *You know you want it.* This was little Luke. The words sickened her. She heard herself say the same thing to Willy, summer before last, that night by the river. Kevin wrapped his fingers in her hair. They hated her now, wanted nothing except to hurt her. She felt a fist between her legs, hands under her shirt. She was bucking, kicking wildly. Darryl leaned close and she snapped at him. Luke was the first to back off. The cigarette had fallen out of his mouth. *Come on*, he said, *this isn't worth it.* Darryl squatted on her a moment longer, then stood and kicked her thigh. Kevin cuffed the top of her head.

Long after their voices faded in the night air, she lay on the ground trying to breathe.

Iona thought of Sharla locked in her father's cellar, saw her bruised legs, remembered her on the couch days later, white belly and streaked thighs, knew that because of this Sharla would understand and not judge, would open her door no matter what Jeweldeen had said. She didn't get to Rosewood Drive until four o'clock that morning, but Sharla was still awake. On her nights off, she kept her usual hours. "Too much bother to switch," she'd said. "Besides, I like the quiet." Yes, Iona thought, and silence is more bearable in the dark.

"I'm not supposed to let you in," Sharla said, "according to Miss Jeweldeen." Iona leaned against the wall outside Sharla's apartment, and Sharla stepped into the hallway to get a better look. She touched the bruise above Iona's eye. "Does it hurt?"

"I think I'm still a little drunk."

"You'll feel it tomorrow."

"And a lot of other things too," Iona said, looking at her scratched feet.

"I'll make us some tea."

"What about Jeweldeen?"

"It's my apartment."

"Is she here?"

"Out cold on my bed. You can have the couch."

"I'm not tired."

"You will be."

"It's almost light."

"That's the best time for sleeping." Sharla put one arm around Iona's waist. "Come on, baby," she said. "You need to sit down." Sharla's body was soft in the middle. Even her arm was soft.

Come on, baby. Darryl said: *How about that rum, baby?* And Iona's mother said: *Sleep, baby, you'll feel better in the morning.* How old was she? Six? Was it chicken pox or just the flu? She couldn't remember. She couldn't remember anything. She couldn't even see her mother's face. When she thought of Hannah, she saw the wrinkled belly, crisscrossed with tiny lines. She saw her swollen feet, the blue, translucent skin, so fragile Iona was afraid it might tear in her hands. But the face of the mother who stooped over the bed to kiss the feverish child was lost to her.

Iona huddled on a chair in the kitchen, tucked her hands under her armpits and shivered, though the room was warm. Sharla filled the kettle, moving slowly from sink to stove, a thick woman with big thighs.

"You want to take a shower?" Sharla said. Iona shook her head. "A blanket?" Iona shook her head again, but Sharla left the room anyway and returned a moment later with a large green shawl. She wrapped it around Iona's shoulders and sat down to wait for the water to boil.

When the kettle whistled, Sharla jumped. "Awful noise," she said. She put two teabags in a fat little pot and filled it with hot water. Iona stared at the empty mugs and the silly red pot as Sharla set them on the table. Everything was ridiculous if you looked at it long enough. Poor Sharla was ridiculous too. She'd painted a mole just to the left side of her mouth, disturbing and dark.

The tea was nearly black. "You want milk?" Sharla said.

Milk and honey, that's how Hannah made it. "No," Iona said, "this is good."

"You want to wash your hands?"

"I guess." Iona started toward the bathroom.

"You can wash them here," Sharla said, pointing to the sink.

Iona stood at the kitchen sink and Sharla stood beside her. Her palms were scraped. The soap stung. Sharla kept her hand on Iona's back, lightly, just enough to steady her. "I know it hurts," Sharla said.

She patted Iona's hands dry with a white dish towel.

"I'll ruin it," said Iona.

"It'll wash out."

They went back to the table to drink their tea. "You want to tell me what happened?" Sharla said.

"Don't you know?"

"Jeweldeen said you took off with a couple of guys."

"Four."

"Did they?"

"One of them left."

"The other three?"

"They gave up. I think I scratched one of them good. They did this instead." Iona pointed to her sore eye. "One of them took a clump of my hair, and another one got a piece of my shirt."

"You can borrow one of mine."

"They took my shoes too."

"You're lucky you got away."

"Yeah," said Iona, "considering how stupid I am."

Sharla peered into her mug. "Sometimes things happen even if you're not stupid." She covered her face with her hands for a moment but was making herself smile when she looked at Iona again. "Anyway," she said, "we all survived."

Iona thought that if Sharla hadn't survived, if Sharla had bled to death on her father's couch, she would have been as much to blame as Jack Wilder. "I'm sorry," she whispered.

"It's no trouble," said Sharla. "I was awake anyway."

"I didn't mean that."

Sharla waited.

"I meant you," Iona said. "I'm sorry about what happened to you."

"No reason for you to be sorry."

"I should have stayed."

"You were just a kid. What did you know?"

"I knew you were sick."

"Yes."

"I should have told my mother."

"He would have made it worse for me later."

"You could have died."

"Yes."

"I wanted to help you."

"I remember. You told Jeweldeen to get more towels."

"But I left you there."

"She told you to get out."

"I didn't have to listen."

"And what would you have done?"

"I don't know," Iona said. "I don't know." She was crying now at last, crying for Sharla and herself and her mother, for all the things she couldn't change. "I could have sat down beside you," she said. "I could have held your hand so you wouldn't be so scared." She wiped her cheek with the back of her hand.

"Did you believe me?"

"Yes."

"Then you're the only one."

"I always liked you, Sharla."

"I know."

"Better than I liked Jeweldeen."

"Sssh, you don't need to tell me."

"What we did wasn't right—watching you when you were locked in the cellar."

"It was a long time ago."

"I meant to come back some night and let you out." Iona still cried, softly. Her chest ached. She saw Sharla trapped in the cellar and her mother trapped in her room; she saw herself pinned to the ground. Now Sharla had her arms around Iona, and Iona sobbed, her whole body heaving, her mouth torn open. The cries hurt her bruised ribs and raw throat, but Sharla held on tight. Iona thought she'd break apart if Sharla let go, but Sharla didn't let go; Sharla wept too, for Iona and herself, for Hannah Moon and her own mother, the woman with the huge blurry eyes, for all the mothers who turned away too soon, who took off their glasses and died, who did not want to see, for all the daughters who spoke the truth too late to be saved, who could only weep and hang on to each other in a bright kitchen on a quiet street.

8

Horton Hamilton hadn't gotten home until two-thirty that morning, so Willy didn't need excuses. At seven the phone rang; fifteen minutes later, Horton left the house. Willy couldn't get back to sleep. Pierce was on duty. Saturday mornings were dead. Usually Fred parked somewhere off Main and fell asleep in his cruiser.

Willy got up at eight. He passed his sisters' room. They were going to live at home forever. Who'd marry them now? Lorena bagged groceries; Mariette answered the phone and made appointments for Dr. Tyler. They got a little fatter every year. Mariette could have been pretty; she had her mother's face, rosy mouth and dark hair. But Lorena never had a chance. She took after Horton: from her long jaw to her size-eleven feet, she was her father's daughter. *Just as well,* Willy thought. What happened to Iona Moon last night was never going to happen to either one of them. If a girl got big enough, she could keep herself out of trouble.

Flo was already downstairs. Her glasses hung on a chain from her neck, bouncing against her chest as she bustled around the kitchen. She still wore her pink robe over her nightgown, but she'd taken the time to paint her eyelids blue and her lips red. She was fleshy—not fat like her daughters, but full. She had a nice waist, and Willy wished that he were still young enough to fling his arms around her from behind and feel her soft bottom against his body.

"You're up early," she said.

"I heard the phone."

"Me too."

"Who was it?"

"Just Fred. Fire east of town, thought he might need help."

"Whose place?" He was relieved. A fire. It had nothing to do with last night or anyone he knew.

"No one's. I don't know why Fred bothered to call. Just a brush fire along the tracks."

Willy stood up so fast his chair toppled and crashed to the floor.

"What is it, Willy?"

His mother was moving toward him, his mother was going to touch his cheek or sweep the hair off his forehead. He couldn't stand it if she did that. "I gotta go," he said, backing away. He was out of the kitchen and up the stairs before she had the chance to ask another question.

The shed had burned to the ground and the flames were out by the time Willy got to the tracks. His father and Fred Pierce walked in circles around the place, wider and wider, looking for clues. Officer Pierce was a twitchy little man with a mustache. So far all they'd found was a broken rum bottle and a crumpled cigarette pack. Willy prayed that his friends hadn't dropped anything else. A wallet would finish them all off. He remembered Darryl saying: *We should burn it down.* But Willy had taken Darryl home himself, dropped him at his front door. When they left the tracks, Matt Fry was out cold and the shed was still standing. Darryl was too drunk to get back here on his own. That meant the kid did it himself.

"What are you doing here?" Horton's voice was soft, but Willy could tell his father wasn't glad to see him.

"Mom told me."

"That wasn't my question, son."

"Matt F-fry . . ." Willy stuttered. "Matt Fry's been living up here." He was too scared to ask if the boy was in the shed, burned to his bones. Maybe he crawled back up here, lay down on his plank bed and lit a cigarette, passed out again and woke in flames.

"Did your mother say that?"

"No." *Just a brush fire.*

"You get on home. Tell her it's nothing."

"Is he?"

Horton shook his head. "No sign."

"Over here," Fred called. He'd found something in the grass: empty beer bottles and the yellow lighter. Willy followed his father to look at the evidence.

Horton Hamilton held the lighter. "Cheap," he said, "a hundred of these in town."

"Kid probably stole it," Pierce said.

Willy almost said it was Iona Moon's. It would have felt good to put the blame on her.

"Must have set it himself," said Horton.

"Why would he do that if he was living here?" Pierce said.

"Crazy boy. Who knows what went through his head in the middle of the night?"

"Looks like he got himself good and drunk," Pierce said.

Horton shaded his eyes and looked down the tracks.

"You don't have any ideas about looking for him, do you Horton?"

"Have to."

"Long gone by now."

"Maybe not so far."

"You're on your own with this one."

"I know."

"As far as I'm concerned, this case is closed," Pierce said. "An abandoned shed burned down last night. No surprise. It's caught fire before. No one's been living here since old man Hardy lay down to rot. You hear what I'm saying?"

"I hear you."

"Let it go, Horton. Even his parents wouldn't want you looking for that boy."

"You're right."

"I'm getting in my car, Horton, and I'm driving back to town. I'm gonna tell the guys they did a good job dousing the fire, but it was too late: every scrap of evidence—burned. I'm gonna write a report that says, 'no suspects, no injuries.' Go home, buddy. Get yourself something to eat."

Willy wished his father would do what Pierce said. But Horton Hamilton meant to stay all day. At five, he'd go on duty. He might catch a few hours sleep after one, but by daylight he'd be climbing these hills again. He'd use hounds if it came to that. He meant to bring the boy home: dead or alive, skinny and wild or zipped in a body bag.

Horton Hamilton felt all his failures slip down around him like the weight of his own belly. He remembered how he'd put his hand on Flo's hip in the kitchen one night after dinner, an old signal. How long ago? But she ignored him, as if she had forgotten. Years now, this absence. He heard himself scolding Willy for the C minus in math and realized his voice had become the voice of his own father, the shamed boy himself. Apples were stolen again after the raccoon was dead, so he knew the animal he'd killed was innocent. And Willy saw this too but never spoke of it.

Horton believed that what had happened to Matt Fry was his fault, just as Flo said, because all those years ago he'd cuffed a child like a man and told his parents: *If your son were eighteen, he'd be on his way to prison for grand larceny.* He told himself that some boys longed to be punished. And he believed it until he saw what they'd done to Matt Fry up in Cross City.

• • •

Willy stayed with his father. He wasn't sure what he was looking for, but he kept his eyes on the ground. He found a ragged piece of blue cloth that he thought might have come from Iona's shirt. His father got a plastic bag from the trunk to hold the evidence: yellow lighter, blue material, broken bottle.

They searched in wider and wider circles. Willy felt light-headed. He should have had breakfast before he left the house. He thought of his mother in her pink robe, the warm kitchen. If only he had put his arms around her the way he'd wanted, just for a few seconds—now there was no chance of it. He saw her in the hours to come, hovering over the stove with her back to him and his father, holding her tongue but hiding none of her scorn.

Willy hoped that his father would see that Matt Fry didn't want to be found. As he climbed through the woods, Willy was certain Matt watched him. The forest was noisy with birds—chattering jays and chickadees. But Matt Fry was an owl, silent, invisible by day though he perched right above your head. In the dark he swooped to the ground, and you still didn't see him until you felt the air move.

Horton called to his son. Willy didn't like the sound of his name as it echoed through the trees. When he got his badge, he was going to call himself Bill. If children stopped him on the street and asked his name, he'd point to the badge and pat their heads.

He met his father at the shed. "Four o'clock," Horton said. "Let's call it a day."

Flo had already heard the news from Fred Pierce; he'd called to let her know where Horton was and not to expect him back any time soon. She had dinner ready: roast beef and boiled potatoes, green beans and chocolate cream pie. She wore a pair of tight lime pants, a stretchy material that made a scratching sound as her thighs rubbed together. Willy saw the lines of her girdle. She was packed in tight, not like this morning when she'd scurried around in pink disarray. Even her hair was pinned up on her head, and her glasses hid her eyes.

Horton shoveled down his food as fast as he could, gulping his milk. He had to swallow hard because he wasn't taking time to chew. Flo served him and let him suffer. She didn't say, *Slow down, honey, you've got plenty of time;* she poured him a second glass of milk, then went to the living room. Willy could see her through the doorway, flipping the pages of a magazine too fast to read or even see the pictures.

He picked at his food. He was hungry, but every bite stuck. He wished he liked one of the guys well enough to pick him up and go for a long ride. One beer wouldn't kill him. He supposed Luke was the best of the lot if it came to that. His father's hat was on the table. His plate was empty. He was lucky. The cruiser was in the drive and he had somewhere to go.

Horton wiped his mouth. "Gettin' to be that time," he said.

Willy cleared his throat. "Dad?" Horton waited and Willy realized he didn't know what he wanted to say. *I know who did it.* "Can I come with you tonight?"

Horton nodded and they left their dirty plates on the table.

It was a quiet Saturday, despite the fact that graduation was only two nights away. Kids partied all over town, but Horton Hamilton wasn't interested in catching them. He did break up a fight at the Roadstop Bar. Usually he would have hauled the men downtown and locked them up till they cooled out, but tonight he let them off with a warning, said he was coming back in half an hour and they better both be gone.

Horton and Willy were up at six Sunday morning. They ate toast and eggs and drank coffee at the Park Inn. "Don't want to wake your mother," Horton said. They headed back to the shed, but there were no more clues than the day before. The boys must have left Iona's shoes somewhere else. A crew had doused the embers a second time, and Horton stomped through the soggy ashes, poking at them with a stick. He and Willy walked up and down the tracks. Willy knew exactly where he'd left Matt Fry, but the grass had sprung back: there was no imprint of a boy's body on the ground.

At night the stars seemed dangerously close; Willy swatted the air with his hands as if sparks flickered against his face. He thought about his mother whispering to God in the dark. Her god would shelter the boy, hold him in his arms, keep him warm at night and invisible by day. The god Horton knew would be stern and still forgive, would call Matthew out of the woods and make him face all that he had done. Only Willy's god could remain hard, impassive to argument or explanation, absolutely certain. His god would chase Matt Fry into the clearing and say: *So, you add rebellion to your sin.*

Matthew hid himself for another night and another day. Late Monday afternoon, he let Horton Hamilton find him. When Horton came out of the woods to beep his horn and wait for Willy, he found Matt squatting in the coals.

Willy was less than a minute behind his father. Horton moved slowly, too weary to chase a scared kid. "Come on out o' there," he said. But the shed had no roof and no walls, no doorway and no windows. So how could Matt Fry come out? He looked at Horton Hamilton, his face and hands covered with soot. "I'm not gonna hurt you."

Matt stood up. He was three years older than Willy but looked younger, fifteen at most. His sleeves were too short, and his hands dangled at his sides, big and strange. His loose pants flapped around his legs. *Jesus.* Willy barely heard the word his father breathed.

The three of them stood there, just like this, waiting. Willy wondered why the sun didn't set. Why didn't it get dark. Why didn't the scrawny boy run or blow away. "I want to help you," the man said. Only a few seconds had passed. Why should Matt Fry believe that? *I got a gun.* Willy wished the boy would charge his father, teeth bared and snarling. Self-defense. Horton Hamilton would have to shoot. Willy was his witness.

And Flo Hamilton would wash the body of Matt Fry as she had washed the body of Everett Fry and the body of Hannah Moon. She would weep for the boy who died, for his scabbed knees and bony butt, for his hands that revealed he was a man, for his wrists that were thin as a child's. She would weep as she swabbed his dirty ears and clipped his broken nails.

Horton saw that Matthew wasn't going to bolt. He didn't have to step inch by inch or lull the boy with soft, repeated words. "Let's go, son," he said. Horton tried to lead him out the back of the shed, straight to the car, but Matt wrenched free and pounded at the air. "The wall," Willy said, "he thinks there's still a wall." Horton turned and Willy pointed to the place where the door had been.

There was nowhere to take him except jail. "But he hasn't done anything," Willy said.

"What do you suggest?"

Willy slumped in his seat.

"What the hell is that?" Pierce said when they brought the boy into the station.

Horton gripped Matt's arm and led him down the back hall to lockup. Willy watched them: the big man in uniform, the skinny kid in torn pants. The boy had a limp, and the man moved slowly, as if his whole body ached.

"Your mother's been calling," Fred said to Willy. "She said to tell you two fools to get your butts home. Graduation's at seven." Willy looked at the clock: 5:45. Fred laughed and pulled at his mustache. "It's gonna take you an hour just to get clean. You better scoot on home, boy."

Willy heard a yell from the hallway, one short bark, then a long, high-pitched wail.

"What the bejeezus?" Pierce muttered. "You need me, Horton?" he called. He had his hand on his gun.

The wailing stopped for a few seconds, then started up again in waves, rising and falling. Horton appeared at the end of the hall; his body waffled beneath the throbbing fluorescent lights as if he were under water. Left foot, right: he had to think to walk. Why didn't he get any closer? The cries washed over Horton's body, pushing him forward, pulling him back, while Willy waited and waited.

"Your wife's been calling every ten minutes," Pierce said when Horton finally stood in the front office, when the door to the hall was closed tight, the howls muffled. "Your kid's graduating tonight. Did you forget?" Fred smirked. "You're gonna be looking at one furious woman. I wouldn't want to be in your boots tonight, buddy." Willy pictured the stupid little man teetering in Horton's huge black boots.

"Willy?"

"Not till seven, Dad—there's time."

But there wasn't time, not really. At home, Flo buzzed from room to room, half dressed, wearing her slip and skirt but no blouse. She said: "What are you wearing tonight, Horton?" She whispered: "Did you find the boy?" She clicked her tongue and hissed: "Fine thing dragging Willy around with you for three days and now this." She turned to Willy. "And you," she said, "you get yourself in the shower—make it quick so there's time for your father." Willy looked at his hands, mud under the nails, soot in the fine creases of his palms. It would take days to wash all this away. "Now, Willy," his mother said, and he felt the burn, the old shame, *not again,* his bedclothes stained; he was that dirty.

He scrubbed himself, dressed quickly. He still felt hot and unclean; his clothes stuck to his skin. When he glanced at the mirror, he saw a blue shirt and striped tie but did not see his own face floating above them.

Horton locked himself in the bathroom. Six-thirty: there was time enough, but Willy didn't hear shoes dropping to the floor, didn't hear water running. Minutes later, Flo stood with her ear to the door, listening to the little gasping noises from inside.

"Let me in, Horton." Glass shattered, and Willy knew his father had looked himself in the eye. Did he break the mirror with his fist or his gun? "Horton—please." Flo sat down beside the door. "I'm here," she said. "I'm right here."

Willy flung himself across the bed. Lorena and Mariette came to his room, both in peach-colored dresses with peach ribbons in their hair. They looked like overgrown twins in those outfits, and Willy was glad no one was going to see him with them tonight.

"Aren't we going?" Mariette said to Willy.

"No."

"You shouldn't miss your own graduation," Lorena said.

"Leave me alone," Willy said, and the girls in peach both huffed, crossing their arms over their chests.

"It's *your* graduation," Lorena said. "Do what you want."

Willy pulled his pillow over his head but still heard his sisters' heels clicking down the hall.

Later, the bathroom door opened. Willy looked from his dark room to the bright hallway and saw his mother slip inside. The door closed again. He knew his mother held his father, rocked him, said: *It's not your fault.* Now that Horton blamed himself, she could forgive him. *Who will forgive me,* Willy thought. *Who will rock me and make me small again.* A car passed on the street. His sisters giggled in their room. He rolled to his back and stared at the black ceiling.

Iona heard about the yellow lighter and knew it was the one she'd tossed to Darryl McQueen down by the river. So she was the one who set the fire. She brought the boys to the tracks. She teased them. She fought them off. If they'd gotten what they'd wanted from her, they never would have gone after Matthew.

Before Horton Hamilton found him, she'd told herself he was free and flying. She thought she'd fly too, and find him again, in some other place—a place where Matt wore clean clothes and combed his hair, learned to talk and got a job. Maybe they'd rent an apartment. And if none of that could happen, they could just dig a cave in the ground, burrow into the hole, lie down together where no one would ever find them.

He was calm now, Iona was sure of that. Two men in a van had come for him, wrapped him in a white shirt, tied the sleeves behind his back. He was safe in South Bend. But a nuthouse was worse than jail because there was no sentence to serve. This time he was gone for good. They'd clean him up and strap him in a chair. In the afternoon, when the sun was warm, someone might scoot him to the window where he could watch the river swirl and splash against the dam.

"What is wrong with you?" Leon said. Iona had already burned her hand on the casserole and spilled her milk. It was Wednesday, and they were only halfway through dinner.

"She's had a feather up her ass ever since her old sweetheart got busted," Rafe said. "She's afraid she's never gonna see him again."

"Unless she goes crazy too," Dale said.

"She's got a good start," said Leon.

Frank Moon tapped his empty glass on the table. "Looks like rain tomorrow," he said. That's as close as he could come to telling the boys to leave her alone. Right then Iona saw exactly how her life was going to be as long as she stayed in this house. She was going to burn her fingers and spill her milk. Her father would talk about the rain or the lack of it. One way or another, her brothers would torment her. *I've got a quarter. What'll you do for a dollar?* Every boy she'd ever known ended up sounding just the same.

As she washed the dishes that night, Iona thought how easy it would be to let the plates slip from her hands. She thought how much sense it made to smash the glasses instead of washing them, to start all over again with one new plate and one new glass: her own.

She smiled as she set the dishes in the drainer, unbroken and dripping, some still slick with soap. What did she care? She was never going to eat off this plate again, or this one. No sense in breaking them when you can just walk away. Hannah would have thrown them to the floor. Hannah would have needed the sound of splintering china because she had nowhere to go.

The highway, the river, the tracks, three ways out of town, but people only leave here by dying. That's what Hannah said. Iona thought about her mother's life on the Flats, sixteen years in a trailer, a tin box that expanded in summer and contracted in winter until the roof cracked and the rain seeped in, until the walls heaved and the wind blew. In the winter, they nailed plywood over the windows and lived in the dark for five months. Sometimes Hannah's father worked and sometimes he didn't. In the summer the children gathered dandelion greens and berries. The boys fished for trout: rainbow, steelhead, cutthroat. They ate well. In the winter they made squirrel stew, and no one asked if the carrots and potatoes had been bought or stolen. No one mentioned that the skinned squirrel looked big and had long legs, like a cat.

Hannah's drunken father drove off the road one cold night, hit a pole and banged his head, just a little bruise the doctor said, he would have been fine, but he froze to death instead, two miles from home. The light outside the trailer burned and burned.

Thinking about her mother's life made Iona ashamed to feel sorry for herself. And this was only the beginning. Hannah lived on the Flats for twenty-five more years, in a big house with a solid roof, with a husband who stayed home when he drank, safe and warm. But the windowpanes still rattled in winter, and sons were not so different from brothers. Hannah's brother Quinte mangled three fingers in a thrashing machine, and Raymond blasted two with a firecracker. *A man and a half.* They laughed and laughed. But their sister Margaret said: *Less than that, not one full life between them.* Though her sons stayed whole, Hannah saw them in dreams: hands bloodied, toes shot off, ears nipped by the spray of BB pellets. She waited for this so long it might as well have happened.

No wonder, Iona thought, no wonder she found a way to leave.

Iona rinsed the silverware and sponged the inside of the glass she was never going to drink from again. She kissed her father's forehead as she passed him in the living room. He patted her arm but didn't look up. Didn't he think it strange? When was the last time she'd kissed him—when was the last time he'd looked at her. "Off to bed so early?" he said.

"Yes," she said, "I'm beat."

At three-thirty the next morning, Iona Moon packed three pairs of jeans and two sweatshirts, four tops and all the underwear she owned. When she passed her mother's room, she closed the door. Her father was right. The rain had just started. She took her denim jacket and a rubber poncho, all the grocery money from the sugar tin in the kitchen, sixty-two dollars: she figured she'd earned it. She carried her suitcase out to the barn and milked the cows. She'd worry all day if she left them full and miserable. How many hours would it take for her father and brothers to understand that she was really gone. How many more hours to decide who would milk the cows tomorrow. They'd fight over women's work. Sooner or later, Dale would lose. *Don't be afraid of her, Iona. A cow likes a girl with a good grip.* She imagined her father standing at the window. Rain streaked the glass. At first she thought he was looking for her, but then she realized he was still looking for her mother. *Breathe when she does.* Her brothers were hungry. Which one of them would open the first can? *Don't take your hands away too fast.*

But she'd already let go.

9

Iona drove the truck to town and parked it in the lot at the Roadstop Bar. Drizzle turned to downpour. She sat on her suitcase for almost an hour before a lady on her way to Coeur d'Alene pulled over. The woman had been on the road all night, she said, and hoped Iona knew how to drive. Coeur d'Alene wasn't exactly on Iona's route, but it brought her closer.

"My kid got busted," the woman said as Iona slid behind the wheel. "Stole a car and headed north. I said, 'Just ship him home.' But they wouldn't do it. Said I had to come get him. Little sonuvabitch. I said, 'Why don't you call his father?' Of course they didn't get the joke. Interstate transportion of stolen property—lucky for his ass he's only sixteen." She bunched up a sweater and rested her head against the window. "Mind if I catch a few winks?"

"I don't mind." Iona thought about her father finding his truck later today. He'd be pissed. But the car wasn't stolen, just misplaced. No one would come after her.

"You sure you know this road?" the woman said.

Fog rolled over the highway. Iona nodded. *Every inch,* she thought.

The woman opened one eye. "I've got half a mind to just leave him in jail."

Iona always wondered about people who admitted they had half a mind.

"Teach the little bugger a lesson."

Yeah, Iona thought, *teach him a lesson. Burn down his shack. Put him in a white shirt. Wrap the sleeves around his body and tie them in a knot. Little bugger.*

"But I've got a soft spot for the kid. Know what I mean?"

Why shouldn't you? Iona thought. *He's your kid.*

The woman stared at Iona, waiting for an answer. Iona said she knew. "Hey," the woman said, "you're not running away, are you?"

"Visiting my sister."

"That's good. That's very good."

She couldn't run away. To run away you had to think that someone might try to find you and bring you home.

The lady fell asleep fast. She snored. No wonder the kid took off. She farted in her sleep. Iona cracked the window and lit a cigarette. The rain had almost stopped and it was growing light.

Getting out of Idaho wasn't easy. No roads cut the forests, only rivers, so Iona had to drive south before heading north, or east before west. She took the eastern route, toward Montana.

A dead skunk got revenge. His scent hung in the fog, filled the car and stayed with them for half an hour. Iona saw a porcupine, two rabbits, five ground squirrels. Some had been stunned but not crushed; they seemed to sleep on the pavement. She remembered a dog with a broken spine. It had dragged itself to the side of the road, and she sat with his head in her lap while he looked at her with his huge wet eyes, big and dark as a doe's eyes. She felt the dog's weight against her, felt the wild hammering of his heart—as if he had become all heart. Then she realized: this wasn't her memory at all, but something Hannah had told her.

Still the woman snored, oblivious to all this death on the quiet road. When they passed the smoking pulp mills of Missoula,

Iona thought it would have been as good a place to stay as any if she hadn't had to worry about her brothers showing up next winter, finding her by mistake, feeling obligated to haul her home.

It was almost two when they crossed into Idaho again. *Nine hours,* Iona thought, *and here I am.*

She was glad to leave the woman in Coeur d'Alene, but she felt sorry for the boy.

A trucker took her to Spokane. Twenty-five minutes and she was across the border, in a different state, free at last. He dropped her at the first exit, and it was almost five before she hitched a ride with two long-haired college boys headed for Seattle. One was blond and tanned, thick as a football player. The other was thin and wore wire-rims. They said their name was Larry, both of them. This made them laugh, and the skinny one rolled a joint.

The road was dry and dusty. It hadn't rained in Washington. Iona drifted toward sleep, then woke, startled. Every time she opened her eyes she saw the same thing: a farmhouse on a hill, a clump of trees, a red truck. The white houses made her heart pound. She kept thinking the boys had turned around and brought her home. She stuck her head out the window to let the wind whip her face.

"You got a place to stay?"

Iona opened her eyes in the dark car. One of the Larrys was talking to her. Now she saw a black lake, a long bridge, buildings in every direction, the yellow lights of winding streets, the glow of living rooms. The bridge wavered. She could be lost here, and safe.

"We're gonna crash with some friends," said little Larry. "Sleep on the floor. They won't mind one more body."

The concrete bridge floated on the water for more than a mile, a mystery, its lights delicate and blue, and Iona wondered why the years of waves hadn't torn it from the shore.

The Larrys took her to a two-bedroom apartment on Olive Street where five other people expected to spend the night. They ate chocolate cupcakes and potato chips, drank wine, smoked pot. Skinny Larry put his arm around her, and no one asked how they'd met. Later he got up to go to the bathroom. When he came back, Iona was lying on the floor behind the couch. She felt him staring. He stooped and jabbed her shoulder. "Hey," he said, "wake up." She played dead. If he was anything like her brothers, he'd give her a kick, just to be sure. But he didn't. Iona heard blond Larry say, "I told you she was a waste of time, and not much to look at so what's the point?"

She woke before it was light; early enough to milk the cows, she thought. She climbed over the bodies in the living room. Larry still wore his wire-rims. The other Larry sprawled on the couch. Three girls huddled on a piece of foam, spooned together—little rabbits, Iona thought. No one had a blanket. She found her suitcase near the door. Someone had opened it and pawed through her clothes.

She walked the streets, looking for signs: *Room for Rent. Help Wanted.* She'd have to wait till nine at least. No sense knocking at six in the morning. Yesterday she was in the barn taking care of the cows. One last time.

She'd turned her life into an accident. If she'd left today she would have gotten a different ride, ended up in another part of town. Everything was luck, good or bad. One wild cell multiplied again and again in a woman's body. One child skated onto thin ice and did a lovely pirouette before she drowned.

She went the wrong way first, along a street of fancy houses with stained-glass windows and wrought-iron fences, past gardens where nymphs frolicked in fountains, and dogs lived in little replicas of their masters' mansions. Every house was as big and still as Jay Tyler's house. Who would let a girl like Iona Moon sleep in one of their clean white beds. She had mud on her shoes and dark stains on her jeans—blood, she thought, a chicken plucked and gutted a month ago.

She circled back past the apartment on Olive, down a long hill and up another. No one had lace curtains in this part of town. She saw a house long-deserted, wood worn silver as an old barn, windows boarded. She knew how easily floorboards rotted, pushed apart by earth and weeds, how quickly thistles took the yard, how big sunflowers grew. She'd seen a roof torn away in a thunderstorm and understood that a house can become a husk in a single hour. She remembered her mother standing in the kitchen, moving from stove to sink. It was summer, a long time ago. The front door was open wide and so was the back. Iona stood on the porch and saw all the way through this house, clear to that burst of light, the bright space behind her mother. She was afraid for Hannah even then, though she couldn't say why.

Night filled the valley like black water. When the house stayed open, she felt the dark pour in.

Now she saw that the mother in this memory was only thirty. Already her oldest boy was big enough to work in the fields with his father, to come home surly and sweaty as a grown man. When Hannah was Iona's age, she'd watched her husband put their first baby in the ground. So no matter what happened to her in Seattle, Iona knew she had no right to pity herself.

She spotted this in a window on Fir Street: *Rooms to Rent.* She sat down on the curb to wait. The house had two stories plus an attic, was white once and now dingy. Soot clouded the windows. This seemed like a good thing; no one would be able to see inside.

"Fifteen a week, due on Monday. Twenty-five-dollar deposit," the landlady said. Iona was still in the entryway. If Maywood Wilder had grown fatter and nastier every year of her life she would have become this woman. Her dewlaps drooped.

Face powder clung in her wrinkles as if she had tried to fill them in. She peered over her glasses. "Well?"

"That's fine," Iona said.

"I'll only charge you ten this week."

"It's already Saturday."

"I'm doing you a favor."

Iona followed the woman up the stairs. She looked over her shoulder. "How old are you anyway?"

"Twenty."

The landlady snorted. "What's your name?"

"Iona Moon."

"Yeah, right," she said, "and I own the sea and the stars. Look, it don't matter to me how old you are or what your name is as long as you've got the cash."

"I've got it."

"Thirty-five today. Fifteen on Monday."

"I remember."

The room was worse than Iona expected, but she pulled the roll of bills from her pocket and peeled off three tens and five ones. There were no sheets on the bed, no blinds on the windows. The mattress was stained, flattened by bodies much heavier than her own. But it was a corner room, and this was a blessing; she had two windows, one overlooking the street, the other facing the burned-out house next door.

"I'm Mrs. Hagestead," the woman said, "by the by. There's no Mr. Hagestead." She put her hand over her heart, or rather over her huge left breast. "Rest his soul." She closed her eyes for a moment and swayed as if she hoped to faint. "But don't think you can get away with any mischief just because I don't have a man around." She leaned forward to make her point. "This is a respectable place. No overnight guests. No cooking in the room."

She dug down the front of her dress and pulled out a chain with half a dozen keys on a ring. She took one off and gave it to Iona. "For the front door," she said. The key was warm and damp. "The one for your room is in the top drawer of the dresser. Five-dollar charge if you lose a key and have to use mine."

Iona locked the door as soon as Mrs. Hagestead was gone, took off her shoes, and fell on the bed.

At four she woke, teeth fuzzy, neck stiff. Afternoon. She only knew because it was light. She had to piss and her head throbbed. Cupcakes and wine. Pieces of yesterday floated back. She remembered where she was. *No cooking in the room.* She'd forgotten to ask about the bathroom. Maybe she was supposed to go out for that too.

She found it at the end of the hall: toilet, sink, shower—a room the size of a closet. *Bring your own toilet paper.* Mrs. Hagestead had neglected to say that. The stink of urine seeped up from the tiles. Somebody had missed. The outhouse was cleaner than this room. In the winter, her brothers pissed in the snow, tried to write their names in great loopy script.

She changed her shirt, stuffed five dollars in her pocket and the rest in her left shoe. She had to find the second sign.

Help Wanted. It took three hours of walking. From the top of every hill, she saw the mountain, a perfect cone, snow-capped and solitary, rising out of clouds—a mirage, a place you could never reach no matter how far you walked.

She finally found the right one on Broadway, barely a mile from where she'd started: *Night Shift. Ask for Manager.* She was going to end up like Sharla after all, working graveyard at a convenience store called 'Round the Clock, sleeping all day, dreading the long nights when she didn't work.

Stanley Dorfman was hardly any bigger than Iona and three times as old. He said she could have the job if she didn't mind working eleven to seven, six nights a week, starting tonight. "Buck forty-five an hour, one eighty-five if you last a month."

She said fine, and he shook her hand. His palm was greasy, like the strands of hair matted across his scalp. He wheezed when he talked, but that didn't keep him from lighting up a cigar as he showed her around the store.

"Ever work a cash register?" he said.

"No."

"Ever work somewhere that you had to make change?"

She shook her head.

He wore jeans and cowboy boots, the tiniest boots Iona had ever seen on a man.

"Ever stock shelves?"

"Only at home."

Stanley coughed and spit into a yellowed handkerchief. "Maybe this would be quicker if I just asked what you do know."

I know how to milk a cow, Iona thought, *and skin a rabbit. I can change a woman's bed while she's still in it.* But Stanley Dorfman wouldn't be interested in any of that. He showed her how to use the coffee maker, and told her to watch the mirrors near the ceiling when kids were in the store. *Just kids?* She didn't ask. He pretended he was a customer, piled chips and milk and sardines on the counter. He asked for Marlboros, soft pack. "Twinkies," he said, "where are they?" She didn't know. "Aisle three," he wheezed, "don't forget."

At eleven, Stanley left her on her own. "I trust you," he said. "Don't prove me wrong."

The place was busier than Iona had expected. 'Round the Clock was next door to an all-night gas station. People who needed gas in the middle of the night needed cigarettes and chocolate too, six-packs of Coke, and large coffees.

Iona watched the man at the pumps. His long dark hair was parted in the center, pulled back and braided. He bounced off one foot when he walked, as if his right leg was stiff and heavy. Iona thought of Jay learning to walk like this, without a cane, without feeling sorry for himself. The man wore sneakers. Even from a distance Iona could see they were twice as long as Stanley

Dorfman's little boots. His jeans were faded, but his loose shirt was a brilliant blue.

By three o'clock the street was dead. The man in the glass cage leaned back, rocking his chair on two legs.

He must have felt her staring, just as she'd felt Larry's glare. *Wake up.* Sometimes Leon sneaked into her room. She took deep, slow breaths. Sometimes he reached under the blanket. She groaned and rolled toward the wall. At breakfast Leon ate fast and didn't look at her. She wanted to ask him: *Did you come to my room last night, or was I dreaming?* The man in the station stood up and glanced at the store. She started wiping the counter. "Always something to clean," Stanley had said on his way out. "If I happen to drive by here, I don't want to see you standing around picking your nose."

The man stretched and left his booth, then headed across the lot. He kept his leg more rigid than he had when Iona had watched him pumping gas, checking oil, washing windshields. Arthritis, she thought, bad joints, like Hannah, too young for that but life wasn't fair. The bell above the door didn't ring when he opened it. He moved up and down the aisles, trying not to limp. He looked at soap and spaghetti sauce. He read a box of crackers—each side and even the bottom. He pulled four different ice-cream bars from the freezer and inspected each one before he put it back in its place. He considered cans of tuna and Spam, studied the lunch meats in their tight plastic wrappers. He was the kind of guy who could slip a can under his shirt every time you blinked, the kind who could stuff every pocket and never show a lump.

"Can I help you, sir?" Iona said.

"Yeah, keep your eye on the station, will you?"

He thought she was stupid. She watched his big hands and silver belt buckle; she watched the mirrors to check his back and front at the same time. Even so, she thought she might be missing something. The blue shirt swelled, filling up with deviled ham and red apples, a quart of milk, a bag of Oreos. But how could she accuse him if she didn't see it happen?

Finally he stood at the counter. His shirt deflated. He'd taken nothing. "How old's the coffee?" he said. She wondered what he meant. For all she knew, Stanley had kept it on the shelf for five years. She shrugged. "When did you make it?"

"One-thirty."

"Then we could use a fresh pot." He had a high, broad forehead, bony cheeks and sharp jaw—as if his skin was stetched thin, pulled too far over his skull. He was dark, as dark as she was. *Dog drag you across the field?* He had that look. If Jeweldeen was here that's what she'd say.

"Pot's half full," Iona said.

"You Dorfman's daughter?" The gas man took a silver toothpick from the pocket of his jeans and scraped at something between his front teeth.

"No," Iona said. Did he think she looked like Stanley?

"Then don't be so tight with the man's coffee," he said, "and make a fresh pot for your pal Eddie."

"You're not my pal."

"Yeah?" He glanced over his shoulder, shaded his eyes and looked out the door. He peered at the empty gas station. "Is there somebody around here you like better?"

"Eddie what?"

"Birdheart," he said. "Used to be Rogers." He didn't explain. "You?"

"Iona Moon."

"Lucky girl," he said. "Now make me that coffee, will you?"

At two minutes to seven, Odette Dorfman arrived. The bell on the door was working again. She looked Iona up and down. "Stanley's done it this time," she said. She was nearly six feet tall, her neck long and sinewy. Her head seemed too small, bobbing so high above her body. Iona imagined Odette lifting little Stanley in her arms. She saw the man, small as a wooden dummy on Odette's lap. In their bed, he might disappear, buried beneath her, tiny sliver of a husband and his big-boned wife.

"What're you lookin' at?" Odette said. The skin around her eyes crinkled.

"Nothing."

"Do much business last night?"

"Some." Stanley could lift up Odette's dress and hide between her legs. Maybe he was there right now. Maybe Odette couldn't feel him.

"What *are* you staring at?"

"Nothing."

"Don't get smart with me."

"I'm not."

Odette's mouth shrank to a wrinkle. "Yes, I can see that," she said.

Iona lay on her mattress, too tired to sleep, smelling the smoke and hair and sweat of the man who had lived in her room before she did. She wondered what had happened to him and hoped he hadn't died in this bed. She tried to figure out how long it would take to earn enough money to buy sheets and towels. By fall she'd need a blanket, by winter a quilt. She thought of Sharla, though she didn't want to. She knew she was lucky to find a job but suspected there was always a graveyard shift for girls like them, girls with no one who expected them home at night. She was worse off than Sharla already. Sharla's bed was clean and so was her toilet. Still it was a relief in a way, to miss all the bright hours, to stop seeing faces in daylight.

She'd have to buy some blinds. That was the first thing. The room was too light. She pulled a shirt over her eyes. And she needed paper and pen, one stamp, one envelope. *Dear Daddy, I'm fine.*

Dear Father.

Dear Frank.

She couldn't even write the first line. It could wait. If she gave him her address, he might think she wanted him to come after her or send twenty dollars. He might be mad about the grocery money, might write to say she owed him. Maybe she'd just send a postcard, no greeting, no return address. *Arrived safely. Got a job. Hope you didn't have too much trouble finding the truck. Love, Iona.*

No, scratch the *love*—just *Iona.*

10

Iona knew the other tenants by their sounds. The man in the attic vacuumed every day. One night the man next door fell against the wall and cussed. Iona pictured him, huddled on the floor, nothing but a few inches of plaster between them. She could see the mirror image of her own room: stained mattress on a metal frame, dresser with three drawers and loose knobs, one lamp, one straight-back chair, a closet without a door, two wire hangers. She heard him stagger to the bed and collapse again. The springs were shot. The mattress sagged. Iona felt his back curve into it and remembered the other room, how it looked afterward, bed stripped, chair empty, though she herself had sat there hour after hour. Dresses still hung in that closet, all but one, and Iona wanted to stand in the close dark, feel rough wool and worn cotton against bare skin, smell the leather of broken shoes. She wished to watch the last line of light disappear as the door closed and she stayed inside.

She heard footsteps, fast and light, the Scavenger Lady—that's what Mrs. Hagestead called her. Iona hadn't seen her but knew she collected treasures and stuffed them in shopping bags, dug in garbage bins, brought home shoes without mates, wheels but no wagon, books half burned. She lined the shoes up outside her door as if she expected the absent half of each pair to walk upstairs in the night.

Iona wanted to know her real name and how she paid the rent. In a dream the woman stood by the bed and showed Iona what she'd found: a piece of green glass worn smooth by water, one suede glove, a child's plastic duck, forgotten at the edge of a pond. The room was bright, but the woman kept her back to the window so her face stayed in shadow.

Iona had been in Seattle five days and Eddie Birdheart was the only person who talked to her. Every few hours he'd drop by to lean on the counter and drink coffee at 'Round the Clock. He needed to talk in the middle of the night—to anybody, she thought, and she was there. He'd stopped paying, but Iona couldn't remember how that had happened. She told him about the Scavenger Lady walking into her dream with those strange gifts.

"My mother could tell you what it means," he said.

"She one of those doctors?"

"No," Eddie said, "just an old Duwamish woman who understands what people see when they close their eyes."

This time, Iona started a fresh pot of coffee before he asked.

"Got you trained already," Eddie said. "I never did get too far with the last girl Stanley hired—neither did Stanley, but Odette canned her anyway. Dumb blonde," he said, "but cute."

Iona stared at the thin stream of coffee as it squirted into the pot. *Trained.* She was going to charge him for this cup.

"I'm out of cigarettes," Eddie said, "can you spare one?"

"I'm out too." She kept her eyes on the coffee.

"You've got a hundred packs under the counter."

"More than that," she said, "but they aren't mine."

"One could be yours," Eddie said, "if you opened it."

"Marlboros?" she said.

"That's more like it."

"Seventy-five cents," she told him, "and twenty-five for the coffee."

"Fine," he said, tossing a crumpled dollar bill on the counter.

Odette Dorfman gave Iona her first paycheck that morning, $61.28 after taxes, enough for a towel and soap, sheets and a blanket, two shades, one bowl. She had that night off, so there was plenty of time to hang the blinds and make the bed, light a candle and smoke a cigarette, time to open a bottle of Coke and drink it from the glass, her own glass, plenty of time to sit at the window and think about the paper and pen she didn't buy, the note she wasn't going to write.

She saw a pair of lovers on a porch across the street, bodies pressed tight and locked, frightening pair, Siamese twins joined from mouth to knee, shared heart and shared spleen, all their blood flowing, one to the other.

At eight, Iona was still at the window smoking cigarettes. Kids played kickball in the road, and teenagers lurked in the tall grass of the vacant lot. At nine she went out. She thought she might walk all night and still not be tired enough to sleep. She went to the hill beyond the Olive Street apartment. The Larrys were gone, hundreds of miles south by now. No one knew her. Smooth-skinned girls lived here, Iona thought. They peered out of attic windows shaped like keyholes, slept on brass beds with cool satin pillows. They wore long white nightgowns and had dreams she couldn't imagine. She thought of Jay Tyler in his prison, a house as big as these but still a cell in the end. Porch swings hung empty, and Iona remembered the wicker chairs on Jay's porch, the ones where he never sat. If Jay had been her father's son, Frank would have kicked his butt months ago, told him to get off his ass or get out—an act of love, neither cruel nor kind.

A pair of stone lions guarded the huge white house at the edge of the park. They roared: jaws opened, chests swelled with breath; in the shifting wind, Iona saw their massive heads turn to watch her pass.

At eleven, she headed down Broadway, just to find out who worked in the store on her night off. He was a pimply-faced kid, tall and bony as Odette. She bought a box of Animal Crackers to get a good look at him. Eddie sat in the station, rocking back in his chair, feet on the desk. He had a cup of coffee from the store. Was the boy trained? She doubted it. From the looks of him he was pure Dorfman, greasy-haired as his father, stingy as his mom. "Take it or leave it," he'd say, even if the coffee had turned thick and oily in the bottom of the pot.

People were still out in Iona's part of town. The lovers had disappeared, melted or drowned, and children were in bed, but the gang of teenagers whooped in the vacant lot. Iona heard laughter and slurred words, a boy's voice saying: *You know the rules.* In the morning, she'd find the grass stamped flat in one place, a circle of dirt where they'd spun the bottle. She'd discover a torched pack of matches and imagine one girl who sat alone, who lit all the matches at once and held the blazing pack until it burned the tips of her fingers. *Truth or Dare: Fire, Kiss, Electric Chair.* She'd see broken glass and cigarette butts, flip-top rings and a pair of lace panties. *You know the rules.* Some dares were more dangerous than others. *Kiss* was just a peck, the lips of a boy you liked, so you were embarrassed but not too scared. *Fire* hurt but wasn't always flame. *Electric Chair* had to terrify, had to thrill you half to death. When brakes squealed and a horn blared, Iona knew that some quick kid had charged into the dark street, that his thigh barely missed metal as he jumped clear. Lying on her bed, Iona felt his young heart drumming in her own chest.

Eddie bobbed into the store at twelve-thirty the next night. He asked for coffee, spinning a quarter on the counter so Iona would know he meant to pay. When she started to pour, he said, "Hey, how about a fresh pot?"

"It's not that old," she said. "Take it or leave it."

"You sound just like Lyle."

"Who's Lyle?"

"The Dorfman kid, the one who was working here last night when you stopped by."

She felt tears at the back of her eyes, but she didn't know why. "I didn't think you saw me."

"I told you—my mother's an Indian, old Duwamish woman, stubborn as a pig and smart as a crow."

"So what?"

"I see things without looking," he said. "I know things."

Her whole body felt hot, as if he'd caught her in a lie, as if he were her own father and was loosening his belt, pulling it from the loops. *Tell me the truth and I'll stop.*

"I'll take it," Eddie said.

"What?"

"Your old coffee."

He came back at three. She relented and brewed a fresh pot. They smoked while they waited, and she forgot to charge.

"I told my mother about your dream," Eddie said. "She says the woman isn't the Scavenger Lady at all. She says your mother's dead and is trying to bring you something. I told her your name, and she said, 'What tribe?' I said you were a white girl, and she said, 'Don't be too sure.'" Eddie dumped three sugars in his coffee. "Is she?" he said.

"Is she what?"

"Dead."

"Yes."

"Mama Pearl knows everything."

"Lucky guess."

"She sees how people die," Eddie said. "She sees what they'll be when they come back. She won't tell me about myself, says I might try to slip out of town, trick Death, but you can't—he finds you. She told me about my father. Stranded on an ice floe. He waves his gun and begs. Nobody hears him. Except Mama Pearl in her dream. He hunts walrus in Alaska, cuts off their heads with a chain saw to get the tusks. That's why I gave my name back to him. Took my mother's instead. My wife says it's not legal. She doesn't care what the man does. Still calls herself Alice Rogers, says she'd rather die than take an Indian name. Mama Pearl laughs. She knows just how that will happen."

Odette Dorfman stood at the coffee machine with her back to Iona. The sharp bones of her shoulders poked at her dress like little wings. She counted the foil wrappers three times before she turned, clutching a pack of coffee in each hand. "What is this?" she said.

"Coffee?"

"Don't get wise. I know what you're up to." Odette had a trace of a mustache above her upper lip, a dozen hairs bleached white. "I've been counting these coffees ever since you started. The night my boy worked he used two packs. You go through four. You must have a drawer full of coffee back home."

"I don't even have a coffeepot," Iona said.

"So why are you stealing my coffee?"

"I'm not."

"Then you must be pouring it down the drain."

"It gets bitter."

"Are you drinking this coffee? Is that what I hear?"

"Customers complain if it sits too long."

Odette had torn through the foil with her fingernails and the grounds spilled on the floor. "Now look what you made me do," she said.

"I'll get the broom."

"You'll get your ass out of here. And you'll learn how to tell customers that coffee's just been made."

Eddie stood at the door. He'd done it again. The bell hadn't rung, and he'd heard the whole thing.

"Mornin', Odette," he said. Iona expected her to snap at him too, but she turned sweet and girlish, gave him her best smile, showed him her big teeth and pink gums.

Iona ducked around him, slammed into the door with her full weight. She walked fast and was two blocks from the store before Eddie pulled up beside her in his beat-up black Ford. He said get in, and she didn't argue. It smelled like her father's truck, leather and dirt, something half spoiled but sweet. Eddie kept his right leg tucked close to the seat and put his left foot on the gas.

"I didn't mean to get you in trouble," he said.

"Don't matter."

"I'll buy you breakfast."

"Why?"

"I figure I owe you."

"Yeah," Iona said, "you do." *I owe you.* She heard Darryl McQueen say the same words and thought of the way he'd paid her back.

The Western Coffee Shop had ten stools at the counter and four red vinyl booths in back. There was a plastic horse on every table, and a poster of a cowboy with a mean-eyed steer on the wall. Eddie and Iona took the last booth. She ordered pancakes and eggs, a side of sausage. "You don't look like you could eat half that," Eddie said.

"I'm hungry."

"I hope so."

Eddie got toast and fried eggs, a plate of hash browns. He squirted squiggly lines of ketchup on everything, including the toast, and they ate without talking. Iona knew she had to get it down fast before she felt too full. A radio in the kitchen blasted songs about drinking and cheating, women who made you crazy enough to kill, so you ended up in jail with nothing but time and regret. Sometimes you forgot she was dead. Sometimes you forgot you'd done it. Iona gulped her coffee and swallowed hard.

"You eat like a starved dog," Eddie said. "Ever seen an animal eat till its stomach explodes?"

"No," Iona said, stabbing her last sausage.

"I didn't think so. You wouldn't eat like that if you had."

• • •

Eddie was right. It was a mistake to eat so much. Iona lay on her back but couldn't sleep. The blinds were too narrow and light leaked around the edges. She hadn't bothered to undress or even take off her shoes. She was too full to bend over. Why did Eddie marry a woman who was ashamed to use his name? *Mama Pearl told me to marry a white girl if I could.* He didn't explain that either. *Birdheart, chicken heart, it's all the same, that's what Alice says. She should know. She's seen the worst. Thought I'd drink myself to death after the accident, but Pearl says that's not the way I'll go. Busted up my leg bad. Guess you can tell. Trapped under a tree. We were clear-cutting, moving as fast as we could. My partner didn't yell. I said I wanted to die, but they pulled me out. You can't imagine. You can't imagine how it felt. Drank myself numb for months. She stayed with me, worked hard, called me a coward. I guess I was. It don't hurt so bad anymore, You'd be surprised what you can live with.* Eddie laughed to make her laugh, but she didn't. He got serious again. *You'd be even more surprised what you can live without.*

The Scavenger Lady flitted down the hall. Iona wanted to call to her, wanted her to come into the room and empty her pockets on the bed. Maybe Eddie's mother was right, maybe Hannah needed to give her something: a jackknife with one short blade and one long, a felt hat, a rusty key. *I've been looking for the box all day,* the woman said.

What box?

She held up the key. *The one this opens.*

11

Stanley kept finding ways to touch Iona. He brushed up behind her as she stood at the register, rubbed against her butt and made a low sound as if something deep in his body gave him a sudden pain. He squeezed her arm when he told her he had a shipment of soup for her to unpack and stock. He stood so close she could smell the grease he used to slick his hair over his bald crown. Iona wondered if she'd always find a man like Stanley—boys by the tracks, brothers in the barn: it was all the same. *You take yourself with you.* That's what Hannah would say. *No matter how far you run.*

She walked down to the bay. The Space Needle hovered, a flying saucer on a pole. Sailors leaned on rails, waiting. She saw the little girls dressed as women, how they tempted, how they wanted the men and didn't want them—at the same time. Clean in their white uniforms, the men looked safe, and the girls with red lips looked wild—dangerous, Leon would say. Now she knew why. Rainier rose from a ring of clouds, pink at sunset, a volcano cool with snow but ready to explode.

When she climbed the hills, she saw the blue lights of bridges flickering across black water: lakes became holes and Puget Sound was the edge of the world.

Again and again she passed the house of stone lions. Strange firs with limbs like monkeys' tails grew in the yard. One night a Chinese man watered the grass. He moved without seeing, pulling his hose. He did not live here. A big dog with long red hair leaned out a window on the third story. He was king, the man his servant. Inside the house, a woman played the piano, her song drifting in the dark, two hands dancing: bass refrain and sweet soprano answer. Iona squeezed through the hedges to peer in the window. A boy sat on the floor, under the piano; he touched his mother's feet as she played, and Iona saw Hannah's feet—saw herself, washing them. A chubby girl in a white tutu and a rhinestone tiara twirled in front of a mirror. She was too short to be a ballerina, already too heavy; but she was lovely in this moment, in this dream of herself.

On Broadway she passed a wiry little man with bowed legs. His face was gray with stubble. He wore a sailor's cap, cropped kimono, loose white trousers. Iona imagined his body, thin, bone-hard, painted with blue tattoos, birds of paradise, and naked ladies, a lizard that crawled when he flexed his bicep, his mother's name, a heart on his thigh for a girl he'd almost forgotten.

If she climbed enough hills, she was worn out when she came to work, calm, so that when Stanley touched her—as he always did—she didn't bite his hand or kick his shin. This was good. She'd lasted a month, and Stanley was going to give her the raise.

Eddie stopped asking for fresh coffee. When it got old, he popped a can of Coke instead. Sooner or later Odette would catch on, but for now she was too busy counting foil wrappers to keep track of anything else. Iona just happened to leave packs of Marlboros on the counter, and Eddie just happened to pick them up. He took her to breakfast once or twice a week. It all worked out. She didn't steal anything for herself until the middle of July. It started with a can of sardines and a loaf of bread. By the end of the month she was swiping tomato sauce and chunks of cheese, party napkins and peaches in heavy syrup. She made a pyramid of soup cans on her dresser. "I don't like somebody thinking I'm stealing when I'm not," she told Eddie one morning. "Odette's been out to get me from the start."

"She knows Stanley, figures he's got his hands on you."

"You'd think she'd be glad for the break."

"No woman alive's glad for that."

"He'd hit on anyone."

"Any*thing*," Eddie said, "anything that squeaked and had a tail."

"I knew lots of boys like that back home." Iona's eggs were cold. She thought of Matt Fry drinking them raw, straight from the shell. "Let's get out of here," she said.

"I'm driving up to Molina," Eddie told her. "Mama Pearl's been calling."

"I can walk home."

"I was wondering if you'd come with me."

"To meet your mother?"

"She wants to see you," Eddie said.

"Why?"

"Who knows why that old woman wants anything."

Molina looked like the outskirts of White Falls: little box houses and dented trailers, vacant lots and dusty roads. Street signs struck by cars tilted or lay flat on the ground. Cows grazed. Two dogs romped in the dirt, their blond fur burning with light. An old man led an earless goat down the middle of the road. Beyond the houses, Iona saw grass and then ocean. The place sea became sky was only a curve in the distance where the green of one gave way to the gray of the other. Eddie said, "It's the wind here that makes you crazy."

Pearl Birdheart lived at the edge of town in a three-room pink shack: kitchen, bedroom, living room. But the kitchen was really only an alcove with a plastic accordion door. The shades were pulled, and the front room was full of smoke. Mama Pearl sat at a folding table playing poker with four men.

"See what I mean?" Eddie whispered.

Pearl wore a man's plaid shirt, sleeves rolled up to her biceps. Her hair was steely gray, one long braid pulled tight, like Eddie's. This woman split her own wood, Iona thought; if her pipes froze, she'd chop a hole in the ice and haul water from the river. She looked as if she could wrestle a man to the ground and keep him there as long as she wanted. But her face was old, cracked like stone, and her eyes were cloudy.

Pearl introduced three of the men, two bulky, bearded brothers—the Johnstons—and a dark, stubby man she called Blue. They nodded without taking their eyes off the cards or the pile of coins in the center of the table. The fourth was Eddie's brother. He stood to shake Iona's hand. "Joey, my baby," Mama Pearl said. He was six-five at least, with a paunch and a wide face; his hands were paws, callused and fleshy.

"Just let me finish this game," Pearl said. "I'm winning. The old boys can't play for shit this morning—too much whiskey last night."

There was a bottle of whiskey on the table now. "Hair of the dog," Eddie said to Iona. "They think it will straighten them out, but Mama Pearl whips them every time."

Eddie leaned against the wall, and Iona sat on the couch. She watched the Johnston brothers, Bud and Moose. They were blond with red cheeks and red hands, barrel chests and big bellies, almost identical except Moose was bigger.

Joey said, "Did Mama tell you she won half a jeep?"

Eddie shook his head.

"Two weeks ago," Pearl said. "My buddy Bud brought one of his pals to a game. Fish and Game Warden, full of himself."

"Talk or play," Bud said.

"See you and raise you ten." She meant cents.

"Mama lets the warden get confident," Joey said, "throws him a few hands, not all in a row, but enough to make him think he's hit a streak."

"We start talkin' real money," Pearl said. "We tell him we just got our government checks. He's so stupid he thinks that means we've got something. I want to ask him, 'How much you think they pay us for living on the reservation?' but I keep quiet, wear the mask. Crazy old Indian woman, that's what he sees. I catch him lookin' at my eyes, thinking I'm half blind besides. I let my hands shake. I drink too much."

"I'm out of this," Moose said. Bud called, and Pearl scooped up another pile of coins.

"I lose fifteen dollars in fifteen minutes," Pearl said. "The warden's flying, wants to go higher. He starts betting parts of his jeep—the radio, the CB. I put my check on the table and so does Joey. He looks at them, laughs, says: 'Is that all?' No matter. He's already bet the radiator and the battery."

Blue dealt the next hand. Iona realized he hadn't said a word since they'd arrived.

"You should have seen him when I spread my hand—full house —kings and tens. So mad he wouldn't even show us what he had. Ready to play all night, win back his car. I took two tires, the rearview mirror, the steering wheel. I let him have a hand in between, gave him back the radio. I start makin' noises like I'm tired. It's getting light. I'm not the only one. Joey opens the shade, looks at the jeep, says, 'Looks like we got half of that, Mama.' Well, the warden snaps, sees he's been taken. 'Goddamn Indian bitch,' he says. Funny how it always comes to that. He doesn't believe we're really gonna take our half. He's pleading with the Johnston boys, saying they should've warned him."

"And we should have," Moose said. He laid his cards on the table, face down.

Blue threw a quarter on the pile.

"So he starts tossing credit cards at me," Pearl said. "I take one, bite it, throw it back at him, say: 'What am I gonna do with this? Whoever heard of an *Indian bitch* with credit?' We laugh. Me and Joey. Joey gets the wrench, the tire iron, a screwdriver, heads out to the jeep, starts takin' what's ours. The warden's almost crying, I swear, saying we can't, we can't. But we do."

"Where is it, Mama?" Eddie said.

"Sold it back to him two days later. Five hundred for parts, two hundred for labor."

"Labor?"

"You think I'd put all that stuff back in for free?" Joey said.

Pearl won two more hands before the Johnston brothers left. She counted her coins—$18.25, a decent day. She said she liked taking money from white boys, especially those two. "Bud and Moose run the bar," she told Iona, "take our money all the time. But they don't own the land," she said. "Lease it from the tribe."

The mute man spoke at last. "White folks don't own nothing here," he said.

"Except our souls," Eddie muttered.

Joey opened the accordion door to get a beer, and Iona saw the sink heaped with blackened pots and smudged glasses, plates crusted with dried food.

Pearl asked if they wanted breakfast. "What kind of offer is that?" Joey said. "All we have is beer and refried beans."

"We ate," Eddie said.

"Why do you always eat before you get here?" Pearl said.

Joey guzzled his beer. "He comes with a full stomach because you never have any food, Mama."

"I'd keep food in the cupboard if he'd stay."

"See, Eddie, it's your fault." Joey patted his swollen gut.

"Might end up like you if I hung around here," Eddie said.

Joey crushed the can and dropped it on the floor. "Yeah, our bad habits might rub off. You might turn into an Indian after all."

Eddie didn't talk to Iona for almost an hour as they drove south. Iona stared out the window. Madrona trees clung to the cliffs, and she wondered how they did it, why the rain didn't wash the sand from the roots, why they didn't fall into the ocean. Bark peeled, leaving new flesh exposed, slick, rust-colored. High, tangled limbs were leafless, wiry as an old woman's hair. Eddie said, "I've been running from them my whole life—and look at me."

Iona did look—at his hands on the wheel, at his red shirt, dark as blood, at his stiff right leg pressed close to the seat.

"My pitiful people," he whispered.

"Mine are no better," Iona said.

"Married a white woman and thought she'd save me. Thought I could be Eddie Rogers for the rest of my life. Alice and Eddie, wouldn't it be sweet? If I dressed right, I could pass. But I have a bird's heart. It beats too fast. It makes me afraid. I hear voices coming from the telephone. I answer them."

"There *are* voices on the phone."

"But I don't pick it up," Eddie said. "I hear other voices. I hear Joey. I hear my sisters, Ruth and Marie. They tell me to come home. They say Mama's sick. I drive up to Molina. I find her at the table, drinking whiskey, stealing money from the white boys and the old man—just like today. She grins. She's missing half her teeth. That's why she eats those damn beans. Do you see, Iona? I'm this close." He held his hand less than an inch from his face. "This close to falling all the way.

"Every time I think: *I won't go.* But I do. I saw her nearly die one time because my father wouldn't let the healer in his house, and Mama wouldn't take the white man's medicine. My sisters came with their beads and their Bibles. Nothing worse than a pair of converted Indian women. They prayed; they said Mama Pearl was being punished for her evil ways, drinking and smoking, playing poker half the night, sleeping till noon. They said me and Joey were being punished too, little heathens. Joey was six. I was ten. The girls were older, from one of Mama Pearl's other lives."

Iona wondered how many lives a woman could have, if the joys of one eased the sorrows of another, or if grief piled on grief until you wished to be cut free.

"She burned. Ruth said the fever in her now was nothing compared with the fires of hell. She made me and Joey touch Mama's body so we'd know how bad it could be.

"My sisters washed us. They said we had to have clean bodies to have clean souls. They ran the water hot as we could stand it—hotter. They scrubbed our heads and our ears, our dirty necks; they scrubbed up the cracks of our behinds. They wiped our penises—hard. They said we were whiter than we thought, once we were clean. Their father was an Indian, their skin dark compared with ours. They told us Mama Pearl might be saved if we asked Jesus into our hearts."

Iona thought of Hannah, how no one pretended she could be saved, so there were no bargains, no wild hopes, only the days of winter, one following another.

"I wanted her to live, more than I'd wanted anything in my whole life. But I couldn't think good thoughts. My butt was raw from all that scraping. I hated my sisters. My heart was so full of hate there was no room for Jesus. Joey cried. He was sore. He kept rubbing his penis through his pants. Ruth slapped his palms every time he touched himself. Finally she tied his hands to the chair to make him stop.

"Jesus never came. My father brought a white man from town —doctor, he said. Papa untied Joey's hands and told my sisters to get out. Best thing he ever did. He and the man smelled of sawdust and beer. No decent doctor would come to a shack in Molina in the middle of the night. But the man had a black bag. He gave Mama a shot. His hands shook; I was afraid. He told me and Joey to keep washing her with a cool rag, and we did. The doctor finished off Pearl's whiskey. By morning her fever broke. Joey asked me if I'd let Jesus in my heart, and I told him the truth. He slugged me so hard I couldn't breathe."

Iona thought of what she and Eddie shared, this knowledge

of their mothers' bodies. But Pearl lived and Hannah died, so Eddie couldn't know, not really.

He didn't take her home. He drove out to the edge of the Sound. "My friend has a boat," he said. "We can go there." Iona didn't ask why. The clouds were low; it had started to rain. Ghosts of buildings wavered in the fog, and the arms of orange cranes stretched across the water, disconnected from their trunks.

"When our father was gone again, my sisters came to visit. They said there was still time for Mama Pearl to open her heart to Jesus. I kept picturing a little Jesus curled up in her chest like a bloody rabbit. I saw another one crouched in the cage of Joey's ribs. I knew my sisters thought they had a Jesus inside of them, and I wondered: *How many Jesuses are there?*"

Eddie parked at the marina. Hundreds of sailboats rocked on the black waves. The rain was heavier now, and the wind whipped off the water. "Which one is your friend's?" Iona said.

"The last dock," Eddie told her. But when they climbed aboard, he used his silver toothpick to release the lock of the cabin.

"I thought you said this was your friend's boat."

"I forgot the key."

The cabin was narrow, a sink and cupboards on one side, a single bed on the other. Rain streamed across the tiny window; the room was dark, damp as a cave.

"Are you tired?" Eddie said.

"Yes."

"Me too." It was almost three.

"It's a small bed," Iona said.

Eddie nodded. "We'll have to make ourselves small too."

"What if your *friend* finds us?"

"He never comes on rainy days."

"Are you sure?"

"I'm not sure of anything," Eddie said, "except I'm tired, and I want you to lie down with me." He sat on the bed. "Please," he said. He held out his hand, but Iona stayed where she was, leaning against the sink, just beyond his reach.

"Won't your wife wonder where you are?"

"I'll stop for a few on my way home, come in smelling like whiskey and smoke; I'll tell her Pearl got me into a game. It wouldn't be the first time."

Still Iona didn't move.

"I'm just asking you to sleep beside me. That's all."

"I know."

"And you're tired."

"Yes," she said, "I'm tired."

Eddie grabbed his bad leg with both hands and lifted it onto the bed, pressing himself close to the wall, curving his body so there was a hollow for Iona to fill. "Just for a little while," he said, and she lay down in the place he'd made.

Eddie slept, but Iona didn't. She watched him, imagined a boy washing his mother.

My pitiful people. She thought of all her people, how none of them could tell her who she was, so she ran away, like Eddie, but they still touched her eyelids when she slept, whispered in her ear; they still tried to pull her back even though they didn't want her. She saw her father washing his bloody hands. The calf was born, the weasel dead, the pig slaughtered and skinned. She watched her brothers emerge from the forest, rifles on their shoulders. They dragged a buck and left a red trail across the snow. Hannah's brothers leaned against the barn the day she died. Their silver flasks caught the afternoon light as they raised them to their mouths. Their hands and heads were bare. When they came inside, their ears burned crimson. Quinte had just told a joke, and Raymond was laughing. Iona thought of the fields, how white they were that day, how the trees looked black, how everybody that had ever walked into the woods seemed to move through the shadows: boys with BB guns and men with axes, lovers and lost children, weeping women. She thought, *How will I know my mother except by dreaming?* A girl stood on the road, defiant or scared, squinting at the stranger who would be her husband. A woman stood at the window, watching a man dig a small, deep grave. *My pitiful people.* Iona wanted to wake Eddie and tell him not to be so hard on Joey and Mama Pearl. "Everybody's pitiful in his own way," she whispered.

Rain pounded the deck and beat on the glass. The boat rocked on the water, and they rocked too. They were very small, just like Eddie said.

12

Willy Hamilton hadn't placed any higher than third all summer. His dives were sloppy, his knees weak. Every time Coach Brubaker yelled at him to lock his legs, he thought of Jay slamming his brakes on the River Road.

So far the only good thing that had happened since school let out was the that Iona Moon had left town. Word had gotten around that she'd pulled a train for Darryl and Kevin and Luke, in that order. Willy was glad she wasn't here to dispute it. He knew the truth, but he kept his mouth shut. *You're an asshole, Willy.* That's what she thought.

Still, he couldn't get free of her. Horton had to haul Leon Moon in for drunk and disorderly one night in July. Now Iona's brother was married to Jeweldeen Wilder. Poor bastard. Jack Wilder didn't exactly hold a shotgun to Leon's head, but everyone knew their first baby wasn't going to take nine months. Having a sister like Iona was bad enough, but being forced to marry her best friend was worse.

Willy was glad he didn't have to worry about that. No girl was ever going to trick him, telling him not to worry, saying: *I'm safe,* then coming to him a few weeks later to say she was sorry, she'd made a mistake, a slight miscalculation that would cost him his life. Flo had told him to watch out for that. *Girls do it all the time,* she'd said, *when they see a nice boy like you.*

Horton said: *The only way to stay out of trouble is to keep your pants zipped.* They talked this way back in the days when he'd parked by the river with Belinda Beller. He wanted to tell them: *Above the neck or below the knee.* She kept him in line. He wondered what he'd do with a girl who didn't say *no.* Resisting Iona Moon didn't prove anything. He never did like her, and still, he'd had to think of old Mrs. Griswold when he felt himself getting hard.

Sometimes he was even afraid of his sisters. When they tripped him in the living room and wrestled him to the rug, he felt the surge of blood and prayed they wouldn't notice. What a hoot they'd have, shrieking and pointing. It wouldn't last long, he could be sure of that. But he didn't know what he'd do if some pretty woman touched his face or leaned close enough for him to smell her hair. What if he started kissing her neck and she let him work his way down to the bones of her shoulders? Whose hand would stop him if she said "Touch me"?

Willy lay on his bed, rolled to his stomach and buried his face in the pillow. He hoped the lack of air would make the feeling go away. Just thinking about it scared him. His sisters giggled. What were they doing? He remembered Mariette telling Lorena that Dr. Tyler had cornered her by the filing cabinets after everyone else had gone home. Maybe she had something more to tell; maybe she was showing Lorena exactly how he touched her—here, and here. He wanted to charge down the hall, burst into their room, catch them tossing and laughing, make them stop.

Jay Tyler sat on the edge of his bed and listened to his parents arguing in the kitchen below him. He didn't need to hear the words. Supper wasn't ready. Again. There wasn't even enough food in the house for Jay's father to make himself a sandwich. *What is it you do all day, Delores?* Jay used to wonder that himself. Now he knew. His days were exactly the same. The most important thing was to stay in bed as long as possible. So much less of the day to fill if you didn't wake till noon. You could spend another hour in the bathroom, standing in the shower, getting dressed. Not that Jay cared how he looked. His hair had grown long, but he shaved every day. Shaving was good. It took time to do it right. He never nicked himself even though the cool razor on his neck gave him ideas. The secret was not to be distracted by your own face. He watched his hand, the blade, his chin, his cheek—but never looked into his own eyes.

At certain hours of the day his mother still cared about her looks. She took her sweet time in the bathroom too, applying lipstick and mascara, a pale foundation so close to the color of her own skin no one noticed the mask. She blended the foundation down her neck. Most women neglected this final step. When they tilted their heads back it looked as if their faces could be peeled off at night.

Usually Delores Tyler went out in the afternoon. She played bridge with her lady friends or met one of the girls for a late lunch. *Girls*—that's what they all called one another.

While she was out, Jay sat in his father's chair and watched television the way his father did, just the picture, no sound. All afternoon women clung to men and wept. Doctors pursued nurses, made silent agreements, and met later in unoccupied hospital rooms. They pulled the curtain around the bed, and Jay saw the shadows of their bodies rising and falling beyond the white veil. Women spit words at other women, hands on hips, lips quivering. Women slapped men, and men grabbed women by the shoulders, shaking them until they fell to their knees and hid their faces in their hands. Hour after hour, men and women embraced. But there were no children in this world, no consequences of desire, no screaming infants, no demanding toddlers, no troublesome teenage sons.

Today, Delores hadn't come home till four. Jay heard her car in the drive and hobbled upstairs. It was too late for her to plan dinner and go to the store, too late to chop vegetables or trim a roast. But it was early for a drink, not yet five and still so light. Winter was more merciful. You could start at four-fifteen and use the dark as an excuse. She padded from room to room and finally put on a record. Jay imagined her dancing, arms hugging herself, a man's high voice, crooning in her ear, soft as smoke. At four-twenty she gave up and went to the kitchen. Jay listened for the crack of ice, the splash of vodka. He preferred whiskey and kept it stashed under his bed.

What is it you do all day, Delores?

I get dressed and put on my face. I play bridge and eat lunch. Sometimes I think of jumping in the river, and sometimes I just go for a drive.

Jay's father did a hundred things in a single day, saw twelve patients or more, examined x-rays, peered at the ghost teeth gleaming in his lightbox. He knew most everyone in town by their fillings and the condition of their gums. He could name the dead, pointing to bridges and bits of gold. Once bones were found in the woods, and Horton Hamilton brought the jaw to him. Dr. Andrew Johnson Tyler injected Novocain into the mouths of terrified children, then drilled holes while his assistant suctioned up powder. Jay thought he should admire his father's clever hands, but he didn't. He was afraid of them in a way. They always smelled of lava soap. He felt his father's thick fingers in his own mouth. *Do it without the Novocain,* he pleaded. He hated the feeling as it wore off, his face dead and itchy at the same time. But his father said that was stupid. He used too much. One side of Jay's face went numb, as if he were paralyzed. He closed his eyes and tasted his father's soapy finger. How many times did it happen? Only once, or more than a dozen? *Please,* he thought, *it hurts.* He couldn't speak. His mouth was stretched wide. The clamp bit into his cheek. *It's for your own good,* his father said.

Andrew and Delores were silent now. This night would be salvaged. Delores found chicken pot pies stashed in the back of the freezer. Andrew ate his in the living room, watching his voiceless television, and Delores ate hers at the kitchen table.

She left the third one on a tray outside of Jay's door. He had
enough whiskey to wash down perfect cubes of carrot and potato,
doughy crust and viscous gravy.

He flushed what he didn't eat. He heard the growl of the
garbage disposal and knew his mother hadn't finished hers
either. They didn't like this kind of food. They liked cupcakes
that dissolved in the mouth whether you chewed or not. They
liked sugar cookies dunked in milk, bread with jam, pints of
ice cream you didn't have to share. Andrew said their gums
would rot if not their teeth. Sometimes, late at night, Jay heard
his mother's steps in the hallway, faint as a whisper, and he'd
open the door to find one of these gifts. Tonight she brought
lemon cake long after Jay's father was in bed. Jay opened his
door and watched her float away, her pale, filmy nightgown
shimmering like the wings of an insect. She paused at the bathroom door and turned on the light. Jay saw her silhouette
through her thin clothes, her loose breasts and full hips, the soft,
scarred belly, the round beautiful belly that was firm and flat
before that butcher in Boise cut him out. Jay had never seen
the scar, but he thought about it night after night as he took
her sweet offerings to his bed and ate alone, slowly, in the
dark.

Willy thought about Jay every day. He couldn't climb the rungs
of the high dive without seeing Jay's tanned legs, lean muscles,
long back. Willy's dives were arms and air, feet and springboard,
head and water—fragments. But Jay's dives were precise pictures in the mind, whole and perfect every time.

Even on his good days Willy knew he had more luck than
talent, skill without vision. He was strong for his size but showed
no grace. He feared surrendering to the logic of the body,
the inevitable spin and fall; he dreaded the moment of entry: the
water would not open for him as it did for Jay. He saw the
surface of the pool, hard as ice—he had to break it every time.
Jay Tyler leaped like a man with faith. In the long seconds

between approach and entry, Jay Tyler was reborn, transformed into the ideal image of himself.

But Jay was a coward in the end. That's what ate at Willy.

Willy hadn't done a decent dive all day, and this one was the worst. His thighs stung where they'd smacked the water. He wished he could stay on the bottom of the pool so he wouldn't have to stand there dripping wet while potbellied Bob Brubaker circled him, gripping his shoulders and jabbing the small of his back, slapping his buttocks to demonstrate all the ways the dive had gone wrong. "You're the best I've got," Brubaker said, "and you are one sorry sack of shit."

Willy's wet suit clung to him. He shivered, though he wasn't cold. Three weeks of practice, three more Saturdays of competition, then he'd never have to put up with Brubaker yelling in his face again. He wanted to say he didn't give a fuck about the speed of his spin. He wanted to say he was joining the police force in September, that high school sports were for kids. But all this was still a precious secret, this picture of himself in uniform. He couldn't risk the disbelief of such a stupid little man. Besides, he knew what Horton would say if he quit now. *I hate to think you're the kind of man who doesn't follow through.*

Ever since that night on the tracks, Darryl and Luke and Kevin had kept their distance. They were friendly enough at the pool; they even clapped him on the back when he hit a good dive at the meets. But in the locker room they were too quiet, and after practice they always had somewhere else to go. Sometimes they took off in three different directions, and Willy was sure they'd tricked him. He imagined them meeting up a few blocks down the street and having a laugh about ditching Miss Priss.

Willy headed toward the showers, and Darryl trotted up beside him. "Brubaker's an asshole," he said. "Your last dive wasn't tight, but it wasn't half bad."

"Thanks," Willy said. It made him feel worse to have Darryl put it that way.

"He's a pig," Kevin said. "Where does he get off, patting your ass?"

"I wouldn't let that fag rub my buns," Luke said as they all stood in the showers.

Willy turned his head up to take the spray in his face. *Brubaker's an asshole.* He felt the sharp pellets on his lips and eyelids. *The best I've got.* The other showerheads went off one by one. *One sorry sack of shit.* He heard laughter and talk echoing against the cinder-block walls of the locker room, snapping towels, metal doors slamming shut, footsteps fading.

He took his time, stood naked under the blow dryer, let the hot air blast. He buttoned his shirt from bottom to top and checked his fly twice, old habits never forgotten, Flo's lessons the first day of school. He looped past Jay's house. He could just pop in, say hello, tell Jay he was having a hard time with Brubaker. He wouldn't stay long. He'd say, "My sisters will eat all the potatoes if I don't get home." And Jay would say that was the last thing they needed. They might laugh. Jay might say, "Drop by tomorrow after practice."

Delores Tyler answered the bell. "Willy," she said, "goodness." She looked him up and down, and he was glad he'd been so careful when he buttoned his shirt. "You've gone and grown up on me." She put her hand on his arm. "I'm forgetting my manners. Please—come in." She stepped back and opened the door wide. The entryway was cool, and the house had a musty smell, as if the family had just returned from a long vacation. When Delores Tyler led him to the sitting room, he almost expected to find the furniture covered with white sheets.

But everything was just as he remembered, the sofa with its muted flowers, the twin gold chairs, his and hers, the myrtle-wood coffee table, the polished oak floor that always looked slippery. A portrait of Dr. Tyler's father loomed above the fireplace, and a photograph of his mother sat on the mantel. Jay

used to say these pictures explained everything, and Willy nodded without knowing what Jay meant.

"Can I make you an iced tea?" Mrs. Tyler said. "Or a
lemonade?"

Willy wondered why she was whispering. "Tea," he said,
"iced tea is good." He kept his voice as low as hers.

"I hope you don't mind instant," Mrs. Tyler said when she
returned with two glasses on a tray. "I'm afraid I didn't brew
any tea today." *I'm afraid.* She had such an odd way of putting
things. "And I'm all out of lemon. I hope you don't mind too
much." *Why should I mind.* "I could give you a splash of lemonade. Shall I do that?" The glasses slipped on the tray as she
lowered it to the table.

"I'm sure it's fine just as it is," Willy said.

His glass was tall, but hers was short, the drink clear. "I'd
offer you what I'm having, but I imagine you're in training."
Her hair was pulled back in a knot, a *French* knot, Jay called
it. Her eyes looked puffy. "You are still diving, I hope."

"Yes, ma'am." He felt proud for the first time all day.

"Please—don't call me that."

"Don't call you what, ma'am?"

"That. That old-lady name. And don't call me Mrs. Tyler,
either." Willy nodded. "I want you to call me Delores." He
wouldn't call her anything. He slurped his tea. It was sugary
and much too strong.

"How is it?" Delores Tyler said.

"Perfect. It's perfect."

"Delores." She stared at him, waiting for him to repeat her
name.

He wanted to run from the house. Andrew Johnson Tyler,
Sr., glowered from his portrait. He rode a white stallion with
a wild mane. Delores looked at the painting too. "Old bastard
never rode a horse in his life," she said. She forgot to whisper.
She downed half her drink in one gulp. "I'm afraid you've come

at a bad time," she said. "Jay's had a touch of the flu. He's sleeping."

Willy set his glass on the tray and stood up. "I need to get home anyway," he said.

"Your mother's expecting you."

"Yes," he said. *How did she know?*

"Well, don't keep her waiting." Her voice was soft again, sweet and cloying as the tea. He was ten years old and she was his best friend's mother.

At the door he said, "It was nice to see you again, Mrs. Tyler." She didn't correct him.

He was relieved to see how bright it was outside; he wouldn't be too late for dinner. "Don't be such a stranger," she called. He turned to wave. Delores Tyler leaned against the doorframe. She looked wilted, older at this distance than she'd looked when he faced her in the dim sitting room.

Jay was glad Delores hadn't called him. He didn't want to see Willy, didn't want to be reminded of all the things his body couldn't do. From the start, Dr. Rush had told Jay his legs would never heal if he didn't exercise every day. Joints freeze, tendons stiffen, bones lighten, muscles go slack—*flaccid,* he'd said, and Jay wondered if he knew about that too.

The doctor had a way of looking very serious and sorry as he asked Jay to lift one leg at a time, to bend and extend. He shook his head without speaking, and Jay thought the whole thing was pointless.

Jay did walk, in the beginning—around and around the rose garden, after dark. Rain streamed down his face, and still he made himself limp for an hour, sometimes more, using two canes, hobbling till the skin of his palms ripped and the sharp pains shot up his shins, radiated through his knees, throbbed in his thighs.

Afterward he sat on his bed, wet hair plastered to his skull, damp jeans making a spot. Delores stood at the door, knowing what he'd done. She said, "It won't always be this way," but he didn't believe her and wouldn't take comfort because nothing ever changed—in her life or his—and it was always exactly this way.

He'd stopped walking months ago. Now he drove to Woodvale Park to watch the divers practice, a private torment. Luke wasn't strong enough, so his dives were soft, unfinished. Darryl was sloppy, too loose in the limbs to go down straight, too cocky to correct the flaws. Burch was just too big to knife the water and too satisfied to try. You had to be hungry to hit a dive. That was Jay's secret. You had to feel a hollow place at the center of your body. You had to suck your stomach toward your back and want perfection more than anything. Willy had lost his concentration. He knew about hunger but couldn't use it.

Sometimes Jay parked on Main to watch women. When he saw Belinda Beller and Susie Endicott bouncing along, arm in arm, he thought about the vision he'd had of himself, graduating then going to college, this summer of freedom in between. Now he was a cripple who would live his whole life in a fancy house at the edge of town. He knew what happened to families like his own who lived in houses that were too big. People grew older and more feeble; they stopped climbing stairs, sealed off one room at a time. Paint chipped, windows broke, porches sagged, lawns grew wild, dust gathered along hallways and under beds, and still no one died and nothing changed.

He saw what happened to sons who stayed in their parents' houses. Joe Baldwin returned from Portland after his pretty wife divorced him. Now he drove his father's hearse, wore white gloves, kept his eyes on the road. Wade Catts got kicked out of seminary school. He watered his mother's garden, drove her to the store twice a week, put up the storm windows in October and took them down in April.

Years ago, Everett Fry sat on Main Street, just like Jay, his hunter's cap pulled down so the flaps covered his ears. He watched women. He stuck a gun in his mouth. Jay wondered if these things necessarily followed one another. He wanted a cap with a visor to hide his face.

Twyla Catts used the window of the bank like a mirror—brushed her hair, made her lips more red. He wanted to ask her: *What did your brother do?* He saw Sharla Wilder. He remembered the year she moved back to town and got her own apartment. He and Willy climbed the tree outside her window and watched her undress. He could see her body even now, unbelievably white, the slope of her breasts, the rosy nipples. There was so much of her, so much doughy flesh, round arms and small white hands, big thighs but slim ankles, huge globes of her buttocks, luminous as moons. She turned toward the window as if she sensed the boys in the tree, but her eyes stayed blank as chips of blue ice.

Now she was heavier, no longer smooth and supple but just plain fat. Still he longed to whisper her name and have her sit in his car, to fill the space with her warm breath and vague words. He knew something had happened to her that made her run away. And something else happened to make her come back. He wanted to ask her now, to say: *Something happened to me too.* He imagined her body above him, enveloping him in all her white flesh.

He saw a pretty little red-haired girl standing alone. He wanted to call to her too, wanted her to move toward his window so he could see the color of her eyes. She was a child, no more than ten, unformed, with a pink bud of a mouth and thin legs. He almost loved her for being so frail, so beautiful; he thought he might still be saved. But before he could open his window and speak to her, a woman swooped down the sidewalk, grabbed the girl's hand and dragged her away. He was doomed. He recognized the woman. Grace Arnoux. The pretty child was Muriel's little sister. *I'll kill you and go to hell.* Worse than that. *I'll cut off your balls and stuff them in your mouth.* His hands were shaking. He gripped the key but couldn't turn it.

* * *

Jay saw the boys go off the board, one after another. They tumbled toward the water, doing half somersaults and quarter spins. Their legs spread, their feet flopped. But no matter how many divers he counted, he couldn't fall asleep.

He heard his father rap on his mother's door. "Delores?" he said. *Come in.* Jay didn't hear those words, but the door clicked open, then quickly shut. Jay knew what would happen in that room. His father wore only a towel. He flicked off the light and let the towel drop to the floor. Delores lifted the covers, and he slid in without a word. Soon he grunted over her, eyes screwed shut, hands pinning her shoulders. She was still dressed, the nightgown bunched up around her waist. Her eyes were open, always, so she saw his bald head gleaming, reflecting the glow of the streetlight. She saw the sweat bead on his brow just before he collapsed. He rolled off her, indulged in min-utes of rest, then slipped out of bed. He gathered up his towel and left the room without saying goodnight. Jay heard water running in the bathroom, his father showering before he went to his own room to sleep, cool and solitary between clean white sheets.

Jay saw his mother lying in the dark, yellow hair matted, eyes still open.

He lumbered down the stairs. The night air was chill; stars pulsed like tiny, brilliant hearts. He drove to the pool and stood outside the fence, wondering if he could really do this.

The wire fence was easy to climb—even for a cripple, he thought. There was only one string of barbs at the top, a symbol more than an obstacle. He stripped quickly, letting his clothes fall in a heap.

His pale body was both skinny and flabby. His legs had lost their definition, his buttocks were loose. His chest seemed sunken and his ribs showed, but there was a slight bulge around his belly, a ring of unfamiliar fat.

He thought of Delores, her ruined body. *Jello on high heels— just like Marilyn Monroe.* This was the final humiliation—the body gone slack and helpless. This was every disappointment turned to flesh.

Each rung made him aware of his limitations. Each time he bent a knee he felt the stiffness. He had an image of himself, his whole body shattered, as if he had dived onto concrete and broken there. Now he was reglued, but each seam pulled and stung. From the outside he looked whole but inside he was brittle: a single breath might make him splinter, might send shards of bone ripping through his flesh.

He was almost there, about to stand on the high board. He thought of Sharla's white flesh, how it weighed her down, sapped her strength. He thought of Muriel, of the way her body had betrayed her, of the way he was to blame. He imagined Iona helping her mother's body move through those last days. He remembered her thin arms wrapped tight around him; he wished she were here now, to walk to the end of the board with him, to hold him on his way down.

The pool glowed, its underwater lights turning the water green as glass and just as hard. He realized he had no chance of hitting even the simplest dive. His body was no longer his to control. He wavered like his mother as he walked to the end of the board. How could he be lumpish as Sharla Wilder and frail as Hannah Moon at the same time. He wondered if Muriel was even more afraid than he was. He lifted his arms. His shoulders ached. He bent his knees. Failure was better than cowardice. He got so little spring, but he was off and flying, forgetting everything except the air whipping his naked body, the water coming closer and closer. He could not twist or roll. His body buckled, and he slammed the water like a half-open jackknife. The pain shot to his balls, centered there and left him stunned. He thought he might drown, but again his body betrayed him, and he found himself floating. How surprising to be alive. Delores must have felt just this way, and Muriel too. After all that grief, you find yourself bobbing on the surface, feeling nothing, and you swim to safety because you don't know what else to do.

In the nights that followed, Jay Tyler lived like a prisoner in his room. He did a hundred sit-ups and fifty push-ups, every morning, every night. He was going to be strong. He heard his father go to his mother's room on Wednesday, and again on Saturday. He hated them. He clumped back and forth down the hall, running with one cane, filling the house with his horrible, three-legged sound.

13

Iona and Eddie didn't go to the boat again, and didn't speak of it either, so it began to seem like an accident or a dream. When they ate breakfast together, Eddie often found some excuse to remind her he was old enough to be her father. "Not *my* father," Iona said. "But old enough," Eddie told her. Yes, if he'd started at seventeen—he knew plenty of guys who had. So did Iona, girls too, and even younger. She thought of Muriel Arnoux who moved away before her time. But people knew. She came home changed, a girl with a wound that wouldn't close, like Everett, who had to wound himself a second time and die so that everyone could see he'd never healed.

When Eddie talked stupid, Iona excused herself and ducked into the bathroom of the Western Coffee Shop. Across from the toilet was a map of the United States with a red pin stuck through every town that had a rodeo. Oskaloosa, Kansas; Lovington, Texas; Rosebud, Montana—she liked the names, liked imagining a life where you didn't stay anywhere too long.

She lay on her bed in the afternoon, too hot to move. No one in Seattle could remember so many days without rain. She needed a fan. The air was dead, heavy as a blanket pulled up over her mouth and nose. But she was saving her money. She stashed thirty dollars a week and kept it rolled in a sock at the bottom of her suitcase. Already the wad had grown fat.

Someone scratched at her door and scuttled away. Iona recognized the fluttery steps of the Scavenger Lady. For weeks
now Iona had found her gifts: a tea tin without a lid, a ham-
merhead without a handle.

This time it was a naked doll with no legs. The doll's face
was dirty, and the paint had worn off her lips. Her glass eyes
rolled as Iona picked her up: one eye drifted to the left and one
peered straight ahead. Iona washed the doll in the bathroom
sink. Its hard plastic body was molded to look soft and plump—
a lie, Iona thought, another broken promise.

The doll seemed more naked after it was clean. Holes gaped
where legs had joined the torso. She was too hard to take to
bed, too ugly to set on the dresser. Iona wrapped it in one of
her T-shirts and laid it on the chair. A lid stuck. The doll stared
up at her with one blue eye.

Iona pulled the blind and went back to bed. She'd never had
a real doll. She remembered stuffing the toes of her knee socks
with rags and tying them off with string. She'd made half a
dozen lumpy-headed creatures. They had long, droopy bodies,
no arms or legs, no eyes or hair. She hid them in her bed and
talked to them at night. She asked them if the land floated on
the oceans or if it was anchored to the core of the earth. *Because
when I start to fall asleep,* she said, *I feel myself being swept away.*
The sock dolls never answered.

She woke after dark. The legless doll was a dream, she
thought, nothing more than a vision, like the visions of
the Scavenger Lady herself, standing over Iona's bed, hands
open, face in shadow. So she was surprised to find the thing,
lying there in the chair, wrapped in her own shirt. Somebody had slipped a note under her door: *You owe me $2 for
the baby.*

Iona grabbed the doll by the head and let the shirt fall to the
floor. She marched down the hall and pounded on the woman's
door. No one answered. She knocked harder. The man in the
next room yelled: "She don't wanna talk to you." Iona stuffed

the note in a leghole and propped the doll against the wall. Its wild eye spun in the socket.

Iona opened a can of sardines and made a sandwich with the last two slices of bread. She wondered if stolen food always had a bad taste. The fish was an unlucky choice. Oil soaked into the white bread. The smell would linger for days. She blamed it on the heat. Everything reeked: the bathroom, the hall. Streets ripened with the stench of garbage, a fermenting mash, cans full of corn husks and apple peels, chicken fat and black bananas.

It was already nine o'clock. She thought of little Stanley. He liked her. In his way. He'd be hurt if he found out about the sardines and the loaf of bread, all the loaves of bread. Odette would have her excuse at last. Someone would be happy. Iona pictured Stanley sneaking nips. That's why he'd told her: *Don't ever be late.* A half hour could destroy his timing, tip him over the edge from buzzed to bombed. He might get sleepy, put his head on the counter. If some kids found him that way, they'd clean out the register and the cigarette rack, and Iona would have to take the blame.

She drank a warm Coke. It was too fizzy, disgustingly sweet, but it cut the oily taste. She swished the last gulp like mouthwash and spit it out the window.

The doll fell into the room when she opened the door to go to work. This time the note said: *You touched it. No good to me now. You owe me $2 I mean it.*

No good to me now. A mother bird won't go back to the nest if a human touches her fledglings. They call to her. All day they peep. Sometimes she circles but doesn't land. She carries nothing in her mouth. By morning they're silent. By afternoon they're dead. *No good to me.*

Iona remembered a sign out back of the supply store where they sold rabbits and chickens: *Don't Pet the Baby Rabbits or the Mother Will Kill Them.* There were other mysteries. Why did her father shoot the skinny dog that strayed into the yard, and why did he make Leon dig such a deep hole to bury it? What pleasure did her brothers find in propping tin cans on the fence and riddling them with bullet holes? Why was it all right to shoot a duck but bad to kill a loon?

When she was a child she thought if she could understand these things she might know if she was safe or in constant danger.

The doll's face was smudged again, and Iona wiped it with her shirt. Poor walleyed baby—who would take care of it? Iona remembered how she'd found the sock dolls one day: their necks untied, bodies turned inside out, all the stuffing strewn on her bed. Her brothers had found them, had pulled them from their hiding place under her blankets. She threw the rags and string away and put her socks in her drawer as if nothing had happened. In bed that night she held up her hands to make shadows on the wall, long creatures with big mouths. One said, *If the land floats, maybe I'll wake up on the North Pole.* The other answered, *The land doesn't float.* Iona closed her fists and tucked her hands under the covers. *But I feel it,* she said, *I feel everything shifting under me.*

She could bang on the woman's door and argue, or leave the doll in the hall again, but she knew she'd find it in front of her room in the morning. There'd be another note, another threat. *I mean it.* She slipped two dollars under the Scavenger Lady's door.

Iona ran all the way to Broadway but was still five minutes late. "I was about to call my boy," Stanley said. He grabbed her hand and stood too close. She smelled his rum, sweet and hot; she saw Jeweldeen, the two of them lying by the river that night in June, miles from here but not so long ago. She should never have gone to the tracks with Darryl McQueen. Stanley rasped in her face. "Remember what I told you," he said. "You got to be on time." He was close enough to kiss her. She could taste his smoky breath. Darryl McQueen put his tongue in her mouth. Darryl McQueen slugged her in the eye. Iona tried to pull her hand away from Stanley, but the little man had a tight grip.

"You owe me five minutes," he said. "I'm keeping track." He let her go and teetered toward the door. "Five minutes," he said. "Don't forget."

"You're an idiot," Eddie told Iona. They were eating pancakes and sausages at the Western.

"It's my money."

"You give her two bucks for half a doll and she'll be leaving you something every day."

"What do you care?"

"I don't," Eddie said, smearing butter on his pancakes. He took the syrup and started to pour. But he gave her that look: *Don't slurp your coffee; don't eat with your fingers; chew your food before you swallow.* He was still pouring.

"I'm not your kid, Eddie."

"Thank God," he said. He slammed the syrup on the table. His pancakes were ruined.

She didn't tell him she wanted the doll. She didn't tell him about her socks with their stuffed heads and their long, legless bodies. When she held them above her in the dark, they seemed alive. If she tossed them above her head, they flew, falling softly against her face and chest.

Eddie was right. Iona found another present when she got home, a toaster with half a cord and no plug. *No cooking allowed.* It was perfect for this place. Iona knew enough not to touch it, not to take it in her room. *No good to me now.* She stepped over it for two days. On the third day it disappeared. Later Iona glimpsed the Scavenger Lady skittering down the shadowy hallway. She was small and wore a raincoat and scarf, though the day had been hot. She walked fast, shoulders hunched, a full paper bag in each hand.

The next day Iona came home to discover a ragged green sweater hanging on her doorknob. There was no way to get into the room without touching it. The sweater was hers. She

knew what Eddie would say. The bill arrived that afternoon—
$1.00.

The Scavenger Lady stood beside Iona's bed. She wore the
raincoat but no scarf. Her gray hair was long and wet, a tangled
mat. She said, "I have something for you." She held up a tiny
pair of shoes. "For the baby," she said.

"But she doesn't have any legs."

"That's your problem."

Iona sat up in bed. The woman was gone. She went to the
door and flung it open. There were no gifts, no small, terrible
shoes.

When Iona cashed her next paycheck she stuffed the money
inside the body of the doll. She took the wad from the sock in
her suitcase and put that through the leghole too, then pulled
her red T-shirt over the doll's head and tied it in a knot at the
bottom. She patted the doll's back; its eyes clicked open and
shut. "Our secret," Iona said.

On the first day in September fog rolled off the water, and mist
became relentless rain. Iona kept expecting Eddie to pop in for
coffee, kept hoping he'd say, "Let's go to the boat in the
morning."

A gang of kids with the munchies burst into the store around
4 A.M. Their hair was damp, their clothes speckled. They
prowled the aisles, three boys and two girls. Iona watched the
mirrors, but they split in five directions and there was no way
to see all of them at one time.

They stole twice what they bought. Iona saw the lumps in
their jackets and jeans. But who was she to act high and
mighty—and what did she care about Stanley's damn Twinkies
anyway? She wasn't going to bar the door and let the boys shove
her to her knees while the girls laughed and kept walking. She
wasn't going to call the police and have them show forty-five
minutes later. Sure, she could remember the license plate, describe the car, a yellow Maverick—who could mistake it? But

the evidence would be eaten, the empty wrappers crumpled and tossed out the window long before the cops found those kids.

Eddie waited in the rain, leaning against the long black Ford. "At last," he said when Iona came out of the store.

"Odette made me mop."

"No," Eddie said, "I mean the rain."

"It's cold," said Iona.

"Yes."

"I won't have to buy a fan."

"Not this year."

"I'll have to buy another blanket instead."

"Get in the car."

He didn't drive toward the rooming house or the Western. He drove toward the marina without asking, toward the place where the blue boat named *Peregrine* rocked on the dark waves and the only sound was rain on wood, rain on glass, rain on water.

They parked at the end of the lot; it was a long walk, but Eddie didn't hurry—Eddie never hurried. The tide was out, so the ramp to the floating dock was steep and he had to grab the rail.

He picked the lock again and didn't say: *I forgot the key*. Inside, they lay down, just as they had before, Eddie pressed to the wall, Iona curved against him. She told him she'd been with lots of boys, but only one had ever held her this way. She wanted to tell him about the cave in the ground, how the roof collapsed in the rain, how Matt Fry ended up in another hole. She wanted to tell him that her mother twisted the necks of chickens and plucked them while they were still warm. She wanted to describe the potato fields in June, tangle of vines and bright heads of yellow flowers.

The rain had died down to a drizzle; waves slapped the side of the boat. She turned toward Eddie, closed her eyes and touched his face. "This is how I'd see you if I was blind," she said. She felt the bones of his forehead and high cheeks, the deep sockets of his eyes; she ran her finger across his brows, backward to feel the stiff bristles of hair. She drew a line down his long nose, over his lips, then from the cleft of his chin to his ear. The ear was twice as big as hers, lovely, firm. She loved Eddie for his perfect ears.

She wanted to tell him about Jay Tyler, how kissing him made her feel full and she had been hungry most of her life, how wrong it was for someone who didn't like you to make you feel that good. She wished Eddie knew about Leon too, about the beautiful little carvings he'd made: roosters and cows and bears, the solid little man with a hat and a shovel that looked just like her father, the little woman with thin arms and sad eyes. He gave them all to Hannah. But Iona threw his knife in Fish Creek, and he never made anything beautiful again. He dug up potatoes and shoveled shit out of the barn. He chopped cornstalks and fixed the fence when the cows broke through. *He could have bought another knife, just as sharp and just as fine.* She needed to say this now, to tell Eddie: *His sorry life isn't my fault.*

She untied the beaded leather wrapped around Eddie's braid and slowly fingered the plait, working it loose until she could pull her hand through his long, coarse hair. She pressed it to her nose. It was still damp and smelled of smoke and oil, a fish just caught, a dog's wet fur: it smelled more like Eddie than Eddie himself. He smelled familiar to her, someone she'd trusted her whole life, but she couldn't tell him how often she'd heard the snap of tiny bones: a chicken's neck, Matt Fry's hands.

She couldn't tell him she remembered Leon's grimy palm over her mouth, his thick thumb. *Mama will hate you if you ever tell.* Long after he climbed down the ladder, she stayed alone in the loft. That's when she found it, her brother's knife in the straw.

She laid her hand on Eddie's neck where his shirt was open, unbuttoned the second button and the third to touch his smooth, hairless chest. "Your heart's beating so fast," she said.

"Birdheart."

Iona thought of the newborn chicks, so small, nearly weight-less, how their whole bodies throbbed when you cupped them in your hand. "Are you scared?" she said.

"I'm always afraid."

She pulled his shirt out of his pants to undo the last buttons.

"Please," he said, "don't."

She put her head on his chest and heard the dangerous flutter. "There's no reason for you to be afraid," she said.

"I'm an old man."

"I'm not a child."

"I have to tell you something."

"I know you're married."

"Not that."

"It's all right if it's just this one time." She laid her palm flat on his stomach. "Potatoes stay warm after you dig them out of the ground," she said, "warm as your belly—for hours, some-times for days."

"Please," he said.

"Tell me," said Iona, "tell me what I need to know."

"My leg," Eddie said.

"Was broken."

"Yes, broken."

"A tree fell on you in the woods."

"Yes."

"And crushed your leg."

"Yes."

"Now you have a limp. You think you're an old man. You don't want me to see your scarred leg."

"Yes."

"I dragged a dead cat out of the Snake River. I carried a rat home by its tail. I saw a five-legged calf born. I watched my own mother die, Eddie." She stroked his chest, her ear pressed close to hear his heart.

"They took my leg," he said. "Bone broke through my thigh. They set it, but it didn't heal right. The bone got infected, oozed for weeks. So they took it, Iona. They cut off my fucking leg. I've got a stump and a piece of plastic."

She started to unbuckle his belt, but he put his hand on hers to make her stop. "You have to let me see," she said.

"No."

"My brother Leon and I got stuck in a blizzard one time. We had to crawl. The ice froze on my face. I wanted to lie down and die. I saw myself dead, Eddie, and I swore nothing would ever scare me again." She unbuckled his belt and unzipped his pants.

"I'll do it," he said. He pulled his pants down slowly. He wore white jockey shorts. He was hard. The stump of his right leg fit in the socket of the smooth plastic limb. It was pink and shiny, ridiculous next to his dark skin. "They don't make these for Indians," he said, rapping the leg with his knuckles.

Iona moved to the end of the bed to untie his shoes and pull his pants over his feet. She took the sock off his left foot. "You have a beautiful foot," she said. The toes were long and slender. "I want you to take it off."

"I did."

"I mean the leg. Will you take it off?"

"Why?"

"I want to sleep with just you."

He stared at the pink thing, stranger in this bed.

"You don't need legs to make love," she said.

He loosened the valve above the knee, and it let out a hiss of air. He grabbed the limb with both hands and rocked it until the suction broke with a pop. When he pulled the leg away from the stump, Iona took it, surprised by its weight, the heavy wood inside. She laid it on the floor, gently, as if it were a living thing.

In this light, the stump was purple at the base, cut by a single scar from side to side, rose-colored, raised off the skin, more like a new scar than an old one. She touched the leathery flesh with her fingertips. "Does it hurt?" she said.

"Not so much anymore."

"But it did?"

"I used to bang my stump on the floor. They put all us cripples together on one ward. So we wouldn't drive the others crazy. Every night you'd hear it, that thumping—some poor bastard with a twitch or a burn. Goddamn nerves don't know the leg is gone. You get a cramp in your missing foot and the only way to make it stop is to hammer the tile with what's left of your leg."

Iona stood up.

"What are you doing?" Eddie said. He reached for her as if he were afraid she might leave him like this.

She pulled off her jacket and shirt. "Getting undressed fast," she said. She took off her shoes and jeans, unhooked her bra, peeled off her underpants, left them where they fell. Eddie took off his shorts too. She had seen her brothers standing in a row, peeing in great arcs, the only contest Dale ever won. They jumped naked in the river and pranced naked on the shore. She watched her father piss in the gutter of the barn while they waited for the calf. She'd felt Jay Tyler's hard penis, gripped his balls and made him come. But she was afraid when she saw Eddie; she wanted to hide him, even from herself.

She lay down, pulled a blanket over them. Rain tore against the pane. He held her, and she felt everything at once: muscles of his arms, hands on her back, curve of his chest, warmth of his belly; she felt his penis against her leg, felt the weight of his left leg over hers and the space in the bed where his right leg had been.

The square of sky in the window above them was dark and yellow. She thought of Everett coming to Sharla in a dream after he died, Everett with a hole in his skull. She reached down to touch the stump, to feel the ridge, hard as the knotted scar on Everett's shoulder.

He said, "I can feel it sometimes, the whole leg, not in the bad way, just a kind of warmth, like the blood going all the way to my toes."

"I feel it too," she said. "It is warm."

They clung to each other like children lost in the woods; and when they kissed, mouths open, eyes closed, the last space between them disappeared. Eddie tried to move inside her, slowly, slowly, and she said it didn't hurt, but it did, and she was surprised because she thought she was past all that. He wet his fingers and touched her until she opened and she said *okay, it's okay,* but it still hurt and she said, *I can't.* His tongue was in her ear, his fingers in her mouth. He tried again, and this time she pushed through the pain. Waves swelled under her buttocks and thighs, lifting her toward him. He was a fish in the tide, pulled into her, washed back. He whispered: *Is it safe?* And she didn't know what he meant, so she said *yes,* breathed the word, *yes.* But it wasn't safe, nothing was safe now. She opened her eyes, but his stayed shut, closed to her. Each time he thrust against her she felt the old hurt, a tearing deep in her chest; she was tossed out to sea, and there was no boat to carry her back. Cold waves broke over her head; black water filled her mouth and lungs till she couldn't speak, couldn't breathe. And though Eddie held her this close, he didn't seem to know how afraid she was, or how alone. She saw her mother's body and her father's hands as he washed her; she saw her mother standing on the back steps at dusk, calling her name. She hid in the barn and didn't answer. She was nine years old. Now she would answer, now she wanted to answer, but Eddie was the one saying *Iona,* and she was digging at the bed, clawing at the blanket as he shuddered inside of her.

14

Iona wondered if making love always forced you to see things you were trying to forget. Afterward Eddie held her for a long time. The pain faded. Her flesh felt tender but not torn. The vision of her mother on the back steps was just a memory like any other, not a voice she still heard, not a hole opening in her chest, not a child whose body was her own. She knew now why she hadn't answered, knew she was ashamed and afraid: she thought Hannah would know what had happened in the barn. But she never guessed, and this was worse. Iona was scolded, in the usual way, neither punished nor protected.

Yes, Eddie cradled her, and all that went away, back where it belonged, until there was no one else in the room, no hands touching her that weren't his. And his hands were gentle. His hands moved from shoulder to buttocks, a smooth line, resting there, lightly, as if she were fragile, almost holy, and he said, "I'm sorry if I hurt you. Next time I won't be in such a hurry."

She wanted to tell him it was all right, it didn't hurt that much, it hardly hurt at all now, and if he just kept holding her, if he touched her forehead and knees, bones of her chest and veins of her hands, as reverently as he touched her behind, she might be healed. But she couldn't say it. She couldn't say anything. All the words had been pushed deep inside of her, jumbled and pressed together until nothing she could say seemed important enough and nothing quite made sense. She tried to stay with Eddie but felt herself flowing away from him, her body cool and thin as water.

At work that night, Eddie came for coffee twice but didn't stay to talk. The first time he said: "Rain's stopped," and the second time he told her: "Might be hot tomorrow." That was all. But she knew it meant they wouldn't go to the boat. He was waiting by the car at seven. The clouds broke in the east, and she squinted at the sun, angrily, as if it had betrayed them. "I'll drive you home," Eddie said.

Iona thought they could have breakfast together. Even if they couldn't risk going on the boat, they could drive to the marina and park by the water, close their eyes and touch each other's faces. "I can walk," she said.

"I want to drive you."

She shrugged and followed him to the car, despising his limp for the way it revealed his weakness. She sat as far from him as she could, leaning against the door. A block from the house a small girl charged in front of the car and Eddie slammed the brakes. She turned, two feet from the grille. She was seven or eight, with delicate bones and wispy blond hair. Her lips parted, her eyes opened wide, her whole body said: *You almost killed me.* She looked toward the sidewalk where the boy who'd been chasing her stood frozen, just as she was. She glanced back at Eddie, wondering which one to blame.

The boy flew down the alley, and she raced after him. Iona hoped she'd catch him, hoped she'd throw her arms around his legs and pull him down on the gravel. He'd have to go home with torn jeans and bloody elbows. He'd have to tell his mother exactly what had happened.

The engine had died when Eddie hit the brakes. It choked and sputtered as he turned the key and pumped the gas. The car jerked forward, and Iona said, "You don't owe me anything."

He pulled up across the street from the rooming house, shifted to park but kept the motor running. "I caught hell when I got home," he said. "She said she could smell what I'd been doing. She thinks I have to pay for it on account of my leg. She thinks she's the only one generous enough to do it with a mutilated man for free. 'I bet you found some Indian whore to do it cheap,' she said, 'one of those thirteen-year-old bimbos who does six boys a night and douches with 7-Up in between. I know you, Eddie,' she says, 'you sorry bastard. Did Mama Pearl let you use her bed? That old witch never did like me.' She said next time I was late she was going to drive up to the reservation and drag me out of any hole I'd found. She said I better watch myself and sleep with my leg because she might steal it anytime, and then where would I be."

"Do you love her, Eddie?"

"That has nothing to do with it."

"You're just a coward."

"A chicken," he whispered, "a man with a bird's heart."

Iona stared at the stain on the ceiling. The blind was down, but light blistered around the edges and the room was still too bright. She wondered how Sharla Wilder got herself to sleep day after day. Did she close her eyes and imagine Everett Fry—did he come to her every time—did he lie down beside her and touch her eyelids, stroke her belly, kiss her breasts? Did he say *I'm sorry* a hundred times? *I'm sorry I was in such a hurry. I'm sorry I have to go.*

At last the Scavenger Lady left Iona the gift she wanted, a jackknife with two blades, one short, one long, Leon's knife returned from the river, rusty and stiff, but a knife all the same, something she could use. She stuffed it deep in the front pocket of her jeans, carried it everywhere, gave it a name: *my sweet,* and paid the two dollars gladly.

• • •

Eddie kept to himself for twelve days, brought his thermos of coffee to the gas station and stayed away from the store. Sometimes Iona went back to her room and ate half a loaf of bread. Being full made her groggy, and she could fall asleep. She figured this was how Sharla managed it. She thought of Sharla sitting in her kitchen, eating stacks of pancakes or slices of toast. She saw her in her bed, popping crackers into her mouth, eating herself to sleep one morning after another. No wonder Sharla grew plump and then fat, swollen up with all the babies she'd never have. But nothing made Iona fat. She was skinny as ever. She didn't like to look at herself. Even when she combed her hair she didn't use a mirror.

On the thirteenth day it poured. At five-thirty Eddie Birdheart put a newspaper over his head and clumped from the gas station to the store. He slid his thermos across the counter. "Can you fill this up?" he said.

"Coffee's old," Iona told him.

"I can wait." He lit a cigarette. His eyes were bloodshot and his hand shook as he held the cigarette to his lips. "I haven't been sleeping so well," he said.

"Me neither."

"It's raining."

"Yes."

"Looks like it'll rain all day," Eddie said.

"Looks like it'll rain forever."

"Mama Pearl's been calling me again," Eddie said, "the usual way—the phone rings, I pick it up. I told Alice I didn't have no Indian girl. I told her I paid white man's money for it right here in town and she shouldn't worry about me going to see my own mother. I told her I was driving up to see Mama Pearl today, make sure she's been to the store and has something in her cupboard besides beans."

"Bad day to be on the road."

"I'm not going," he said.

"Coffee's ready."

"I don't want it now."

"You mean I made this for nothing?"

"I'll come back at seven."

"For the coffee?"

"Yes, for the coffee."

"I'll keep the thermos," Iona told him. "I'll have it ready for you."

She met Eddie outside, but he wouldn't take the coffee. "You hold it," he said, so she got in the car and held the thermos between her legs.

As they drove toward the marina, they talked about the rain, how cold it was today, how the sky seemed to be falling.

Eddie couldn't run from the parking lot to the boat. He had to hop and skip on his good leg, swing his right leg to catch up, then hop again. "Don't ever get in trouble with me," he said, "I won't get away."

Their clothes were wet, so they undressed quickly without touching each other. He sat on the edge of the bed to release the valve on his leg and rock the stump out of the socket. Iona thought of Alice's threat: *You better sleep with your leg. I might steal it anytime.* Leaving it on the floor was the bravest thing she'd ever seen Eddie do.

He was already hard. He had a condom this time and was slowly rolling it over himself. It seemed to take all his concentration, as if his penis were a separate person, a small man in a rubber suit who might try to flee if he let go.

Iona had seen plenty of condoms, flattened in their cases, stuffed in wallets. Boys started carrying them at twelve and hoped to need them before they were fifteen. She had seen used ones lying on the bank of the Snake River, limp and sodden. She thought she should tell him she'd had her period last week. In the days before it came, she remembered Sharla crouching on the cellar floor and wondered if she could do what Sharla had done. She thought he should ask, but he didn't, and she wanted to hit him, thinking how afraid she'd been. She pushed him back on the bed and kissed him hard instead. She bit his lower lip and sucked his tongue into her mouth, kept sucking so he couldn't pull away, and she knew it hurt but didn't care. He pushed himself inside of her, and that hurt too, but not as much as the last time. She thought the rubber would stop him or slow him down at least, but they were moving against each other, struggling to get something. She saw her father's dogs tugging at their chains in the yard, nearly choking themselves to get a scrap of meat or bare bone. They shredded the pig's entrails, devoured its balls. They fought over a bloody piece of cloth, a rag from the truck that Leon had used to wipe his hands after gutting a rabbit. Eddie's face was red, his eyes pinched shut. Iona gasped, but there wasn't enough air for both of them. Her lungs tightened, squeezed small as fists as the rain hammered the window and pounded the deck, as the rain pelted the water, as her body turned hard and black as the waves and the rain pierced her back like icy slivers. Eddie pulled her down, hid his face against her chest and moaned—terrible, that sound, Angel's hopeless cry. Iona saw her father's arms, dripping blood and mucus. She saw him put his whole arm inside the cow, and she felt it too, felt herself opening wider and wider, but there was no hoof to grab, no blind calf to save, only the carved hollow of her empty body and Eddie inside of her. He arched and heaved, cried out to God though she knew he didn't believe. A ripple moved through him, chest to thigh, then he lay still, and she lay on top of him. She felt small as a child, floating on his belly, rising and falling with his breath; she was weightless, insubstantial, a man's dream. She saw her mother holding Angel's head. She felt her mother stroking her own cheek. Her hands were cool, and Iona's face was hot with fever.

She thought Eddie was falling toward sleep, already slipping out from under her, but his pelvis began to move again, slowly; "I'm still hard," he whispered. He kissed her palms, her wrists, the tender underside of her forearms. He kissed her neck and bony shoulders, licked behind her ears and at the corners of her eyes. He held her tight to his chest and barely moved, only rocked, as the boat rocked on the water, as the earth wafted on the sea. Iona felt her body growing big again. She clung to Eddie but seemed to hold all of him inside of her, as if they had become the same thing, parts of the same body. Her skin was cool as rain but there was a warm place spreading from her thighs to her belly, a pool, hotter than blood, flowing into her chest and down her legs. Someone was crying. Someone was saying, *Don't, baby, please don't cry*. But the sobbing didn't stop, and the body that was theirs moved faster and faster, against itself. She closed her eyes and saw the square light of the window flashing in her mind with each thrust, bright though the day was dark, brighter each time she moved until the glass exploded, bursting behind her eyelids. The hot pool flooded her brain, and she knew what Everett felt when the gun went off; she knew what Hannah was trying to say.

She couldn't stop sobbing, and Eddie was afraid. Her hands were cramped like claws and her face was numb. Her scalp burned, as if her hair had caught fire, and she saw herself standing at the trash barrel after Hannah had shaved her head. She threw fistfuls of her own hair into the can and struck a match. Eddie kept asking a question she couldn't answer or understand. Her hair sizzled and stank. She wished he'd leave her alone. Hannah stood, watching, beyond the smoke, beyond the mesh of the screen door. Iona wanted to fall into the dark. The ground would be hard when she hit bottom, a well gone dry, too deep, too black to see anyone. She'd lie alone, curled into herself, beyond all voices.

"Sonuvabitch." Iona thought the word came out of a dream, her mother cussing at her father, blaming him. She opened her eyes and felt the boat rolling on the water. She was in the wrong place to hear her mother's voice. "I can't fuckin' believe this."

The voice was male, not a dream at all. "A gimp and a piece of jailbait." Eddie pushed Iona away from him and leaned over the bed, reaching for his leg. "Don't even think about it, asshole."

Iona saw the outline of two men, one tall and thick, the other wiry, half a foot shorter than the big man. The heavy one used his flashlight like a weapon, following the lines of their bodies, slowing to inspect the stump of Eddie's leg, blasting between his thighs to be sure nothing was missing there. The beam hit Iona's breasts and neck before it slammed against her face and blinded her.

Eddie tried to pull the blanket over them, but the little man yanked it from his hands and ripped it from the bed. "You're in deep, asshole." He spat the words.

"Breaking and entering. Contributing to the delinquency of a minor." The heavy man had a soft voice, matter-of-fact.

"Statutory rape." The way the nasty little one said it made the words seem true, and the light in the other one's hand cut a bright line from Iona's chin to her crotch.

Eddie leaned over the bed again, grabbing for his pink leg. "Don't do it," the hefty one said.

"I'm just getting my leg," Eddie told him. "Can I put on my leg?"

He sounded like a child awakened from a bad dream. The light on his stump made the skin look violet; the old scar flared. Everyone on the boat was having the same dream.

"Yeah, cover up that damn thing." The big man was sensible at least. "We're taking you downtown," he said.

"You too, sweetheart." The scrawny one lurched toward Iona and she jerked. "Look at that," he said. "She'll fuck a one-legged Indian, but she's scared of me."

Iona had never dressed so slowly. Her fingers seemed twisted, joints swollen. Eddie put the two-holed stocking over his stump and eased himself into the socket of the leg. He stood, threading the stocking out the valve hole. His pink leg was more naked than he was, stark and frightening in the glare of the flashlight.

The men watched him instead of Iona, and she wondered if Eddie's missing limb made them afraid for themselves, sorry and angry at the same time.

They were in uniform but didn't look like real policemen. Just security guards, Iona thought, the worst kind, men who had to act tough to make up for all the things they couldn't do, for the guns they didn't carry.

She couldn't tell what time it was. The square of sky in the tiny window had been dark all day, as if the sun never rose but only moved along the edge of the horizon.

The nasty one jabbed Eddie with his nightstick. "Let's go," he said. Outside, Iona saw their sedan—brown, like their uniforms—it said: *Waterfront Security, Inc.* The fat man was old, sixty at least, big but not strong, his bulk a burden. Iona believed he was sorry and wanted to let them go.

The skinny one was a kid, barely older than Iona but almost bald. He wanted to cuff Eddie, and the weary one said, "Relax, Dave, he ain't going anywhere."

"We've been waiting for you," Dave said. "We knew someone was using this boat."

When they got to the car, Eddie said, "Let her go. I told her it was my friend's boat."

"The boys downtown can decide about that," Dave said.

Iona leaned against Eddie in the backseat but couldn't look at him. He hid his face in her hair, whispering words she didn't understand. She thought she had lost something precious, these last tender phrases, apologies or regrets, promises he could not keep.

At the station, they emptied their pockets on the concrete counter, and Iona was surprised to see the knife. *My sweet,* she muttered. It looked small to her now, useless and rusted, too stiff to open fast, too dulled to do any harm. Still, it was the one thing she didn't want to give up.

She was taken one way and Eddie the other. She looked over

her shoulder and saw his straight back, his long, dark hair. She wished it was pulled back, tightly braided, safe.

Fingers in ink, photos against a wall, the guard who took Iona was small and efficient, a girl scout grown up. They walked an endless hall of beige tile. A steel door rumbled along its tracks, closing behind them with a clap that echoed, fainter and fainter but never ceasing. Somewhere a phone kept ringing. Seven rings, and then eleven—*pick it up,* she thought, and some-one did, but in a moment it was ringing again.

She landed in a cell with three women. Two hung together, like sisters. They wore high heels and short skirts. One had a black leather jacket and bright red hair. The other was a fake blonde with a fake fur. The third woman looked like the Scav-enger Lady but much older, a hundred years older, her face crinkled as brown muslin. She lay stiff on the concrete bench, pretending to sleep, clutching her shoes to her chest, priceless shoes, cracked and muddy, but real leather, the only thing she owned that was worth stealing.

The redhead and the blonde looked Iona up and down, trying to figure out why she was here. They smoked. Iona wanted a cigarette too, but she'd lost her pack.

Finally the blonde said, "What'd you do, baby face, steal some candy?"

"Breaking and entering," Iona said. It sounded important.

"Bullshit." The blonde had crooked teeth and hard red lips. "So what'd you get?" she said.

"Nothing. We were just using the place."

"We? We? Listen to that," the blonde said, nudging her friend. "The scrawny babe has a sweetheart."

"Leave her alone, Rita."

"Don't call me that."

"It's your name."

"I don't like it when you call me that."

Iona crouched against the wall. The toilet was clogged, full of piss and paper. The phone wailed again in the distance. She heard voices in other cells, cusses and cries, one refrain: *You fuckin' bitch,* said over and over at different pitches.

A guard waddled down the hall. This one moved like a man; her hair was clipped short, almost a crew cut, but the hard cones of her breasts defied her. She unlocked the door and pointed to Iona. "You're out o' here," she said. Iona expected the big woman to take her to a room with a table and no windows. She thought she'd have to answer questions: *How many times did you break into the boat—what did he tell you—how long have you known him?*

But they were letting her out. The man at the desk gave her the change she'd emptied from her pockets, her keys and lighter, the knife, the comb. She knew Eddie had taken the rap, told them it was his idea and his fault. She knew they didn't believe him but pretended they did: he was saving them a lot of paperwork. And he was an Indian. That made it simple. Iona wished one of the policeman were as bad-tempered as the little security guard. He'd make her take her share of the blame. She hated Eddie for getting her off. She wanted to be locked up, safe in the same way he was. She had nowhere to go except the bare room on Fir Street.

The rain on her face was sharp, a thin drizzle cutting her cheeks. Buildings made a deep canyon down Fifth Avenue. Streetlights hummed. She thrust her hands in her pockets. She'd find a store, buy some cigarettes, get to work on time, make Stanley happy.

She didn't go straight to Broadway. She walked to the rooming house first. Hills loomed, steeper with each step, and she was tired, so tired, her body buzzed with adrenalin and now drained. She passed the Mission-with-a-Heart. Men leaned against the building. A red light in a third-story window flickered and went off, one heart beating out. The men didn't bother to ask her for spare change, and she realized she looked as bad off as any one of them. Yellow fog hung heavy in the glow of streetlamps;

yellow fog rolled down the dark streets, followed her under the viaducts, carried her all the way to Fir Street, where she stared up at her own dark window but didn't go inside. She was scared. Of what? She didn't know. A single word from Mrs. Hagestead might break her. So she headed down the hill, fifty blocks, a hundred, no, only a mile, but so far tonight, so far in the icy rain.

She was seven minutes late. "You're getting yourself in debt, little baby," Stanley said. He pinched her cheek as if she really were a baby. She fondled the knife, deep in her pocket. "My sweetheart," Stanley said, "don't make Daddy mad."

"You better watch your ass." Those were Odette's first words to Iona the next morning. "Stanley says you were late again last night, and you're filthy besides. I got my eye on you, girl." Iona imagined Odette with only one eye above her nose, a huge eye, the white yellowed as an old egg, the iris cloudy. She wanted to knock every can of soup off the shelf, right now, while Odette peered at her with her one eye. But she didn't. She knew that if she ever wanted to see Eddie again she had to come back here tonight and tomorrow and the next tomorrow. She had to be patient and good. She had to wash her clothes and comb her hair and wait for Eddie.

Lying on her bed, Iona felt the room rocking. There was a pressure deep in her head, inside her ear, water in her brain, a steady sloshing. She closed her eyes and the boat capsized. She and Eddie struggled in the black waves; his pink leg bobbed on the water, floating out of reach.

On the third night, Eddie appeared. Iona watched him in his glass box, smoking cigarette after cigarette, drinking coffee from his thermos. She stared at his hands. Having seen him naked, she couldn't look at his bare hands without remembering all of him. He gazed at the pumps or out toward the street. At five he finally came to see her. His braid was gone, his dark hair neatly trimmed above his ears and collar. He wore a white shirt and a plain leather belt. His skin seemed paler, as if the red glow had burned out. He could pass, Eddie Rogers, husband of Alice Rogers, son of a white man who sawed off the heads of walruses, no relation at all to an old woman named Pearl Birdheart.

"She bailed me out," he said. "I didn't have to spend the night."

"Neither did I."

"I know."

"Yeah, thanks," Iona said.

"Her father found me a lawyer. Cut a deal over lunch, five hundred bucks and no trial—I've got six months to pay it off."

"I've got some money," Iona said.

"I'm not telling you this to hit you up for cash," Eddie said. "I'm telling you this so you'll understand."

"Understand what?"

"Some people die in prison," Eddie said. "Some people shrivel if you lock them up. They think they'll never get out even if you tell them how many days they have to serve. I was afraid— can you see that?"

Iona nodded. Eddie Birdheart would stop eating, squat in the corner, piss his pants and die a little more every day. She thought of Matt Fry. Eighteen days—it didn't take long to kill some men.

"I'm a cripple," he said. "I can't run away."

That morning, Iona walked down to the bay. The rain had no drops: air itself had turned to water, mist beading on her face and in her hair. Two old women sat on a bench. They leaned forward to draw pictures in the sand with their fingers, then erased them with their feet. Long-legged sandpipers skittered to the water's edge. Their paths made pictures, too, as they fled the rising waves.

The women moved down the shore, arms linked. A fishing boat returned from the sea. The man on deck wore a yellow slicker and yellow boots. Iona imagined his load, the hold full of silvery fish with black, open eyes. She could smell those fish. The sea washed up all the dead: carcasses of trees, stumps and bleached roots; broken shells and strands of kelp, their amber bulbs swollen with fluid. The ocean smashed bottles and battered boats, destroyed everything if given time. Waves tossed whole trees against the seawall. Their trunks were thirty feet long, thick as three men, but the sea threw them lightly, heaved them up as easily as children's toys. Seaweed clung to the roots like tangled hair. Waves lapped the shore. Waves splashed in the ear, relentless, a tormenting tide.

Gulls circled, descending on a single piece of garbage. They pecked one another's chests, crawing and complaining; they flapped their wings, then hunkered along the shore, heads tucked down like little hunchbacks.

The clouds were gray, and the water was gray too. The sky sank and the waves rose and the fog rolled along the shore. This was the beginning of the day and the end of the night and the start of all days to come. This was the sky without rain that was always raining.

Iona Moon's life in Seattle without Eddie was different but no better than her life on the Kila Flats. *You take yourself with you.* She figured that was why Sharla came back to White Falls, and she knew for sure that was why Everett shot himself. Some people were split in half, like Eddie, so it seemed as if he could get away from his old self. But Iona knew Pearl Birdheart would talk to Eddie through his telephone some day, that it wouldn't ring and he wouldn't pick it up, but he'd hear her voice all the same. She felt sorry for him: she imagined Alice kicking his leg out from under him when he came home loaded, smelling of smoke and his mother's house.

She barely slept for a week. It was the ear that kept her awake. It throbbed, filling the left side of her head, pounding, as if a separate, swollen heart beat there.

At work she felt weak, pulled off center. Kids came into the store, joking and jabbering. The boys pretended they didn't see her. Pretty girls stared with pity and fear, wondering how they could stand themselves if they looked like Iona Moon. Perhaps they insulted her. She couldn't be sure. Words were muffled. After they left, she whacked the side of her head and her skull filled with light—brief and blinding.

By October, she was stealing things from the store that she didn't want and couldn't use: a jar of popcorn kernels, a bottle of vinegar, newspapers with stories about two-headed babies and passionate aliens who landed in cornfields to visit lonely house-wives in Iowa. She got a thrill fooling Odette, walking out of the store with the newspapers crackling in her jeans, taking a scolding for her sloppy sweeping while an icy box of frozen peas dampened her shirt and chilled her belly.

Stanley was always glad to see Iona. He called her sweetheart, rubbed her arm while he talked to her. Somehow he'd found out about Eddie and the boat. He had hopes for himself. One night he told her there was a carton of milk leaking in the dairy case. "Would you clean it up?" he said. He'd had too much rum and lurched as he followed her down the aisle. When she bent over to peer in the case, he pinched her ass, the same way he'd pinched her cheek many times before, only harder. She turned, slowly, the punctured carton in her hand. The long strands of hair that Stanley had greased carefully over his bald spot had slipped, revealing his shiny scalp. He lunged, kissing her hard on the mouth, crushing the carton of milk between them. *Sweetheart.* She dropped the milk and the carton broke, splattering on the floor, squirting their pant legs. *Sweetheart.* The burn in her ear made her half-deaf and giddy. He forced his tongue inside her mouth and she let him do that too. She

tasted cigars, the salami sandwich he'd eaten at seven, the last
hot swallow of rum. He put one hand on her left breast and
squeezed, poor little Stanley with his thin chest and mean wife,
desperate, drunk, wheezing Stanley, such a small favor for a
dying man. It wouldn't last long. What did she care? One more
kiss, one more pinch—but she did care; she could have pulled
the rusty knife from her pocket and stuck it in his belly. *For a
quarter, I would;* that's what she thought. "Iona." He choked
on her name, doubled over, coughing, and never knew how
close he'd come to the knife, never guessed that as he teetered
away from the girl, she imagined blood spurting from his stomach, staining his shirt while he pressed his hands to himself,
weak and bewildered, trying to hold it all inside.

15

The next time Willy Hamilton found himself in the Tylers' house, he and Delores sat in the kitchen. It was late October. He accepted the drink she offered, a short one just like hers, vodka on the rocks with a squeeze of lime. He was still in uniform and knew what his father would say. *You're on duty until the minute you step out of those pants.* But Horton Hamilton wasn't there. He called Mrs. Tyler *Delores*, lightly, as if he had called her that his whole life. *Thank you, Delores.*

"You're so tall, Willy."

"It's the boots."

Those were their first words, and they almost deflated him before he was even inside the house. He was seven years old again, putting his feet in Horton's big shoes, drowning in his father's clothes.

"You look very handsome."

The boots fit. His boots. He tipped the hat. "Thank you, Delores."

Now he was sipping his vodka, sitting across the table from a pretty woman who just happened to be his best friend's mother. "How's Jay?" Willy said.

"The same."

She didn't make excuses this time, didn't pretend he was asleep, didn't say he had the flu. *The same.* Willy had never understood how awful those words could be. They were the soothing words the doctor used at the hospital when his grandmother was dying. *The same.*

Delores Tyler cupped both hands around her drink and stared at the ice splitting in the warm vodka. It was only five o'clock but almost dark. The air turned murky and Delores blurred. Willy wondered if one of them might be drunk.

"I'm afraid I haven't been much of a mother."

"It's not your fault." His words came too fast and sounded false.

"Lousy wife, lousy mother—I made a mess of things." Even in the fading light, Willy could see that her hands were unsteady. He almost reached for her, but she blinked hard, gripped her glass, and drained it. "I'm afraid I've had a few too many." She laughed. "So you can't hold me responsible for anything I say." He had never seen her with her hair down, curling around her shoulders. "Or do," she added.

She filled her glass again. "You don't mind, do you?"

"Why should I?" But he did mind. The boy who was Jay Tyler's friend and his own mother's son wanted to take the glass from her and toss the vodka and ice into the sink. This boy wanted to dump his own drink too, but there was someone else here, someone who thought of himself as a young man. He was reckless and scorned the other Willy for his prudish rules; he drank fast and poured himself another.

"I tried in the beginning," she said. "The good wife part, I mean."

"It's getting dark," Willy said.

"Yes, he'll be home soon."

Willy heard footsteps above his head, then a thud, the dull sound of a body dropping to the floor.

"Jay," Delores said. "He must know you're here."

"Did he fall?"

"Maybe."

"Shouldn't we see if he's all right?"

"He does it all the time." She raised her glass. "Like mother, like son—much to his father's dismay."

Willy thought of the Jay he knew, the Jay who said drinking destroyed the body, who wouldn't touch a drop when he was in training.

"Because of the pain, you know," Delores said. "It started because of the pain."

Willy imagined Jay's legs, the shattered bones, the months in bed. He realized he had no idea how much it hurt, no knowledge of pain beyond scraped knees and a bruised forehead, a cut on his foot that took a month to heal and left a scar an inch and a half long.

"That's how it started with me too," Delores said, "because of the pain."

Willy didn't want to know, didn't want to hear anything about the pain of a woman.

Never talk about sorrow in the dark, his mother said, flicking on lights all through the house before she sat down to tell them their grandmother was dead.

"I was pregnant with Jay. I found a handkerchief in Andrew's drawer. A brand-new handkerchief with his initials embroidered in one corner, the kind of thing he'd never buy for himself, a gift—do you see what I mean?"

Willy nodded. He wondered why she was telling him this. He heard more steps above him, the awkward three-legged gait of a man with a cane.

"I moved it to the back of his drawer, so he'd know that I'd found it, that I knew he had a girl."

She poured her third drink and topped Willy's too.

"I thought he'd see what a fool he was, that he'd look at me some night, pregnant with his child, and realize he loved me. The handkerchief would disappear.

"But that didn't happen. The next time I put his clothes away it was in the front of the drawer again, right on top. He wanted me to know that he wasn't going to stop seeing her. This was our life now, our *vow*.

"I imagined crying myself sick. I thought he'd come home and find me that way, on my bed, in the dark. That he'd see he'd been a fool. But Andrew wasn't like that. It's not in him to be sorry. He would have said, 'Pull yourself together, darling.' So I didn't cry. I made myself a drink and cooked dinner. I got drunk, Willy, and I discovered I didn't give a damn if he was sorry or not."

Willy heard a door open and close.

"I figured out who she was. The next time I stopped by his office, I knew. His receptionist was wearing red shoes. What kind of girl wears red shoes? As soon as I saw them, I knew."

Willy would never understand women. He was sure Delores was right about the girl but couldn't imagine how a pair of shoes could reveal the truth.

"I hated those shoes. I wanted to spit on them. I wanted to tear them off her pretty little feet and jump up and down on them till the polish cracked and the heels snapped off."

Willy thought of Mariette. Delores was safe. He knew for a fact his sister didn't own any red shoes. But he remembered her giggling with Lorena. *He cornered me by the filing cabinets*. Was it true?

Andrew Johnson Tyler stood in the kitchen doorway and cleared his throat. "Fine thing," he said, "for a man to find his wife alone in the dark with a policeman."

Dr. Tyler put on his southern drawl; *policeman* was a joke in his mouth, one more thing in which a medical man didn't believe. He hit the light switch, and Delores covered her eyes. "I'm sorry," he said. "Is that too bright for you?" *It's not in him to be sorry*. "What's for dinner, darling?" He bent down to kiss her cheek. "No, don't tell me—let me guess: chicken pot pies?" He massaged her shoulders so hard she flinched. "My wife's a wonderful cook," he told Willy. "We'd ask you to stay for supper, but I'm sure she doesn't have an extra pie. Am I right, sweetheart?" He squeezed her shoulder again, and Delores gazed at Willy, a silent plea.

When Willy stood, he felt the floor tilt and remembered Coach Brubaker circling him, poking him between the shoulder blades, smacking his butt, thumping his chest. *You are one sorry sack of shit.*

"I hope I'm not driving you out," Dr. Tyler said. "I hate to be the spoiler." He still had one hand on his wife's shoulder.

"No, sir. Time for me to get home for supper anyway." He saw his mother's table: fried chicken, potatoes, vegetables— something green and something yellow: *For my hard-working boy*, Flo would say, and he would want to cry. A boy, yes, as long as he ate dinner in his mother's house.

Delores Tyler had no intention of cooking dinner for her husband. She wasn't even going to slide a chicken pot pie into the oven. He knew where the freezer was, could turn on the damn stove. "You made a fool of yourself," she said.

"Did I? I thought I was quite congenial. Not as congenial as you, of course."

"I'm tired."

"You had an *exhausting* afternoon."

"I'm going to lie down."

"Why don't you, darling?"

Delores lay on her bed and wished she were still talking to Willy. She kicked off her shoes. He was a nice boy. She wished she'd explained that she hadn't always been this way. *I could have forgiven him*, she imagined herself saying, *for the handkerchief, for the girl, for the red shoes. But he wouldn't let me.*

She thought of the day her marriage ended, a hot Saturday in July. Jay was only three. They all drove down to the river, to a bend where the water eddied into a calm pool. Andrew waded in the shallows with Jay. He didn't like to swim; he sank, heavy bones and no fat. Delores was a good swimmer, light and strong—buoyant.

She let the current pull her downstream. When she was a hundred yards away, Andrew called to her to come back. *I pretended not to hear.*

At first she thought she would work her way back to shore, but the thought passed. The cool water numbed her limbs. Even now, lying on her bed all these years later, she remembered how good it felt just to drift, to stop fighting. *I knew I could get back to the bank.* She saw the rushes sweep past her. *Anytime.*

Andrew ran along the river with Jay in his arms. She heard her name bouncing on the water and saw herself as he did, a head bobbing in the distance.

The flow grew swifter; the riverbed was strewn with boulders. Sometimes a whirlpool sucked her under and she thought she'd be smashed against a rock. She pictured her own body popping up hundreds of yards downstream, nothing but a bruise on her forehead, like a boy she'd known as a child, a boy whose brother had killed him with a stone, an accident. There was no blood, no open wound, just the swollen place above the brow, the pale violet bloom on his white face.

Slowly she worked her way toward the bank, swimming at an angle, not fighting the current, letting the river do the work, being swept farther and farther downstream.

Soon she sat among the rushes along the shore. *I didn't mean to hide.* Andrew was barely fifty feet away. *But I was hidden.* Jay clung to his chest. *I let them pass.*

Andrew knew he had to turn around. If he waited too long there would be no hope. *I knew what he was thinking.* He was imagining the long ride to town, his own muddled explanation, the shame of it all, the way other men look at you when you admit you've lost your wife, when you say: *She swam away from me.* He envisioned the men in boats, dragging the river till dusk drove them to shore. He'd worked with such men before, peering into cloudy water. He knew how terrible it was, how every clump of weeds looked like a woman's hair, how the nets and hooks dredged up all that should stay at the bottom of a river: a rusty fan, a child's shoe, a punctured inner tube.

She was sitting on her towel when he came into the clearing. She saw him before he saw her, his chest streaked with the white trails of salt sweat, as if his whole body had been weeping. Jay toddled beside him, rubbing his eyes.

"There you are," Andrew said, fear already turned to fury.

"Yes, here I am."

"I was looking for you."

There was still time, Willy. I thought he might say the right words, that he might drop to his knees beside me.

Jay rushed to her open arms and she hugged him tightly, too tightly, until he squirmed and fussed and tried to get away.

"Time to go," Andrew said, the words hard and precise, three pellets spit on the ground.

Why couldn't he tell me he was afraid? Then I could have said I was afraid too. Every time I opened his drawer I was afraid. She thought that the great sorrows of life were all the things you imagined saying but didn't, all the fears you carried alone, the words unspoken that day at the river, this story untold even now.

Delores Tyler drifted on her white bedspread and saw herself through all the long evenings of that hot summer. She imagined standing in the kitchen after supper, listening to the moths as they fluttered against the screen door. They hung on the mesh, their bodies fat and gray, their pale wings tattered.

16

Willy Hamilton got the news on Halloween. He was on his way home, wondering if his mother had bought enough Tootsie Rolls and M&M's to last the night. He'd already stopped at the store once today—for a Dracula mask with fangs. Now Fred Pierce's voice cracked over the radio with the word that Matt Fry had busted out of the hospital in South Bend. "He's bound to head this way—sooner or later. If he's got two brain cells left to rub together. Keep your eyes open, Willy."

Willy. He'd tried to be Bill, but what good did it do if everyone he knew still called him Willy? A light snow had begun to fall. It was going to be a cold night for the kids. Damn Pierce. Why tell him at the end of his shift? *A policeman never goes off duty*. That's what Horton would say. Did they think Matt Fry might put a sheet over his head, stand on the stoop of the Hamilton's house, and ring the bell? Maybe a boy who was already a ghost wouldn't bother with a costume. *He's one of our own, Willy*. His mother was always reminding him. Better to be a policeman in Spokane or Seattle—even Boise. Here in White Falls everyone was one of your own: your neighbor, your cousin, a bad girl you knew in high school, your best friend—everything happened to you.

He slipped in the back door of his house, wearing the mask. Flo sat at the kitchen table. He bent down, nibbled at her neck with his plastic fangs. She neither yelped nor giggled. Her cheeks were red, her eyes brimming. Horton had called, so she already knew that Matt Fry was out there alone, wandering in the dark.

Willy lifted the mask and let it rest on the top of his head. He wished his mother had never forgiven his father for what had happened to Matt Fry last summer. He wished Horton still needed to keep his secrets. She was crying now, saying his name, *Oh, Willy,* but he knew her tears were for the other boy, the one lost in the snow.

Lorena and Mariette pranced into the kitchen. They were already in costume, matching outfits: black tights and black leotards with glow-in-the-dark skeletons painted on front and back. Their bodies bulged, giving their spines dangerous, unnatural curves.

"Watch this," Lorena said. She hit the light and danced with Mariette, bone people, twirling hand in hand. The skeletons did glow, bright and narrow, and the girls disappeared—but Willy heard their heavy feet as they thudded across the room.

By nine o'clock the doorbell had stopped ringing. All the little goblins and witches had gone home. Snow fell in wet clumps, and the streets were slick and white. Flo fretted. She worried about Horton cruising the side streets. She worried about children darting in front of cars, ghosts in the snow, invisible until it was too late. She couldn't help seeing her own hands on their sweet, cool faces. Willy remembered how she'd wept the day she washed and dressed ten-day-old Miranda Arnoux and laid her in her tiny baby coffin. He was eight. Horton said, "Maybe this work doesn't suit you, Flo." But that only made her cry harder. "You don't understand," she said. "You've never understood what's important to me." Hands deep in pockets, forehead creased, Horton turned and walked out the back door to stand in the yard, looking at the sky before he drove away in the dark.

Willy knew he had the right to leave just as his father did, without explanation or goodbye. He could drive away through the snow—leave his silly sisters and joyless mother—if only he could figure out where to go.

Flo would fuss about him, out on these icy streets, and he was glad for that. He took the Chevy. He was Willy Hamilton, citizen, definitely off duty, no matter what Horton said.

He didn't realize that the Dracula mask was still on the top of his head till he looked in the rearview mirror to back out of the drive. He tossed it on the seat, stupid thing—he hated it now. Flocks of children fluttered along the sidewalks, scurrying home, clutching bags full of goodies. He saw a horse head with a boy's body, a sheet that walked, a troll with hair down to her knees. On Main Street, a group of teenage girls clustered on a corner, smoking cigarettes. Snowflakes melted in their long hair. They were in costume too: leather jackets and cowboy boots, thin white faces, black lips.

He crossed the river to circle the trailer park. There was plenty of space: an irregular border of pines on one side, an endless stretch of field on the other. But the two dozen trailers were packed close together, fifteen feet apart, three perfect rows. Some had pink awnings over the windows or a screened porch built onto the door. But these additions did not disguise the tin boxes, quite the opposite—decoration made them all the more pitiful.

A stuffed man with a pumpkin head sat in a lawn chair at the edge of the park. He looked human at first but too still, sitting outside in the cold, wearing jeans and a flannel shirt, not flinching as snow piled on his shoulders and bare head, as snow fell into his eyes and into the hole of his mouth.

Willy Hamilton had choices: south to the reservation, north to the wilderness; he could drag Main like the high school boys or head out to the Roadstop and drink like a man. A couple of beers might settle his nerves, but by the time he got to the bar he remembered the last drink he'd had, the vodka with Delores Tyler. That hadn't calmed him down at all, so he turned around in the parking lot and drove back downtown. Tricksters had vanished but left signs: graffiti soaped on windows, tires slashed, pumpkins crushed against concrete.

He took a side street and found himself on Willow Glen. Not habit or coincidence, he knew—the thought of Delores Tyler had led him here. He wanted to see her, and for once he knew why: Delores understood failure. He needed to see her weary face and feel her soft hand on his arm. *You're not the only one.* Who would say it first?

He was glad for the mask—a friend after all. There wasn't quite enough time to feel like a fool before Delores opened the door. "Willy," she said.

"Trick or Treat."

"We're out."

"Then it's trick," he said.

"I never bought anything."

"I just wanted to say hello." He started to lift his mask.

"No," she said, "I like it." He wondered why she didn't ask him inside. "Dr. Tyler's out for the evening, overnight in fact. Boise—on *business*." Good, he thought, it was good to be out here, breathing clear, cold air. "I'd offer you a drink," she whispered, "but I'd rather go for a drive." She reached for his hand and squeezed his fingers. He'd forgotten his gloves. Her hand was small and warm. "You're freezing," she said.

"I'm all right."

"Let me get my coat."

He waited in the entryway. They were going for a drive, but he couldn't remember if he'd agreed to it or not. Puddles formed around his feet as the snow melted off his boots. His hair was damp. He took off the mask and rubbed his chilled hands together.

"Where do you want to go?" he said when they sat beside each other in the car.

"Away from the lights."

He drove toward the river. She slid across the seat and sat close. "To keep warm," she said.

He parked in the clearing overlooking the Snake, the same place where he'd parked with Jay and Belinda and Iona, the same place where he'd come with Darryl and Luke and Kevin the weekend before graduation. He wanted to laugh at his former priggish self. *Boot the sucker out of his car and let's have some fun, boys.* Delores pulled a flask from her purse, and he drank greedily, grateful for the way the thick sweet liquid burned all the way down his throat and warmed his stomach. "Cognac," she said, "for winter nights."

She had her hand on his thigh and her head on his shoulder. He wanted to tell her about Matt Fry and his mother, about his friends who got Matthew drunk and dragged him along the tracks before he torched his shed. He knew Delores already and could almost hear her say: *It's not your fault, baby.* He thought of driftwood washed up on the bank of the river, how it heaped on the shore like piles of bone.

Snow fell on the hood of the car and melted from the heat of the engine. Snow fell on the river and disappeared without a sound in the black water. Willy felt a weight against his chest, as if he lay at the bottom of the river. He handed the flask to Delores; she didn't drink—she screwed the cap back on and kissed him instead, lightly, near his mouth.

He gasped, but the weight pressed on all sides, the air dense as water, too thick to breathe, so he grabbed her and held her tight, kissed chin, neck, nose, opening his mouth wide to feel her whole mouth inside of his, forcing his tongue between her lips. He tugged at the buttons on her coat, frantic lover, impatient child. He had never kissed anyone like this. He thought of Belinda pushing his hands away each time he strayed. *No, Willy.* A voice from his past told him to stop, warned him about adultery, reminded him of the wages of sin. But Delores wasn't fighting—she was helping him undo the buttons. The voice muttered but no longer made words. Delores whispered: *Yes, baby.* Now his hands were inside her coat where it was warm, so warm. He remembered Iona Moon's torn shirt and small breasts that night by the tracks; he remembered the day he discovered Belinda Beller's bra was stuffed with tissue. Delores Tyler's breasts were real, heavy when he cupped them in his hands. He clutched the front of her dress, wanting to rip it open.

"Slow down," she said, taking off her coat, guiding his hands to the long zipper down the back. He tugged. No zipper had ever seemed so stubborn. His fingers felt numb, as if his hands had fallen asleep.

It was impossible to kiss Delores and get the zipper down at the same time, so he focused all his attention on her clothes. Now that her mouth was free, she laughed, and Willy knew the whole thing was a mistake. The zipper gave. She pulled her arms from the sleeves, unhooked her bra, let her breasts spring loose. She lay down on the seat with her dress bunched around her waist. Willy pressed his whole face against her chest. He thought he might smother but didn't care. He moved hard and fast. There was no time to wrestle with pantyhose, no time to unfasten his belt or wriggle out of his pants. She gripped his balls through his jeans, and he exploded, biting down on her nipple to keep from screaming. She had to swat the side of his head to make him stop.

Lying on top of the woman in the cold car, Willy Hamilton was already sorry. He covered her breasts with his hands. "I'm half frozen," she said, so he helped her hook her bra and zip her dress. She pulled her coat around her shoulders. He remembered Iona's tires spinning in the mud and knew things could still get worse.

But he wasn't stuck. Delores had found her flask again. She didn't sit so close to him on the way home, but she touched his arm and said, "Don't worry, it's always like that the first time."

The first time. He couldn't look at her. He was a virgin and a fool. *The first time.* Surely she didn't think there would be a second time.

He meant to just drop her off, but she said, "Please—walk me to the door. I'm a little tight."

Whose fault is that? he thought. And his father's voice answered: *Every woman deserves to be treated like a lady*. How could Horton believe that? Because he had never done what Willy had done, had never found himself with a woman like Delores Tyler.

Willy left the car running. He walked around the back to open Mrs. Tyler's door for her, offered his arm as she climbed out and held her steady up the long walk. "Will you be all right?" he said.

"My husband's not home."

"I know."

"My son's asleep."

He felt sick to his stomach and blamed it on the cognac.

"I know it's silly," Delores said, "but I'm afraid to go in alone. This old house is so big at night."

It's a man's duty to protect a lady. Willy hated the ring of Horton's words and wanted to ask: *Who will protect the man?* But he knew his father could never understand that question. *What kind of man needs protection?*

So, he was going to see her inside, flick on a few lights, blow the ghosts out of the corners. It was past midnight. Halloween was over. He thought of the Dracula mask. He couldn't remember where it was—in the car or still on the table. Jay might have discovered it already. Perhaps he knew everything and was sitting on his bed in the dark, wearing the rubber face, waiting to scare his mother.

The mask was on the table. Delores was safe, moving down the hallway, hitting every switch she passed. "Let me make you some tea," she said.

"I left the car running."

"Just a quick cup."

He looked at her smeared lipstick, her wrinkled dress. He had done this. He had bitten her nipple, much too hard.

"Please, Willy, sit with me for a minute or two."

He nodded. He owed her this.

They didn't make it to the kitchen. Jay wobbled down the stairs. Willy stared at his friend, and thought he might not have recognized him on the street. Jay's dirty-blond hair was pulled into a scraggly ponytail. He clenched the banister with one hand and his cane with the other. Willy wanted to embrace him so that he wouldn't have to see Jay's squinting eyes and furrowed brow, so he wouldn't know how much each step hurt him.

"Has my mother been filling you up with her sad stories, Willy Boy?" Even his voice had changed, had turned thin and cruel. Did the pain in his legs cause that too? Jay looked from Delores to Willy. He knew where they'd been and what they'd done. He probably even guessed that Willy hadn't managed to get his pants off. "How the mighty have fallen," he said.

Delores Tyler's face crumpled; every line deepened.

Jay limped down the last steps, into the light of the hallway. He had aged too, in a sudden, brutal way. He was red-eyed but not drunk.

Delores covered her face with her hands. Her shoulders heaved, but there was no sound. "We've upset my poor mother," Jay said.

Willy touched Delores's arm, and she batted him away with one hand, revealing half her face. Mascara ran down her cheek in gray streaks. "Go," she said. "Just go."

He drove too fast, slammed the brakes too hard, skidded at every stop sign. He was halfway home when he saw one of those damn kids sprint across the street, a stolen jack-o'-lantern tucked under his arm. He longed to hit the siren and scream out after him, but of course the Chevy had no siren. The kid was fast, climbing fences, cutting through backyards, but Willy kept catching him, a narrow shadow moving through the long beams of his headlights. He spun into a curb and leaped from the car to chase the boy down an alley. One block nearly finished him. He was stiff, out of breath, no match for the lithe child. But he had luck on his side, his father's just god. The boy stumbled and the jack-o-lantern flew from his arms. He sprawled; the pumpkin burst, an explosion of orange shards and splattered seeds. Willy was on the kid in a second, straddling his backside. "What the fuck do you think you're doing?" Willy said. He gripped the boy's neck and pushed his nose into the snow.

"I didn't do nothin'."

"Goddamn thief."

"It was mine."

"Then why you running?"

"I'm late," he said. "My pa's gonna whup me for sure."

Willy wondered if this might be true. The child was younger than he'd thought: ten—twelve at most. Halloween was over and it was just a jack-o'-lantern, after all. "Come on, kid, I'll give you a ride." Willy stood and the boy scrambled to his feet.

"No fucking way," the kid said. He looked older again, mean, a thief for sure. "You're a crazy motherfucker."

Willy wanted to choke him for that, but the kid was off; Willy didn't have a chance. The car door had swung open. From a distance, the yellow light of the dome made the Chevy look submerged in murky water.

He sat on the cold seat rubbing his knee. He must have bashed it when he jumped the boy. *How the mighty have fallen.* Now he remembered the mask lying on the table in the Tylers' entryway. *Motherfucker.* He'd forgotten it a second time, left it for everyone to see: Delores, Jay, Andrew Johnson Tyler. His frightening disguise was false and harmless, his own face ridiculous.

17

Jay sat on the edge of his bed, wondering if Delores had told Willy how pretty she used to be, and slim. He imagined her crying softly, explaining how the doctor carved her belly to get him out. Perhaps she showed him the scar Jay had never seen. He wished he knew Muriel's god and believed in this night of prayer and hope, the eve of All Saints' Day. He remembered Muriel lighting candles for the dead trapped in Purgatory, saying her Hail Mary's and Glory Be's, whispering: *Our Father*.

He felt a flutter in his chest, his heart a flame, guttering in a drafty room. Muriel said: *He won't ever look at me again if I do this.* She had one Jesus small enough to hold in her hand at night under her pillow. His pinpoint eyes revealed neither grief nor rage. But the tiny body twisted, rising off the copper disk, full of misery. She lay awake in the dark, feeling that body, touching Christ's little hands and perfect feet, fondling the piece of cloth, a thin wrinkle of metal that hid his sex and kept him safe and separate even in death.

On the lawn in front of her house a plaster Mary draped in blue stood watch, nose chipped, fingertips broken. She bowed her head as if to confess: *Even I have not been chaste.* Jay believed the child of his sin was trapped in Purgatory, waiting for his candle to be lit so his soul could rise up to God, waiting to be born again, to the right mother at the right time.

To the right father. Jay couldn't make himself say those words. He was never going to be a father to any child except the one she gave away. Sometimes he was hard when he woke, but when he touched himself he felt a pain shoot down his thighs, all the way to his torn knee and cracked shin. He imagined his mended bones splitting and knew that if he made himself come he would break apart again and again.

Delores stayed downstairs; Jay imagined her in the kitchen, drinking from her silver flask. He knew all about his father's *business* in Boise. He'd heard the argument that morning, heard Andrew say: *I'm going;* heard Delores answer: *Someday I might not be here when you come home.* That made his father laugh, and Jay wanted to fly down the stairs, bash him with the cane to make him stop. *Sonuvabitch.* But he knew his father would turn on him, cool and mocking, knew just what he'd say, smirking with the pleasure of his own joke: *Actually, you're the son of a bitch—literally speaking.* Now he felt the vast empty space between his dark bedroom and the bright kitchen; he heard the rush of air like wind whipping down a gorge in this fatherless house.

Horton Hamilton was awake, waiting for his son to come home. Willy saw the light and knew he was in for it. *You worried your mother half to death.* He slid as he hit the brakes and almost missed the turn. For once he wasn't afraid to face his father. What he'd done tonight was much worse than anything Horton might imagine. He felt giddy, freed by his secrets, like the boy who had stolen money from his mother's purse but was punished for tracking mud on the living-room rug. The five-dollar bill burned in his pocket. He was eleven years old, elated and full of guilt.

He'd bought a G.I. Joe with the money he'd taken. By Christmas it was abandoned, given to the Salvation Army so that some younger, poorer boy would find it in a box under a tree. Flo touched his cheek, and Horton whispered, *My little man.* They couldn't read his mind. He was relieved, then disappointed. Only God knew everything. God made him hate the doll. Serious and firm, the god of childhood forced him to give it away but did not demand that Willy expose his crime.

He wouldn't have to tell them about Delores Tyler either—or the boy in the alley—but he wondered what penance his old god might exact.

He remembered Flo, sitting beside her mother's bed, weeping. *I'm sorry, Mom.* Over and over—*sorry*—though his grandmother couldn't hear. What had Flo done? He couldn't imagine. But he saw his grandmother's teeth in a jar of blue water and knew this was the small white room of his own future, knew for certain he would find himself saying the same words.

He stood on the steps stamping snow off his boots, watching Flo and Horton through the window. As soon as he was inside, Flo said, "Your father found him; he's okay. No gloves or hat, just a thin jacket—who knows how he got here—but he's all right. He was walking back and forth across the bridge, as if he couldn't decide whether to come to town or head out to the Flats." Willy wished he'd seen Matt Fry. There would have been no visit to Delores Tyler, no drive to the river, no vision of Jay hobbling down the stairs, no skinny kid sprawled on his belly.

"And do you know what your father did?" She waited for Willy to shake his head. "He drove Matthew straight out to his parents' house." Her throat tightened. She couldn't finish the story.

"They said they'd give him another chance," Horton said. He was both humble and proud, too shy to look at his own son.

Willy knew his ironic god would punish him, but had never guessed how swift and simple the blow would be.

Alone in his room, he gazed out the window, at the snow

falling on the street and on the lawn, on all the lawns as far as
he could see. Would Matthew learn to talk again, get a job,
make his parents glad—or would he take his mother's car for
another joy ride and end up in the river? Maybe he'd set the
drapes ablaze—one more time—light the whole goddamn
house some night while his mother and father slept, forever safe
in their beds upstairs. Sometimes the object itself forces you to
act. A knife demands to cut: to whittle a stick or open a fish,
to stab the dirt or draw blood from your own thumb. Perhaps
that's how it was with Matt Fry. The river called and the car
answered. The match said: *Strike me*, and the curtains said: *I
want to burn.*

The next morning, Willy took a drive out to the Frys' place.
He remembered how Clifford Fry had boarded up the basement
windows years before to keep the boy from breaking into his
own house. Now the boards were gone. The Frys put Everett
in the attic. This time they took the opposite approach. *The dark
is merciful.* Willy wondered about the room downstairs. If a
child cried out in his sleep, would his parents hear?

He drove slowly but didn't stop. The snow was melting, and
it had started to rain. Ruts of the road ran with muddy water.
The dark is merciful. A lie. The dark leaves its own memories,
more powerful because you cannot see: flowers crushed in a
sweaty palm, a woman's perfume, the taste of cognac in his own
mouth, the taste of it in hers.

And the dark made its own claims. That night, long after
his trip to the Flats and hours after he was off duty, Willy
Hamilton found himself turning down Willow Glen Road. If
he'd known what he wanted, he might have had the courage
to stop. But he wasn't even sure who he wanted to see. He
imagined himself burying his face between Delores Tyler's soft
breasts, begging her for another chance. He saw himself running
up the stairs, pounding on Jay's door, telling him to get up off
the goddamn bed and start living his life. He knew he couldn't
do both, so he did nothing at all.

He thought he had been braver as a child. At least he could act. Once he heaved a stone, broke a school window. Because he wanted to do it. Because the window said: *Break me*. Terror thrilled him. He'd made this—not a sculpture but a hole, still undeniably and completely his. The alarm sent him reeling, and he ran faster than he'd ever run, faster than he could run today. When he heard the wail of his father's siren, his heart seemed to stutter, off beat; he didn't know if he was wild with happiness or fear.

Hunched under the covers of his bed, Willy thought of Delores, how surprised he was when she lay down and her breasts flattened, turning loose and flabby, not at all as he had pictured them. Her body scared him; he didn't know why.

None of Willy's imaginings could bring him close to the thoughts of a woman. How could he guess that she waited for him to come again. How could he know her shame, how it hurt her to think of taking off her clothes in front of him, how the difference between them was a cruelty he did not mean to inflict, how his lean body reminded her of all the things she could never be and never have. She touched her own scarred belly, her fat thighs, her white dimpled buttocks. How could she ever bear to let him see. No, if it happened again, it would be exactly as it was the first time. They would be in a car by the river. She would hike up her skirt and pull down her pantyhose. No man would ever gaze at her, full of longing, while they made love in a rose-lit room.

One day passed and then another. He drove by her house. She stood at the window. She saw him, but he did not stop. It snowed again. His headlights carved a pair of yellow tunnels in the street.

The calls started a week later. At first he only breathed while she said, "Hello. *Hello?*" The third time he called, she said, "Willy, is that you?"

He hung up and thought about the kind of girlfriend he wanted, one with smooth skin and silky hair, a girl with a nice smell who would sit beside him at the movies and hold his hand, a girl who would be afraid of men on the screen but not of him. He wanted this girl to kiss him passionately in his car by the river, her tongue exploring his mouth, her body arching against his until he grew hard and she said: *That's enough.*

The girl he dreamed had round cheeks and big eyes, a small nose and pretty little mouth. Her eyebrows were high and light. She was fair, not necessarily blond, but pale. She didn't look like anyone in particular, and Willy realized that the face was childlike, unformed. As soon as it began to take on more definite lines, the fantasy dissipated and the girl said things he didn't want to hear: *Don't worry, baby. It's always like this the first time.* She kept a flask in her purse and drank too much. She moved from shadow to light, and he saw that her face was lined and the skin beneath her eyes was so dark it looked bruised. She unbuttoned her own blouse. No one said: *That's enough.*

He didn't call for two days. On the third day, he rang. She said, "Hello," and he said, "Are you alone?" Just like that, an obscene caller without a name. She knew him, knew what he wanted, not like the little girl in his fantasy who didn't know anything, who could always say *no.* "Do you want to come over?" He was nodding. "Willy?" He realized she couldn't see him. "*Yes,*" he said. "Then come."

She'd fixed herself up, lipstick and blush, yellow hair pulled back and pinned in a French knot. It had been a long time since he'd seen her in daylight. "You look nice," he said, and it was true.

In the car, he asked her where she wanted to go. She answered quickly; everything had been decided. He wondered how this had happened and if he should be afraid, but he drove west, toward South Bend, just as she said.

He said, "Shall we have lunch?" And she said, "I know why you called." He waited. "It's only fifteen dollars." For a moment he thought she meant he'd have to pay. "For a room," she said.

Until now his worst crimes had come from trying to be too good. He remembered fourth grade, how he tattled on Roy Wilkerson when he saw the older boy copy from his spelling test. And Roy was punished by Mrs. Finch, struck on both palms with a ruler, as if the hands themselves were bad. Willy watched the fat, sobbing boy, feeling every blow in his own body but still believing he'd done the right thing.

What he was doing now was wrong. He thought of Iona, what she wanted, what she tried to make him do. He saw that this was God's punishment for the pious, to give him the desire he'd judged most harshly.

His first silent call had set this in motion, and now he couldn't stop—they were here, climbing three flights of stairs at the South Bend Hotel, putting the key in the lock, opening the door. He knew what Flo said, that God heard only silence and hushed words. It was too late to pray nothing would happen, so he prayed to be kind.

The day was overcast, already dark, but Delores pulled the blinds. She'd brought a candle. Stains on the bedspread, dirt on the rug, in this flickering light almost invisible. *Merciful*. She pulled the pins from her knotted hair and shook it loose. When he sat beside her on the bed, they kissed, lightly—there was time now. She took off her coat and he reached under her sweater. Her camisole was satiny, smooth as skin over skin.

She touched his shoulders and his arms. *Beautiful boy*, she said, and the words shocked him. She told him to take off his clothes, and he stood before her, completely naked, unashamed for the first time—because he was beautiful; in her eyes, he was. She guided him to parts of his body he'd barely known, arch of the foot and inner thigh, the delicate space between each finger, the hollow between each rib—he came too fast but grew hard again and was amazed when he moved inside of her, so warm there, so different from his own hand; nothing had ever felt like this. And he was surprised by his own tenderness, his longing—a desperation to make her feel what he felt.

She still wore the red camisole, afraid her belly would frighten him, ashamed to think her breasts might remind him of the vast gulf of age between them. He felt too good to her, a sting, flesh on flesh, the long muscles of his legs, tongue in her mouth, fingers in her hair, the bones of his hips pressing into her, an imprint she would feel for days. She didn't want to scream, didn't want her face to contort or turn a brilliant red, so she held herself back and still she came, a ripple of small shocks that racked her body. It had been so long since anyone had made her come—she wanted to weep with gratefulness.

He came a moment after her, thrusting hard. The second orgasm left him limp, exhausted. He curled around her, one leg over hers, soft cock nuzzling her thigh, face pressed to her neck under her damp hair.

The candle flickered out while they slept. They woke in darkness and made love again, but the afternoon was wearing on and they were both thinking of the night. He strained to come quickly, to be done with it. He heard Mrs. Stiles say: *An animal act,* and thought of the old woman's dry hands, the ropes of blue veins, how her hot blood seemed to leap into his body where she touched him. His hands pressed the sheet as he moved against the woman in this bed. He did not kiss her or look at her. He thought only of himself, of his own breath, the way that sound filled the room.

Delores showered alone, and Willy lay on the bed, listening to the water. He smelled her now, on him, and wished he had been the first to wash.

While Willy was in the bathroom, Delores turned on the light to gather up her clothes. He found her that way, on her knees, white rump in the air, looking under the bed. They dressed quickly and slipped out the back entrance of the hotel, their hair still wet.

In the car on the way back to White Falls, they had nothing to say. He parked in front of her house, hoping she would climb out quickly. "Call me," she said.

Willy drummed the steering wheel with his fingers. "Sure," he said, "of course."

Driving home, he thought of the welts on Roy Wilkerson's palms and wished he could kneel now to take those blows.

18

Iona stared at the stain on the ceiling. It opened and spread, the shape of a womb, dark as dried blood. The man upstairs was vacuuming again. She thought of him, moments before, lying on his bed, fighting down his urge the same way she fought hers. Muscles tightened around his ribs. His breath came fast and shallow. He had already swept the floor, dusted the windowsill, vacuumed the rug. Panic rose in him like a hand inside his chest, reaching up, a fist in his throat. He peeked under the bed, crawled to the dresser, ran his finger along the ledge of the frame above the closet door. *Yes, dirty.* Now the frenzy began.

The wheels of the little machine rolled across Iona's ceiling. She pressed her pillow to her ears, but it was too late. The legless doll sat in her chair peering at Iona with her one good eye. Seven o'clock, four hours to kill before she had to relieve Stanley. She hated it when the doll looked at her that way. It still wore the red T-shirt, tied in a knot over the holes in the torso. All her money was stuffed inside, crumpled bills wadded together. She no longer cared how much there was. Enough, she thought, enough to get away.

Later Iona saw that the kids had started a bonfire in the vacant lot. She stood at her window, watching the flames lick higher and higher. Soon the fire trucks would come to douse the weeds, but for now the kids were dancing in a circle, stamping and shouting. One boy waved a burning stick, painting a fire, sculpting a blaze. Sirens howled in the distance. By the time she left for work, the black grass was wet, beaten flat, the street deserted.

Alice visited Eddie in the middle of the night, brought him a bag of food as she had every night since the arrest. She never got out of the car. Iona saw the big head, wide shoulders, one pale hand holding the paper sack. It was easy to imagine the rest: wide feet cramped in a pair of pumps, thick legs, big-boned Alice, full breasts and full belly.

Eddie was getting a bit of a paunch himself, eating that extra meal, sandwiches and apples, boxes of raisins, slices of pie. Iona remembered how he'd felt his whole leg in bed with her, the lost calf, the knee that still bent, warmth of blood all the way to his toes. He said: *This never lasts.* Iona understood how a man could stay away from her—but his own leg, how could he abandon that?

She imagined him growing huge and round, swelling with his wife's food. They'd lie on top of each other, Eddie and Alice, too bloated to move, hopelessly separated by the humps of their stomachs.

Iona wanted to eat herself numb. She stole a box of cereal, a quart of milk. Alone, in her room, she found it difficult to chew, nearly impossible to swallow. The first bite was good, the second disappointing. The third bite exhausted her, and she set the bowl on the floor.

One night she climbed a tree to see in a window of the house with stone lions. The mother brushed her daughter's hair, slowly, tenderly. Iona thought of Hannah, yanking her hair, pulling it tight to snip it close to the scalp. *I know where you got this, Iona.* She remembered standing in front of Jay Tyler's house, late fall; the trees were bare, the grass yellow, matted and muddy from a snow that had melted. She didn't want to see Hannah's hair, but she did, brittle yellow strands wound in the brush. Still the woman brushed her child's hair, fifty strokes, a hundred. People didn't die in houses like these. They went to hospitals and died in rooms with white sheets and white walls. No daughter here wiped her mother's bottom or stripped her mother's bed. No girl ever stood in an empty room and whispered: *Where is she?* She wished the kids from her block would build a bonfire in this yard, that the flames would rage, devouring wood and paint, curtains and piano; she longed to hear the pop of glass and a child who was not herself screaming.

By the middle of November, Stanley stopped trying to get his hands on Iona every time she moved in front of him. "There's nothing left to grab," he said. "Why don't you help yourself to a salami sub tonight—or a pint of ice cream?"

Just thinking about the fat-pocked salami made her feel sick, but ice cream seemed like a good idea. It was smooth, easy to swallow. She didn't get around to it, though. Eating was too much trouble. As soon as Stanley was out of the store she broke open a carton of Chesterfields and started smoking instead.

It was the cigarettes that did her in. Odette noticed the split carton before she even said hello. That saved her the trouble of a greeting all together.

"Just the other night," Odette said, "just the other night I was lying awake waiting for Stanley to get home, making a list in my head of things that were missing, knowing that any day now I was going to catch you red-handed. I've seen it from the beginning. I told Stanley, 'Just look at her eyes—the girl's a thief.' "

"Aren't you even going to ask me if I paid?"

Odette pushed the cigarettes toward Iona. "Did you?"

The lie would have been easy. But Iona was tired. So tired. She slipped the carton under her jacket and headed for the door. She glanced over her shoulder. "I didn't pay for them," she said. "I didn't pay for the fucking cigarettes."

• • •

They owed her a week's wages. She figured she'd get it from Stanley tonight. Yes, it was important not to forget the money. But right now she had to go home.

The mattress rocked. She needed to sleep but couldn't. Her head felt twice its size, swollen with fluid. The sky was dark by six, the streets slick with rain.

When she left the house again, her big head threw her off balance. She was hungry—limbs jittery, stomach raw—but the banging made her dizzy, too nauseous to eat. She'd forgotten how it felt to live without this ache, the steady pressure behind her face, her skull too small for its brain. The pain burst as she walked down the hill, a shot fired into her ear and out her eye. She had to stop to catch her breath, lean against a telephone pole until the wave passed and she could move.

The lions roared, calling to her. She knew she shouldn't go to them, knew she should go home, take a warm shower, crawl under her covers, wait. But for what?

The house was empty; black glass wavered, catching headlights. She stood in the yard, hidden by the trunk of an elm. Someone would be home soon. She felt the deep grooves of the bark, the rough skin of the tree.

She closed her eyes. Impossible to think she slept, standing there in the rain, but when she looked again, the parlor was lit. The mother sat at the piano with the boy on her lap, his tiny hands resting on her large hands so he could feel her play. Iona pressed the side of her face against the gnarled bark, let it bite her cheek as she thought of the woman's soft hands, how warm they were, how lightly they moved. She didn't know how this could be. How could people be this warm while she stood in the rain. How could a mother's cheeks be full and flushed. How could music be so sweet.

She hunched against the rain, soaked now, and headed back to Broadway. The money—Stanley owed her. Her head bulged with blood—huge, hot. People jostled her on the street, or she butted into them—she couldn't tell, but they were the ones to swear.

Stanley cussed too, under his breath. He reached for something below the counter. A gun? She asked for the money. Stanley shook his head. No fucking way. He clenched his teeth, hating her—no wrath like the wrath of a man scorned. Iona wanted to laugh. *Pretty baby.* He wouldn't call her that now. *All my kindness and you repay me this way.* He didn't say that either. But she knew. "You're not getting a dime from me." Motherfucker. She didn't feel like laughing now. She fingered the knife in her pocket. Nothing mattered. Her pulse banged at her temple, and she imagined a hundred capillaries bursting with every heartbeat. She remembered: his fingers tight around her wrist, all his stolen kisses, his cock growing hard when he rubbed against her—nothing she'd taken compared with that. Darryl pushed her to the ground; Leon pinned her in the straw; Jay pressed her to the vinyl seat; Eddie left her rocking on the black waves. In her mind, the blade of the knife was long and silver, smooth, just polished. She saw the pig strung up by its hind feet, blood pouring from a hole in its neck. She saw a string of rabbits with no eyes and no skin. It was so easy, the knife so fast, if only Stanley knew how he tempted her.

But this knife was rusted, its blades short. Neither Stanley nor Iona moved. She thought she said, "Just give me the money." She thought he answered, "Get the fuck out of here."

She grabbed a six-pack of Coke on the way out, heard him yell, felt the air behind her move as he charged. She was out the door and the six-pack was sailing back toward the store. The front window exploded in a million icy shards. Sound filled the street; sound filled the whole night, as if the sky itself had broken and fallen on the wet pavement. She saw Stanley's face at the door. She saw Eddie's face rising in his glass cage. She saw the glow of a hundred streetlights ahead of her and felt her feet flying.

• • •

A hole opened—black, tempting—a tear in the sky, and she passed through it, to the other side of her life, where streets had familiar names but everything was strange. She crashed in an abandoned warehouse on Western Avenue, thinking she'd be safer here, buried under a pile of old newspapers. Her hand was sticky with blood. She thought of the rusty knife and wondered if she had used it after all, if some part of her memory was lost and Stanley was lying on the floor, bleeding.

In the morning, she walked up the hill. A man had made a home for himself under the viaduct—just a board stretched between two struts, but he slept there, all he owned tucked beneath the plank: shoes and radio, a wooden box, a piece of chain.

"Look what the cat dragged in," Mrs. Hagestead yelled from her kitchen. She acted as if she'd been waiting for Iona. "Man's been looking for you." Stanley? Iona wondered. Maybe the police. Mrs. Hagestead didn't say *police*. She would, if that's who it was. Iona climbed the stairs, holding the rail, dragging herself up, one step at a time. Her father. What if her father had found her. No, he wouldn't come. But he might send Leon. And what would she do if Leon were sitting on her bed when she opened the door. The knife felt heavy in her pocket. After all these years. Would she stab him in the belly, or offer him this small gift.

The room was empty, dark, the blinds still down. She opened them. The street was deserted. No one was coming for her. She set her cigarettes and saucer on the floor beside the bed so she wouldn't have to get up if she wanted to smoke. She wanted a cigarette right now but knew she'd be asleep by the third drag. Then she'd be a story in a newspaper: *Girl Sets Rooming House Fire*. There might be a photograph of Frank Moon. She imagined him, blinded by the flash. *Smoker Was Teenage Runaway from Idaho*. People would feel sorry for him, bewildered father of a

wayward girl. They'd say he lost his wife less than a year ago.
And now this. Lost his wife. Why didn't he look for her? Iona
saw him gazing out his window. Yes, she was sure of it. He
saw her leave, saw her duck out of the barn and run toward
the truck, suitcase in her hand, poncho flying. Why didn't he
call her name? She pulled the blanket to her chin. She still wore
her jacket and her shoes, but she was cold. So cold.

Wind roared and snow blew in her face. She was on her
knees and Leon was beside her. They were going to die. They
might be two miles from home or two hundred feet. But it
didn't matter, because they couldn't see an inch in front of their
faces. She lay down in the powder but wasn't cold, not at all;
even the snow itself didn't feel cold. She pulled herself out of
the dream. The wind still howled. She was in her bed. Sun
streamed through the window. Not wind, only the growl of the
vacuum in the room upstairs.

She reached for the cigarettes. She was thirsty too. There
were four Cokes on the dresser, the last of the supply, but she
didn't want to leave the bed to get one. She saw the doll in the
chair and said, "Bring me one of those Cokes, will you?" She
smiled. Good joke. She knew the doll couldn't bring her the
pop. "I'm not that crazy," she said. "I know you don't have any
legs."

She leaned over the bed to snub out the cigarette in the saucer.
Blood rushed, left her body, filled her brain. If she fell, who
would pick her up? She burrowed down under her covers. *I'll
show you something.* She crawled into the cave with Matthew.
They weren't ever coming out. Rain battered the roof until the
ground softened and collapsed around them.

Someone knocked at the door. The Scavenger Lady looking
for money. What had she left this time? A legbone, a skull. *I
think this is yours.* Iona slept. *I don't need it. I don't need anything
now.*

When she woke again, the room was almost dark, her throat

so dry it hurt. But if I drink a Coke, she thought, I'll have to pee; I'll have to leave the room. She was hungry too. Her stomach hurt. Bodies were too much trouble.

She closed her eyes. Hannah cried as Iona lifted the bedpan to slide it under her buttocks. *I'd rather piss the bed.* The doors of her house blew open. Snow drifted into the hallway, filled the silent living room. Angel was still alive; Angel bore another calf that grew to have eight teats and gave forty quarts of milk a day, just like Hannah said. Iona kicked the blanket from the bed and it fell in a heap on the floor. "Let me have my own dreams," she whispered.

The chill was gone. She was hot now. *I almost burned my hand when I touched her.* Sharla tore the sheet away from her naked body. Her legs were streaked with blood. Iona put her hands on her own damp thighs. *I'd rather piss the bed.* She scolded Matthew. *Are you too lazy to step outside and unzip your pants?*

Hannah sat on the edge of the bed to tell her the story of a man cursed to live as a bear by day and a man by night. He had a young man's longing for a beautiful girl, a desire so strong it nearly broke his great bear heart. The witch who'd cursed him said he might be a man again if he could make the girl love him as a bear.

He carried her into the woods and was kind to her, kept her warm against his fur, fed her fish and berries. But she didn't love him. She was afraid of his huge paws and hated his bear smell.

She slept beside him because she was cold and needed him. One night she woke and saw a man, a beautiful man with a red mouth.

She kissed that mouth.

He opened his eyes and wept. *Now there's no chance,* he said.

The sun rose behind the trees. The sky turned pink. Hair grew on his face and back. He couldn't speak.

Why didn't he wait till night, Iona said, to be a man again?

Because he needed the girl to love him just as he was.

Couldn't she learn to love him?

I don't know, Hannah said.

Why not?

He left her there; he walked into the woods, still weeping.

Maybe she found him.

The hunters found him first.

What do you mean?

They shot a bear, Hannah said, and found a man in the snow.

But it was still day.

It is the wounded heart that makes us human in the end.

Everyone she'd ever known was close, crowded in this room.
Hannah cradled the legless baby; Sharla curled on the floor.
Her three brothers found her sock dolls and untied their necks.
Frank stood at the window, his back turned. Matthew pulled
the hair from her mouth.

The air beside her bed thickened and grew darker; the body
of a man kept sliding in and out of focus. Finally Everett lay
down beside her. *I know exactly how you feel,* he said. He rocked
her in his arms. His breath was sweet, like cinnamon. His skin
smelled of almonds. She touched the back of his head. The skull
wasn't shattered. *I'm whole,* he said, pressing himself against her
thighs, *I'm whole.* She let herself fall. Now it was safe to sleep.
Everett would catch her.

Someone had curled inside her head and was using a hammer
to beat his way out. She felt him pound on her temple again
and again, always in the same place. The sound became a light,
a bright crevasse opening in her brain. Everett was gone, and
the smell he'd left behind was sharp as acid.

"Open up." Now the pounding was outside of her and had
a voice she almost recognized. "I've got a key." Iona didn't care.
"I'm coming in." She wondered who needed a key. Last night
her room had been full, and no one used the door, no one asked
before he entered.

The door split. Two shapes filled the entryway, a squat woman, a tall man.

"You've got a visitor," the woman said. She waddled to the bed to stare at Iona. "Jesus H. Christ. She's pissed herself. If she's ruined my mattress it'll be another twenty besides the rent." The one at the door didn't answer. "You've got ten minutes," the woman said, "and you'll keep this door open. I'm making an exception letting you in here at all. I don't like my ladies having male guests, don't allow it, in fact, so don't be getting any wrongheaded ideas." The woman looked at Iona again and muttered, "You are one fine mess."

Iona couldn't understand why the pounding hadn't stopped. It came faster now, not a single blow, not a hammer at all, dozens of tiny hooves, silver flashes behind her eyes. The man sat on the edge of the bed. He was heavier than Everett. Iona felt herself sliding toward him. She was chilled. She thought she remembered being hot, so hot she could barely stand it. That must have been a long time ago. The man picked the blanket off the floor and wrapped it around her. "It's me, baby. It's Eddie." He touched her cheek. "I've got to get you out of here," he said. "But you're going to have to help me. I can't carry you down the stairs—my leg, you know. You'll have to lean on me. Can you do that?" She nodded. "That's my girl," he said. "I'm going to pack your suitcase, then we'll go."

She watched him drift around the room, stooping for the suitcase, opening all the drawers. There wasn't much to pack. "The doll," she said. It seemed very important.

Something dry and brown flaked off her palm. Blood, she thought, and looked for the wound. She remembered the skinny little man, remembered wanting to do it.

Eddie closed the suitcase and came back to the bed. "Can you sit up?" he said. He put his hands beneath her back and lifted her; her neck was weak, a baby's neck, and her heavy head rolled. "Come on," he said, "we just have to get to the car." He swung her feet over the edge of the bed. They looked as if they were touching the floor, but she couldn't feel the wood: everything dropped out from under her. She giggled. The hooves struck harder, and she almost fell.

She moved one foot and then the other. Even her shoes seemed too big. She shuffled like an old woman, like her own mother the last time she got out of bed, put on her slippers and scuffed to the bathroom at the end of the hall. "The suitcase," she said.

"I'll come back for it."

The woman appeared in the doorway. "Your ten minutes are up," she said.

"We're going," the man told her.

"Not until you pay me for the mattress," she said, "and she owes me a week's rent whether she's staying or not."

"I have to come back for the suitcase," he said. "I'll pay you then."

"I'm watching you. Don't think you can sneak out of here. I wrote down your license."

Iona and Eddie stood at the top of the stairs. She tried to see the bottom, but the stairs folded into one another. The harder she tried to focus, the sicker she felt. She closed her eyes.

"One step at a time," he said. "Don't look at the bottom."

Couldn't he see her eyes were closed? "That's good, baby. One more. See? See how easy it is?"

The bones in her legs bowed outward. Any second one was going to snap and she'd roll to the landing and be done with it.

"Five more steps," he said, "that's all."

If she fell, she'd bring him down too.

"My girl," he said, "that's my good girl." She had just walked from her mother's arms to her father's, three baby steps. *My good girl.*

They were passing through a doorway, into light so sharp it sliced through her closed lids, pricking her eyes. She'd be blinded if she opened them, even for a second. *Don't stare at the eclipse,* her father said. *The light will be gone, but it can still burn your eyes.* But she did look. She opened her eyes and saw flares, bursts of yellow and green around the dark circle where the sun had been. She wanted to fall on the ground. She was sorry. She wanted her father to forgive her. When she looked up, she saw his dark silhouette, brilliant flashes exploding behind him. Yes, he was the shadow moving across the sun. Her eyes were burned blind.

"We're almost there," Eddie said.

Now he was lifting her. She smelled the familiar leather of the seat. Daddy's truck. He was putting her in Daddy's truck. He was going to drive her home, and everything would be forgiven. She lay down on the seat and breathed in the sweet animal smell. Daddy's gun was behind the seat, with the hacksaw and the coil of rope, with the calfskin gloves and a small ax, light enough for a child to swing.

She felt dirt in her hair and between her fingers. She tasted it under her tongue and breathed it up her nose, dirt from the potato field. She'd felt the hard clumps of earth raining against her chest; now she sank deep in the ground, drifting in the dark, a room with soft walls and no doors. She was becoming a child again. She was no longer a young woman. She was only a girl, her ten-year-old self, shrinking still, becoming seven, six. She clutched the legless doll beside her and was afraid: she was almost that size. *She was so small,* Hannah said. *Why did you have to bury her?* She didn't mean Iona; she meant the other one. *She should have disappeared inside my body.* Now she was smaller than the doll, the girl child born too soon, Hannah's first and best-loved daughter. The doll rolled toward her, its wild eye spinning, its legless body tumbling into the hole, pulling clots of dirt behind it.

She woke, knotted in a sheet, arms pinned to her sides. The blankets smelled of wool and mothballs. A voice said, "You've been dreaming—but the fever broke a few hours ago." Iona realized the sheets were clammy. "You've got to drink something. You've lost a lot of fluid." A woman put her hand on Iona's forehead. "I'll make tea."

"Please," Iona said, "unwrap me." The woman pulled the blankets down, tugged the twisted sheet free. "Who are you?" Iona said.

"It's me," the woman said, "don't you remember old Pearl, Eddie's mama?"

Eddie, yes, Eddie came to her room and made her climb down the stairs. Eddie talked too much and had leather seats in his car.

The tea Pearl brought tasted foul, worse than the dirt in her mouth, and Iona wanted to spit it back in the cup, but the woman was so kind, holding her head up so she could drink, raising the cup to her dry lips. "All of it," Pearl said, "one sip and then another. It goes down."

"It's awful," Iona whispered.

"I know."

"But I have to drink it?"

"It will make you well."

Pearl came with her tea again and again. Sometimes only a few seconds passed between visits, and sometimes days. Once Iona woke to find Eddie lying beside her. He was not just the man called Eddie; he was someone she knew. He kissed her face, but they didn't talk. When she woke again, he was gone. Dogs barked in the yard. Coyotes howled in the hills. She slept and Hannah died.

Days began to form in the square of window, a swell of light rising and sinking, the safe dark spreading across the sky, then the light again, thin and pink on the horizon, predictable and painful, almost insistent, a voice that called her back from the edge, demanding ordinary things, instructing her to eat and piss and speak, to walk to the kitchen when she wanted a glass of water.

Once Eddie sat on her bed and told her the weather had turned in Seattle, that it was spring in December, not warm exactly, but warm enough for grass to come up green and flowers to bud. "It's not right," he said. "Everything will freeze."

She thought of Idaho in winter, white and black, forever and ever, white sky and white ground, black birds and black trees in the distance, slow river running, the color of slate, the shadows of trees wavering on the surface, the river freezing white. She depended on this.

She began to count the days, to mark them in her mind. She waited for Eddie's visits. On the tenth day, Eddie's brother came instead. Joey played blackjack with Mama Pearl while Iona sat on the couch and watched the old woman cheat. Outside, the wind whipped the water into the rocks of the seawall, rippled the tall grass so it moved like waves, carried the smell of kelp and dead fish across the field; the mindless wind beat at the little house and rattled windows till Iona could hear nothing else. Still Pearl and Joey slapped their cards on the table, laughed in pantomime, spoke without voices, as if nothing were happening, as if they weren't afraid that the house would rise off the ground and spin away.

Later, Pearl went to the store. The wind died. Joey sat beside Iona. He put his arm around her. He said, "You're still sweet on my brother, aren't you?" He nuzzled her neck, nipped her ear. "You're wasting your time," he whispered.

And she answered, "So are you."

That night Eddie came and lay on the bed beside her. They both stared at the blank ceiling. It was dusk. The plaster looked gray and fuzzy, no longer solid, turning to sand, turning to dust, falling on their faces, a dry rain, falling forever, covering their bodies, burying them on this bed. Eddie kissed her eyelids, pressed her hand to his face and kissed her palm. He asked her what she wanted, and she only knew that she didn't want to be like him, running from one thing to another, his bird heart racing.

"I have to go home," she said. "I have to finish something."

She lay still as driftwood on a beach, her porous limbs bleached by years of sun. She knew this was the last time she'd lie in the hollow of Eddie's arms. The tide flowed toward her, to wash her away a second time.

Eddie stayed, but he didn't take off his clothes. Iona thought of his scarred stump, the bright ruby flesh. She imagined touching it with her fingertips, and Eddie saying, "I feel my foot—it's warm."

Sorrow came in soft waves. She saw that the smallest sacrifices were the ones that drowned you in the end. She had never imagined a life of joy together, but she expected to see him one more time, standing by his car, waiting for her in the rain. This was the loss that buckled her, the image of Eddie's face, his hair long again, wet around his shoulders. This was the absence she could not bear.

She knew the exact moment when he slipped away in the dark. She pretended to sleep, understanding he could never leave if he thought she was awake.

In the morning, the doll sat in the chair, eyes wide open, T-shirt untied. Iona's money was gone, and there was a note: *I'll find you a good car to get you home.*

That was all.

19

    The three little girls pranced around Jay Tyler, touched his hand, his sleeve. He had the bottle tucked under his jacket, and they grabbed for it. They had violet lips and green eyelids. They looked ghoulish under the yellow street-lights and weren't really so little, but Jay thought of them that way because he felt so far beyond them, decades older, living in another country.

They ran away as soon as they had what they wanted, the pint of brandy to mix with their soda. He'd only made two bucks buying their booze for them. Next time he'd charge them double. Business, after all. And there was some risk involved.

He'd bought a pint for them last Saturday, and they were waiting for him this week, sitting in the parking lot of Marty's Liquor—Tina and Dory and Kim, blowing on their hands to keep warm. That first night he limped away and heard one girl say, "He gives me the creeps."

"How old is he anyway?" This voice was higher.

"Eighteen." That was Kim, Kim Beller, who was nothing like her sister, Belinda.

"Bullshit."

"My sister knew him." Past tense. No one still knew Jay Tyler.

They'd flirted in the beginning. *I'm Dory, I'm Tina, I'm Kim,* smiling, pulling their hands through their long hair so he'd notice and want to do the same. *We forgot our I.D.'s.* He nodded. *Do you mind?* Kim took care of the negotiations. She was tall and slender, her jeans so tight she must have put them on wet and let them dry to fit her shape and no other. She had a nice butt, high and round, a little too big, perhaps, considering how slim she was; maybe her fine ass would be her undoing when she was older and heavier, flabby instead of fit, but right now her bum was perfect and she knew it. She was leaning against the car, backside turned toward him when Jay returned. *Keep the change.* That's what she'd said. Tip for the errand boy. Three dollars that night and only two tonight. He was slipping. Next week he'd make new rules. Next week he'd tell them: *Stay in the car.* He didn't want them twittering and tugging, didn't want to see Kim's long legs or Tina's little white hands. He didn't want Dory to stare at him with those wide dark eyes. Maybe he'd tell them to forget it. He'd say, "Listen, I can't take the risk. My I.D.'s a fake." They'd laugh. *Who'd card an old cripple like you?* He didn't need the money, so why bother? *He gives me the creeps.* Little bitches. He'd like to really give them the creeps. He thought of them parked out on the Flats, some deserted road, half-moon reflecting on snow the only light for miles except the distant glow of farmhouse windows. He contemplated following the girls, headlights off. He knew their stories, how terror brought delight when it didn't press too close. But he meant to press close. Very.

He imagined them this way: Kim telling the one about the man with a hook for a hand. He came after pretty girls, just like them, threatened to put the hook through their throats if they didn't do exactly what he said. Kim swore she knew some girls he'd almost caught. They were on this very road, telling this story—a mirror reflects a mirror endlessly. They got scared and drove away, those girls in the past. Kim said, "When they got home they found his hook hand hanging from the door handle. He was that close."

The girls all saw the same image, a man on his knees in the snow, howling in the night with the pain of the bloody stump and the anguish of thwarted desire.

Tina locked the doors and peered across the white fields. Dory saw a dark shape rolling into the ditch. They pleaded. "Let's go." Kim took a long pull of brandy straight from the bottle. "Please." Jay could see her now, head tilted back, golden hair frosted white at the tips, bristling like fur. *Sissies*. And just as she said it, he'd put his face to her window, smash his nose and mouth and cheeks flat so she wouldn't know him. He'd shatter the glass with a rock, unlock the door, drag the girl out of the car, pull her kicking and screaming into the snow.

Of course he wasn't really going to do this—even as a joke. It took far more energy than he had. And what did he care about three giggling girls—what did he care that they reached inside his coat, trying to grab the bottle with their cold hands? *I'm Dory, I'm Tina, I'm Kim*. Cheerleaders. *Keep the change*. Old man, that's what they thought. Pathetic cripple. *Creep*. Men with canes, men with metal plates in their heads or hooks for hands; men with knots of scars on their backs, bits of shrapnel forever surfacing, leaving spots of blood on their shirts: the maimed have nothing left to lose, he thought, and are always dangerous.

He was ready for them the next time. He'd bought the brandy and was sitting in his car, patiently, so they had to come to him. He cracked his window, said, "Get in." When he saw them hesitate, he started the engine—so they'd see he didn't give a damn. Kim knocked on his window and got into the back seat.

"Ten," he said.

"Ten what?"

"Dollars."

"Cost you four," she said.

"Right."

She dug in her pocket. "I've got eight."

"Ask your friends."

Dory and Tina had backed away from the car. Kim opened

her window and called to them. "I need two bucks," she said. They squeezed their fingers down the pockets of their tight jeans, pulled out quarters and dimes, seven pennies. Kim counted in the backseat. "Nine-thirty-seven," she said. "That's it."

He pretended to consider this offer. "Too bad," he said.

"Please," she said, wheedling. He looked at her in his rearview mirror. He hated whiners and didn't give a shit about her nice ass. "Please, Jay," she whispered, her voice suddenly soft. She had never said his name before. A hole opened in his chest, as if her voice carved his body, as if her small hand tore muscle from bone. His head throbbed with the strain of holding back tears. *Please, Jay.* Muriel's voice this time. *I can't.* But they did anyway. He passed the pint to the girl in the back seat, took the wad of bills and coins and turned quickly so she wouldn't guess what she'd done. He wanted to say, "Don't look for me next week," but he was afraid his voice would break if he tried to speak.

Kim slammed the door. She looped her arms through her friends' arms. "He's an asshole," she said, loud enough for him to hear. The girls ran toward their car, skidding and squealing across the icy pavement.

Willy saw the dark Chrysler careening across the bridge around midnight. Horton had been on his case all week: *You haven't written a ticket in ten days.* Now it was sixteen days. He couldn't believe his luck. Bad, that is. How could he arrest Delores? He couldn't just write a ticket and let her drive home. Not in her condition. She'd do a U-turn and jump the rail, go flying into the frigid Snake. How could he explain? He hadn't seen her since that day in South Bend. Sixteen days. A coincidence. And hadn't called, either. He hoped she understood but knew she didn't. In a way he was relieved to catch her this way. It restored order: she was drunk; he was a policeman.

He hit the siren and set the blue light flashing. She punched the gas and surged ahead of him, speeding toward the Flats.

He hadn't expected this, had imagined instead that Delores Tyler would pull over carefully, sorry and contrite, that she'd climb in the back of his cruiser without any trouble.

The road was slick, puddles frozen in the ruts. He chased her for a mile or more until they were alone on a black road.

She stopped. So this was the point of it all, to be alone. The door opened—not Delores. He'd never considered this. Jay headed toward the cruiser, limping but powerful.

Willy got out too. "You crazy sonuvabitch—you could have gotten us both killed."

Jay didn't answer and kept coming. Willy thought he might have to take a swing to make him stop, but he couldn't imagine hitting a man with a cane. What would Horton do? No words of wisdom came to mind.

"Motherfucker," Jay said.

Willy's face felt hot despite the cold. *Motherfucker*. He heard the kid in the alley, saw the crushed jack-o'-lantern, knew the simple truth. *Motherfucker*.

Jay leaped before Willy had a chance to brace himself. Both of them went down, and Jay pinned Willy to the road. Willy remembered wrestling in the grass, how good it felt, nothing like this, a hot summer day, their bodies slippery with sweat, wearing cut-offs and nothing else, moving against each other like fish. Jay wasn't playing now. His elbow hit the center of Willy's chest, a soft spot that took Willy's breath and left him stunned.

Jay kept pressing. He leaned close and Willy saw his face, every muscle tensed, jaw clenched tight forever, tendons popping in his neck. He smelled Jay, bitter, not just his breath but his skin, a burned smell that made Willy taste hot metal. He thought of Horton: *When you catch a whiff of that, you better have your hand on your gun.* But Jay's knees dug into Willy's arms, held them to the ground. He wanted to tell his father: *If you're close enough to smell a man, it's already too late.*

"Buddy," Willy whispered, "it's me."

"Goddamn right," Jay said. "I fucking know it's you."

Willy twisted, arched his back. Jay smacked his chin and rolled off him, grabbing the cane he'd dropped in the snow. Willy took one breath. He thought it was over now, but the quick pain blinded him and a brilliant yellow pool spread in front of his eyes like blood. If he'd had any air he would have screamed, and the cry would have carried across the fields to a girl's house on the Kila Flats, up the tracks to a burned shed, across the river to his mother's house, along the tree-lined streets to Delores. She would see them, clearly and without doubt, her lover lying in the snow clutching his balls, her son crumpled to his knees beside him.

The yellow pool bled thin enough for Willy to see sky, but the clouds looked yellow too. Snow melted beneath his back. Snow melted under Jay's knees.

"Fucking cop," Jay muttered. "Whatever happened to your god-damn sense of duty?"

Those were his last words on the road, and he remembered them now, just a week later, when he realized he needed Willy Hamilton. He was a policeman, after all. This was his job. Jay didn't want to make it official by filing a report with Fred Pierce or Horton Hamilton. He didn't want half the town out looking for his mother, waving their flashlights in the woods, shouting her name in the dark. Besides, she'd left the house at noon and it was only eight. She wasn't a missing person for another sixteen hours—just an absent mother. *A woman needs some privacy once in a while,* that's what Pierce would say, implying Delores was shacked up with her lover for the night and Jay Tyler was a fool.

Jay didn't have to explain much to Willy. He told him his father was in Boise again and that Delores had been out all day. He said some pills were missing, and Willy said he'd be right over. Willy remembered how Jay felt about Everett Fry: *Why'd he have to make such a mess?* Jay thought Everett should have jumped off the bridge or swallowed a handful of barbiturates, done it clean and fast, so no one else would have to get down on her knees to wash the tiles. Even then he was more worried about Everett's mother than he was about the son who'd died.

, Jay was waiting at the curb when Willy came by the house. Willy thought of Delores waiting for him three weeks ago, just this way. "What kind of pills?" Willy said as Jay got in the car.

"I don't know. Sleeping pills."

"How many?"

"How could I count them if they're gone?"

They headed out the River Road, toward the bridge. "I know how you are," Jay said. "You'll want to blame yourself. But you're an arrogant bastard if you think one roll with you could make a woman miserable enough to do this."

Willy nodded. Jay was right. He did want to blame himself. He was an arrogant bastard.

The Chrysler wasn't parked on the bridge. Jay told Willy to stop and got out of the car to look at the water. Snow on the bridge had frozen to a hard crust. The moon was bright, three-quarters full, and the crescent left in shadow cupped the fuller part, a dark hand holding the yellow head in the sky. Jay peered down at the black water and stony bank. He thought of the story Muriel had told him, of the sisters Mary and Martha, how angry they were when Jesus finally appeared, how they each said to him: "If you had come sooner, Lord, my brother would have lived."

He called her name, and it bounced off the water: *Delores*. "But Jesus wasn't too late," Muriel said, "and he led Lazarus from the tomb, though he'd been dead four days."

Jay used the loud voice of a man, but inside a child cried: *Where are you?* This child was lost in his own house. There were so many rooms. He went from one to another, opening closets, peeking under beds, as if this was a game. But he wasn't having fun. He felt that frustration now, the panic in his chest as he ran up and down the stairs. His legs were short and tired. He was four years old.

"Where to?" Willy said when Jay got back in the car.

"To that place where we always parked."

As much as Willy wanted to find Delores, he hoped she'd gone somewhere else. Maybe he was an arrogant bastard to imagine he had anything to do with her unhappiness, but it would be hard not to blame himself if this was the place she'd chosen.

Jay and Willy both thought of the woman who'd jumped from the bridge and was saved. They saw her red coat billow around her, a small parachute slowing her fall, a preserver that kept her afloat when she hit the water. They saw her blue lips when the men pulled her from the river. They saw her breathless body and knew that she was dead in this moment. But the man struck her chest. Water spurted from her mouth. He pressed again with both hands until she sputtered and gagged. He breathed into her, covered her nose and mouth with his mouth, called her back with his own breath, gave her his own life. *Damn you.* Her words of gratitude, the only ones the curious boys heard. She moved away a month later, left her husband and five kids in their trailer. Jay wondered if she was thankful in the end, if leaving her troubles was better than leaving her life, or if her problems followed her to every little room, if one night she leaped from a window instead of a bridge, to cement instead of water. He wondered if Lazarus lived long and joyfully, or if he grew sick and bitter, if he cursed the Lord and wished there had been no miracle.

There was one car parked by the river. Willy thought the Pinto with the fogged windows belonged to Twyla Catts. He hit the car with his high beams but no heads appeared. They were down on the seat for sure, eyes screwed shut, bodies locked. If a flood swept their car into the river the divers would find them this way: arms clutching, legs entwined, hair tangled together. Willy laid on his horn, and Jay grabbed his wrist. "Save it," he said.

"Any other ideas?" Willy said when they were back on the road.

"Just drive west for a while."

Every time they rounded a curve, Willy expected to see the Chrysler hunkered on the shoulder. Maybe she'd slid into the ditch and had been out cold for hours. She might wake at any moment, confused and afraid. He imagined her running on the road, her blond hair blowing. He drove slowly so he could stop in time.

Jay said, "I'm sorry about the other night."

And Willy said, "Forget it."

"Lost my head."

"I deserved it."

"Maybe," said Jay, "but not from me."

"She's your mother."

"I haven't treated her so well myself."

They were halfway to South Bend and had only seen two cars coming toward them on the narrow road. Each time they thought it must be her, heading home. But the cars were unfamiliar, driven by strangers who didn't know how cruel they were to drive this road, to give boys hope and snatch it back.

"This is stupid," Jay said. "We won't find her this way. Maybe the pills rolled under the bed—why should she off herself when she can just leave?"

But they both knew she didn't have the courage for that: running away meant making a new life. "Let's check the bars," Willy said.

"Yeah, why not."

They stopped at the White Bull and River's End on Main, but no one had seen her. As they veered east, Willy suddenly felt certain they'd find her at the Roadstop, drunken Delores about to fall off her barstool, leaning up against any guy who happened to sit beside her. They'd scold her and take her home.

They'd laugh in the car, pretending they weren't that scared.

But the Chrysler wasn't in the lot. "She's not here," Jay said.

They drove to the bridge again but crossed it this time and headed toward the Flats. Willy slowed as they passed the cluster of trailers. The stuffed man with the pumpkin head still sat guard, but the head had rotted and begun to shrivel, sinking into the shoulders.

Jay said, "Take me home. I think she's at home." Willy saw that Jay's cheeks were wet.

"It's not your fault," Willy said. He thought it was important to say this now, before they found her. Jay nodded. "If she's not there, I'm going to call my father."

"She is," Jay whispered. "She is." He saw her, curled in the basement. That's where he'd found her the other time, wedged in a dark corner under the cellar stairs; he poked at her with his small hands, but she didn't wake.

The memory of the sirens was so close he had to cover his ears. He was sure he'd find her in exactly the same place. Maybe she'd been there all along. Maybe she'd driven the car away to fool him and had sneaked back later, like a thief in her husband's house, tiptoeing down the stairs to steal her own life. Her name welled in his chest; the sound of it filled his whole body.

The Chrysler was in the drive. Someone had turned on the porch light. Willy followed Jay, up the walk and into the entryway. At the end of the hall, light burst from the kitchen.

She sat at the table, hair loose at her shoulders, just as Willy had imagined, hours before on the River Road. She wore an oversized cardigan and hugged herself to hold it wrapped around her.

Jay stood in the doorway, eyes filling with shame and gratitude. Willy peered over his shoulder.

"I'm drunk," she said.

"I was afraid," Jay whispered.

Delores heard those words at last, the ones Andrew could not say at the river. "I didn't have the guts," she said.

"We've been looking for you all night." He gestured toward the doorway with his head. Willy backed into the shadows of the hall. He saw mother and son through a haze, as if a veil had fallen in front of him, and he couldn't find the place where it parted to let him in. He realized she had spared three lives tonight, that he and Jay had been saved, pulled from the freezing river at the last moment.

He hurried toward the door, his own footsteps so loud they frightened him. He glanced back as he stepped outside. The house was quiet, but the light burned in the kitchen, fierce and steady.

20

Eddie found Iona a 1966 Plymouth Valiant for two hundred. "Takes a long time to warm up," he said, "and it idles too fast." The passenger side had been rammed and never repaired. Now rust bloomed where the metal creased. "Don't open those doors," he told her. "Tank's full and tires are good. She's no beauty, but she'll get you home."

Iona packed her suitcase. She was leaving with the same things she'd brought: poncho and denim jacket, three pairs of jeans and two sweatshirts, four tops and a pile of underwear. She took the red shirt off the legless doll and hid the wild-eyed baby in the closet. It felt right, somehow, to travel so lightly, to forget towels and sheets, spoon and bowl, to abandon the hard plastic doll.

Firs stood stark and black on mountain slopes as she crossed the Cascades. She felt small, alone in her car and unbearably human.

Snow fell on the rolling hills as she drove south and east. Snow fell on solitary farmhouses. The earth was white; the houses were white; Iona's hands on the wheel, white. The road was gray and long, a ribbon of memory unfurling one blank mile at a time. She saw a house, barn, toolshed, chicken coop— a clump of trees, an endless field of dark ground pocked with snow. She saw a man walking in the distance. He carried a shovel over one shoulder. His gait was slow, uneven, his head bare.

The heater in the Valiant blasted warm air in her face, but her feet were cold. She imagined standing on her father's porch, knocking on her father's door. It would be rude to go to the back door, to enter the familiar kitchen—now she was a guest, almost a stranger—so she would wait at the front until someone answered, until someone said: *Come in.* Through all the open doorways she saw her mother at the sink, back curved, arms weary. She spoke her mother's name, and Hannah turned but did not answer.

She had counted out sixty-two dollars plus three dollars interest. It was right there in the pocket of her jacket, the left one over her chest. If Frank asked about the money that was missing the morning she disappeared, Iona could put the bills in his hand and be done with it.

She knew how Leon would look at her, from feet to head, then back to her belly. He'd wonder what had brought her home. She was too skinny to be pregnant. Rafe and Dale wouldn't care about her reasons as long as she cooked biscuits and eggs in the morning, as long as she milked the cows and scoured the tub.

How could she explain? *I haven't come back for that.*

Her heart was fragile as ice on the river in late spring, so thin a pebble thrown by a careless boy could shatter it. She was glad for the cold outside, glad to be alone, away from the water, traveling on the hard ground of winter.

Snow fell, light and dry, on the backs of cows in the fields. Wind whipped white swirls across the road and dropped them in shallow ditches. Snow fell over the Cascades behind her and across the Rockies beyond her vision. Snow fell on an unmarked grave at the edge of a potato field and on the blue lids of her mother's eyes.

When Iona reached South Bend, she knew she'd meant to stop here all along. She was scared now, imagining how she might find Matthew, strapped in a chair at the window, drugged and docile, his hair shaved close to the scalp, eyes milky, spittle at the corner of his mouth and down his chin.

Too late to see him tonight—no visitors allowed after dark, she thought; everything's safer in the light. She checked into the South Bend Hotel. She was just going to lie down for a minute, rest, then go out again, get something to eat. But as soon as she closed her eyes, her brothers came to the foot of her bed. They were smiling, all three of them in a row, waiting for her to wake. They raised their arms and she saw that their hands were gone, cut off at the wrists. No blood spurted from the stumps. These were old wounds.

She jerked up in bed and flicked on the lamp. She was alone. The hotel was quiet. If she opened the door, she knew no one would be standing in the hall outside her door.

She lay back down but left the light on. The pillow smelled of someone else, faint oil from a man's hair. She remembered now. Rafe and Dale made gifts at school, pressed their hands into wet plaster, pressed so hard every line of their palms was revealed; and when the white clay dried, each finger's imprint, each fingertip's unique whorl was rendered distinct and unmistakable. Hannah hid the plaques in a drawer. *Nice present for a woman who lives in town,* she said. They reminded her: one brother's hand mangled by the thrasher, the other brother's fingers black at the root, blown off, a firecracker held too long. Plaster spilled blood in the brain. Iona made a cast of her hand too. Everyone did. But she didn't bring it home. She smashed it on the road and kicked the pieces into the gutter.

Now she thought her mother was wrong. It was not a bad thing to remember the lost limbs of mutilated boys. She hoped that somewhere, a long time ago, Eddie Birdheart had found a sidewalk smeared with soft cement. She hoped he had taken off his shoes and walked across it, leaving behind the perfect prints of his two bare feet.

Just before dawn, Iona's father came to her and stood in the doorway. He was black with mud: hands and face, boots and hair—his whole body dripping, only a ring around each eye wiped clean. All afternoon he'd been in the field, trying to pull Belle from a sinkhole. He'd tied ropes and chains, had gotten her to the brink twice but lost her again both times. *Belle, my beauty.* She was the cow he'd named himself: *because she's the most beautiful and knows it.* When Iona saw him look at Belle's sad face, she thought he loved the animal more than he loved her. Now he stared at Iona but didn't see. Now he said: *Get me my gun.*

"That boy's long gone," the woman at the desk told Iona the next morning. A little white hat perched on her head like a child's paper crown.

"What do you mean?" Iona said.

"Just what I said." The woman pushed her glasses up her nose with her middle finger.

"He was released?"

"Not exactly."

"Tell me," Iona said, "*exactly.*"

"All information on our patients is confidential."

"I'm his sister."

The woman gave herself a push and her chair rolled backward toward the file cabinet. She wore white shoes and heavy white stockings. Her legs were thick, shapeless as sausages in pale casings. She stood to open the top drawer: A–F. The key was on a chain around her neck, and she didn't take it off, she only bent over to free the lock. The tiny crown never moved.

Iona wondered if Matt was well and strong, gaining weight and speaking in full sentences. *Not exactly.* She wondered if they'd sent him somewhere else, a place for wild boys who needed separate rooms with padded walls, a place where you could scream all day and not be heard.

The woman pulled a folder from the drawer, leafed through the thin file, then slid it back in place and closed the cabinet.

The lock clicked, a final sound, and the woman dropped heavily into her chair, wheels squeaking as she scooted across the floor. She peered down at her desk and started making tiny red *x*'s in the squares of a chart. "What's his middle name?" she said.

"Delancey."

"Yes." The woman looked up and nodded. "That's right. That's very good. But Matthew Delancey Fry doesn't have a sister." She went back to her charts. "One brother—deceased."

"Please—I need to know where he is."

"Confidential." The woman kept making *x*'s.

"I'm his only friend."

"He's gone. Climbed the fence and walked away. But you didn't hear it from me."

"Where'd he go?"

"Look, I don't know and I don't care. You're his friend. You tell us."

Iona walked toward the river and stood on a cliff overlooking the dam. Ice jutted from the shore. She was his friend, but she didn't know where he'd go. The roof of the cave collapsed, the shed burned to the ground, the basement windows were boarded shut. She hoped he really was free this time, and hated herself for what she knew that meant.

Sometimes she wished she were as brave as Matthew. She saw him gun the engine and plunge his mother's Buick into the Snake. The windows were rolled up tight; the boy in the bubble howled with laughter. He had time to decide: *Do I want to die?* The car floated for a moment, hung in the water, then sank, nose first, the weight of the motor pulling it down to the bottom. Matt saw the riverbed, churning water, jagged rocks, jagged teeth in his brother's mouth. He stayed calm, rolled down the window an inch at a time, let the water pour in slowly, so there was no fierce wave to drown him, no rush of current to toss him senseless. When the window was down and the car full of water, he simply swam away.

Iona imagined his face and hands, his naked feet, pale and bright as the crescents of little moons in the dark water. *What have you done with your shoes, you little shit?* His mother slapped him, as if the shoes were the most important thing, more valuable than her car, more precious than a boy's life.

Perhaps he'd thrown himself in the river without a car this time. You can always stop the pain if you're willing to make the jump. Now he was trapped beneath the ice near the bank. He'd rise up with the first thaw, bloated and blue.

What else would this river give up in the spring? She saw the skinny yellow cat with its spiked fur, bobbing among beer cans and used condoms. She saw a dog with a bony white head, paddling upstream, exhausted, afraid. She was seven years old. His head went under and came up again, his eyes dark and terrified as her own eyes in the mirror hours later. The dog disappeared a second time and never broke the surface again. *A stray,* Hannah said, *don't waste your tears.* She wiped Iona's face with the corner of her green apron. The cloth was rough and smelled of the fish her brothers had caught and her mother had gutted.

Iona stared at the ice. She saw dark shapes forming beneath the surface, the shadows of clouds moving across the sky, the vague outlines of drowned animals.

21

Jay Tyler made himself walk, hobble, that was more the truth, though he hated the word, that image of himself. He remembered a child's riddle: What walks on four legs in its youth, two when grown, three when old? Now he knew the simple answer. He banged his cane into the cement—he'd just gotten to the last stage faster than most.

A week ago he'd seen Matt Fry scuffling across the bridge, miles from home. Jay was driving that day, and he pulled over, said: "Hop in—it's cold." Matt kept moving. He was thicker than Jay remembered, still thin but no longer frail—a grown man. "It's on my way," Jay said, which was true, since neither one of them seemed to be going anywhere in particular. But Matthew didn't answer, didn't even nod.

Now Jay limped from one end of town to the other, till every muscle ached, till his bones hummed like tuning forks struck hard, ringing through his body. Sometimes he stole Darvocet from Delores when he got home, to numb the pain, and sometimes he stayed awake with it, to feel the throbbing, to know his body again.

This morning was raw and clear, the gusts on the bridge fierce as they whipped down the canyon of the Snake. He saw how people looked at him, quickly and with disgust, as he himself had looked at Matt Fry. His denim jacket was flannel-lined, not nearly warm enough. Even so, the armpits of his T-shirt would be ringed with sweat when he got home. His jeans hung loose in the butt. He no longer bothered with underwear, and the wind seared through the cloth, shriveled him—that was the part no one saw, his only secret. He wore fingerless gloves, like a beggar, a wool watch cap, sneakers, two pairs of socks. When he got home his toes would be stiff and cold, bright red. His hair stuck out from under his cap, long light hair, not just blond, streaked with gray now, already, old man.

Cars buzzed past him, swerved close enough for him to feel the rush of air pushing him toward the rail of the bridge. Day after day, he imagined himself falling—but, didn't fall—kept walking instead, growing stronger, hoping to be muscular and lean, his old self, though he knew that was impossible, that he might be strong enough, in time, but he would never again approach his former elegance, never shoot toward the water, limbs perfectly aligned.

The little girls reminded him—Dory, Kim, Tina, dark eyes, honey hair, little hands—they drove past on Main Street, big in their car and safe. They honked to scare him because they were afraid. People moved out of his way as he lunged down the sidewalk. He took up more than his share of space, wild man with a stick, so women cringed against buildings, averting their gazes, clutching children to their thighs.

Sometimes he saw Willy Hamilton rolling past him in the cruiser. He thought he caught Willy looking in his rearview mirror, not once but many times, even blocks away, when Jay would be small as a broken toy in the distance.

He knew he looked mean, lurching along the street—eyes narrowed, teeth clenched, stick jabbing. When the women cowered, he wanted to whack them with his cane, to give them what they expected. But he longed for one to speak to him, to look at him as she would look at any other man, with kindness. He wished to be among the living, to pass close enough to the bodies of others to feel their warmth. Where shoulders rubbed or thighs brushed some small part of him might be healed, some tiny bit of rage might drop away. He was startled by the way he understood Matt Fry—clever Jay, who was going to college; pretty Jay, loved by the girls for his beauty; graceful Jay, who could spin toward water and fill the crowd with awe—how had he fallen so far? He remembered Iona Moon, what he'd heard about her and Matt when they were kids, and he wondered if she might be merciful enough to lie down with him too.

Cold wind in his face made him think of his mother. The pity he felt for himself tangled with the pity he felt for her, inseparable, twisted tight. She'd told him her river story that night in the kitchen after he and Willy had imagined her dead. She told him how she swam away and his father ran down the shore. Jay's memory of this came from the body, not the brain; he felt himself pressed against his father, smelled the bitter odor of fear, tasted salt sweat. He felt the terrible heat and the damp matted hair of his father's chest.

Seeing how they shared sorrow made Jay feel less alone for a moment but more afraid. She was just a woman, a person like himself; not a mother, just sweet Delores, who was once a girl waltzing with her father, dancing on his toes, a child who wanted life to be that simple and that good always, who was amazed by the disappointments of her life, how numerous they were, how small. He stood on the bridge, looking down at the water, and realized he was amazed too.

He thought of the prehistoric flood, Lake Bonneville ripping open this canyon of river, leaving behind giant boulders, cutting sheer walls that dropped sixty feet or more, five stories—you might as well leap to cement as hit water from that height. But there were cliffs he'd climbed to jump into the swift river. He remembered clambering up the hillside, the dry grass scorched by sun, so hard it sliced his feet. Swallows had built their nests in the shadows all along the canyon walls, mounds of mud and tiny stones, little pebble caves. Eagles soared with the updraft.

Downriver, he knew he would find the fish hatcheries, trout

268 / Melanie Rae Thon

farms; at feeding time, fish churned the water, whirled it into a frenzy, and he thought of that whenever he jumped, what it would be like to swim among them, thousands of trout, to hit water thick with fish and feel their bodies everywhere rubbing against him in the dark river.

He had a vision of himself, now, flying off the cliffs again, his body lithe and straight, never broken. He wanted to soar, wanted to leap and spin into the green water, to be sucked down toward the sharp hidden rocks, dragged underwater, spit up downstream. You had to swim at an angle, yes, just like Delores had said, at an angle against the current, steady but strong, toward the bank, toward the place where you could clutch the rushes and pull yourself to the safe shore.

His chest ached from breathing so hard in the cold; his right knee had turned rubbery, and he had to lock his left to keep from slipping on the ice. He had gotten himself too far from home.

It was noon, and White Falls was only thirty-two miles away. Iona Moon had plenty of time, too much time, and she wondered why she was trying to go home at all. Perhaps all her brothers would be in Missoula, working at the pulp mill for the winter, and she'd find her father in the house alone. She imagined knocking, then saw that the door in her mind was unlocked, open a crack—her slightest touch opened it more. She called their names, but no one came and no one answered. In each bedroom she found the bed neatly made, the white curtains washed. Who had dusted these dressers—mopped these floors—who had folded the clothes so neatly and put them all away? A Bible lay on the nightstand in her father's room. She wanted to go inside and see the last words he had read but was afraid he'd find her here, sitting on his bed, holding his book. She opened her mother's room last. The chair sat close to the bed— her chair, just as she'd left it. Leon's carvings stood in a line on the dresser: little bear, little bird, perfect man, little woman. But the bed was stripped, the closet empty. She went to the window, saw her father below her, walking from the barn to the house. She ran down the stairs to greet him, and they stood in the kitchen, face to face. His sleeves were pushed up around his elbows; blood streaked his hands and arms. He had just delivered a calf. "Where were you?" he said at last. Then he turned to the sink to wash himself.

She crossed the bridge to Route 2, where the trailer homes clustered in the park. She thought of the girls she'd known in high school who might have married already and moved here, believing they'd found freedom. But babies came fast in tin houses. Each year a trailer grew tighter until it felt like a can of people, all lying on top of one another, smothering in the dark.

She made a U-turn back toward town. The buildings seemed shrunken, with flat roofs and small windows. There was one new sign on an old store: TATTOOS. She wondered how business was. She cruised out to the Roadstop Bar. Maybe she'd go shoot pool tonight, throw darts and drink beer. She saw herself laughing, head thrown back, one hand on her hip, cue stick tapping the floor while the jukebox moaned and a man confessed that he'd shot his baby by the river. She might talk to some boy who knew her by reputation, one of those older boys who had noticed her long ago but had never actually spoken to her until this night when he challenged her to a game of pool. Later, they'd go out to her car for an hour or two. She wished she had the blanket from Mrs. Hagestead's. When the boy was gone she'd wrap it around herself and go to sleep. She'd have a dream and forget.

She passed Woolworth's and the hardware store, the Mercantile and the White Bull. She saw the Park Inn, a bright yellow shack covered with white signs, the entire menu printed outside: fried shrimp, cinnamon rolls, burger deluxe. She hadn't eaten since yesterday morning. She wanted to sit down with

Eddie and eat a stack of pancakes, five high, a side of sausage, endless cups of coffee thick with cream. She wanted to hear him say: *You don't look like you could eat half that*. Then they'd be at the beginning, and everything could start again. But she knew there was no point—because it would always end exactly the same way.

She drove out Willow Glen Road and finally stopped in front of Jay Tyler's house. There were no footprints in the snow of his rose garden. She longed to touch his scarred legs and say: *Now I understand*. She wanted to tell him about Eddie, to explain the difference between grief and self-pity: the first makes you sad and strong, the second leaves you bitter. She wanted to say she hadn't forgotten his body, that one lover did not erase another, that no matter how much he thought he had changed, his bones were still his bones, his blood his only, and if she touched him blind, she would know him even now, the unmistakable curve of his shoulders, the exact length of his arms.

She headed back to the numbered streets. Every yard had a fence. What were people trying to keep out? The most dangerous thing in this town was drifting snow. On Seventh, she expected to see Willy's sky-blue Chevy, but instead there were two cruisers in the drive, and she knew what he'd done. *Poor Willy, you could have spared us both that night last June, and Matt too, if only you hadn't taken us to the tracks*. She knew he meant to pay for this mistake the rest of his life; he'd chase down reckless drivers and rescue children lost in the woods, find old ladies who ran away from the Lutheran Home, pull despondent drunks off the bridge—he'd save them all, but not her, and not himself.

She kept driving. There was only one place she could go, one refuge in this whole town.

"Jesus," Sharla Wilder said when she opened the door. "I thought you were gone for good, Iona." She wore a tattered robe. Her mascara smeared into dark circles around her eyes. "What time is it?"

"Three o'clock."

"Tell me everything."

"Can I come in first?"

"I'm an idiot," Sharla said, stepping back to open the door wide. "I just woke up."

"I'm sorry."

"No matter." Sharla bustled down the hall, and Iona followed. "You hungry?"

"Starving."

Maywood still hovered in the kitchen, her head floating on the yellow wall above the table. She watched her daughter scramble eggs in the skillet. She heard the kettle whistle and saw the toast jump out of the toaster, crisp and dark. Sharla slathered it with butter, scooped eggs onto a plate, stirred instant coffee in a mug of water, and whirled around to set this meal before the skinny, dirty girl. If Maywood Wilder had had hands instead of just a face, she would have covered her eyes to keep herself from witnessing her child's weary defeat: Iona Moon had laid her head on the table and fallen into quick, deep sleep.

When she woke two hours later, Iona found the plate of cold eggs and a note from Sharla: *Gone to the store. No work tonight — called in sick. Home soon.*

In the bathroom, she stripped without looking at her body; if she caught herself in the mirror by accident she'd be surprised by a bony girl. Water ran over her, lukewarm at first, then hotter and hotter, as hot as she could stand it, and when she finally turned it off, her arms were sore and pink.

Sharla rapped at the door. She had clean towels and a spare robe, wool socks and a long T-shirt. "Thought you might need these," she said.

Iona rubbed her hair with a towel, roughly, the way her father had when she was small. She tried to comb it, but it was too snarled—the comb snagged; her arms ached.

She found Sharla in the kitchen again, cooking macaroni and cheese. "Sorry about the eggs," Iona said.

"No need to be."

"I want to be glad to see you."

"I know."

Iona could only eat half of what Sharla gave her before she felt too full to swallow. Later they sat together on the couch, and Sharla poured a glass of wine for each of them. "Drink up," Sharla said, "I've got something to tell you."

"Bad news?"

"No—a blessed event."

Iona glanced at Sharla's belly.

"Not me," Sharla said. "That *would* be bad news. Jeweldeen. Your old friend Jeweldeen is going to have a baby. Got married last summer—August—baby's due in February." Iona counted the months on her fingers. *First one can come any time.*

"Who?" Iona said.

"Leon."

"Leon who?"

"Leon, your brother."

"No," Iona said, "she wouldn't."

"Well she did."

"Where are they living?"

"With your father."

"Where do they sleep?"

"I don't know. Does it matter? Leon's room, I guess."

But Iona knew they wouldn't sleep there. Jeweldeen wouldn't stand for it, that cramped, cold bedroom with its single bed and thin northern light. No, why would they sleep there when Hannah's room was bright and twice the size?

"What's wrong?" Sharla said.

"Nothing."

Iona lay awake in Sharla's bed thinking of her brother and Jeweldeen. *Dangerous,* Leon had said. Did he think of that the

first time he lay down with her? Did the word echo weeks later
when she said: *I've got one in the oven?* Iona remembered Jeweldeen's body the summer they were ten, how they rubbed
against each other, naked on the floor of the cellar, the very
place where Sharla lay, years later. *Dangerous.* Leon had it
wrong. A man's danger was a small thing. But she figured
Jeweldeen and Leon were a good match: they both thought of
sex the same way. She hoped they'd each learned something
since they'd been with her. Still, Iona preferred Jeweldeen to
Leon— at least her skin was smooth, her hands clean. Maybe
Jeweldeen had taught him to feign kindness. Maybe he wouldn't
have to move so fast or rub so hard if he took the time to get
his pants off. And he'd done that. But she wondered anyway.
Did Jeweldeen lie beneath him in the hayloft, as stiff and scared
as Iona? That summer in the cellar, Jeweldeen said: *This isn't
so great.* Her body was pale, much softer than Iona's. She was
plump and almost had breasts; her hair smelled sweet as sugared
apricots. Boys already liked Jeweldeen, and the man at the candy
store gave her licorice whips.

Later, Iona learned that even boys who didn't like you much
might want to suck your lips and leave red marks on your neck.
Boys were all knot and bone, push and shove; boys were sharp
elbows, hard thighs. Their wet hair smelled like dog fur; their
hands smelled of gasoline. They whispered names. But not your
name.

Iona Moon. He thought he had seen Iona Moon today. He sat
by the window watching dusk come, then dark. He didn't take
a Darvocet. His body ached: from shin to thigh, across the pelvis
and up the spine, down the arms all the way to his fingers—
pain cut to the bone and had no prejudice, no part of the body
it preferred. He didn't take a hit of whiskey, though his throat
was dry and he longed for it. He wanted to remember—the
smell of the car, her hands on his chest, the sound of the river.
He wanted to stay awake and fully alive.

22

"*Two conditions,*" *Sharla said,* "if you want to stay here with me." Iona figured that number one was a job so that they could split the rent, and number two was doing her share around the apartment. Later there might be other conditions: not drinking too much, not having boys in the bed while Sharla was at work. *You wanna do that shit, use the couch.*

"First thing—you have to drive out to the Flats and tell your father you're living with me," Sharla said. "I don't want Jeweldeen finding you here by surprise."

Iona hadn't expected anything like this.

"Number two—you stay here, you go back to school."

"They can't teach me anything I need to know."

"Didn't say they could. But they won't even hire you at the phone company if you don't graduate. You look at me, you say Sharla Wilder don't have any kind of life you want. I say, *fine.* You don't care about making a living, you can get married instead, go hide in one of those trailers over the bridge, put a herd of plastic deer in the yard, have one baby after another until you're too sick to do it anymore—or too fat, and your husband leaves you alone. Who knows? You might get lucky like your friend Jeweldeen. Get a farm instead of a mobile home. Four men to take care of instead of one."

Iona nodded. "I get your drift." She tasted Mama Pearl's foul tea and felt the sting of kerosene after Hannah shaved her head; she smelled the iodine as her father painted her scraped legs. And she heard every one of them say: *It's for your own good.* Now this. One more thing. *And one more,* Hannah whispered. "I want a job," she said. "Pay half the rent."

"You can start paying after you graduate."

"It's important to me."

"Yeah, okay. But if your grades go, forget it."

"You're not my mother." She spit the words, but she already knew she was going to do this thing—*for my own damn good,* she thought.

"No, I'm your friend, and if you weren't such a pighead you'd just thank me."

"I s'pose." Iona thought of her father, how slowly he read, running his finger under the words to keep them in line. She thought of Hannah, who could only read what she'd memorized, who sat in her hot bed on a summer night and said: *Why don't you just stay here and read to me?*

"But you don't have to thank me now," Sharla said. "Just go see your father tomorrow. That's how I'll know."

The dogs yelped and tugged at their chains. *Nothing changes.* But when Jeweldeen answered the back door, Iona realized that everything had changed.

She remembered all the old insults. *You fall in the slop bucket?* For once Miss Jeweldeen was the one who had to hold her tongue. She was the biggest pregnant lady Iona had ever seen, the kind of woman doctors put to bed for the last month.

"Jesus, Iona." At least Jeweldeen still sounded exactly like herself. That was something. "Quit that barking," she yelled over Iona's head. "Goddamn dogs," she muttered, "don't mind anybody except your dad." *Don't lie to me, Iona.* She saw the raised hand and knew why the dogs whined and grew still.

Jeweldeen looked her up and down. *You sleep in the barn last night?* She didn't say it. "Well get your ass in here and tell me everything."

"You look like the one with a story to tell."

Jeweldeen patted her belly; her breasts rested on her hump. "Nothing to say that this don't explain."

"I didn't even know you liked him."

"He'll do. You want some tea or something?"

"Not right now."

Jeweldeen and Iona sat facing each other at the kitchen table. "I'm not due till February," Jeweldeen said. "Can you believe it? Two more months of carrying this load around. Me and the damn cow, due the same day. Shit, I am a cow. I hope the friggin' thing pops out early. It's big enough, I swear." She wiped the sweat from her upper lip. "You sure I can't make you tea?"

"I'm fine."

Jeweldeen reached in her apron pocket for her cigarettes. "The boys are all out," she said. "Made a run to the dump and promised me a Christmas tree. *Hunting* for a tree, that's the word they used. *Boys—*" She shook her head and smiled to herself.

"Does he treat you all right?" Iona said.

"Who, Leon?" Jeweldeen lit her cigarette. "Yeah. He treats me all right. Feeds me—as you can see. Roof over my head, all that." She took a long drag. "He's okay. And I like the boys too, and Dad—your dad, I mean."

How does he touch you? Iona wanted to say. She couldn't help hearing Leon's breath, a gasp close to her ear. *Did he hold you down in the straw the first time? Does he know your hair smells of apricots?*

"If they come back," Jeweldeen said, "pretend the cigarettes are yours. He thinks it's bad for the baby."

Iona looked around the kitchen. There were new canisters in a neat line on the counter. The top of the stove gleamed, scrubbed and white. Pretty yellow towels with embroidered leaves hung on the rack. "When do you expect them?"

"Anytime." Jeweldeen snubbed out her cigarette. "I'll make tea." Iona didn't try to stop her. Leon's wife waddled to the stove. Her buttocks had swelled as much as her stomach, and Iona wondered if she'd ever be the same again.

"Did you hear about Matt Fry?" Jeweldeen said.

"I know he got out."

"I never thought they'd take him back."

"Who?"

"His parents. You don't know?"

Iona shook her head.

"Where'd you think he was?"

"Just gone."

"Dead?"

"Maybe."

"Like you?"

"I wasn't dead."

"We wondered."

"How'd he get home?"

"Walked, I guess, or hitched. Horton Hamilton found him wandering around in the snow one night, took him to his folks' place, talked them into giving him one more chance. Can you believe it? Old Horton finally did something that turned out right."

The tea was too strong. "I'm not much of a cook," Jeweldeen said.

"It's only tea."

"Sharla did most of the cooking at home. I never learned anything." She gestured toward a pie at the far end of the counter. Violet juice oozed from the crust. "Huckleberry," she said. "Leon's favorite."

Iona added cream and sugar to her tea so it was sweet and bitter at the same time, cooled from the cream.

"First pie I made I used salt instead of sugar." Jeweldeen

giggled, covering her mouth with her hand, a delicate gesture, girlish and shy, but her fingers were thick, stained blue from the berries. "Well how was I supposed to know?" She lit another cigarette. "He's just the same," she said.

"Leon?"

"Matt Fry."

"What d'you mean?" said Iona. She had a crazy hope.

"You know—he doesn't talk. Stays in the basement when he isn't walking from one end of town to the other. They made him a room down there. Leon went to see him, but he wouldn't come out."

Iona wondered if the truth was always this simple and this disappointing.

Jeweldeen heard the truck first. She nudged the pack of cigarettes toward Iona and crushed the one she'd been smoking. "Remember," she said.

Leon was the first one through the door; Rafe and Dale were right behind. All three had bushy winter beards and plaid hunters' jackets. *A matched set.* Hannah was still laughing. Iona wanted to fling herself in her brothers' arms—just because she hated them didn't mean she wasn't glad to see them. But she sat too long, and they stood at the door without moving toward her. She remembered how her brothers had ignored her the long year after she stopped taking their money in the barn. What good was she to them if she wouldn't twirl or let them touch her? She was just a nine-year-old kid again, pest, baby sister.

Frank came in last, stomping his boots and rubbing his bare hands together. His face was clean-shaven. Snow had melted and frozen again in his thick eyebrows.

"Look who's here," Leon said.

Frank stepped toward Iona, her name forming in his mouth. She almost stood, but something moved between them, cold and quick. He saw the dirty puddles of melted snow tracking Jewel-

deen's clean floor and stooped to untie his boots. "Where've you
been?" he said.

"Seattle." She sank back in her chair and gulped the cold tea.
The sugar had settled at the bottom and the last swallow was
the worst.

"I figured," Frank said. "That's where I'd go."

Dale was the least shy. At dinner he asked Iona where she'd
lived and what she'd done. It came out easy: a convenience store,
night shift, rooming house on Fir Street.

Jeweldeen sat in Hannah's place and popped up every time
one of the boys grunted. She got more potatoes for Dale, the
ground pepper for Rafe. She stood behind Frank's chair for a
moment with her hand on his shoulder. "Can I get you anything,
Dad?"

"I'm fine," he said.

"Leon?" she said.

"I could use more gravy."

"You'll get fat."

"Like you?" Leon said.

"No, like Dale," said Rafe, poking his brother's belly. Dale
swatted Rafe's hand, and Rafe jabbed Dale in the ribs.

"Boys," Jeweldeen said, "please."

Everyone started eating again. Nothing had changed, Iona
thought. The boys still had their petty fights. *Boys*. Jeweldeen's
boys. Not her worry now, thank God.

Later, Jeweldeen washed the dishes while Iona dried. "I hate
being pregnant," Jeweldeen said. "I'm so fat."

"You'll lose it when the baby comes."

"I've gained fifty pounds. The baby's gonna weigh less than
eight. I'm fat, Iona. I'm gonna be fat forever."

"Leon doesn't seem to mind."

"You don't know." The steam from the hot water made

Jeweldeen's face sweat. "It's not my fault, you know. I'm hungry all the time. Leon took me fishing last month, out on the lake, just before it froze. He was casting from the shore, no luck. I built a fire on the beach. I ate the bait. He was using scraps of beef, hoping to snag a pike, and I kept spearing pieces on a stick, jabbing them in the fire till they sizzled and curled, crunchy, more gristle than meat, almost black. I thought I'd just eat one or two pieces; Leon wasn't watching me. But I ate one after another. I ate every goddamn scrap there was. Lucky for me the fish weren't biting anyway. He was mad though. Hasn't taken me fishing since—or anywhere for that matter, not even to town."

"I've got a car," Iona said. "I'll pick you up some afternoon, bring you back to Sharla's or take you shopping. Whatever you want."

Jeweldeen scrubbed at the greasy frying pan. "I'm fine. It won't be long now."

Driving back to White Falls, Iona thought she understood her brothers. She remembered her father whipping Leon, their old fights: Rafe and Dale could be fools, but the oldest son had to be a man. *I'll beat it into you if I have to.* So Leon rode Rafe, and Rafe rode Dale—they all harassed her. There was always someone smaller. She cut the head from a snake because Leon said it would grow two heads. She knew this was a lie but did it anyway.

So she knew, what of it? She swore she forgave Leon for everything when he saved her in the blizzard. But she saw now she had not. Marriage had not softened him, merely given him someone else to ride, pretty Jeweldeen, no longer pretty.

She wanted to leave forever. But more than that, she wanted to love them all. This was the wound in her chest that never healed, this simple longing to love, not just anyone, but them: Rafe, Dale, Leon, Frank. She wished they would do something small and kind so that she could believe, at least, in the possibility of love. She wished Hannah had protected her so she wouldn't have to hate them now.

She thought of her father, sitting in his chair while her brothers struggled to get the tree in the stand. He'd said, "You can stay if you want."

And she told him, "I've got a place in town."

"There's room here." He didn't look at her.

There was a crib in her bedroom, a double bed in Hannah's room. So the only place left for her in this house was the drafty corner room with its small, high windows and its cold northern light.

The face of the half-moon disintegrated behind a wisp of cloud. Her headlights seemed weak. Beams bounced off snow, the drifts of the fields, the ice of the road. She was afraid of animals in the woods, afraid they'd leap in front of the car and there'd be no time to stop. She saw herself spinning out of control, plunging down a ditch or into a pole. But she wasn't afraid for herself, only for the animals, the living creatures she might kill.

23

Iona looked for Matthew. She couldn't just go to the house, knock on the door. Even if he agreed to come upstairs, she didn't want to sit in the living room with Matt and his mother, watching Mrs. Fry's mouth twitch and tighten while her only son hunched on the couch, hands tucked under his thighs. She knew she'd see him walking. "One end of town to the other," Jeweldeen had said, "two, three times a day. Never takes a ride from anyone."

But he did get into Iona's car. That was something. She'd been in White Falls less than a week when she spotted him, not roaming the streets but just over the bridge, heading up the embankment toward the tracks. She called to him from the road, and he stopped and turned, then stared down at the car without moving. She thought he recognized her voice but not the Valiant, so she climbed out to let him see her. The look on his face didn't change. She said, "It's me, Matt—Iona, Iona Moon." He waited, so she said, "Where're you going?" He tilted his head to the left, the slightest gesture, less than an inch. *Down the tracks. Who needs words?* Iona thought. "You wanna ride?" she said. "I'll take you there." She meant the place where the shed had been.

He slid down the bank. She moved away from her door so he could get in first, but he went to the back instead, opened his own door. She figured that's how he rode with his parents if he rode at all; that's how he'd ridden with Horton the night he came home.

He was different. His whole body was bigger—wrists and thighs, jaw and shoulder—as if every bone had thickened. He was a man now, like Leon or Frank, like his own brother, and Iona thought it must be terrifying for a boy like Matthew to live in a man's body. His clothes were old. She remembered the plaid wool jacket, was sure it was Everett's, the trousers too— thin at the knees and frayed at the cuffs.

It seemed dangerous to give him his brother's clothes, a curse—that lingering smell—an itch, a burn. Why not just hand him the gun?

She watched him in the rearview mirror but didn't torment him with questions. His broad white hands rested in his lap, unfamiliar to her. Were they strange to him too? He had a scar on his left cheek that she didn't remember, and the skin of his face was rough, red from the cold. His eyes looked smaller, as if he were still squinting, but she realized it only seemed that way because his face had more flesh.

She pulled to the shoulder near the place where the shed had been. "There's nothing left, Matt, you know that?" He sat for a moment, and she thought he might answer, might nod at least, that the memory of one particular night might break him at last. But she was dreaming. This was not the boy she loved, not the one who'd led her to a cave dug in the earth, not the one whose body curved around hers as they lay in the musk of damp ground.

Matthew Delancey Fry simply got out of the car and shut the door.

She found the other one too: bent against the wind on the bridge, stabbing the snow with his cane. Then again on Main—his blue Chrysler, her rusted Valiant, stopped at the same light, facing each other. That night, she passed him as he came out of the

White Bull, leaning on the cane, his strongest leg. Three times in one day. Coincidence. For a moment, they were the only ones on the street, and she almost spoke, but the door burst open behind them. Two women staggered onto the sidewalk. He moved out of their way, quick now, surprisingly steady, a shout away instead of a whisper, so she kept quiet.

If he recognized her, he pretended he didn't. Maybe he thought she was following him. She wanted to say: *It's a small town.* She wanted to tell him: *I don't need anything from you.* But she did. She needed Jay to look at her as if he remembered who she was and what they'd done.

Willy wasn't happy to hear Iona Moon was back in town. First Matt Fry, and now this. *Every man makes his own hell.* That's what Horton would say.

And Horton was on him too. Willy still wasn't writing enough tickets. *Not that we have a quota, son.* He was overlooking too much or sleeping on the job. Pussy ass or loafer, two options, nothing gray.

Flo said, "He's barely started, Horton. Give him a chance to settle into the job." This was Sunday, at breakfast, the first meal together all week. Usually at least one of them was missing, but here they were, all five, the happy family. "Stay out of it, Flo. This is business."

"Then don't do it here."

They minded each other. Flo kept to her work: juice and milk, a plate of bacon, more coffee. Horton stayed quiet, concentrating on his food, shoveling it down fast. Grease soaked into the paper towel under the bacon, and Willy wished he had a place of his own, away from his silent parents, away from his sisters who chattered now to fill the air. How many mornings had he hunched at this table, skinny and hungry, his stomach shrunken to a knot, just as it was now. How many times had his sisters romped in the yard, shouted from the street, while he sat in the stifling kitchen, his father's words hanging above him: *You're not leaving this house until you finish what your mother gave you.*

Just before midnight Buck Caudill called Willy out to the Road-stop to break up an argument. Some poor loser didn't want to pay his pool debt, and the winner was threatening to punch the cue stick in one ear and out the other.

Willy was glad to have a mission, a life to save: this was better than six tickets; Horton would be proud. But by the time he got to the bar the debt was paid, and the two guys were slapping each other on the back, buying beers for the house, setting up the balls for a rematch.

"Sorry to drag you out here," Buck said.

"No bother—better to play it safe."

"Wish I could offer you a drink."

"Some other time." The trouble with Delores started because of that first mistake: drinking in uniform. Horton was right. *One false step leads to another, and the path of evil is long and dark.*

Sitting behind the wheel of the cruiser, Willy counted thirteen cars in the lot. He tried to recall the faces of the people inside. *A good policeman sees without looking.* He was a lousy policeman. He could only picture four faces: the laughing men who had just quarreled, the tall girl in a yellow miniskirt— no, he didn't see her face: he saw the curve of her buttocks as she bent over the pool table, shooting imaginary balls with an imaginary stick. And he remembered Buck, of course, Buck's slack, weary face, Buck's big hand setting a shot glass in front of a customer at the bar as he talked to Willy. Buck had the look of a heavy man who had starved himself; the flesh of his cheeks hung loose, and his mustache drooped. Seeing Buck hardly counted, so he'd only noticed three people. Was there a blond at the bar? Man or woman? *I don't know if you're cut out for this line of work.* The girl in yellow was underage. Most likely. He should have asked her for some I.D. But if she didn't have it, Buck was in trouble too.

Willy scanned the cars again. The red Mustang belonged to Luke Sweeney. Graduation present. Short men need hot cars. He hadn't seen Luke. Maybe he was taking a piss. Yeah, maybe half the guys in the place were in the damn john. Willy banged the steering wheel with both hands.

At the end of the lot, he saw the Chrysler and parked again.

"Change your mind?" Buck said when he spotted Willy.

"Mind if I use the facilities?"

"Be my guest."

This time Willy looked at everyone. He walked quickly toward the restrooms but watched each face. The blond sitting alone at the bar nursing a drink wasn't red-faced Delores, half in the bag. It was Jay.

He looked gaunt, his face drained of color. They hadn't spoken since the night they'd found Delores. It was difficult to tell if Jay was tight or dangerously sober. *Can I give you a lift home?* He'd see through that. Willy believed Jay had forgiven him but no longer loved him. No—never loved him. Willy was surprised at the word—*love*—his word, unbidden, what he'd felt for Jay since they were boys rolling in the grass, arms and legs entwined, what he'd felt from the first time he saw Jay Tyler hit a perfect dive—love and awe, that too, what he'd always felt but left unnamed till now. Willy almost touched him as he passed, but Jay didn't glance at the thin man in the blue uniform.

He splashed cold water on his face and dried himself without looking in the mirror. When he came out, Jay was gone.

He glimpsed the Chrysler on Elm, killed his lights, and followed it all the way to Willow Glen. Jay slipped the car into the dark garage. Home safe. Willy hit his high beams. He wanted to set the blue light flashing, wanted the keening siren to wake everyone on this dead street, everyone in this ghost town.

He looked at his watch: half past twelve. He could go home. Home, where his mother was sleeping. Home, where his father was sleeping. Home, where his sisters pressed themselves into their own dreams, swollen with desire. If he didn't make any trouble for himself, he could just go home.

Iona knew she could never go home, not really, and she couldn't stay with Sharla too long either. They'd grow alike. Spinster sisters, twins with a secret language no one else understood, a way of praying, these words between them. It was simple and tender and terrifying.

She kept her promise and started school in January. Three nights a week, she flipped burgers at Doolie's Drive-in, wore a pink polyester uniform and knew Sharla was right: she'd rather die than do this for the rest of her life. So she went to class and took notes, passed her tests, tried not to get caught smoking in the girls' room.

They shared the bed. Iona slept while Sharla worked, and Sharla slept while Iona was at school. Leon asked about that the second time Iona came to visit. "You sleep on the couch?" he said. He was nervous because of what he'd done with Jeweldeen. He grunted when Iona explained.

"What did you think?" said Jeweldeen, nudging him with her elbow.

"Nothing," he said. "I was just asking."

This was the middle of January. Jeweldeen still had a month to go but looked ready to bust. "Sometimes I want to reach inside myself, grab its foot and yank it out," she told Iona. "Seventeenth of February—that's my day. If I'm late I'm gonna pop my own water."

Jeweldeen and Tessa were both a week ahead of schedule. Frank Moon spent the eighth of February in the barn with his cow, and Leon rushed to town with his wife. The calf was male, the baby a girl. "Bad luck for both of us," Leon said.

The child was so small and red that Leon wouldn't touch

her. He watched her squirm in Jeweldeen's arms, watched her suckle and sleep. He felt pity and envy, a desire to pull her from his wife, a need to protect her from himself.

Iona wondered how it was that Jeweldeen always knew exactly what to do. Even when the baby's tiny face twisted, even when she screamed and her whole body trembled with frustration, Jeweldeen could calm her, could lift her from the crib and still her sobs. No wonder Leon was jealous: he saw the mystery but had no part in it.

Every time Iona went to her father's house she expected to startle Hannah in the barn, find her sitting on a stool, bent under a cow. She looked for her mother in the root cellar. Flinging back the door, Iona was sure she'd see Hannah rise from the dark room, climbing slowly, her apron full of potatoes and beets. But it was always Jeweldeen who emerged—Jeweldeen with her broad face and strong shoulders, round arms, thick legs—good wife for a farmer, not at all like Hannah, who moved fast as air, a wraith in the woods of Iona's mind.

Once Iona imagined Hannah had locked herself in the bathroom. She sat in the hall by the door, waiting, listening to the snap of cards, Hannah laying out a game of solitaire in the only room where she could have her privacy. Iona was patient, completely still. Finally she touched the door; it wasn't locked, not even closed tight. Curtains flapped in the breeze from the open window.

If she were quick and quiet enough she might catch her mother at the kitchen sink. But she missed her again and again. She kept feeling someone had just slipped out of the room; someone had left her apron tossed carelessly over the back of a chair. Soon, Iona thought, it will be tied around a waist again. On the table, half a cup of cold tea made a rust-colored stain on white china. *Will it always be this way, late afternoon, late winter. Will I always come into a room she's just fled.*

Moving through the house, Iona felt weary, too weak to keep

standing: she had to stop and steady herself, had to grab a door frame to keep from falling. She was amazed that such a small thing—dust motes swirling in a shaft of light—could unstring her: snow on the ground, this winter light, bright rectangle on the floor, and Hannah upstairs, forever dying. Later, outside, she pressed her back to the trunk of the maple in the yard, and even then she felt herself sliding down, as if her bones were blood, flowing out of her.

You watch your own brothers carry a pine box, and you know that's where your mother lives. But a green ribbon in yellow hair destroys you, just a girl on the street, young and rosy, nothing like Hannah, except for the ribbon, except for the hair. Sun strikes blond wood. This is what you remember most of all, how you wished to touch it, smooth, lovely wood, how you longed to lie down and feel it, the whole length of your body.

She stood in the barn. Four cows chewed their cud in the half-dark. Belle was still alive. Under the eave of the tool shed the last wood of winter was stacked. She sank down, crouching in the damp shadows, promising herself she would wait now until someone found her. She stayed a long time—a day, she thought, a minute. She gazed out at the fields. No one came. The black limbs of the maple were full of crows. Beaks stabbed gray air. She walked back to the house and up the steps, into the bright kitchen where Jeweldeen sewed at the table, basting a blue satin edge on a tiny wool blanket.

Leon sat beside her, rubbing mink oil into his boots. His hands were stubby, fingers short, palms broad. Strong hands but not an artist's hands. She wanted to remember him carving, wanted to see the grace of those hands as they turned a block of wood into a delicate woman. But she realized she had never witnessed this magic, that he must have whittled alone—in his room at night or behind the woodshed.

She burned, jealous of him for making something Hannah loved. That was the part she did remember: Hannah holding the bear in her hands, closing her eyes to feel ridges of fur, opening them to see that the bear was smiling, slightly, so he looked sweet instead of dangerous—Hannah was smiling too, she who smiled so rarely. And it was Leon who had worked this miracle. Dull, brutal Leon. Iona tried to imagine how the same hands carving feathers or fingers, lips or eyes could cover her mouth. *Don't you ever tell, Iona.*

Leon looked up from his boots and caught her staring. She was ashamed, as if she'd seen something she was never meant to see: his thick fingers rubbing those boots, oil soaking into leather.

"What?" he said. But she did not answer.

In the night, Jeweldeen and Leon filled Hannah's room with their sounds. The baby cried in Iona's room. The baby cried in the living room and in the kitchen. The baby laughed. Everyone held her, sweet baby Louise, round, hairless Louise. Where could Hannah hide in this house full of noise? She stood at the edge of the woods where her own child was buried. She climbed in the hills where coyotes howled. Iona knew that when fall came, when the tamaracks moved gold and brittle in the wind, she would see Hannah stooping in the fields, lifting potatoes from the earth. Her mother brushed away the dirt. *See,* she said, *see how warm it is.*

In a trunk in the attic, Iona found her mother's cotton dresses and wool sweaters. She pressed them to her face, but they smelled only of mothballs. She found the clay plaques, her brothers' handprints, hated and saved. *What mother needs to be reminded? What mother wouldn't recognize the smallest part: lock of hair, bony ankle, scraped knee, sunburned shoulder?* Iona looked for relics like these, but Hannah Moon had left nothing of herself behind.

Leon's carvings lay at the bottom of the trunk. She stuffed the little farmer and the tiny woman in her bag and took them back to Sharla's. At night she put them on the dresser and watched them in the dark. Sometimes they moved toward each other, sometimes away. *I just want you to be happy,* the woman whispered, and Iona thought this was strange, because she had never known anyone who was happy.

She remembered the long morning silences of her father's house, sheets of rain, endless rivers, the wide lake opening forever. Mother bent over the stove, and Father sat in his chair, hands cupped around coffee. Just by the curve of Hannah's shoulders Iona could see that some word or absence of words had passed between them; her mother had turned, and meant to stay turned, busy with her woman's work, cracking eggs, spooning dough onto the pan for biscuits, emptying coffee grounds to make a second pot before the boys woke. She resented her chores and was glad for them, for the excuse to keep her back to the man at the table. He lifted his mug slowly, sipping noisily. Even his slurping made Hannah flinch, despising the fact of him, the unavoidable body. His hands were chapped, raw and bloody at the knuckles. Iona didn't know why they'd argued. A word or a touch could stiffen her mother's spine, though he was the one to go out in the cold rain for firewood; he was the one who took the chill from the house.

In this moment, he was the one Iona pitied. But he was not the one she loved.

Iona knew that seeing her father holding the baby should make her happy, but it didn't. She felt a space opening inside her, a hole dug at the shore, filling with muddy water.

Leon took the baby from Frank. He was tender now but still scared, and Iona felt sorry for him, remembering how he stood at the window, chewing tobacco, unable to touch Hannah, unable to look at her with open eyes. Louise was more than a month old, but her own father still touched her as if he expected her to break or scream. Often Louise did yell when Leon picked her up. How could she trust him, this clumsy man who was afraid of her?

"That's how you were with me," Frank said to Iona one

evening in late March. "You wouldn't have anyone but your mama. When your grandma had her stroke, Hannah left you here with me for five days, and I swear you howled the whole time."

"I remember that," Leon said. "She wouldn't let any of us near her." He seemed satisfied by this, putting blame where it belonged, showing Iona it was her fault, after all.

Leon held Louise and rocked lightly in his chair. The baby stopped crying and laid her head on his shoulder.

"Good thing your mama came home when she did," Frank said. "Another week and you might have starved."

Iona felt a pressure behind her eyes that made her head pound, a place that still hurt, where a white scar and a memory of snow converged. She wished she were Louise, that Leon and her father would hold her this way, that she would be free to love them.

Her headache started at the old wound and spread: her brothers said they were just running, and she said they were trying to ditch her, and it didn't matter either way because her head got split open all the same. Ice glazed the rocks. Her brothers ran, far beyond her reach already. Frank called from the woods, angry—that's when it happened, when she looked back and kept running. She saw herself falling, as if she were a hawk and the shadow of a hawk at the same time, in the air and on the ground. She heard herself yell. Then something struck the back of her skull, and she must have blacked out because time folded in on her, and the next thing she remembered was looking up to see her father and her three sorry brothers standing in a circle around her. Her father said: *Wiggle your toes for me, Iona.* He smiled. He was very proud of her for doing this one, small thing. *That's my good girl.*

She saw that despite the pain—or perhaps because of it— this was a good memory, because her father held her and talked to her as sweetly as he talked to the cows when they were almost ready and he knew their sorrow.

Now Iona watched Leon stroke the soft down of Louise's

tiny head. Later, after supper, after the dishes were washed and
the baby was in her crib, Frank sat on the porch alone, smoking
his pipe. Iona stopped on her way to the car.

"Leaving so early?"

"School tomorrow."

"I always forget."

Iona nodded. He had other things on his mind.

"How's it going?" he said. "School, I mean."

"Fine." She wanted to tell him how much she hated it, how
the girls stopped talking whenever she came into the bathroom,
how Mr. Fetterhoff still made jokes under his breath, private
jokes that only she understood, how she and Muriel Arnoux
brushed against each other in the cafeteria and looked away,
pretending they had nothing in common. She wanted to tell
him that even the younger boys asked her if maybe she wanted
to go to the river. "Smoke some cigarettes," they said, "drink
some wine—you know." She wished she could say that she'd
found a picture taped inside her locker, a photograph from a
magazine, a dark-haired girl naked on a bed, playing with
herself, one hand on her crotch, one hand in her mouth. Someone
had scrawled *Iona Moon* across the girl's belly. She tore it down,
crumpled it in a wad, stuffed it in her pocket. Who knew her
combination? She heard laughter behind her but didn't turn,
didn't let them see what they'd done: her red face burning, her
tears of rage.

"Aren't you cold?" she said to Frank.

"I suppose I am."

"You should go inside."

"Smoke bothers Jeweldeen."

"She's not—"

"No," Frank said, "it's too soon."

"I'll see you next week." She longed to kiss his forehead but
she put her hand on his shoulder instead. *Nite, Daddy.* He seemed
to slump beneath her touch, weaker, more frail than she remembered, and she was worried for him, living in this house

with three strong men. She wondered if Leon might turn on him one day, pay him back for all his childhood pain. She saw her father just as he was, no longer the colossus, no longer the bear in the fairy tale, forever terrifying and tempting, turning to a man in the dark, waking as a bear every morning.

He patted her fingers without looking up. His skin was rough, his touch heavy. She would recognize those hands anywhere, at the edge of any sleep. "I keep thinking I'll see her," he said at last. Iona knew that his grief for Hannah went far beyond her death, that he mourned the girl she'd been before the first child died, the girl who'd loved him for a single year. "Every time I come in the house," he said, "I look for her."

Iona stroked the back of his head. "Me too," she said. "Me too, Daddy."

24

Willy saw Delores pinned to a wall, struggling with a man in a loose black coat. She dug at his shoulders, kicked at his shins. Willy shouted, but his voice was garbled, a record at the wrong speed. She moaned. He remembered that sound, remembered looking at her just this way. When she felt him watching, she opened her eyes. Slapped the man. Pushed him away. A show for Willy's sake. Now she was tall, bigger than the man; he shrank under her gaze. The little man turned, and Willy saw it was himself, a boy wearing a foolish mask.

He really did see her once, the last day of March. He was at Pick-n-Pay with Flo, rolling the cart down the aisle as he looked at the shelves. That's how they collided, his cart bashing into hers, so his first words were: *I'm sorry.* Everyone was very polite. Flo asked about Jay, and Delores said, "He's fine—much better"; and Flo said, "That's good," and they all smiled as if they believed it.

Willy envied the women, the way Flo and Delores touched each other's arms, so casually, the way they spoke in fragments of sentences and understood though they had never been friends. Women had a language he didn't know, and he felt as clumsy as his father, as dense as Roy Wilkerson.

At first he was ashamed, imagining how his mother might see Delores, supposing pity or soft judgment, thinking Flo would notice the slight tremor of her hands. He wanted one of them to forgive him. But Flo Hamilton didn't look at Delores Tyler that way. She had washed the bodies of old women and shaved the cheeks of handsome boys; she had tied ribbons in the golden hair of little girls. She looked at the body and beyond it. Life was a mystery to her; death was certain.

What were they saying? Something about June. The month, or a woman they knew? It didn't matter. It was nothing that concerned him. He saw how unnecessary he was, how easily ignored, by his mother, his lover, how it had always been this way with women: his sisters tormented him, then ran away, slammed their door while he stood in the dark, forever on the other side. He knew, suddenly, that this was his father's sorrow too, that Flo depended on him but did not need him.

He longed to touch Delores, remembering her skin, all of it, neck and arm, surprising and soft, her belly under the satin camisole. In that room in South Bend, he was changed, *beautiful boy,* and she was everything he wanted. For an hour he was completely satisfied. He couldn't recall another time in his life when he had known exactly what he wanted, couldn't remember satiating any hunger. His life was a string of small denials, a succession of little *no*'s, an endless catalogue of moments when he'd said *stop* before he was full.

The women's talk had shifted to weather—blustery today; and fruit—overpriced; and husbands—who expected certain things on the table in certain quantities but who were tight with money. Willy had imagined seeing Delores a different way—drunk, dancing at the White Bull or careening through Wood-vale Park. And in those scenes he always knew just what to do.

But sober under the harsh lights of the store, she was graceful and needed nothing from him. She was a grown woman, mother of a crippled boy, wife of a cold man—long-suffering woman—lovely, sad, wearing blue shoes to match her blue jacket, all her golden hair pinned perfectly in place.

He knew she might be drunk tonight, in disarray, one shoe

lost under the bed, stockings torn. She might sit alone in the kitchen; she might pass out on the couch. But that was a private matter.

Here, at midday, she was expert and efficient. She could touch his arm as they parted, lightly, with her fingers, lift them, quickly. She could say: "Don't be a stranger, Willy," and seem to look at him—but not look, could turn, wheel her cart away, not teetering on her high heels, not hurrying, but moving swiftly away from him while he stood, staring stupidly at the seams of her stockings, so his mother had to say: "Willy?"

He was sure Flo guessed everything. But of course she didn't, and that was worse, because even he could see how unbelievable it was to imagine that a woman like Delores Tyler would desire anything from a boy like him.

He wanted to run after her, wanted her to drop her groceries in the parking lot so that they could kneel together and pick them up. He wanted to ask her if he could come by sometime, but he couldn't bear the answer, couldn't stand it if they only talked in the bright living room, sipping tea or vodka. And he couldn't stand it if they drove away, if they climbed the stairs to another room where he could stroke her soft belly and hear his own name whispered while the candle guttered and burned out.

He would have been surprised to know how close his thoughts were to hers, how proud she was of her self-control, how grateful for Willy's silence. Driving home, she gripped the steering wheel and leaned forward to see more clearly. She knew she could have swayed the moment, touched his arm a second longer, held it more tightly, looked in his eyes when she spoke. She could have lingered in the store and struggled with her bags until he had to help.

But for once, just for once, she spared herself all that, the questions and the longing, his hands in the dark, hers in the light.

• • •

Much later that night, Willy dragged Main in the cruiser. He hoped he'd see the Chrysler and he hoped he wouldn't. He wished the kid in the white Bel Air would jump a red light so he could write a ticket, wished he'd catch three teenage girls drinking beer in the alley behind the Mercantile. He wished one thing would happen. Then he'd get a coffee to go and sit on some side street with his lights off.

He saw the Bel Air pick up speed as it rounded the loop behind the courthouse. He pressed closer. He finally had one. Thirty miles per hour, then thirty-two. The greasy-headed boy had hit forty by the time he ran his first red light, and Willy's siren started wailing.

The kid ran a second light and kept accelerating. Willy stayed on his tail, edging past fifty, wondering if this was worth it, wondering if he was the one making trouble by starting the chase.

By the time they jumped the city limits, the boy in the Bel Air was doing sixty-three and showed no sign of slowing down. He was steady, a good driver. Focused, that's what he was. He wasn't thinking about deer leaping onto the highway; he wasn't distracted by the lights of oncoming cars. He and the car were one machine, one animal; he watched the strip of road, nothing else.

Already Willy was losing his nerve. Every time they rounded a curve he expected the kid to tap his brakes. He saw himself slamming into the rear end of the Bel Air, imagined both cars spinning, plunging toward the river. But that boy had skill, new tires and no need to slow down. Willy was losing him. Twice he thought he saw dark shapes moving across the road; twice he lifted his foot off the gas and felt the cruiser drift to the right.

He couldn't do it. He saw that now. Tomorrow he could track down the license number, go to the kid's house. But he knew he wouldn't do that either, knew he couldn't tell his father: *I gave up.* He let himself fall behind—three car lengths then

five. Did the boy know what was happening? The taillights
of the Bel Air burned in the distance. Willy followed those
lights for another mile, until they disappeared over the crest of
a hill.

He pulled to the shoulder. Gravel spit under his tires. He
tried to clutch the wheel tighter to stop shaking. Even his fingers
were weak. Loss of courage or will—was he a coward or a lazy
sonuvabitch? He turned and headed back to town, never pushing
past thirty. He imagined sleeping on the job, like Fred Pierce.
How long till it came to that?

He saw the lights of White Falls glittering along the black
river. Nothing would happen now. But he remembered Delores
and Flo in the grocery store, how little they needed him. He
realized why Horton did it, this job—saw that it gave his life
order and sense, one clear purpose. He could come home and
tell Flo: *I found Matt Fry*. And for a night or a week she would
see that he was necessary, to her, to this whole town.

This was all Willy wanted: to be necessary, in his mother's
eyes and in his own. He wanted to make up for his failures, for
deserting Iona that night last June, for leaving Matt Fry on the
tracks and driving his friends home, for sitting in the car while
Delores walked to her door.

He stopped at the Park Inn for coffee and drank it at the
counter. It was well past midnight, already April. *Fool's Day,*
he thought, *five hours till dawn*. He heard laughter behind him.
Someone knew. He spun on his stool, a half turn, and saw two
girls in the back booth eating giant cinnamon rolls. Just drunk—
they weren't laughing at him. Sharla Wilder and Iona Moon.
Why tonight, he thought, why her? He threw a dollar on the
counter. As he left, he caught his reflection in the glass door, a
boy drowning in his father's uniform.

Two weeks later, Iona imagined Willy on the streets again. She
was already half cocked and had no intention of stopping. If
she swerved on her way home, took her corners too wide, she

knew that Willy—Officer Hamilton—would be the one to drag her downtown. *For your own protection,* he'd say. And she'd tell him: *You should have thought of that the last time.*

She and Sharla were at the Roadstop, tossing darts. They came here often, whenever Sharla had a night off, shot pool and drank beer till one of them missed the cue ball and they laughed so hard they had to hug each other to keep from falling. Sometimes Sharla's laughter turned to sobs by the time they got to the parking lot, and on those nights Iona felt suddenly sober and wished she lived alone.

Sharla's dart stuck in the wall instead of the board. That was the end of the game. Buck Caudill yelled over the bar, told her she was through, and two men in cowboy hats took the rest of the darts from Iona.

"Assholes," Sharla said.

But Iona knew they had to do it and blamed Sharla: she might nick somebody's ear the next time.

The smell of sawdust and spilled beer mingled with the smell of sweat. Only ten, Iona thought, but she felt trouble already, a fight about to spark. It wasn't just the smell. It was the heat too, this warm night in April, balmy almost, more like July, so everyone was on edge, and she felt something prickly moving over her bare skin, as if the air itself had a charge.

Jay Tyler sat alone at the bar, drinking tequila by the shot and chasing it with a draft. Iona wished she could say: *Glad to see you out.* But no matter how she put it, the words sounded sarcastic.

Sharla couldn't get a turn at the pool table and wanted to go. Iona said she felt like getting looped. "We can get bombed at home," Sharla said. "You can drink rum and Cokes till you fall out of your chair." Iona couldn't face the thought of another night in Sharla's kitchen with Maywood watching over them. They'd smoke cigarette after cigarette, lighting one from the other until their faces blurred.

Once, through this haze, Sharla had whispered: "I used to

think she did it on purpose." She meant the mother on the wall.

Maywood said: *I don't want to know.*

"She was sick," Iona said.

"She was unhappy."

I don't want to know anything.

"She died of pneumonia, Sharla."

"She wanted to be gone."

Maywood closed her eyes. *What did you expect me to do?*

The dim bar was safer than Sharla's place on nights like these. Bodies stayed whole even when faces turned fuzzy. Iona watched a gang clustered at a table. Bright lips, wet teeth—mouths fluttered too fast to read words. Boys picked tobacco off their tongues with one hand and reached under the table with the other while the jukebox played the same song over and over: footsteps and slamming doors.

Iona stared at Jay. His mouth was closed, a thin line. Even when he drank he barely parted his lips. Bodies wavered, blocking her vision, and Sharla said, "I'm out o' here."

Iona didn't know which was worse—imagining Sharla and Maywood in the kitchen alone or sitting there with them. But she knew how she'd find Sharla hours from now: asleep in the chair, her head on the table, the fluorescent light humming. Iona swayed, almost dancing. "Think I'll stay awhile," she said, and Sharla muttered, "I figured."

Iona pictured herself dancing with Jay, pulling him from his stool, holding him close enough so he wouldn't need his cane. She inched toward him. None of this could happen. She knew that. But she still had five dollars in her pocket. She thought she might offer to buy him a drink. Funny idea: dirt-poor daughter of a potato farmer buying a shot for the pretty blond boy with perfect teeth. Pretty, like Jeweldeen, not anymore. Someone had started the song again, a torment, a joke: no more footsteps after all, no more jeans on the floor. Twyla Catts plunked herself down on the stool next to Jay, and Darryl McQueen sat on the other side of her. At first Iona thought it was coincidence: they couldn't be together. Surely Twyla hadn't given up a linebacker and a second baseman to hang out with a gangly guy from the diving team. But Darryl put his hand low on Twyla's back, slipped the tips of his fingers inside her pants. He wasn't even a good diver.

Twyla leaned close to Jay. She wore a low-cut top, white with red stripes. Iona thought her breasts might pop out any minute, might spring free of the stretchy cloth like a pair of jack-in-the-boxes.

Twyla's high voice cracked above the chatter of the crowd. "Didn't you used to be Jay Tyler?"

Darryl slapped the bar and hooted. "That's a good one," he said, " 'used to be.' "

"I just meant—" Twyla was too wasted to know what she meant. *Didn't you used to do double somersaults off the high board? Didn't you used to be the best-looking guy in school?*

Jay spit a single word in Twyla's ear, downed the last shot, threw a five on the bar, and headed for the door.

Twyla puffed up red, cheeks and chest ready to burst. She yelled after him. "You can't call me that." He pounded his cane into the floor with each step. "Fucking cripple."

The last word hit Jay like a stone flung at his back. He stumbled but kept moving. People got out of his way. Darryl grabbed Twyla's wrist. "Sit your ass down before I knock you down," he said.

The space Jay had opened with his swinging cane closed quickly. Twyla pulled her jacket around her shoulders, and Darryl yelled to Buck, "I'm dry, buddy."

Iona squeezed through the crowd. She found Jay outside, propped against the first car in the lot, a long tan Oldsmobile, somebody's daddy's car.

He pretended he didn't notice her, but he stared at her feet, her unbroken legs, and she felt him blaming her. "I don't know if you remember me," she said.

He looked at her face now. "I didn't crack my head," he said, "just my legs."

"That's not what I meant."

"I remember you," Jay said. "What of it?"

"She's a bitch."

"I used another word."

"You shouldn't let people like her bother you."

Jay hit the car with his cane. "She doesn't." He whacked the car again, harder, and Iona thought she heard the cane split. "You know what bothers me?" He hit his right knee with the cane. "This bothers me." He swung again, smacking his left thigh. "And this." He raised the stick as if he meant to strike her, but whirled instead to hit the car. "This goddamned car bothers me. Whose fucking car is this anyway?" He pounded the hood until the cane splintered and hung limp. "Look what you made me do," he said, turning to face Iona.

He started down the lot and Iona followed. "Let me drive you," she said.

"I may be a fucking cripple," he said, "but I can drive. Even a fucking cripple can drive a fucking car."

"You're drunk. Let me take you home."

"Your place or mine, baby?" He sounded mean, even to himself.

"Wherever you want to go."

"You're not scared of me, are you?"

"No."

"Nobody has to worry about a cripple."

"Let me drive you."

He said, "I don't want to go home," but he walked to her car with her, limping, unsteady without his cane.

"Where to?" she said as they pulled onto the highway.

"Just drive."

She headed toward the Flats, and they didn't talk. She wanted to say: *I know you.* She wanted to tell him about crawling through the snow, how Leon showed her that even when you're on your knees and frozen to the bone, you can choose to live. She had almost forgotten at times; but when she did, Leon swatted her butt, whispered in her ear: *Not this way, not this way, God.* And even when she didn't believe in God, she believed in her brother who had saved her with those words.

She started humming the song that had played over and over in the bar.

"I hate that tune," Jay said. He flicked on the radio, and Iona let him run through the stations before she said it didn't work.

"Me neither."

"Doesn't matter to me."

"No, I s'pose not." Jay whistled a rift of the song he said he hated. "It's stuck in my head," he told her.

Iona nodded. A lot of things were stuck in her head: stars flung in a summer sky the night Jay gave Willy Hamilton directions to her house and got them lost; a day, months later, when she stood behind the wire fence and watched Jay leap, first air, then water. She saw it all: Willy pinned to the hood of the car and Jay saying, *Sorry, buddy, I'll make it up to you.* And he did. His knees bent, his feet slapped the blue surface. Jay came up grinning, and Willy won the day. Only Iona knew this was deliberate and just, reparation for a dirty girl with crooked teeth.

Jay stared at Iona's hands, thinking of all the times she must have washed her mother's body. No wonder she wasn't afraid. He remembered how she held him in the back seat of Willy's Chevy, how skinny she was, how strong.

"I was an asshole," Jay said.

She nodded. She thought he meant tonight, outside the bar.

"I should have beat the crap out of him."

"Who?"

"Willy."

She realized he was talking about that other night on this road. "I didn't blame you," she said.

"You should have."

"He was your friend."

"So were you."

Friend, she was amazed to hear him call her that.

He watched her, looked at her body—yellow arms and dark face, tangled hair and sharp nose, all her frail bones almost visible. Strange comfort, this girl, but it did comfort him to think of her ribs and knees, her bony pelvis, all the parts of her he would feel if he lay down beside her, nothing soft and simple, just the hard fact of this particular girl, this night, this body against his own.

She punched off the lights as she turned up the rutted road that led to her father's house. "Don't want to wake them," she said.

"What are we doing here?"

"I want to show you the barn and the outhouse. I want you to smell the cows. I want you to know how we live, out here on the Flats." She hit the brakes and put the car in reverse, started backing up the road. "But I can just take you home— if that's what you want."

"We're here. I might as well see."

"Don't do me any favors." *Friend*. She remembered but didn't trust him, thought he might do the same thing all over again.

"I want to see."

"We should leave the car."

"I don't mind walking," Jay said.

The night was cool now and fog filled the valley. Damp air smelled of the fields: fertilizer and black earth.

One of the dogs growled, and Iona whispered, "It's only me." Her familiar voice made him whine. "Stupid mutt." He growled again. She said, "Hush, baby, I didn't mean you." The dog whimpered.

She lifted the latch on the barn door and took Jay inside. The smell of dung was dense, sweet, stronger than it was as it blew off the land. The cows stamped in the dark. She led Jay to each stall, to Ruby and Myrtle, to pretty Belle, to Tessa and the new calf. "Born the same day as my niece," Iona said. "Have you ever watched something being born?"

Jay shook his head.

"I used to milk these cows every morning—before I came to school."

"Who does it now?"

"Jeweldeen. Leon says he married her because a wife's cheaper than a milking machine."

"I heard he had to marry her."

"It's a lie," Iona said. "Machine's cheaper than a wife."

"It's so quiet."

"Do you want to stay?"

"Where else would we go?"

"Back to town."

"I'm in no hurry."

"Can you climb a ladder?"

"What d'you think I am? A cripple?"

They climbed up to the loft and lay side by side in the straw. "I wish we had a blanket," Iona said.

"Are you cold?"

"Yes."

"Me too," Jay murmured.

He rolled toward her and laid his head on her chest. She took his hand in hers and slid it under her shirt so it rested on her belly. "See," she said, "see how warm it is?" The words rose up in her, her mother's words to her father when he was still scared of the girl in his bed, her mother's words to the child as she handed her a potato just dug from the earth. All these months she'd been trying to find Hannah, trying to turn fast enough to catch her. *See how warm it is?* Hannah was right here all along, inside of her, tender and alive.

Jay's body curved to hers, his hand on her stomach, one leg over her legs. "I remember this," he said, "all this time, how you felt."

They were warm enough and they slept.

Hannah said: *All your kindness is never going to change him.*

She was right about Matt Fry and had come to warn Iona again.

But it will change me.

Dentists don't marry the daughters of potato farmers.

He's not a dentist.

Son of a dentist.

I don't want to be married.

But you want to be loved.

I just want to love, the way Daddy loved you, with that little doubt.

And you think you love this boy.

I know him.

It's not the same.

It feels the same to me.

He'll break your heart.

Tell me about the bear, Mama.

Iona woke before dawn. Her left leg was numb, asleep beneath the weight of Jay's leg. She saw Eddie, though she didn't want him to be here, Eddie naked on the narrow bed, dark hair splayed on the blanket, dark chest, his arms the only warmth in the damp cabin of the boat, his fingers in her mouth, salty, feeling inside, the most delicate place, *soft,* he said, *so soft,* and he was the one moaning as if touching her there took him outside his own skin, out into the water, terrifying and deep. She smelled his wet hair, and later she saw him from a distance, behind the glass of the station, his blood-red shirt. Cars moved down the street in the rain, and she heard the lonely sound of tires hissing through water, then she was on the boat again, endlessly rocking, feeling that his touch could shatter her, his breath could tear her open, throat to bowel, and the day that had never been light was growing dark around them.

"We have to go," she said to Jay.

"It's early."

"They'll be up soon."

"So?"

"I don't want them to know."

"Are you ashamed of me?"

He was mocking her. Hannah was right. Jay Tyler would go home, scrape the shit off his shoes; buy a new cane, ebony or oak; he'd cut his hair and remember who he was.

He said, "Can we come again?"

She nodded.

"Promise?" He sat up beside her.

"Sure," she said. "Why not?"

"What's the matter?"

He was looking at her as if for the first time, watching her lips, waiting for her eyes to open fully, to take him in, she thought. *That's all: he wants me to look at him.* She hit her own thigh with her fist. "My leg's asleep," she said.

He rubbed her calf and then her knee, worked his way up slowly to the thigh. She felt his hand deep in her chest, at the base of her neck, in a sore spot on her palm. He seemed to reach everywhere by touching her legs, and she was afraid because it felt good, because he didn't know that she could feel his fingertips behind her eyes. She thought of Eddie, how his leg returned to him. She believed this must be the greatest mercy, to restore another's body, to give back what had been lost. She bathed Hannah, making her whole each time. She remembered the dog on the road, its eyes wide with pity, the gratefulness of a dying god.

"Iona?"

The sound of her name jolted her.

"Better?"

She nodded.

"Happens to me all the time."

"I suppose."

"I rub my own legs."

She nodded again.

"Is your leg all right? Can you climb down?"

"I should ask you."

"My legs are fine," he said, "nearly healed."

"Then you go first."

He did seem better, but she didn't know why. Nothing had changed in the night. Still, they darted across the muddy yard, and he seemed to move as easily as she did. The sky had cleared; a ghost moon drifted above the pines, almost full. The dogs barked. Already there was one light shining in an upstairs window, Jeweldeen nursing the baby before she shambled outside to milk the cows.

In the car, they both watched the road, as if they thought it might slide out from under them, crumbling from both sides, a narrow strip eroding behind them as they sped toward the safe paved streets of White Falls. He sat inches from his door, leaning toward her, till the pressure of the air between them felt like waves moving over her body, too light to bear.

She wished that he had not touched her that way, back in the loft. She couldn't guess that he was as scared as she was, startled by his own body. He saw himself swept down the river alone, and he believed this was his own fault because he had left Muriel to struggle without him, abandoned by her capricious God, sacrificed by her furious father. The child was with her always, their child, a body she carried everywhere now, their silent, unforgiving son. Somewhere a blond boy romped in the yard, rocketed down a slide, pulled an imaginary gun from his pocket, his own pointed finger, to shoot his mother dead. This mother fell down laughing, but Muriel, the real mother who would never see her son again, fell down without a sound except the thudding of her own heart.

He thought of Delores. They strapped her to the table, shoved the hard rubber bit into her mouth. *This won't hurt at all.* But the blue light lifted her off the table, shot through her bones till she stiffened, arms rigid, legs locked. *You would have been fine if you hadn't locked your legs.* He slammed into the doe and his own bones snapped. Delores lay limp on the table. Jay lay limp in his bed night after night. *One more time, Mrs. Tyler.* And they did do it—one more time. *That's when I died, Jay.* He knew now what they'd asked of her, knew how he would have wept and pleaded if someone had asked him to hit the doe, one more time.

He wanted to tell Iona that he couldn't touch himself, that he hadn't since the accident. He saw himself climbing the ladder of the three-meter board, he remembered his own taut body, rippled muscles of his stomach, a hundred sit-ups every morning, a hundred more every night. He was beautiful and had pictures to prove it, Jay Tyler leaping into the air, Jay Tyler spinning toward the water. He took this act of faith for granted until he knew its absence. He was a priest who'd lost his god, who woke at dawn to his own doubt, who discovered at dusk he'd stopped believing. He wished he could describe the hollows of his body to Iona Moon; he wished she knew about the empty space between his legs, the weightlessness of his belly, the hole in his chest where his devoted heart had been.

The sun rose over the violet mountains in the east, streaking the sky pink and orange. Down the road, the fine leafless limbs of a weeping willow waved like a girl's golden hair underwater. Iona's sister said: *It hasn't been easy for me either.*

All you had to do was watch.

Yes, she said. *Just imagine if your eyes were always open but you had no hands.*

Iona's eyes filled. She didn't slow down as she crossed the bridge. The lights on Main flashed yellow. She thought Jay had forgotten everything already, the bare skin of her stomach, the warm place under his hand, her promise, that he had forgotten his own words: *I remember this, all this time, how you felt, everything.* She turned east to take him to the bar, where his Chrysler would be parked in the lot, its windows beaded with dew.

"Shit," he said.

The last hope collapsed under her: she was the girl spinning on thin ice, plunging into dark water. He would say nothing kind when they parted, though it would cost so little now.

"You've got a pig on your tail," he told her.

She looked in the rearview mirror. Sure enough, she saw the light spinning. She pumped the brakes and pulled over before the siren whined. "Just a piglet," she said, watching the mirror, "your old pal Willy."

She rolled down her window and waited.

"Iona," Willy stammered. "I didn't recognize the car." He took out his pad to write the ticket. "Do you know how fast you were going?"

She shook her head. "Tell me," she muttered.

"Forty-three. Limit's twenty-five."

Jay leaned over. "Hey, buddy," he said.

Willy stopped writing. "Jesus—Jay. I didn't see it was you."

"Do you have to write that? I mean, I guess you do—it's your job and all, but it's my fault, you see."

"She's driving." Willy pointed his pen at Iona.

"I told her to step on it. I gotta piss."

"What am I gonna do with this?" Willy waved the pad with the half-written ticket.

"Tear it up?"

"They're numbered." Willy tapped the corner with one finger. "We keep track of the numbers."

"Let him finish," Iona said. "It's no big deal."

"A warning. I'm just going to write out a warning."

Jay grinned. "Thanks, buddy."

"It's not a favor. It's fair—first offense, you know."

He tore the ticket off the pad, and Jay said, "We were thinking of stopping at the Park Inn for breakfast."

"We were?" Iona said.

"Yeah, well I was gonna ask you."

"Don't forget to take that piss," said Willy.

"You hungry?" Jay said to Willy.

"I'm on duty."

"Pretty quiet out here."

Willy nodded. "I'll follow you."

So they turned without getting Jay's car, headed west with Willy Hamilton right behind them.

They sat in the corner, Jay and Iona on one side, Willy on the other. They ordered pancakes and sausage, scrambled eggs and coffee. "Lots of coffee," Jay said to the waitress. Iona thought of Eddie and hoped he'd eat a big breakfast this morning when he got off work, that he wouldn't go home hungry, that he and Alice wouldn't fight.

"Horton's giving me shit," Willy said, spearing a sausage and waving it on his fork. "I haven't been writing enough tickets. That's how I got graveyard." He cleared his throat to make his voice low. "'Not that we have a quota, son.'" He popped the whole sausage in his mouth and chewed hard. "Jesus." He swallowed enough so that he could talk. "I'd be better off working here—fry cook—or bagging groceries at Pick-n-Pay."

"Nothing to stop you," said Jay.

Willy slurped his coffee. "Except Horton Hamilton."

"He doesn't own your ass."

"Easy for you to say."

"What d'you mean?"

"You don't have to work."

Jay put his hand on Iona's leg under the table, squeezed it just above the knee. "I don't know what to do," he said.

"Finish school," Willy said, "go to college like you always planned."

They were all thinking the same thing: a man with broken legs better learn to use his brain.

"I've got a year and a half. I can't face it."

"Yeah," said Iona, "and what about facing the rest of your life?" She sounded just like Sharla, but she thought she meant it. "It sucks. But you do it. One day after another. And it ends. Sooner or later it ends, and you've got their precious piece of paper." She saw the picture in her locker; she heard Mr. Fetterhoff's jokes. She remembered smoking herself dizzy in the bathroom and wondered if it would end soon enough.

"I'll make you a deal," Willy said. "You go back to school, I'll look for another job."

Jay reached across the table and nearly knocked over the syrup. "Shake, asshole." They were both laughing. Iona laughed too, and Jay kissed her on the cheek, right there in front of Willy, right there in the Park Inn where anyone could see. He whispered in her ear, the same two words he'd whispered that first night in the back of Willy's Chevy. *Thank you.* But this time he meant something entirely different, and she felt they had almost drowned but now they were swimming to shore, rising out of the water in each other's arms, breathing into each other, suddenly and completely alive.

Angel grew wings and jumped over the moon. Angel flew back to earth. Iona saw she had eight teats and her udder was full, so she sat down and started milking. She filled one pail and then another; still the milk came, sweet and warm, and Iona said: *See, Mama, everything's all right.*

Later, Willy and Jay and Iona stood on the bridge, dropping stones in the water, watching the dark river swirl beneath them. Iona felt sorry for Willy. She saw that even he had his grief—everyone did. She knew he blamed himself for what had happened by the tracks. She wanted to say: *Listen, Willy, it's not your fault. I could have stayed at the river with Jeweldeen. If you are to blame, we all are: you, me—your three friends. And Jay's to blame for not being there. And Horton for sending Matt off to Cross City. And Everett is to blame for sticking the damn gun in his mouth and giving his brother an excuse, an example to follow. And Matt himself is to blame—because no matter how sorrowful your life is, there are always choices. We must all be forgiven.*

She looked down at the water and saw three fragile shadows, broken by waves on the Snake River. Jay imagined himself flying off the bridge and Iona pictured herself running barefoot down the tracks, pursued by drunken boys or chased by dogs. Willy saw his own blue lights flashing on the dark road of the life he still might choose. Wind gusted at their backs, and the scud of clouds rolled into the valley. The only thing that kept them from their solitary flights was the fact that at this moment they leaned together, close enough to put out their hands and break the fall.

At dusk, Iona and Jay drove out the River Road, parked in their old place. Iona thought Jay would be surprised if he knew she was almost a virgin, that Eddie was the only one, that she felt like a virgin now: she was that scared. She wanted to tell him that making love meant carving a hole in your own belly, so the other person can crawl inside. It meant feeling the bones of your face dissolve, turning to air between two bodies, becoming one breath, your lover's only word.

Hannah said: *Why do you want to lie down with him?*

Because I have a body. Hands and spine, blood and skin. Have you forgotten?

The night was cold, but they rolled down the windows to feel the wind move over them, to hear the river in the dark, the relentless rush of water, washing everything away, wearing down riverbank and stone, but pushing everything toward them too, the silt of memory, forever shifting.

Iona said: There was a bear who loved a girl. He carried her away in the woods and held her while she slept.

Jay said: He kept her warm.

One night she woke and saw he was a man.

Beautiful.

She kissed his mouth.

He woke.

And wept.

She loved him.

He needed her to love him by day, to love his furred face and bear smell.

He reeled through the trees, blind with tears.

The first shot struck his heart, the second his head.

Were the hunters surprised to find a man—did his bright blood in the snow make them kneel with shame?

They buried him beneath the snow in the silent forest, and more snow fell, covering their bloody tracks.

But the girl found him, dug her way down to lie beside him. She whispered: *It is the wounded heart that makes us human in the end, my love.*

Then she slept, and the snow fell on her cheeks and on her breasts, and the snow fell in her lover's hair.

Jay and Iona touched carefully, finger by finger, word by word. Rain tapped the roof of the car, then hammered till it seemed to rain into their ears and through their ribs, till it poured through open windows, rained into their eyes, rained and rained into their bodies. Their lives rushed to the banks of the river. A white dog swam against the current. His head went down, came up again, then under for the last time. Matt Fry drove the Buick into the roiling water, and could have drowned right then, but chose to live instead. Jay pinned Muriel to the seat. Iona held Jay to her chest. Willy leaned toward the door, trying to escape. A bottle broke against a car. A boy shouted. Darryl McQueen said: *I'm out, baby*. Darryl McQueen lay down in the grass beside her and they passed a cigarette between them. Iona squeezed a burning butt between her arms, not once but many times. Jay touched the knots of those scars with his fingertips now, asking what they were and why. And when she said she wanted to feel something, just to see if she still could, he understood and pulled her close, rocked her in his arms and said: "Me too, Iona, me too." A woman jumped in the river and her red coat billowed out around her. Sometimes the Snake gave you a second chance whether you thought you wanted it or not. Jay imagined his own leap, the arc and spin of a perfect dive, knowing that when you finally decide, you either kill yourself, or you fly.

Dutton   **Plume**

ENGROSSING FICTION

☐ **LAURA by Hilary Norman.** Erotic obsession and nightmare betrayal intertwine in this vividly imagined novel of adult passion and taut suspense. The emotional landscape of Laura Andros's heart was already strewn with mines of tragedy when she met the incredibly rich and attractive Roger Ambler. But too soon she realized she had made the deadliest mistake a woman blinded by love could make. (937838—$22.95)

☐ **MIDNIGHT IS A LONELY PLACE by Barbara Erskine.** A riveting psychological thriller of love and murder. Author Kate Kennedy thinks leaving London for a remote cottage on a wild stretch of coast will give her time to heal from a broken relationship and the privacy she wants to work on her next project. But she never suspects that her life will become intertwined with haunting and vengeful past lives. (938621—$20.95)

☐ **SECOND VISION by Ralph Vallone, Jr.** This remarkable novel teases the mind with a suspense-filled story about a dead man's second chance to put his life in order—and to find out who murdered him. The result is a contemporary ghost tale, at once shocking and delightful. (93765x—$22.95)

☐ **BLOODSONG by Jill Neimark.** Lynn is a young Manhattan journalist, cool, professional, and both sexually experienced and untouchable—until she meets Kim. Kim is a man who refuses to lower his mask of mystery even when he becomes her lover, and who remains distant even as he takes her to a new level of searing physical intimacy. In his arms what begins as an erotic experiment becomes an erotic obsession. "Seductive and luxurious."—*Entertainment Weekly* (272963—$9.95)

Prices slightly higher in Canada.

PLUME

GREAT MODERN FICTION

☐ **JAZZ by Toni Morrison.** The story of a triangle of passion, jealousy, murder and redemption of sex and spirituality, of slavery and liberation, of country and city, of being male and female, African-American, and above all of being human—from a Nobel Prize-winning author. "Mesmerizing . . . a sensuous, haunting story of various kinds of passion...A MASTERPIECE."—*Cosmopolitan* (269652—$10.95)

☐ **LA MARAVILLA by Alfredo Véa, Jr.** The desert outside the Phoenix city limits is a world of marvels spilling out of the adobe homes, tar-paper shacks, rusted Cadillacs, and battered trailers that are otherwise known as "Buckeye." *La Maravilla* is the embodiment of belonging to two worlds, and being torn between love and fear of both. "A vibrant and colorful tale of magic, history, and human sorrow." —*San Francisco Focus* (271606—$10.95)

☐ **PAGAN BABIES by Greg Johnson.** This powerful novel traces the turbulent, but enduring, relationship between a man and a woman, growing up Catholic in America, spanning three decades, from the fleeting optimism of Kennedy's Camelot to the fearsome age of AIDS. "Thoughtful, engrossing . . . Combines deeply serious intent with compulsive readability." —*Washington Post* (271320—$10.95)

☐ **BLACK GOLD by Anita Richmond Bunkley.** "A poignant look at the African-American experience in 1920s Central Texas . . . in the end, it is the same moral courage common to the best of all of us that triumphs."—Clay Reynolds, author of *Franklin's Crossing* (937528—$21.95)

Prices slightly higher in Canada.

Buy them at your local bookstore or use this convenient coupon for ordering.

PENGUIN USA
P.O. Box 999, Dept. #17109
Bergenfield, New Jersey 07621

Please send me the books I have checked above.
I am enclosing $_____ (please add $2.00 to cover postage and handling).
Send check or money order (no cash or C.O.D.'s) or charge by Mastercard or VISA (with a $15.00 minimum). Prices and numbers are subject to change without notice.

Card # _____ Exp. Date _____
Signature _____
Name _____
Address _____
City _____ State _____ Zip Code _____

For faster service when ordering by credit card call **1-800-253-6476**

Allow a minimum of 4-6 weeks for delivery. This offer is subject to change without notice

DUTTON

COMPELLING NOVELS

☐ **SINGING SONGS by Meg Tilly.** Written by the acclaimed actress, this novel is a masterful realization of a young girl's journey to adulthood in a world of chaos, abuse, and fragmented love; an affirmation of a child's ability to use her judgment and imagination alone to guide her through that world. A profound statement about the dark and secret places of family life.   (937781—$19.95)

☐ **THE BOOK OF REUBEN by Tabitha King.** In this novel, the author writes with stunning intensity about the coming of age, marriage, divorce, and hard-won independence of one of Nodd's Ridge's most popular citizens, Reuben Styles. Moving through the still waters of the 1950s and the shock waves and aftershocks of the 1960s, it captures time and place even as it weaves a timeless story of personal awakening.   (937668—$22.95)

☐ **RIVER OF SKY by Karen Harper.** This magnificent epic of the American frontier brings to vivid life one woman's stirring quest for fortune and happiness. This is Kate Craig's story—one of rousing adventure and heartbreaking struggle, of wildfire passion and a wondrous love, as strong and deep as the river itself. It will sweep you into an America long gone by.   (938222—$21.95)

☐ **MIAMI: A SAGA by Evelyn Wilde Mayerson.** Spanning a hundred years of challenge and change, this breathtaking panorama of Miami, Florida traces the tragedies and triumphs of five families—from the hardy homesteaders of the post-Civil War era to their descendents who bravely battle the devastation left by hurricane Andrew in 1992.   (936467—$22.95)

Prices slightly higher in Canada.

Buy them at your local bookstore or use this convenient coupon for ordering.

PENGUIN USA
P.O. Box 999, Dept. #17109
Bergenfield, New Jersey 07621

Please send me the books I have checked above.
I am enclosing $_____ (please add $2.00 to cover postage and handling).
Send check or money order (no cash or C.O.D.'s) or charge by Mastercard or VISA (with a $15.00 minimum). Prices and numbers are subject to change without notice.

Card # _____ Exp. Date _____
Signature _____
Name _____
Address _____
City _____ State _____ Zip Code _____

For faster service when ordering by credit card call **1-800-253-6476**

Allow a minimum of 4-6 weeks for delivery. This offer is subject to change without notice